"Lowell's finely wrought characters don't have it easy when it comes to navigating restrictive Victorian society, but even their most outrageous actions ring true. Readers will be swept away by this entrancing, intelligent romance." —*Publishers Weekly* (starred review)

"It's a lush, sensual, and outstanding romance that makes the heart ache in the very best way." —*BookPage* (starred review)

"Impeccably researched, Lowell's latest emphasizes justice. This love story tackles weighty issues but remains suspenseful and spellbinding."
—*Library Journal* (starred review)

"Lowell's prose is vivid and evocative, and issues such as class inequity, women's rights, and alcohol addiction complement the intense on-page evolution of the love story. . . . Those looking for a happy ever after for complex and passionate characters will be very satisfied here. A new voice in historical romance that will keep readers riveted." —*Kirkus Reviews*

A SHORE THING

JOANNA LOWELL

BERKLEY ROMANCE

NEW YORK

BERKLEY ROMANCE
Published by Berkley
An imprint of Penguin Random House LLC
penguinrandomhouse.com

Library of Congress Cataloging-in-Publication Data

Names: Lowell, Joanna, author.
Title: A shore thing / Joanna Lowell.
Description: First edition. | New York: Berkley Romance, 2024.
Identifiers: LCCN 2023057903 (print) | LCCN 2023057904 (ebook) |
ISBN 9780593549728 (trade paperback) | ISBN 9780593549735 (ebook)
Subjects: LCGFT: Romance fiction. | Queer fiction. | Novels.
Classification: LCC PS3618.U568 S56 2024 (print) |
LCC PS3618.U568 (ebook) | DDC 813/.6—dc23/eng/20240102
LC record available at https://lccn.loc.gov/2023057903
LC ebook record available at https://lccn.loc.gov/2023057904

First Edition: June 2024

Printed in the United States of America
1st Printing

Book design by Katy Riegel

To the queer ancestors.

We know you were there.

Dear Readers,

This book is a romance, and thus ends happily, with abundant happiness along the way. Characters do, however, struggle on the page with Victorian society's patriarchal notions of identity and sexuality. In the book, readers will encounter incidents of transphobia, including deadnaming, and homophobia, as well as PTSD and the past death of a parent. The emphasis isn't on oppression but resistance, and the ways people create joy and find love.

As a cis-queer historical romance writer with a transmasculine partner, I have found myself wanting to read a story like mine set in the past. I wrote A Shore Thing in close conversation with my partner, a gender and sexuality historian. The representations of queerness and trans identity come out of our lived experience, and our conversations with each other, and with our friends, as well as archival research. Even so, getting at the interiority of characters involves risky imaginative leaps and choices that foreclose other options. Kit embodies a single possibility among many. There isn't, and never has been, only one way to be queer, trans, or anything else. Fortunately, there are ever-increasing examples of literature and art exploring a broader range of lives. The more stories we have, the better we'll be able to imagine a just and equitable future.

Happy Reading,

Joanna

A SHORE THING

1

SEAWEED WASN'T *MY* first choice either."

Muriel said it with an air of apology, wobbling slightly on the uneven rock, and cast a regretful glance into the gleaming pool of water. Seaweed *wasn't* her first choice, most definitely not the botanical topic about which she'd prefer to lecture upon arrival in New York. But marine plants *were* strikingly beautiful, undulating ruby fronds and green silk frills and tiny tufts of lilac. She could watch them float for hours.

Apparently not without a full-scale mutiny on the part of her oldest friend. James had assumed the desperate look of a man about to do something unspeakably rash. Despite his wideawake hat, his face showed signs of sunburn and his eyes were glazed.

"We'll head back to the hotel," she said. "We can climb up to the cliff path and take the long way round. It's shadier."

"The long way round." James spoke in a disbelieving whisper. "My lips are dry, or I'd laugh."

He lifted his arm, and, with it, the gutta-percha-lined basket filled to the brim with her specimens. She'd been overenthusiastic. Muriel could admit that now. This was their first day in St. Ives, after all. She might have foregone collecting and idled away the morning. She and James could have sat in those wicker beehive chairs on the hotel terrace and played cribbage and caught up more thoroughly on everything they'd missed in each other's lives over the last three years. Instead, she'd all but dragged him out of bed and onto the shore for a gruelingly prolonged march in unforgiving footwear. She'd gotten him soaked, leading him into the waves, so she could hook promising algae with a stick. And then she'd led him farther and farther away from the other holidaymakers, and lost track of time, hovering over the tide pools, while he crisped in the noonday sun, holding her basket.

"Seawater." His voice sounded stronger and more ominous. "Do you know the poem? *Water, water everywhere, nor any drop to drink.*"

"Sounds familiar." She gave him a bright smile. He knew she wasn't much for poetry.

"Familiar?" His lips weren't too dry for a rather exaggerated frown. "Try apropos."

She kept smiling. She *had* meant to pack a few provisions, but he'd come down so late to the dining room, and the tide had already ebbed, and her haste made her forgetful. Seaweed spoiled so quickly.

"Here." She handed him another jar, seawater, yes, and a rosy little Callithamnion. He tucked the jar into the basket, where it clinked against the others—a reproachful clink.

"James," she attempted. "I wish I'd brought tea and biscuits. Particularly because I'm the reason we missed luncheon." Contrite, she reached for the India rubber bag at her waist. "I collected an edible species. If you're quite famished, you could—"

"Good Lord." He did laugh. "You promised me a seaside holiday. And here I am, half-expired on the least hospitable stretch of shore for miles, and you're suggesting I revive myself with a mouthful of *kelp.*"

"Not kelp. Irish moss. It's very good, as a jelly."

"I believe it's chiefly used as a mattress stuffing."

"Shall I pile some in the shade of the cliff, then?" She sniffed. "You can lie down and take your rest."

He looked at her darkly. "How many times am I going to let you trick me into this kind of situation?"

"I don't know." She felt a little burst of relief. She'd worried for a moment that she really had pushed him too hard, but, while his sunburn was real, she could tell now that his outrage was, as usual, largely an act.

"I suspect we'll go on like this," she added, "until you stop secretly loving it." She closed up her bag—Irish moss was absolutely punishing raw and worse unrinsed—and crossed her arms, arching her brows at him.

"Blast," he said, but without pathos. He enjoyed complaining in her company, perhaps because he was called upon to display unflappable calm and stern decision in everyone else's. Perhaps because they'd played together as children and never outgrew their formative dynamic.

"We don't have to go the long way round," she conceded, turning to look in the direction from whence they came. The waters of the bay were impossibly blue, edged with golden sands. Striped tents dotted the main beach, and the narrow, crowded houses of St. Ives rose above.

She turned back to James, who was knuckling sweat from his brow, expression resigned. "I simply thought it might be better," she explained. "More exercise, less sun. Isn't it the sun you find objectionable?"

"The sun objects to *me*." James sighed. "We had a falling-out of sorts. Haven't seen much of each other."

Muriel's gaze sharpened as she studied him. James had always been lean, with a thin, strong-boned face, all nose and cheekbones. His features fit him now. He was handsomer at six and thirty than he had been at sixteen. The new silver streak in his dark hair struck her as the epitome of dashing. But he'd grown gaunt and pallid, and his broad shoulders stooped.

"You and the sun are going to reconcile." She nodded firmly. "That's why I invited you."

"Like hell it is." James tilted back his head, surveying the steep slope up to the headland, the tumbled slates and scrubby vegetation. "You wanted an assistant."

"Yes, well, I could have asked someone else." A few of her botanical friends had even offered to make the trip. Any one of them could have provided more substantial assistance when it came to the collection and classification of British seaweeds. But she'd lived so many years abroad, traveling in Asia on commissions from plant nurseries and Kew Gardens, that those friends existed for her most fully on paper, as passionate but impersonal correspondents, their letters filled with taxonomies, enclosing seeds rather than sentiments.

James was still the person she knew best, the person who mattered most to her. She'd wanted an assistant, but she'd also wanted to feel, for these weeks, as though she were *home*. Home wasn't Hampshire, not anymore, but it wasn't Hong Kong either. It wasn't any place. It was *this*, if it was anything—squabbling with James, a stone in her boot, and a sudden lump in her throat.

"I'm happy we're here," she said. "You're happy we're here too."

"Humph." He grunted but didn't deny it. How could he? Some aspect of his London life was whittling him down, visibly.

James was a brain surgeon. Perhaps it was the long shifts in the operating theater? Horrors encountered during experimental investigations into neural tissue? Patients lost? Competition with colleagues?

Questions she'd held herself back from asking formed suddenly on her tongue. Before she'd settled on the right one, he creased his forehead and brushed past her.

"Upsy-daisy," he muttered, and started for the slope, picking his way slowly. Within moments, she'd outpaced him and was charting their course, showing admirable self-restraint as she passed an unusual sedge.

"Do you know there's no hospital in St. Ives?" James called up from below. "Mr. Trevaskis told me."

"That's why you were up until dawn?" she called back. "You cornered the hotel manager and interviewed him regarding the local medical facilities?"

"Lack of facilities. There's a general practitioner, but that's hardly sufficient. Down by the harbor, people live cramped as the pilchards in their barrels. Visitors have no idea. And then there are the mining accidents up on the cliffs."

The way became steeper, and she had to concentrate, proceeding upward via a series of ledges.

She was panting slightly as she responded. "You have enough people to worry about in London. This is a holiday. No operating on the fishermen."

"Your trunk is stuffed with microscopes, chisels, and pickle jars. And you're sniping at me because I brought my surgical bag. The hypocrisy."

"The *lies*. You brought your surgical bag! You swore you wouldn't."

"*You* swore you wouldn't devote thirty-six hours a day to botany."

"I'm not." She huffed hard enough to blow a strand of hair out of her eyes. "Obviously. That would be impossible."

"You would if you could, which is my point. Muriel." His tone made her stop short and face him.

"This doesn't *feel* like a holiday," he said. "If you're botanizing, I'm operating. Fair's fair."

She crossed her arms. "You do manage to aggravate me thirty-six hours of the day. Somehow *that* is possible."

"Botanize all you want." He looked suddenly sincere. "But promise me you will engage in *one* impulsive, thrilling, holiday-worthy activity before we leave St. Ives."

She opened her mouth.

"That doesn't involve plants," he added.

She scowled at him and began to climb again, increasing her pace.

"I see where this is going." She threw the words over her shoulder. "And you're not convincing me."

"Mr. Trevaskis is a bachelor. Rather handsome, wouldn't you say?"

"He's all yours."

"You are the soul of generosity."

She heard a rock clatter down the slope as James started after her.

"Luckily, bachelors are abundant," he continued. "The beach is crawling with them."

"I'm not here to collect bachelors."

"Pity."

A nearby gull, soaring up on the breeze, shrieked in emphasis, and Muriel gave it a dirty look.

"At this point, I'm most likely to do something impulsive to you." She twisted to direct her comment down to James. "And you won't enjoy it."

"At this point, I'm most likely to *operate* on myself as well." James sighed. "After I tumble down this bloody cliff."

She twisted back around. "We're almost to the top. I can see a few easels." She was wearing her collecting outfit, an indecorously short serge dress, the hem hitting well above the ankle, but even so, she had to hike her skirts for this last effort.

"Easels!" James's shout sounded less breathless than she might have expected. But then, he was a natural athlete, however weakened his state. "You claimed this route was better because we'd have more shade. But in fact, you're hoping to find your *artistic prodigy*, your *transcendent genius*, the *indispensable collaborator* upon whom your stratagem depends."

She made a face. James was right. She did harbor the foolish, overeager hope that she'd stumble upon the artist she'd come to St. Ives to commission. There was no need to stumble upon him—or her, as the case might be. Mr. Bamfylde would supply the relevant information when they met for tea on Monday, and she'd act upon it promptly.

But neither was there need for James to mock her with her own tipsy descriptions—he had nefarious taste in sherry—so she ignored him, aided by the convenient excuse of a stitch in her side. Then she was cresting the slope, catching her breath, the green sweeping out in front of her, the grassy patchwork of farmland divided by hedges. A picnicking couple was strolling along the path. The gentleman shot her a startled look that veered swiftly into disapproval.

"How do you do?" She took her hand from her side and waved.

The gentleman thinned his lips and dipped his chin, a minimal motion, due to scantness of enthusiasm, and also, scantness of chin.

"George." The lady peered around him. "Tell me that shocking-looking woman didn't just pop up over the side of the cliff."

"It appears she did." George spoke out of the side of his mouth, but his voice carried as clearly as the lady's. "Keep walking, Margaret."

I don't bite, offered Muriel, but only in her head, because truly, what was the point? She eyed George's basket, which contained a sweating bottle and several wrapped parcels, sandwiches or strawberry tarts. Begging a glass of wine for James was out of the question.

The couple walked on. There were three artists in the near vicinity, easels facing the bay. Not one turned his head to glance in Muriel's direction.

Monday. It wasn't so long to wait.

Nonetheless, she drifted toward the nearest artist, tall and bearded, kneeling before his easel, head jerking as he shifted focus between the scenery and his canvas.

Even more foolish—this notion that she'd recognize her *transcendent genius* by the work itself. She'd seen but one example! But as she peeked at the bearded man's picture, she dismissed him instantly as a possible candidate.

The picture was competent, surely, but bland. It left her entirely unmoved.

Whereas she'd shivered at the sight of the genius's watercolor, a strange heat building behind her eyes, despite the unprepossessing quality of the encounter. She'd been in Pimlico visiting a colleague, sipping a cup of Miss Bamfylde's botanically complex but unpalatable tisane, when she'd spied the watercolor hanging crookedly on the soot-streaked plaster wall, surrounded by newspaper clippings.

It was unsigned, small, a study of a columbine, the pink flower nearly translucent, glowing with the light that fed its cells. Somehow the genius had combined unstinting morphological accuracy with the ineffable mystery of being.

As art, as science—she'd never seen its equal.

She'd known instantly that the person who'd painted it was the one, the guarantor of her lecture's success.

The bearded man coughed—not at her—but she gave a guilty start and retreated.

And that's when she saw it.

She blinked, momentarily uncertain, wondering if she'd made too little of her own thirst, if mild dehydration could produce such a vision.

But no. She was staring at a columbine. It grew on the other side of the path, close to a low stone wall. Among its green leaflets, a single blossom nodded in the breeze, pale blue petals, deep blue sepals and spurs.

Columbines were plentiful in Cornwall. But they flowered in the spring, never in August.

Her heart flipped in her chest.

Nature was indifferent. Violent thunderstorms had nothing to do with the fury of the gods, just as a flower blooming out of time and place didn't mean that fate smiled upon her.

But this unseasonable bloom—she felt its import like a bolt from the heavens.

Her lecture would be a triumph.

She'd make a home in Manhattan, a real home, at last.

And live happily ever after.

Laughable, and yet she stepped toward the columbine, stepped into the path, and a bell began to ring.

For an instant, the chimes confused her, merging with the giddy music singing in her blood. By the time she realized a bicycle was bearing down upon her, it was too late. She stood rooted to the spot. Luckily, the rider's reflexes were quicker. He turned his handlebars sharply, and crashed, not into her, but into the wall. The bicycle stopped, but he continued on, his body an arc against the sky, before he dropped out of view.

2

MURIEL CLAMBERED OVER the wall and crouched beside the crumpled rider. He lay hatless, face down in the grass, and she put a tentative hand to his shoulder.

"Are you all right?" she asked. "My friend is a doctor. Lie still, and I'll fetch him. It will only be a moment."

The man rolled over, his palm and fingers pressed to his eyes.

"Lucy?" he groaned.

"No." Muriel sat back on her heels. "Is that your wife? I'll fetch *her* if you like."

The man made a low, negatory sound of distress. After a decade of travels through harsh and varied terrains, Muriel had learned the rudiments of first aid. If necessary, she could clean and dress a wound, no matter how gruesome, trusting that her nerve wouldn't fail. In this instance, there was nothing gruesome to confront. The man's skull was intact. He'd given it a good knock, though—how good a knock she couldn't say.

James could say. But where was he?

She looked behind her. Stone wall. Blue sky. Two white gulls hanging in the air. James wasn't vaulting toward them, and those three artists weren't either. Were they so absorbed in their painting they'd missed the bells, the crash?

"Sophia," murmured the man.

"Erm." She looked back at him. "No."

"Clara?"

"*No.*"

"Margaret?"

She narrowed her eyes and swept him with a glance. He wasn't particularly large, but he was well-muscled, his body encased in gray trousers, white waistcoat, gray jacket, and mauve cravat. It was emphatically fashionable attire, better suited to promenading in Hyde Park than cycling through Cornwall. It suited *him* very well. His hand covered the middle of his face, but the angles of his jaw and the full lines of his mouth made it easy to anticipate the rest.

He was attractive as sin.

"Phoebe," he sighed.

"You're delirious," she told him, and paused. Delirious, and in his delirium calling out for . . .

Well, Lucy wasn't his wife, and she doubted Phoebe was his mother.

She was flushing slightly as she continued. "I am Muriel Pendrake."

"Muriel." He rolled his head from side to side, demonstrating an encouraging lack of neck fracture. "Muriel. With the little garret in Chelsea? You can see the river from the bed, through the French lace curtains . . ."

He had a husky voice and it trailed off as his lips tipped up in a faint smile.

She frowned. "Not that Muriel. You've never been in my bedchamber, I guarantee it. And not least because I don't have a residence in London."

She tried to speak briskly and without judgment. The man was quite possibly concussed. And if he'd been in the bedchamber of every woman who *did* have a residence in London, as seemed increasingly likely, it wasn't her concern.

"Can you move your arms and legs?" she asked. "Is anything broken? Wiggle your toes."

"Muriel." He didn't move, his stillness more pronounced and thoughtful. "Muriel. I paid the ransom for your pug. *Princess.* That was her name."

"I don't have a pug." She couldn't help it. Briskness edged into exasperation. "And if I did, I wouldn't call her *Princess*." She paused, breathing a bit too hard. This semiconscious man possessed peculiar powers of annoyance.

She reminded herself that *semiconscious* required certain concessions.

"I am sorry," she said, "to hear that *Princess* was dognapped, and I'm sure it was very kind of you to pay the banditti."

"Yes," the man agreed, and lapsed into a silence so protracted she wondered if he'd transitioned from semiconscious to completely insensible.

"Muriel," he whispered. "With the ticklish knees?"

"Oh, for God's sake." She bit her lip, annoyance battling with curiosity. Raised in the country and married young, she'd never before met a bona fide rakehell, unless you counted the gin-soaked second sons who slimed around British legations, or the occasional dapper diplomat.

This man was a different variety altogether. He belonged in the pages of a romantic novel, everything about him louche and seductive.

How many *Muriels* had he bedded? For that matter, how many *Marys* and *Elizabeths*?

She decided on a safer line of inquiry. "How many fingers am I holding up?"

The man spread the fingers that covered his left eye, and she saw a gleam of iris before his fingers snapped closed.

"I can't say. It's terribly bright."

She scowled and leaned over him. A lock of chestnut hair flopped across his forehead. She'd have to push it back in order to tell if a knot was forming.

She brushed at his hair with her fingertips. It was soft as silk, its thickness and slight curl giving it spring. His skin felt hot.

No abrasion. No swelling.

She realized she was hovering over him, rather as though he were a tide pool, enticing her with the promise of beautiful secrets. This embarrassing thought didn't trigger any impulse to pull away.

Her nostrils flared as she detected his scent, not heavy cologne as she'd expected, but something bright and fresh, similar to the delicious fragrances of the West Country summer itself—green leaves, sea air, sun-warmed heath.

She leaned closer. All at once, he lowered his hand and looked her straight in the eye. His eyes were gray, framed with long black lashes. Their gaze was piercing.

"What are you doing?" he asked, and she toppled backward, cheeks flaming. What had she been doing, indeed?

"I was inspecting you," she answered, with as much dignity as she could muster. "For injury. I assumed you were delirious. But perhaps that's the way you talk usually?"

"Perhaps. Were you bowled over by my charisma?" He rolled onto his side, propping himself on his elbow, angling a glance at her from under those lashes. "I'm usually charismatic."

"Then you must have been delirious."

"There's a blow." He grinned. "You were doing such a marvelous job nursing until now. I should call you Florence."

"You've called me by several names already." She gave him a tight smile.

"Apologies." He rose to sitting with a wince. "There must be a mental equivalent to the funny bone. I think I hit mine on that stone. My thoughts went odd. I couldn't place your voice."

"Because you'd never heard it before." She felt obscurely outraged. "We don't know each other."

He was looking around him, scrubbing a hand through the disordered waves of his hair. "And I couldn't recall where I was. Has that ever happened to you? It's a sensation I associate with early mornings, when you first wake up, and everything is shadowed, and innumerable rooms seem to exist at once, superimposed. The door is to your left, or the door is straight ahead. There's a garden outside the window, or a busy street, or . . ."

"The river in Chelsea," she interrupted. "I think I understand why you might feel some confusion upon waking."

Rakes didn't blush, of course. But this one was regarding her with increasingly acute focus.

"Oh?"

"All the women." She cleared her throat. "The various garrets."

"I only mentioned one garret."

"You're a rake," she said, annoyed again. "I'm sure the garrets have been multiple. But the same thing does happen to me. I wake up bewildered."

The admission surprised her. It wasn't that she wouldn't have revealed such a thing to James, but the opportunity hadn't arisen, and so she'd never spoken of the minor disorientations she experienced daily.

She'd lived for so long without fixed address, in hotels, in makeshift camps, in houseboats, in farmhouses, in the mansions of expatriates, politicians, and grandees. Not to mention the cumulative months at sea. The bed was narrow in James's guest chamber, and all last week, she'd woken expecting the floor to sway.

The rake was still regarding her.

"I very much want to discuss this bewilderment. But something else you said weighs upon me."

No doubt. She grimaced. "I'm too blunt."

Her tendency for frank speech got her into trouble. She tried to temper directness with good humor, which softened sharp remarks and reduced insult—sometimes.

Results were mixed.

The rake didn't look *insulted* exactly, but his scrutiny had a sharp edge.

"Ignore what I said," she suggested.

He didn't. "You called me a rake."

Drat.

"Yes." She sighed. "I'm aware."

He folded his arms. "So. Am I a good rake or a bad rake?"

"I can't say." She folded *her* arms. "The terms want defining. Besides, we've established I don't know you."

"You know me enough to know I'm a rake."

It scarcely required pointing out, but . . .

"You listed a half dozen women in fewer minutes," she said, "with reference to their beds and knees."

"In my defense, we've also established I was delirious at the time." He paused. "I referenced a pug as well."

"You referenced *saving* a pug. I suppose that makes you a good rake. Unless you perform good deeds to bad ends? That's not uncommon."

He shook his head gravely. "Saving a pug is an end in itself."

Her laughter burst out. It was the deep, loud, *grating* laughter that her husband, Esmé, used to loathe. But she couldn't hold back. The rake—good or bad—was powerfully annoying, but there was something disarming about him too. His inflated self-regard had a tongue-in-cheek quality. All told, he seemed a frivolous, harmless young man, whose pretty looks would serve *him* worse, in the end, than anyone else, providing him with a substitute for character, leaving his inner resources entirely undeveloped. Probably he was rich, and it didn't matter much one way or another.

He was grinning at her again.

About those pretty looks . . .

He was attractive as *mortal* sin, the kind worth the hellfire.

Those other Muriels hadn't stood a chance.

Thank the Lord, *she* wasn't susceptible to rakes, merely intrigued by their ways.

"How would you define *good rake*?" she asked. "If that's what you aspire to be."

"Good rake," he repeated. Either he shifted forward, or the intensity of his gaze gave the impression of narrowing distance. His face filled her vision.

"A good rake defies social mores." He spoke softly. "He defies them not only to free himself but to free others. He's not debauched so much as divergent. If he falls below the prevailing moral standard, it's because he's a fugitive from morals, searching for other fugitives, with whom he can forge a new kind of ethic, based on a love that knows no shame." His lips curved. "A good rake loves love, shamelessly."

She'd stopped breathing. The sun blazed overhead, and it didn't seem impossible, in her parched, dazzled state, that she'd suddenly combust.

"Well," she managed, a rasp in her voice. "You do seem . . . shameless."

"Thank you," he said.

She looked away. The grass was flattened where he'd sprawled. He'd barely missed the nettles. She could feel him watching her, and her throat constricted.

An image rose in her mind, the green bottle in that disapproving gentleman's picnic basket, the beads of condensation on the glass.

Her chin snapped up.

"Margaret," she said. The rake *was* watching her. She met his eyes.

"Muriel," he corrected. "You're Muriel. I'm not delirious any longer. I know your name, and that you don't live in Chelsea, or own a pug. As for your knees . . ."

"They're not ticklish," she responded automatically.

He tipped his head. "For some reason, I don't believe you."

"Fine. They're moderately ticklish. There is a *more* ticklish region of my person, but I won't reveal its location on pain of death."

His gaze traveled over her, palpable as touch. It didn't tickle. It set her nerve endings on fire.

Clearly, something had walloped the mental equivalent of *her* funny bone.

She shouldn't loll in a field with a rakehell, however perversely interesting the experience. She should fetch James, as she'd intended. She *would* fetch James.

But not quite yet.

"You mentioned *Margaret*," she returned to the previous topic, "and a Margaret walked by, not twenty minutes ago, with a George."

"Her husband?"

"Presumably."

"You're wondering if she's the Margaret I mentioned? And perhaps—wondering more generally if I conduct adulterous affairs?"

He didn't mind inappropriate questions. No, he encouraged them. His eyes were gleaming.

She nodded, disquieted by her nosiness but unable to curtail it. "Does a good rake respect the sanctity of marriage?"

"It depends," he drawled. "Wrong Margaret, by the way." For a moment, he ran his knuckles lightly over the clover, back and forth. His eyes grew brighter. "Are *you* married?"

"I was." Her inexplicable elation faded. This conversation had gotten entirely out of hand.

The rake seemed about to speak.

"My husband died," she said abruptly. "A long time ago now."

She stood, to avoid the awkwardness of condolences—too rapidly. Sparkles danced in the air around her, and she swayed.

"There you are. Muriel!" James came striding up to the stone wall and set down the basket. "Are you scouting for land plants? I call foul play. You gave me your . . . *hullo*." His voice dropped an octave. "And who is this?"

The rake was standing now, at her elbow, *holding* her elbow, to keep her steady.

Muriel inhaled and stepped away.

"I'm not sure," she said to James. "I've been calling him *the rake*."

"How jolly. I hope he seduced you." James leaned over the stone wall, squinting. "James Raleigh. I've been prescribing seduction to Muriel for years."

"Does she follow the doctor's orders?" The rake looked between James and Muriel, adjusting his jacket. His white waistcoat, Muriel noticed, was embroidered all over with white lilies.

"Ha," James retorted. "Never. She's a terrible patient."

"I seduced *him*, if you must know." She almost clapped a hand over her mouth. Botheration. She knew better than to let James goad her into absurdity. The rake couldn't *mind*, though, could he, if she imputed to the situation a little extra rakery?

"It was incredibly impulsive of me," she plunged on. "And thrilling. And it didn't involve plants. So, Dr. Raleigh. I believe I've heard the last from you on the subject of my summer activities."

"You seduced him?" James raised a brow.

Muriel dared a glance at the rake. He'd also raised a brow.

"Just slightly," she said. "But it counted."

"Slightly," echoed James. "What does that mean, exactly? A *slight* seduction?"

What indeed?

She shifted her feet, cheeks flaming.

"It was like . . ." She cleared her throat. "A low dosage of seduction."

"It was like this," said the rake. His voice vibrated in her ear, and she startled. She hadn't realized he'd moved so close. The air around her felt different. It *buzzed*. Some part of her wondered if bees were circling her feet, but she couldn't tear her eyes from his face.

His gaze drifted down, lingered on her mouth. His irises—they were a subtle shade of gray. The muted, moody color—the only subtle thing about him.

Her breath stopped.

Slowly, he leaned over her. His lips touched hers, the pressure light and warm. She froze, then her lids fluttered down, plunging her into velvety darkness.

This was a kiss. Dear God, how long had it been?

Some voice inside her answered instantly.

Forever.

How long since she'd felt *this*?

Forever. Forever and a day.

Heat streamed through her. She was melting. She must be melting, because the rake's muscled arm wrapped her waist and he was holding her upright, already lifting his head away, breaking the kiss. Their mouths had only been in contact for the briefest of moments.

Her eyes flew open.

"More or less like that," said the rake, turning his head to James, who looked flabbergasted.

Muriel broke away and stumbled back, heart pounding. The rake was looking at her now—no, *smirking* at her.

"You can thank me later," he said, too low for James to hear, and winked.

"He hit his mental funny bone," she blurted, as though this could explain everything, *her* behavior as well as his.

"Sounds serious." James appraised the rake narrowly. "Did you lose consciousness?"

"No." The rake shrugged. "My trousers are ruined, but that's the worst of it." He glared down at his grass-stained knees, then straightened. "Pleased to meet you both. I'm Kit Griffith."

His smile crinkled the corners of his eyes.

He was older than she'd thought, within a year or two of her age, perhaps three and thirty. His skin was fine-grained, but lines bracketed his mouth.

His mouth.

Muriel swallowed with difficulty.

The rake's gaze was knowing. He flicked it back to James.

"You're also visiting from London?" James asked.

The rake—Mr. Griffith—approached him.

"Permanently. I live here." His chin pointed toward the basket. "You're on a picnic?"

James snorted.

Muriel shook herself and started forward . . . just as another bell began to ring.

3

"OBSTRUCTION IN THE path!" The man roaring was perched high on a penny-farthing. He kept pedaling, barreling toward James with the speed of a locomotive.

Griffith jumped the wall in a lithe motion and tackled James around the waist. Muriel barked her shin on the stone as she followed, stumbling gracelessly into the center of the path. She held up her palm.

"Halt!"

The man on the penny-farthing skidded to a stop. He didn't dismount. His front wheel was easily five feet high, and he twitched it left then right then left again to maintain his balance.

"Madam," he boomed. "It is highly irresponsible to leave your bicycle in the path."

Muriel's gaze dropped to Griffith's bicycle, which lay tipped on its side between them.

"We thought you were calling *James* the obstruction." She glanced at James, who was accepting a hand up from Griffith.

"He was also obstructing the path," said the man. "Paths exist to facilitate movement. If it's not moving, it shouldn't be in the path."

"Deighton, isn't it? James Raleigh." James flicked a leaf from his hat. "We met at dinner. Your party is staying at the Towans. So are we—Mrs. Pendrake and I. Arrived yesterday."

"We *dined* at the Towans." Deighton's glare was incredulous. "We *stay* in my family's summer residence, Titcombe Hall."

"How delightful for you." James gave him an idle smile. "Hall ownership is such a boon to a man's social life. Now that you mention it, I recall your friend saying something about Titcombe Hall. It's haunted, perhaps? By a murdered eighteenth-century smuggler? Bracegirdle was foggy on the details."

"Butterfield."

"Butterfield. That's it. Nice chap, Butterfield. Avoids pastry and takes cold baths. We had an interesting talk."

"He's in training." Deighton swayed on his penny-farthing. "Can't eat pastry when training."

"I don't know," said James blandly. "What if you're training as a pastry eater?"

"We are not." Deighton spat the words. "We are training as wheelmen. I'm the captain." He removed a hand from the handlebars and tapped one of the badges affixed to his jacket, the one shaped like a wheel, with gold spokes raying out against a blue enamel background. "Mutton Wheelers Cycling Club. We've toured all over England, recorded hundreds and hundreds of miles."

"Well done." James coughed. "You should call yourselves the *Well-Done* Mutton Wheelers Cycling Club. What do you think?"

He looked at Muriel for approval, and she gave a slight shake of her head.

"I thought it was rather good," murmured Griffith.

"Enough of this." Deighton's square-jawed face reddened. "What's good is an unobstructed path." He began to flick the lever on his bell.

"Mr. Deighton." James ignored the tinny noise. "Some physicians believe that cycling decreases indigestion, but increases chronic diseases of the heart and arteries."

"For God's sake, clear the way!" Deighton fairly bellowed it. "I have the heart of an ox!"

"And I have a sphygmograph at the hotel." James clapped his hands. "I'd love to study your pulse. Butterfield's too, if he's amenable, and whoever else."

Deighton tipped dangerously and compensated with a rather savage jerk of the wheel. "Mr. Raleigh," he snarled, in a lower voice. "Please assist the lady in clearing her bicycle from the path."

"It's not my bicycle," said Muriel. "It's Mr. Griffith's."

"What?" Deighton's eyes bulged. "You're joking."

Muriel glanced at Griffith. He stood beside James, on the edge of the path, looking faintly—rakishly—amused.

They'd *kissed*.

She was now Muriel of the slight seduction. Muriel of ticklish regions unknown.

Mortifying.

At least she'd shocked James.

She wasn't *gawking* at Griffith. Was she?

"It *is* my fault the bicycle's in the path." She snapped her eyes back to Deighton. "I stepped in front of Mr. Griffith, and he tried to avoid me and was thrown into the field."

"I don't know what's more disgraceful." Deighton stared down at Griffith with a horrified sneer. "Riding a *safety*, or getting yourself unseated."

"It didn't seem particularly safe," observed Muriel, and bent to right the bicycle. It was surprisingly heavy, the metal frame warmed by the sun. Griffith was there in an instant, taking it from her hands.

"Starley & Sutton's latest," he said. "The Rover. Their finest machine yet."

Even upright, his bicycle was dwarfed by Deighton's.

He patted the leather saddle. "They call these low-mount models *safeties*. The Rover has direct steering. A chain drive. Wheels of roughly equal size. It's going to revolutionize cycling."

"*Ruin* cycling, you mean." Sweat was rolling over Deighton's brow as he jerked his handlebars from side to side. "It's a sport. It's not for women, children, or the elderly, or the *infirm*. They can recreate, within limits, on tricycles and safeties. But *real* cycling necessitates an ordinary, a high wheeler, like this one. *Real* cycling is for men with dexterity and skill. The day we cease to value the achievements of the strong so we can cater to the whims of the weak—that day is the day I die. The day our society dies."

"I wish I had my sphygmograph now," murmured James. "Mr. Deighton, I can *hear* your circulatory system."

"I hire out Rovers." Griffith addressed himself to James. "If you want to try one yourself." His gaze brushed Muriel's. "Either of you."

"*You* are the proprietor of the St. Ives bicycle shop?" Deighton listed precipitously and came back to equilibrium with notable strain. His thighs looked ready to burst the seams of his knickerbockers. "I saw the advertisement. You give lessons! And you can't even ride."

"I can ride." Griffith shrugged.

"Riding a safety—even if you *aren't* unseated—isn't riding."

"I can ride a high wheeler as well. I've raced high wheelers. I have three at the shop."

Deighton lit up. "A competition, then."

"You want to race?" Griffith's brows lifted. "There's no track. We could—"

"Joust!" crowed Deighton.

"*Joust*," echoed James. "As in, joust?" He cut his eyes toward Muriel. "Aren't you glad I brought my surgical bag now? I say, old boy." He looked back at Deighton. "Do you always travel with lances?"

"I'll fashion the lances." Deighton bared square, white teeth. "Tomorrow, then."

"Tomorrow's Sunday." Griffith inclined his head. "*Remember the Sabbath.* They certainly do in St. Ives."

"Monday, then."

"Brilliant." Griffith smoothed his cravat. "Shall we say four in the afternoon?"

"Brilliant."

"The pasture at Rosewall Farm?"

"Brilliant."

"None of this is brilliant," interjected Muriel. "Diverting, possibly. Brilliant, no."

"Will you attend?" asked Griffith. His eyes locked on hers, their expression unreadable.

A tingle started at the top of her spine and ended up in her toes. What would it be like? A seduction that wasn't . . . slight.

She turned toward the stone wall, to retrieve the basket, and her eyes fell to the mangled plant at the wall's base.

The accident did have a casualty. The columbine had been shredded by the tire of Griffith's bicycle. The flower was gone, as though it had never been.

Time to remember she wasn't superstitious.

And to remember she had a purpose here.

She picked up the basket and turned back to Griffith.

"I have an engagement on Monday," she said. "Sadly, I will miss the joust."

She hurried to James, and Griffith wheeled his bike to them, and, at last, the path was clear. Deighton launched forward with a howl. The air he displaced as he hurtled away smelled of hot rubber and grease.

"We're going this way." Muriel pointed.

"I'm going the other way." Griffith pointed, and a little pause ensued. "Enjoy your picnic."

"Impossible." James shook his head. "It's Irish moss and seawater. Enjoy your joust."

"I believe I will," said Griffith, and he dinged his bell. His smile was wide and somehow indecent, far too transfixing for ordinary interaction.

The backs of Muriel's knees went damp.

And then he was pedaling off.

She released her breath, and James glanced at her, eyes dancing. He looked away, then back. He drew a breath.

"Don't," she warned. He began to laugh.

"Stop." She nudged him, so hard the jars clinked in the basket. "I thought your lips were too dry."

"They are," said James, and kept laughing.

4

❧

IT WAS THE light that drew so many artists to Cornwall. The great marine painter J. M. W. Turner had inaugurated the tradition. He'd toured the West Country at the beginning of the century, walking or riding the whole of the way, nearly as far as Land's End. The golden views he put to canvas inspired future generations, and the railway bridge made their treks west swifter and more comfortable. Now a dozen trains crossed the Tamar a day. You could chug out from Paddington Station in the morning and step off the Cornish Riviera in St. Ives in time to set up your easel and capture the sunset.

That's what Kit had done, two years ago. He'd sent his luggage to Tregenna Castle, the Great Western Railway hotel, and raced down to the foreshore of Porthminster Beach, wedging his easel between the seine boats, painting until it was too dark to see his brushstrokes.

He'd come for the light, like Turner, for the breathtaking natural beauty, for the scenes the local industry provided, fisherfolk at work.

He'd come for the chance to be himself, *fully* himself. To introduce himself as Kit Griffith to everyone he met. To hear himself called the same. To answer to it. To go months without hearing that other name, Kate Holroyd, the sound of which set his teeth on edge.

Riding away from the scene of that unexpectedly agreeable smashup, the wind in his hair, light streaming down from the sky and reflecting up from the sea—he could feel it again, the joy and ease, the sheer relief of those early days.

He'd begun to sign some of his pictures *Kit Griffith* long before St. Ives. Putting that masculine name to his work—it felt true, a way of expressing something about how he experienced the world he represented on those canvases. But he'd maintained a separation, in his mind, between Kit and Kate. Perhaps because he'd known society enforced such distinctions. Perhaps because he'd feared collapsing the tension, collapsing alter egos into one identity—the choice and additional sacrifice required.

He'd endured the irritation, the slight abrasion of *wrongness*, until the repeated chafing burned like fire.

Geography had offered a solution—all those miles between London and St. Ives. He could be Kit here, at the very edge of England. And Kate there, with his friends and his family. His friends at least accepted that Kate wore trousers, and his parents tolerated it as best they could.

They accepted and tolerated *her*.

He turned off the path, the Rover juddering, and pedaled over the heath, the smell of wild thyme rising from beneath his wheels. Miners' paths crisscrossed the land, and he picked one up and spun along, curving back toward the cliffs, until the huer's hut rose before him, round and gray.

Such huts dotted prominences on the Cornish coasts. From high above the harbor, huers watched for shoals of pilchards, sending up cries and directing the boats below to the glinting silver mass of fish.

He jumped off his bicycle and pushed it to the nearest boulder. He scrambled up the lichen-spangled granite and stood gazing out at the horizon, the blurred line where airy fathoms churned into the thicker blue of the Atlantic. Luggers with rust-brown sails drifted toward the bay.

Wind blew steadily, drying the sweat that had gathered under his collar. He spread his arms, coolness pooling in their hollows, then he probed the ridges of his brow, walking his fingers up to his hairline, smiling despite the painful tenderness.

Nothing like getting staggered by a beautiful woman. And what a woman.

Blunt and bossy, her coppery hair nearly metallic in the sun. That hair, and her strong profile, put him in mind of Roman statuary.

Muriel Pendrake looked like a goddess cast in bronze. If a goddess wore a scandalously short yachting dress with boys' shooting boots, tall and stout and coated in rubber.

She was an odd duck, bewitchingly outré. She'd been collecting seaweed with Raleigh, the sunburnt doctor. He should have guessed even before Raleigh had pointed to the jars in the basket. She'd smelled of rosemary soap, but also of the ocean, and her skirt was crusted with salt, and, then, by God, those *boots*.

He'd seek her out at the rock pools. He'd carry a picnic basket filled with scones and pots of raspberry jam and lemonade and Pimm's, to appease Raleigh. Then he'd whisk her away to a secluded cove where they could pursue any number of summer activities.

First, though, the joust.

He half climbed, half jumped down from the boulder and righted his bicycle.

That Deighton was a muttonhead, exactly the kind of entitled blighter he lived to vanquish. His old self—*she* had thrilled every time she'd asserted her presence in a place she'd been told she didn't belong. Every time she'd taken a medal for drawing, or run the table in billiards, or made some braggart shut his mouth.

Kit's impulses hadn't changed, even if his dearest friend—former friend—Lucy Coover, now the Duchess of Weston, refused to believe it. But his triumphs landed differently—they didn't undermine assumptions about female capabilities. They didn't blaze new trails. More often than not, they partook of the very privilege he'd once envisioned himself helping to dismantle.

For example, his solo exhibition at the Grosvenor Gallery this past November. A tremendous critical success. The least picture went for twice the amount commanded by Kate Holroyd's best.

Had his painting so improved? Or did the Consulting Committee, the critics, the public value it higher by virtue of the signature, the abbreviated biography that played so neatly into societal myths about the solitary male genius?

People were keen to attribute visionary greatness to a mysterious young man. If you believed the gossip, even the reviews themselves, Kit Griffith's refusal to attend his own opening was as radical and interesting as his merging of form and color.

He'd allowed himself to relish the achievement regardless.

And then his life broke. Or rather, his two lives collided.

It had been Boxing Day, his third day back in town for the Christmas holiday. When he'd fulfilled his family obligations, he'd walked to Weston Hall, rare London snowflakes drifting down, whiter than gray for once, almost sparkling. Nose cold, blood hot, he'd taken stomping, twirling steps, had been laughing as he'd charged up the stairs to bang on Lucy's door. He'd been so excited to see her after his long absence, bursting with stories.

She'd confronted him with his exhibition catalogue, voice icier than a thousand winters.

Tell me this isn't you.

But it was. He couldn't deny it, and he couldn't find the words to explain. As students at the Royal Academy of Arts, he and Lucy had formed an artistic society, the Pre-Raphaelite Sisterhood. They'd exchanged praise and criticism at the easel. They'd entered into passionate collaboration with fellow artists—*women* artists—evolving new styles. They didn't exhibit behind each other's backs. They celebrated each milestone together, for what it meant for them, and for what it meant for women generally.

I can't believe you'd do such a thing. I can't believe you'd betray us all.

The ice in Lucy's voice traveled through his veins until it reached his heart.

He'd intended to stay in London until Twelfth Night. He could hardly remember the excuses he'd given his parents. The next morning, he was on the train out of the city.

Motion caught his eye. Two men were hailing him from the edge of the cliff, waving from behind their easels. Johannes Bernhard and Shigeki Takada.

Last summer, they'd drunk barrels of ale in each other's company and covered miles of canvas with paint. This summer, Kit was keeping his distance.

He waved back, but he was already rolling his bicycle in the opposite direction, hopping onto the saddle.

After that shattering confrontation with Lucy, he'd found himself unable to sustain focus on large pictures. He'd spent the late winter and spring dabbling, producing but a few small color sketches.

Until the fifteenth of May. That was when he'd finally written Lucy a letter, formally withdrawing from the Sisterhood.

I can no longer be your Sister, he'd written. *But I hope to remain your friend.*

He hadn't managed so much as a scribble since. For him, art was over.

He pedaled for home, where he could hide from all this goddamn painterly light.

ONCE HOME, HE spent the remainder of the afternoon taking apart his best high wheeler—a New Rapid, the same model as Deighton's—and putting it back together, assuring himself that his mechanical steed was in peak condition. Reassembly complete, he considered decoration. For a joust, destriers wore rich caparisons embroidered with heraldic symbols. He could paint gold bezants on the black steel, to signal that he rode for Cornwall.

His fingers trembled, then closed into a fist. No, he wouldn't—couldn't—paint gold bezants, or anything at all.

His nails were cutting half-moons into his palms when a decisive knock made the door jump in its frame.

Muriel Pendrake's face appeared before him. He could feel the ghost of her kiss, butterfly soft. Her lips had opened beneath his. In that moment, she'd wanted more.

With a good rake, seduction had a tonic effect.

A low dose wasn't always sufficient.

He hoped she'd decided to follow the doctor's orders. That she'd come to find him. That she'd come for more.

He wiped at the grease on his hands with a rag.

The door jumped again.

His heart jumped too.

Florence, he'd say. *I've been expecting you.*

"Holroyd?" Another knock. "Blast. Sorry. Bungled it. *Griffith,* I mean. Griff, it's me."

The unmistakable voice sent Kit rocketing around his worktable. He flung open the door and stared, disbelieving, at the one old friend in the world he could greet without fear.

5

"Homas Everett Ponsonby!" He launched forward to clap
Ponsonby hard on the back. Ponsonby wrapped him in a bear
hug, then dragged him out of the doorway. They wrestled for a
giddy moment, both hooting like schoolboys. Ponsonby was several
years younger—Kit had already gained admission into the Upper
School of Painting when Ponsonby'd entered the Royal Academy as
a probationer—and their friendship remained incorrigibly laddish.

"I say." Ponsonby stepped away, panting and laughing. "Quite the
formidable tower you've got yourself."

"It's an engine house." Kit grinned up at the tall, narrow building.
"Part of a tin mine originally."

He'd bought the granite shell for next to nothing, then drained
down his trust fund to hire the carpenters and masons who'd in-
stalled floors and pierced the walls with windows.

"Perfect studio." Ponsonby nodded approval. "Wonderful light."

Kit's smile slipped.

Ponsonby was craning his neck and didn't notice. "By God, will
you look at that sunset?"

The sun itself had disappeared behind the headland. Cirrus streaks
layered the sky with orange and rose, shading into gray.

Kit gave a grunt. "Picturesque." His fingers were closing again, his hands fists at his sides. "So." He cleared his throat. "When did you arrive?"

"Yesterday." Ponsonby lowered his chin with a happy sigh. "I plan to stay a month at least. I'm a guest of the Oatridges."

The wealthy London family summered in an elegant white villa perched high above the harbor. Kit hadn't known they were acquainted with Ponsonby, or vice versa.

"I still can't believe you're here." He shook his head. "Of all the days to forget to check the paper."

The *St. Ives Weekly Summary and Visitors List* came out every Saturday. It reported on the local artistic community, the artists' achievements and Show Days, their comings and goings, and their guests. The *Visitors List* was how Kit knew when to avoid parties and public houses, when to ramble off to Penzance for a week, whatever it took to avoid awkward—or worse than awkward—encounters with people who still called him by another name.

Today he'd been distracted, by another visitor to St. Ives.

Muriel's face formed again, and he had to blink the image away.

"Well, *I* checked the paper," said Ponsonby. "Imagine my surprise when I saw your advertisement. I hollered so loudly Mrs. Oatridge came running with bandages. Apparently, the garden chairs sometimes unsheathe rapier-sharp sprigs of wicker. A previous guest was horribly gored." He rubbed his flank absently. "I confirmed I wasn't pouring out my life's blood, and she confirmed that Kit Griffith the bicycle retailer was also Kit Griffith the painter."

A little pause drew out.

"I didn't think you'd mind if I turned up." Ponsonby was watching him, his exceedingly agreeable face—all freckled mirth—suddenly serious. "You know I'd never . . . I did call you *Holroyd* just now. That was a bungle." He flushed to the roots of his red hair, hesitating.

"Hell's bells," he said at last. "*I'm* a bungler. People say that, and they're not wrong. But I'd rather die by wicker then let down a friend. I don't—"

"They are wrong," Kit interrupted. "You're not a bungler."

A clown in his youth, Ponsonby might not have matured into the pragmatic, responsible paragon his eldest brother Cecil, the pater-familias, wanted him to be. He'd learned to listen, though, and to keep his mouth shut when necessary. He was the sort of drinking companion to whom it was seldom a bad idea to confess your secrets.

Over the Christmas holiday, the winter *before* last, Kit had meant to tell Lucy about his other life as Mr. Kit Griffith and ended up telling Ponsonby instead, on a night of carousing that had taken them from theater box to tavern bench to gambling table. By the time they'd stumbled to a feeding place to sober up, Ponsonby was slapping Kit's back and slurring to the lamppost that *Griff* was his best mate.

"You're my best mate." Kit said it experimentally, and Ponsonby made a face.

"Bosh. That's Coover. By my count, I'm your fourth-best mate. It's all right." He batted the air, fending off any potential objections. "You're my second-best mate, really. What matters is that we're mates." His lips twitched now. "I'm *not* a bungler?"

"No." Kit tipped his head. "You're a trump. I trust you with my life. And may a sprig of wicker pierce my heart if it isn't so."

"You're a trump too." Ponsonby grinned. "But you're bollocks at hosting. I've been standing here for long minutes, coated with the dust of the road, my throat cracking."

Kit couldn't help but laugh. "Let's see if I have a chair that won't gore you."

Inside, Kit beelined for the bottle of whiskey on the worktable. There was one glass, clean enough. Kit filled it. When he raised his head, he saw that his friend hadn't followed.

Ponsonby had stilled just over the threshold, staring at the rack of Rovers.

"I don't understand." Ponsonby's perplexity intensified as he surveyed the room.

Kit looked too, trying to see it the way his friend would. Tires hung from pegs in the wall. Tables and shelves held pedal shafts, oil cans, and wrenches. Cyclometers and lamps. Jars of ball bearings.

He'd purchased extravagantly, investing his earnings from the Grosvenor show in the business.

"This is the shop," he said. "Living quarters are upstairs."

"I expected bicycles, but . . ." Ponsonby raked a hand through his disheveled red hair. In his overlarge tweed suit, he looked achingly familiar. Kit could anticipate his next words.

"Your drink," he said, delaying the inevitable. When Ponsonby approached and claimed the glass, he clinked it hard with the bottle. "Cheers."

"Where are the pictures?" Ponsonby glanced at the glass, then at Kit, then again around the room. "Where's your easel?"

"Burned it." Kit swigged from the bottle, the sear of the liquor spreading through his body in tandem with the memory.

"You're not serious."

"Grave as a mustard pot." Kit swigged again. "Art bores me."

"That's a lie." Ponsonby blinked. "Some art bores you. Maybe *most* art bores you. But you've always been fiendishly impressed with your own. Not that I blame you. If I could paint half so well, I'd be twice as insufferable."

Kit was beginning to regret opening the door. "I'm still insufferable, don't worry."

Ponsonby gulped his whiskey. "What does Coover say about this? And the rest of your Sisterhood? Didn't you all pledge to transform the art world?"

"We did." Kit reached out with the bottle and refilled the glass. "As women artists."

"And you're . . . You don't . . . Right." This time the whiskey went down the wrong pipe. Ponsonby coughed until his eyes watered. "I hadn't thought it through. Too heady. Sorry, Griff."

Kit shrugged.

"I wish Lucy had told me you were in St. Ives." Ponsonby fiddled absently with the iron vise at the end of the table. "We talked about my trip, at Burgess's salon, but she didn't let on."

Kit said nothing. Ponsonby assumed Lucy knew where he was living. And shouldn't she? Only miserable gits lied to their best mates. Kit had lied to everyone about his time in the West Country, claiming for himself a merry, Turneresque itinerancy designed to stave off visits.

He cycled to different towns to mail his correspondence and supplied, for a return address, the post office in Camborne, where he paid a clerk to hold letters and parcels.

Lately, they'd been few and far between.

"I understand why." Ponsonby sounded only slightly grudging. "She didn't know *I* knew. That you go by Griff."

"I don't." Kit rolled his eyes. "No one calls me that but you."

"Hmm." Ponsonby looked pleased.

Kit wondered how he'd react to the truth.

You knew before Lucy.

He'd probably feel more confused than flattered.

"I sent her a telegram." Ponsonby missed Kit's violent start. He was wandering toward the New Rapid.

"You . . . what?" Kit's heart hammered.

"I sent a telegram to Coover. Turns out I found you without her help. I had to rub it in a bit." Ponsonby ran a finger along the rim of the New Rapid's front wheel. "Shiny." He turned and caught Kit's eye. "Is something wrong?"

Kit tipped the bottle, whiskey rushing down his throat, taking with it the ugly stream of curses.

Thomas Everett Ponsonby, trump and bungler of the first water.

He'd wired Lucy.

"Did *I* do something wrong?" Ponsonby's face was falling.

Kit had to massage his neck to coax out an approximation of human speech. He wanted to roar. Instead, he croaked, like a rook.

"Not your fault." He set the bottle carefully on the table.

"But what—"

He cut the question off with a wave. "In any event, it's not of any consequence."

Lucy hadn't responded to his letter. So what if she learned his location? His guilt made for a disproportionate reaction. She wasn't going to leave her husband, her *children*, and storm to Cornwall to dress him down in public for abandoning the Sisterhood, even if he deserved it.

But did he? *Had* he betrayed her? Or had she betrayed him?

God, it was heady. Too heady for tonight.

"The New Rapid." He joined Ponsonby at the bicycle. "I'm riding it in a joust."

"Joust." Ponsonby regarded him warily, searching for signs of anger. Presumably, he found none. The tension in his shoulders eased. "*Joust* joust? With lances?"

"Sticks is my guess."

"If they're wicker, you're doomed."

"I'll forfeit at the first sight of wicker." Kit smiled. "How would you like to be my squire?"

"I'd like it almost as much as I'd like dinner." Ponsonby's jollity was entirely restored. "Mrs. Oatridge extended you an invitation." He drew out his watch. "We can't walk, though. It will take far too long. We'll miss the soup."

As Kit fitted Ponsonby for a Rover, he related the story of his accident: beautiful Muriel Pendrake in the enormous boots; her friend, the flippant physician; and Deighton the lunkhead, captain of the undercooked Mutton Wheelers. They were both half-drunk and wheezing with laughter by the time they set off, cycling for town, their lamps lighting the way across the dark fields.

It felt like old times.

Except Kit wasn't thinking about the past, about the Sisters he'd lost. The night air was scented with roses, and herbs, and the faint brine of the sea, teasing his senses, electric with possibility.

He was thinking about that kiss.

6

"I CAN'T BELIEVE IT." James began chortling before Mr. Bamfylde had closed his front door.

"Shhhhh." Muriel gave him a surreptitious shove. "He'll think we're laughing at him." Mr. Bamfylde had the kind of fragile self-importance that reacted furiously to slights even when none were intended. Five minutes in his company had made it perfectly clear why his sister, Eva Bamfylde, avoided it.

"I'm laughing at *you*."

"I know that. But he doesn't. He's a buffoon."

"Shhhh," said James, and chortled louder.

She accelerated away from the cottage, clambering over the stile into a long green field dotted with brown cows.

"I can't believe it," said James, catching up.

"You've already expressed your disbelief."

"It was nothing easy, prying the name from him. My God, he made you work for it! Interrogating you about his sister's activities, like he thinks collecting moss is a form of devil worship."

"I remember. James, this just happened. It's a bit soon to reminisce."

"I'm not reminiscing. I'm relishing. There's a difference. Oh, he's beastly. An obvious skinflint to boot. And he claimed he bought the watercolor at auction as a charity! Hard to credit. Why do you think he gave it to the sister? My guess is she asked for money."

"Why did I take you with me today? That's the question on my mind."

"Moral support." He shook his head, beaming. "I can't believe it. Never have I been so richly repaid for an unpleasant errand involving tea with a tyrannical nitwit."

"Stop. Now."

But he hadn't even gotten started.

"The *rake*. A genius. *Your* genius. Kit Griffith—the very artist you sought!"

She didn't respond.

"Can *you* believe it? Did you suspect? Your eyes were glued to him, but I thought his cheekbones had caught your fancy. Was it his prodigious talent?"

"I am as surprised as you are."

"But are you as *delighted* as I am?"

"I sincerely doubt it. You're about to turn somersaults."

"I haven't turned a somersault in thirty years. But you know, I'd consider it, if this suit weren't white flannel." James spread his arms. "I could caper instead. What constitutes a caper? I think it's a kind of skipping. Skipping in a circle, perhaps?"

He dropped his arms and bumped her with his shoulder. "Muriel. Are you in shock? It often manifests first as stupor. If I had my sphygmograph, I'd check for hypotension."

Muriel gazed past him, across the fields and rolling hills toward the sea. Perhaps it *was* a clinical syndrome, this bizarre sensation—a sizzle cased in ice.

Would that make it easier to treat?

James took her wrist.

"Are you counting my pulse?" She jerked her arm away. "I'm not in shock. I suppose I might have guessed he was an artist. It's artists who move to St. Ives. But he didn't seem like an artist."

"Because he wasn't sitting at an easel? What are artists like?"

She thought of the artists she'd known. Chen Wei, who cultivated dwarf trees in his gardens—some bent ingeniously into the shapes of animals—and contributed satirical cartoons to the newspapers. Pamela Richard, the watercolorist with whom she'd traveled along the Min River, never married, and never long in any one part of the world. Nrityalal Dutta, the woodcut printmaker with the press in Calcutta. A handful of botanical illustrators, most of them botanists themselves, their pictures scrupulous, their personal lives, varied. And then there were the plein air painters she'd observed in St. Ives. Some looked like gentlemen, and others looked like bohemians, and two of the women wore tam-o'-shanters.

"Never mind," she muttered. "I have no generalization to offer about artists. He's not what I was expecting, that's all. Don't ask what I expected. I'm not sure."

"Someone less rakish." James started whistling. A cow stood nearby and swung her neck to look at him.

"Hello, darling," he said, then narrowed his eyes at Muriel. "You should offer him a night in your bed in exchange for the paintings."

She tripped and took a short hopping step, her scowl aimed unfairly at the cow. "That's absurd. I will offer him financial compensation for his paintings, as is generally done."

"Then what's the point of his being a rake?"

"There is no point," she muttered. "Not as far as I'm concerned. It's an extraneous fact."

Nonetheless, her heart began to pound. Over the past day and a half, she'd thought of the rake far too often—not *the rake*. Griffith. It would help if she didn't think of him as a rake at all, and certainly not as a good rake. A fugitive from every stifling convention, luxuriating in voluptuous freedom, daring her to join him with the glint in his eye, with the curl of his lips.

Not *her* in particular. That much was clear.

"He's had at least three lovers named Muriel already." She spoke with too much heat. "He's always in and out of women's beds. The exchange you propose doesn't even make sense. It's backward. I should offer something for a night with *him*."

"Blimey." James stopped short and faced her. "You should."

She cleared her throat. "I didn't mean I *should* should. I was critiquing your logic. I meant a night with me isn't a sufficient incentive for a man like him."

"Muriel." James put his hand on his heart. "We've known each other a very long time. But believe me when I say you're a raving beauty."

She wrinkled her nose. "I might believe you. If you hadn't once said I resemble a trout."

"I never said any such thing." He sounded indignant. "But now that you mention it, you do sometimes give me a troutlike look, a sort of open-mouthed frown. Like right now."

"James."

"Trout are beautiful creatures. Those big, bulging eyes."

"*James.*"

"Oh, hell." He slouched. "In any case, you've a brilliant mind. And a winning personality."

"I can't bear another of your compliments. They're lacerating."

"Perhaps we tease each other too much." He tipped his head and spoke in a sober voice. "I adore everything about you. You are outlandishly lovable."

She met his eyes. They were hazel in the city, but in the countryside, they reverted to emerald green. His gaze felt warm as the summer day.

James loved her. Her mother had loved her. Esmé had taken her for granted. It was thanks to him, though, that she'd escaped her cousin's shop, the dreariness of stocking onions, years spent sweeping the same length of floor. Their marriage had opened so many doors. Enlarged her world by powers of ten.

"I am outlandishly lucky," she said, and she meant it. If she felt at times that something was missing—well, so did everyone.

She started walking again, and James matched her pace. She bumped him with *her* shoulder.

"We've got each other," she said. "We've no need of rakes."

"Speak for yourself." His flat tone took her aback.

"Oh." She slowed. "Well. Maybe there's a rake for you too." Her cheeks flamed. She'd spoken as though she *had* a rake. But she'd worry about that slip later.

James was gazing up at the clouds. "It's not quite as easy, is it?"

She bit her lip. Comparisons were so fraught. James was a man, a doctor, the son of a baron. No one ever simply looked at him and doubted his intelligence or closed him out of their conversations, clubs, societies, seminar rooms, or offices. He enjoyed legal rights denied her—the right to vote, for example.

But his love affairs carried specific risks.

"Few worthwhile things come to us easily," she said, and he cut her a sardonic glance. She dropped her eyes, feeling foolish. She didn't like platitudes either. But she'd nothing else to offer if they didn't address the subject directly.

"James," she began. "I can tell something has been troubling you. Is it about—"

"Does it look like rain?" James was gazing at the sky again.

"Um." Muriel cast a critical eye at the puffy white clouds. "Eventually."

"That's what I thought," said James. "Eventually, rain."

She sighed. They walked on, turning down a hedged path, and the strain left James's face as they summited the hill. There was a farmhouse below, and barns, and a well-grazed pasture.

A cheering crowd pressed against the fencing.

And in the pasture . . . those weren't *cows*.

Muriel did a double take.

Two men on bicycles were pedaling toward each other at top speed. The spokes of their enormous front wheels glittered in the sun.

James let out a hoot. "A rake, a genius, and a most proper knight!"

He turned to Muriel, grinning, then bounded a few steps down the hill. His gleeful narration carried back to her.

"The combat has begun, and our Griffith rides forth most gallantly. No, he is not faint of heart but spurs faster and faster, and lo! His golden shield doth shine in the sun!"

James stopped and whirled round. "They don't seem to have shields, actually. Hope Deighton didn't sharpen those lances."

And he was off, bounding the rest of the way down the slope.

Muriel hitched up her skirts and followed. There was no overtaking James on this occasion. He disappeared into the throng as she reached level ground.

She'd bet the beaches were empty. Every holidaymaker in St. Ives seemed to have turned up for the joust, as well as several of the artists—at least she assumed the tweedy men in deerstalker hats were artists. As she squeezed between them, she could smell the turpentine.

A roar erupted.

She went up on her tiptoes, peering between shoulders.

Griffith and Deighton were pedaling a collision course. Each leaned low over the handlebars, reducing his opponent's target. Deighton's face was contorted in a snarl. Griffith wore a faint smile.

They whooshed past each other, Griffith swerving at the last minute, Deighton's lance glancing off his shoulder.

"Are those billiard cues?" James materialized at her elbow.

"Every chalk mark is a point," explained an excited, half-grown boy. He was no doubt imagining staging his own joust at the earliest convenience.

A man had climbed the fence. "Go, go, go!" he was yelling, pumping his fist in the air. He called down to a younger man in a matching striped jacket. "Deighton'll chalk him good this time."

Muriel caught a glimpse of his thin face, dominated by a mustache of surpassing lustrousness. A wheel-shaped badge glinted on his lapel.

She asked James, "Is he in Deighton's cycling club?"

"That's Butterfield." He nodded. "We're among Mutton Wheelers."

Muriel noticed two other men in striped jackets, then her eyes strayed back to the pasture. Griffith and Deighton were riding toward each other again.

James touched her elbow. "Shall we move along?"

Before she could answer, a collective gasp rose from the crowd.

"No, no, no!" shouted Butterfield.

She pushed forward and got her foot on the lower slat of the fence, climbing up then leaning out to see between the waving arms.

Griffith and Deighton were moving now in the same direction, Griffith hurtling forward on his bicycle, Deighton propelled backward off his, the tip of Griffith's billiard cue pressed to his throat.

The thud was swallowed by the cheers and the groans.

"Let me through!" That was James, swinging his leg over the fence. "I'm a doctor!"

7

THE CROWD SWARMED the fence, and Kit leapt to earth, letting his New Rapid wobble on, riderless. Within moments, the bicycle was surrounded by laughing young men—tony trippers from London, excited to muck up their brogues. They lifted it above their heads and paraded around the pasture.

"Well met!" yelled Ponsonby. Kit looked in the direction of the voice, saw a flash of red, his friend's bright hair bobbing toward him.

Bloody hell but there were a lot of people.

He'd imagined a handful of spectators, and that's what he'd said to Wilmot Curnow when he'd asked the farmer for use of the pasture.

He hadn't asked for this.

This was chaos.

Deighton's fault, obviously. He must have made a circuit of the best hotels, bragging about his tourney in lobbies all around the bay.

Well, he'd hoisted himself upon his own petard.

Unfortunately, this wasn't the time to gloat.

If Curnow's cows got out, Kit would find himself hoisted as well.

He could hear Deighton distinctly now, bellowing.

"Let's go again! That was the first of three!"

"He never said three." Ponsonby elbowed his way up to Kit, flushed like a man in the throes of fatal apoplexy. Or like a ginger on a hot day in a crowded cow pasture.

Kit's sudden surge of alarm evaporated.

"It's not very sporting of him." Ponsonby frowned, then brightened instantly. "If the cheating duffer wants to get knocked down two more times, why not?"

"The joust is over." Kit pulled Ponsonby out of the path of the parade. The train of hilarious young men was longer now. "God almighty, it's like Hyde Park in here. Curnow will have my head."

"All right, then." Ponsonby nodded. "Joust's over!" He cupped his hands on either side of his mouth and shouted. "Shove off!"

No one acknowledged him. The parade paraded on.

"Good effort, mate." Kit clapped him on the shoulder. "I'll convey the news to Deighton direct, though. Might be more effective."

They struggled through the crowd.

"I shouldn't tell you this." Ponsonby yelled directly in Kit's ear. "She said not to tell you."

Kit stretched his neck, moving his head as far from Ponsonby's mouth as possible.

"But it's a day of glory!" Ponsonby gave a mighty yawp. "Are you ready?" He didn't wait for a response. "Coover wired back. She's coming to St. Ives!"

Kit's head snapped around.

"I don't believe you can ruin a surprise." Ponsonby winked. "A surprise is a surprise. Now is as good as later. Watch your feet." He laughed and tugged Kit's arm, steering him around a cowpat. "And you know Sisters travel in force. You'll reunite! And I'll de-bungle things with Nelly." Ponsonby's yawp was mightier than the yawp before.

The roar in Kit's ears had nothing to do with Ponsonby's yawps, or the murmurs of the crowd.

Did Lucy plan to berate him, her outrage reinforced by Gwen and Nelly?

His innards shivered, a sickly motion.

Did she plan to *expose* him?

Before Boxing Day, he'd believed her the last person on earth who'd ever do him harm.

When? He tried to ask but couldn't speak. Perhaps he hadn't caught his breath properly. All that frantic pedaling had winded him.

He tried again and managed it. "When?"

"What?" yelled Ponsonby. "When? Oh, I don't know. It was just a telegram. Not for a little while. At least a week, a week and a half, perhaps. Coover has that opening, remember? The New Gallery? Ouch."

Ponsonby stumbled to the left, helped along by a shove from the person with whom he'd collided.

And Kit found himself face-to-face with Deighton, so close that the toes of the bigger man's shoes overlapped his own.

"That wasn't a joust," Deighton growled. "That was a farce. The terrain is all humps and ditches and dung. The mud threw me, not *you*. Let's meet on the road."

"Are you sure? The road's much harder. When you take a cropper, you're more likely to split your head."

"I won't be the one taking a cropper!" Deighton snatched off his cricketing cap and wadded it in his hand. His sweaty blond hair lay flat on his scalp. He looked like a child about to tantrum, except ten times the size. He loomed even closer, grinding Kit's toes.

"Have I got your name down correctly?" Arthur Hawkings from the newspaper pushed between them, shoving his notepad under Deighton's nose. "Colin Deighton, from Bristol? Your bicycle club is the Mutton Wheelers?"

Deighton stiffened. "Colin Deighton, Captain." He stroked his hand over his badges. "You're not going to write that I lost the joust? In the *paper*? I'll sue for defamatory libel."

Hawkings withdrew the notepad. "I'm happy to quote you as refusing to concede defeat. Any quote from you, Griffith?"

Kit shrugged, except his shoulders didn't move. He felt as though a bag of sand weighed them down.

Ponsonby's voice was repeating in his head, making it difficult to concentrate on what was being said around him. *A week and a half. A week and a half.*

He could picture Lucy, Gwen, and Nelly marching toward him, their skirts snapping around their ankles.

"You should write about our club run." Deighton thrust his chin at Hawkings. "I've been planning it for months. We'll be the first to circle Cornwall, coast-to-coast. We're going west to Land's End, south to the Lizard, east to Kingsand, north to Bude, west again to St. Ives. Ten days of riding over sandy road, and mud, and stone. Griffith wouldn't last on his *safety*."

"Is that a challenge?" Hawkings asked. There was a little hush.

Challenge?

"Not much of one." Kit focused. "I could do that ride on a safety with no hands."

Deighton laughed. "Only if you grasped onto my coat so I could tug you along. But I doubt you could reach."

"The safety is low to the ground." Kit acknowledged the obvious. "But that makes it faster than the ordinary. You're not so much buffeted by the wind, and your position relative to the pedals allows you to exert more force with less fatigue. *I* could complete your tour." He paused. "And so could any of the riding students I've trained, women as well as men."

"Women?" Deighton laughed. "Women circling Cornwall on two wheels?"

"That's what I said."

Deighton returned his cap to his head, yanking down on the brim. "Here is the challenge, then. We leave Tuesday after next. If Griffith can train up a *lady* who completes the ride with us . . ." Deighton's expression darkened as he thought. "The Mutton Wheelers will switch to safeties and admit female members. And if she doesn't complete the ride, or if it takes her *longer* than ten days . . ."

"I'll turn over my business." The roaring in Kit's ears quieted. He felt, suddenly, as though he stood in the eye of the storm of his life.

Lucy was coming to St. Ives.

He'd ride an infinite gyre if it meant he could avoid her.

"I'll take the bets!" someone shouted, to a smattering of loud guffaws.

Deighton's hand swooped at Kit like a hungry gull.

"Who's the intrepid lady?" Hawkings flipped to the next page of his notepad, pencil poised.

"Excuse me. Coming through." The crowd rippled. Kit turned. A breathless woman in a straw hat drew up to him. She wore no shoot-ing boots today.

"I am the intrepid lady," she said. "Muriel Pendrake."

MURIEL'S DECLARATION WAS still hanging in the air when a furious farmer appeared out of nowhere, flanked by two equally furious dairymaids.

"Man alive!" one of the dairymaids cried. "Where are the cows? They 'aven't broke loose?"

"Lor!" cried the other. "They 'ave!"

In the commotion that followed, Muriel was separated from Griffith, carried along as the crowd streamed for the fence. When she'd attained the road, she turned about, scanning for James. He wasn't doctoring, was he? Deighton didn't require medical attention, but perhaps that poor farmer had fallen into a fit. Dozens of shoul-ders, heads, and hats blocked her view of the pasture. She realized people were looking at her, their gazes curious, or—in the cases of several ladies—frankly envious.

Well, she'd made a spectacle of herself, volunteering to tour around Cornwall on a bicycle with a pack of rowdy yahoos and one devastatingly attractive rake. Instinct had spurred her forward. Her brain was just now catching up. Nonetheless, as she considered the ramifications of her action more coolly, she wasn't entirely displeased. Problems proliferated, but also possibilities.

"Who wants to walk to Zennor?" A fresh-faced girl in a cotton print dress and a hat trimmed with seashells was trying to rally a contingent of similarly attired young women who, if they weren't older, were at least doing their best to appear considerably more jaded. They smirked and yawned and fanned themselves, waiting for a preferable cue.

A few families had begun the walk back to St. Ives, or rather the mothers and fathers walked while the children skipped or gave each other chase. Others—members of the artistic-looking set—were striking out in twos and threes, following narrow paths through the fields. A tartan tam-o'-shanter bobbed along between deerstalkers.

"Doesn't anyone care to see the Giant's Rock?" pleaded the girl.

Muriel crossed the road, starting up a grassy slope. From the hill-side, she'd be able to survey the scene, pick out James, and . . . She turned.

Griffith.

A gasp exploded in her throat. He stood just below her, head tipped back, sun gilding his hair and the tips of his long lashes.

"Mr. Griffith." She recovered her breath, but her heart kept racing. Thank God, James wasn't here to study her pulse. She felt like a hummingbird in the presence of a buddleia flower, not only because Griffith seemed to favor fabrics in shades of pale purple.

At least her common sense prevented her from sipping at his skin, although it looked petal soft where it stretched across his cheekbones, gleaming with a light sheen of sweat, making her wonder if he tasted like honey or salt . . .

"Mrs. Pendrake," he said, and she blinked. Had she been listing toward him? Dratted gravity. It was never wise to converse on an incline.

He shook his head, a glint in his eye. "How formal we are, considering."

Considering. Considering their kiss.

The sun seemed to shine brighter.

"I'd rather call you Muriel," he continued, his silky voice conveying immense satisfaction. He was dazzling, and he knew it.

She frowned.

"I'm sure you would," she said tartly. "Women's Christian names conjure such happy memories."

An infuriating grin spread across his face, and she bit the inside of her cheek. Blast. She'd remembered his attractiveness but not his powers of annoyance. Already she'd let him ruffle her feathers.

She put her hands on her hips. "I don't want you saying *Muriel* while picturing a legion of ticklish knees."

"All right." He angled a look at her from beneath those absurdly long lashes. "Show me where *you* are ticklish, and I'll picture that."

She let her arms drop and laughed, another of those unguarded, booming laughs that emerged from the depths of her diaphragm. He was too ridiculous.

"The soles of your feet?" he guessed, peering down at her shoes with interest.

"I'm not telling." She curled her toes. "You can call me Mrs. Pendrake."

"Penny," he countered. "It suits you. Your hair is the color of new pennies. And I've never known a Penny. I'm a blank slate, no memories. *Yet.*"

She ignored this last, and the way his lips quirked. God, he was smug. She ignored, too, the odd little flutter in her belly. No one had ever given her a nickname.

"Penny." She repeated it disapprovingly. "I believe it's a diminutive of Penelope, not Pendrake."

"Is it?" he asked wryly. "Too bad. I *have* known a Penelope."

"Spare me the details of her garret."

"No garret. Her father's a banker. She lets a rather large apartment by King's College and takes courses in the Ladies' Department. Terrific bluestocking."

Bluestocking.

Muriel's brows pulled together. "Is her pug named Pugnacious?"

He gave her an appreciative glance. "No pug either. She has a cat, a fluffy gray puff of a thing named Athena. And among friends she goes by Poppy."

She spoke without thinking. "I shouldn't like to be called Poppy."

"Too whimsical?"

"Too deadly serious. Poppies. *Papaver somniferum.* The seeds are tiny, but . . ."

She waved her hand, which seemed the only way to finish the sentence, here, with him, a near stranger. This wasn't the time, or the place.

It had taken her years to understand the scale of the devastation those tiny seeds had unleashed, on India, on China. And it had taken her even longer to understand that her peaceful, disinterested scientific work depended on the British Empire's exploitation and violence. She'd been too focused on minutiae, too concerned with plants as biological entities, too willing to ignore the fact that nothing was purely natural, detached from social and political realities. If it weren't for Chen Wei's cartoons, she might never have recognized that her presence in his garden was less than innocent.

Art was potent and could transform perspectives.

That's why she needed Griffith now.

He was watching her intently. "Go on."

She hesitated. Probably his conversational range extended beyond outrageous flirtation. She'd judged him frivolous, but his painting proved he had hidden depths. Perhaps she could talk with him about topics weightier than French lace curtains. Perhaps she would.

If they traveled Cornwall together on bicycles, they'd have plenty of opportunities for conversation. For all sorts of things.

"It's nothing." She shook herself and smiled. "Penny, then. But only if I can call you *Griff.*"

"Griff?" He started. "Good God. It's catching, isn't it? *Griff.*" He shuddered, his wickedly handsome face alight with humor. "You drive a hard bargain."

He reached out, took her hand, and shook it. His grip was warm and firm, and she could feel his calluses where they pressed the flesh of her palm. She seemed to have more nerve endings in her palms than she could credit. Or was James right about the rain? Perhaps a storm was gathering.

Her whole body crackled with electricity.

"Penny and Griff." He didn't release her hand. "Renegades of the Rover. A shame we don't have badges."

"We'll ride together, then? It's settled?" No hummingbird's heart had ever beat so fast. "You don't mind that I inserted myself into this tour?"

"Mind? You're a godsend." He let go of her hand and brushed at the chalk dust on his heliotrope jacket. His boutonniere had come through the joust unscathed, a white carnation. "What would I have done if you hadn't stepped forward?"

Waited five seconds for another woman to step forward.

Her voice was dry as sand. "What indeed."

He looked at her, eyelids lowering a fraction. "You *can* ride a bicycle?"

"I'm certain I can." She straightened her spine. "I cannot say as I have."

"And you're just as certain you want to spend hours a day doing so?" He cocked his head, expression suddenly doubtful. "I don't know the exact route Deighton has proposed, but I do know Cornish roads. They'll rattle your teeth."

"I have no worries about my teeth. And also—I have an ulterior motive." She confessed it with a combination of excitement and dread.

"Ah." The huskiness of that one syllable made her neck prickle. He arched his brows. "Must you rack up another impulsive activity to please Dr. Raleigh? He wasn't satisfied by *slight seduction*?"

Her stomach lurched. Of course, he was too provoking not to refer outright to what had passed between them. Just as well, though. Good to clear the air.

"About that." She gripped her skirt. "I owe you an apology. It was beyond presumptuous, my claiming to have seduced you. But James had been pestering me about spending too much time on my work."

"Which meant any rake who strayed into your path was fair game for demonstrations of your commitment to leisure?"

His smile was ironic.

"I made a claim." She hesitated, cheeks burning. "*You* performed the demonstration."

His brows rose higher. "With your participation. To support you in your ruse."

She smiled weakly. Her ruse? Lord but this was lowering. She knew she'd been spouting nonsense that afternoon. But apparently, in some small, secret, vulnerable pocket of her being, she'd been harboring the flattering delusion that she *had* seduced him, slightly, ever so slightly. That she'd intrigued and tempted him. That his kiss had been more than a favor.

Embarrassment rushed through her, a milder version of the shame she'd felt on the occasions she'd approached Esmé in her nightgown, only to have her tentative overtures quelled with a look.

"Most obliging." Her mouth tasted sour. "Chivalry is not dead."

"Two modern-day knights just charged each other on iron horses, wielding billiard cues." He shrugged. "Chivalry is alive and well, and God help us all."

She couldn't interpret his expression. He drew closer, a step up the hill that simultaneously made his height increase by inches.

"Tell me the real reason you want to ride," he murmured. "Ulterior motives are the most interesting."

"It's you," she blurted, and swallowed hard, flustered by the knowing glint in his eyes. "Rather—it's that I know who you are."

He drew back sharply. "What do you mean by that?"

"You're not the proprietor of a bicycle shop, or not primarily."

His expression was hardening, the points of his jaws standing out, the lines around his mouth cutting deeper.

Misgiving stirred within her, speeding her words. "You're an artist. An astonishingly good one. Your watercolor of the columbine— I've worked as a botanist for over a decade, but it changed how I thought about plants, about their cells and the light. I could see the sun *inside* the leaves."

What did *he* see? He was staring at her as though she'd sprouted another head.

"I am giving a lecture in September, in New York." She grew more nervous by the instant. "It is on British seaweeds, and my dearest hope is to commission you for botanical paintings."

Griffith stood like a statue. His stillness had an ominous quality, gave her the impression of hostility tightly leashed. It made no sense. He'd practically purred over Poppy the bluestocking. Clearly, he didn't object to women studying. Did he object to women pursuing careers?

"Our aims find perfect complementarity in this bicycle tour." She used her lecture hall voice, carrying and confident, but she was breathing too fast, and the pitch of her delivery wavered. "You want to scupper Deighton, which I can guarantee. I am indefatigable. Ask James. And given that we'll travel miles and miles of coast, I am sure to encounter more seaweed species than I would if I simply walked around St. Ives."

Griffith's mouth was turning down at the corners.

She rushed on. "I'll only collect the very rare ones. You'd make the paintings in St. Ives, obviously. But if you did a few sketches along the way, we could—"

"Impossible," he interrupted her. "No one has yet discovered a method for collecting seaweed while bicycling. Or sketching while bicycling, for that matter."

As objections went, it seemed deliberately obtuse.

She spoke calmly. "We will dismount the bicycles, of course."

"Thereby falling behind the Mutton Wheelers."

"But who cares, as long as we reach our destination each night? As long as we get back to St. Ives on the tenth day?"

"I am not a flower painter." Griffith sounded cold. Without the teasing animation in his face, he looked supercilious, as though his beautiful features had been fashioned for haughty disdain.

"The watercolor you mentioned," he said. "I did it for a fundraiser. A fishing ship had been lost, name of *The Columbine*. That's the only reason I painted a flower, as a tribute. Something pretty, in commemoration."

"Are you saying you won't take the commission?" Her body felt leaden. "I wasn't suggesting a trade, my riding on the tour in exchange for your paintings. I would pay you, of course. Name your price."

"I'd do it for pennies." He gave her a strange smile. "If I were going to do it, I'd do it for Penny."

"But you're not going to do it."

"I'm not."

"Why?" It burst from her. "Because you think too highly of yourself? Because most flower painters are women?" The unpleasant sensation in her chest coalesced into anger, more anger than she had any right to feel. "Because you prefer more exalted genres? I suppose you specialize in scenes from history. Hulking oils that take up whole walls."

He shrugged. "I paint scenes from history on occasion. Not lately."

"Nudes?" She crossed her arms. A rake *would* paint nudes.

"Often." He shrugged again. "Also, not of late."

"Do you lack for subjects?" This wasn't London, after all. Cornish women were Methodist, too pious to pose in dishabille. And modeling might strike his lovers as dangerously indiscreet.

Discretion meant nothing to her. She was poised to depart the continent.

The idea sprang from her mind to her lips with scarcely a moment's friction.

"If you take the commission," she said, "and paint the seaweeds, I'll let you paint me too. Nude. However you like."

She raised her chin, blushing fiercely.

Only his eyes moved, flicking over her.

"I cannot accept the commission," he said slowly. "Or your generous offer."

His refusal hit her like a slap.

"Well, then." She jerked a nod. "I will have to find another artist."

"There are plenty in St. Ives." His voice was polite.

Hers was trembling. "And you, sir, will have to find another intrepid lady."

Surprise flashed across his face. It made her angrier still. Had he thought she still intended to ride with him? That she'd do it for the pleasure of his company? The privilege of gazing upon his handsome form?

The tour was a waste of time without his collaboration.

She didn't care if he lost his bicycle shop.

In fact, she rather hoped he would.

She narrowed her eyes. "Good luck choosing amongst the Muriels and Margarets."

A crease notched his brow.

"Penny," he began, but she spun on her heel. This meant plodding up the hill, but it was better than returning to the road at his side, awkward and humiliated and crushingly disappointed.

How had it gone so wrong?

She wasn't being strictly reasonable, or fair. She'd pegged all her hopes on Kit Griffith, but he hadn't been party to her plan. He'd made her no promises. He owed her nothing.

Still, his bewildering reaction stung, more than stung. He'd spited both of them, for what? For his arrogant masculine pride.

She didn't want to dwell on the wound to her own pride, why it burned like fire, why the rejection touched such a tender place inside her.

She watched the grass bend beneath her feet and concentrated on putting more and more distance between herself and *Griff*.

"GRIFF!"

Kit watched Muriel's tiny, tense figure as she climbed the hill, shoulders rigid, a lock of penny-bright hair curling in the center of her back, like an upside-down question mark.

She had a temper. And she was stubborn, marching off in the most strenuous direction, which would also extend her walk back to St. Ives. Did she even know which way she was headed? His muscles twitched. He could overtake her before she reached the summit.

"Griff!"

He turned. Ponsonby was legging it toward him, stride matched with that of his companion, a lanky, dark-haired man in a sharply tailored white flannel suit. The doctor, Raleigh. Ponsonby stopped, but Raleigh passed Kit by, sparing him a quick, keen glance. Inquiring, not adversarial.

"Bloody fast, isn't she?" Raleigh tossed the comment over his shoulder, his grin wider than his face.

Kit wasn't in the mood to smile back.

What exactly was the nature of Raleigh's friendship with Muriel? It didn't matter.

Kit watched the man's long legs devour the ground. He'd catch up with Muriel in no time. And she'd tell the good doctor that Kit thought too much of himself to paint flowers, that he was too manly for watercolors and scoffed at commissions.

She'd jumped to conclusions, but he hadn't disabused her. His desire to evade questions had made him surly and defensive, rude.

It didn't matter.

None of it mattered.

"I like that fellow." Ponsonby was catching his breath. "We fixed the fence together. My one act of service for the day. He's a surgeon, though. He'll probably deliver a baby before morning. What do you think it feels like to be so useful?"

"No idea." Kit stalked down the hill. He wasn't in the mood for anything. The sun beat down, but ice had spread through his chest, the feeling familiar. Whiskey didn't warm it, but at least it blunted his thoughts.

He'd go home, drink half a bottle, tinker with his Rovers, and forget the drama that he'd watched play out across Muriel's face—a blaze of eager hope reduced to stricken cinders. Hurt and contempt in her eyes.

Their expression had reminded him of Lucy's.

In the distance, he could see Martha Curnow leading a cow toward the milking barn. Thank the Lord. Things could be worse.

The Curnows' herd could be halfway to Penzance.

"Barmy bet you made." Ponsonby fell into step with him. "I was thinking—maybe you could joust again instead, like Deighton suggested."

His jaw tightened. "There's no changing the terms of a wager."

"To hell with all that. You can't just ride off. It's beastly timing. What about Coover?"

"Give her my regrets."

"Your bicycle's over there." Ponsonby gestured, the motion of his arm conveying frustration.

Kit quickened his pace as he changed course.

"I'm sure they'll stay until you're back." Ponsonby quickened his pace too. "Or we could cable and tell them to postpone."

"I don't want them to stay." Kit's feet carried him forward, but he felt detached from his body, as though his limbs moved of their own accord. "I don't want to see them. To that end, I hope I can rely on your help."

"Griff." Ponsonby grabbed his shoulder. Kit tensed, then swung to face him.

"What are you saying?" Ponsonby wore a look of confused apprehension. "I don't understand. We haven't all of us been together for ages."

"You're bloody right. And that's by *design*." Kit raked both hands through his hair, only barely resisting the urge to rip handfuls up by the roots. "Christ. This little reunion is a frolic for you, but it's hell for me. Why do you think I'm living at the edge of the fucking world?"

"Because . . ." Ponsonby had paled, his freckles standing out in dark clusters. "Because of Turner's Cornish sketchbooks." He tilted back his head. "The light really is extraordinary."

Kit made an impatient noise.

"And because London can be a wretchedly small place." Ponsonby said it softly, returning his eyes to Kit. "I expect you have a hundred reasons. But we're talking about Coover."

"I could explain." He looked past Ponsonby at his high wheeler, propped against an oak.

Ponsonby followed his gaze. "You'd rather not, though."

"Not at the moment, no." It hurt too much. The ice in her voice. The horror in her eyes. The idea that he'd begun to fear her—*Lucy*. His best mate.

"You'd rather we make haste to the nearest pub, where I will perform my *second* act of service for the day."

Ponsonby's pause was expectant. Kit glanced at him.

"Which is?" he sighed.

"Reviving your spirits, mate." Ponsonby folded his arms. "By letting you best me at billiards."

"Ha." Kit's jaw muscles eased.

"And then I'll beat whoever steps up next."

"Have a care." Kit started walking again, his steps more fluid. "Your spirits might never recover. Let alone your purse."

Later, at the Smack, after he'd been stood a drink by every joustgoer in the house and made thirteen points on a single shot at the billiards table, he wedged himself in a corner, wondering if his spirits had, in fact, revived. His eyes felt hot, and his lips felt numb, and tiredness stole through him with blissful languor.

A petite woman with upswept blond hair was gazing at him across the crowded room. She wore a narrow silk dress in the latest London fashion. Her smile was bold, perhaps even intrepid.

He considered making his way to her, discovering her thoughts on bicycle touring, and her availability for the week after next. Instead, he let Ponsonby put a fresh tumbler in his hand and pull him into conversation.

He wasn't ready to look for a new riding companion.

But surely he'd feel differently tomorrow.

8

~⚬⚬ᔓ

"Y OU ARE THAT gel."

Muriel barely registered the starchy voice. She'd chosen a table near the window, so she could eat her breakfast looking out at the bay.

"Reginald," came the voice again. "Is it not that gel?"

Muriel turned her head and met the gimlet eye of the older woman seated at the nearest table. Her high-collared black gown looked costly and too warm for the weather. She was studying Muriel with her thin brows angled down and her lips pursed.

Muriel gave her a slightly puzzled smile.

"I believe you are right," said the woman's breakfast companion, lowering his paper to reveal a youthful face, round and blandly pleasant.

"I believe you are wrong," offered Muriel, as politely as possible. Her head was throbbing. She'd risen with the sun and spent two disappointing hours at the rock pools, before a dog with matted fur and a frenzied bark sped her down the beach and up to the hotel.

A poor start to the day. She'd hoped to avoid dining room chitchat.

"Reginald," said the woman. "What did that gel say?"

"She believes you are wrong," the man responded.

"But I am never wrong. Tell her."

"Excuse me," said the man, louder. "Sir Reggie here. This is Lady Chiswick, my mother. She is never wrong."

Muriel frowned.

"I am hardly a girl," she informed Sir Reggie. "I have reached the far side of thirty."

"Have you?" Sir Reggie raised his brows, impressed. "Dang it. Well preserved. I say."

"You've said quite enough, Reginald," said Lady Chiswick. "What is your name, gel?"

Muriel tried not to sigh. "Muriel Pendrake."

"The bicycle gel!" Lady Chiswick nodded triumphantly. "Just so."

Bother. She should have known.

Lady Chiswick leaned forward. "You plan to bicycle scads of miles with the Mutton Chops."

"Legs of Lamb," corrected Sir Reggie. He tilted his head with a thoughtful frown. "Or was that the dance troupe I saw that time in Leicester Square?"

"I know why," continued Lady Chiswick, ignoring her son. "You are one of those gels who loses her head over men in uniform."

"What's this?" Muriel's cheeks heated. "You don't mean—like Lydia in *Pride and Prejudice*? I think the phenomenon is specific to regimentals. Officers, not . . . *bicyclists*."

"You cannot fool me, gel. I could tell which one caught your fancy." Lady Chiswisk persisted. "Your eyes were out on stalks, like a lobster's."

Muriel willed the floor to open. That was just how she felt when she looked at Kit Griffith. Was it so very obvious to everyone? Did her eyes really seem to pop from her face?

"He is as handsome as he is rich." Lady Chiswick's gaze hardened. "And he is not for you. My Clarinda has caught *his* fancy. It is to be expected. Clarinda has every advantage." She allowed a pregnant pause. "I have decided to encourage the attachment."

"Are you sure that's wise? Looks and money aren't everything. The man is a rake." As soon as she said it, Muriel's stomach gave a tiny kick. Good Lord, was she really joining into the spirit of this nasty, nonsensical competition?

"Nothing doing." Sir Reggie piped up. "We were school chums. I'd never say he's a *rake*. More of an axle." He chuckled at his own joke while both Lady Chiswick and Muriel stared. "Axles allow wheels to rotate," he explained. "And he lives and breathes bicycles. So, he's an axle, not a rake. The humor depends on the other definition of *rake*, which is—"

"He is neither a rake nor an axle," interrupted Lady Chiswick. "He is a bachelor of pleasing appearance and address, good family, and large fortune. And since their fateful meeting last year at Lord Etherington's ball, he has been in love with your sister."

"How do you figure?" Sir Reggie wore an expression of earnest inquiry.

Lady Chiswick made a vague gesture. "He shows the telltale signs."

"Right-ho." Sir Reggie returned his attention to his plate. After a brief moment, he lifted his head, and his fork. "Such as?"

"Such as . . ." Lady Chiswick looked cross. "He was speechless to see her again."

"Oh, but that was because he couldn't place her." Sir Reggie explained around a mouthful of fried whiting. "Then he saw me and twigged."

Lady Chiswick spoke more coldly. "He invited her to call on him at Titcombe Hall."

"Did he? Where was I?"

Lady Chiswick said something sotto voce in reply, but the exchange already had faded from Muriel's notice. Her brain whirred along its own track.

Clarinda. It was a pretty name. How did Griffith think of her? Was she *Clarinda with the school-chum brother*? Or did he associate her with the marriage-minded Lady Chiswick? Or something more intimate, a heart-shaped birthmark beneath her left collarbone?

She glared down at her dissected toast, a jumble of angular fragments and dark crumbs. Had Griffith lied to this Clarinda, pretending to offer something more permanent than a tickle? Or had he lied to *her*? Led her to believe that no particular woman claimed his affection, when he was all but engaged to a young miss?

Either way, she felt confirmed in her negative assessment of his character. Of course he had a large fortune! He was only playing at being an artist. Even his talk of shamelessness amounted to nothing. It was a spoiled rich boy's fantasy of rebellion, a bohemian spin on sowing one's wild oats before landing at the altar. He was detestable, but typically so, his every action evidence of the shallow purpose and lazy hedonism that characterized men of the upper echelons.

She'd wasted too much time thinking about him already.

"I pray Clarinda does not lose *her* head," she said, rising from her chair. "A bit of rational evaluation will shatter her illusions. Better now than later."

"How do you dare?" Lady Chiswick paled. She put so much starch in her voice it creaked. "Your temerity astounds me."

"I have heard that before," Muriel admitted, feeling suddenly tired. Doubtless, she'd hear it again. In New York City, as her professional prospects crumbled.

"Good day, then," she said, and turned away.

"It is unnatural!" Lady Chiswick cried after her. "A woman astride a bicycle. Only one thing comes to mind."

Muriel turned back.

Lady Chiswick sat straighter. "The *thing* that unnatural women have been known to straddle."

Sir Reggie went purple. He coughed violently, sipped his tea, and coughed again.

"A broomstick!" Lady Chiswick threw back her head. "Think on that, gel."

Muriel stood stock-still. After a moment, she gave herself a shake.

"I will," she promised. "If I figure out how to make a bicycle fly, you will be the first to know."

She spun on her heel to the sound of Lady Chiswick's harrumph.

As she sidled between the tables, she could hear Lady Chiswick address her son, the command resounding.

"You will take Clarinda to Titcombe Hall *today*."

Sir Reggie's protest followed, floating on the air: "I certainly will not. The poor fellow's parents are due this afternoon. Everything about them makes him savage. He used to open letters from home and straightaway break a window, or torture a cat. Best steer clear until the dust settles."

Muriel stopped short. *Torture a cat?* And to think, Griffith had smirked affectionately about fluffy gray Athena!

"Today, Reginald." Lady Chiswick's voice snapped like a whip.

Muriel marched on, sparking with indignation. Horrid rake! And horrid lady! Did she truly intend to encourage an attachment between her daughter and a cat-torturing libertine? Had she no soul?

The beau monde was a blight on humanity.

Once she'd exited the dining room, Muriel scoured the hotel grounds for James, who was, in a sense, an emissary from the beau monde, for all he'd been raised in a backwater.

"You have a soul, James," she said when she found him, sprawled in a caned chaise longue in a shady corner of the walled back garden. "How?"

"Don't ask me." James rested his book on his lap. "I'm a brain surgeon. All I know about the soul is that it doesn't reside in the pineal gland." He shaded his eyes to gaze up at her. "You're looking peaky. The fried whiting didn't agree with you?"

"I didn't have the fried whiting." She dropped into a chair and recounted the scene at breakfast.

"My God," he said when she'd finished. "You might have been burned at the stake."

"I'm going to burn Griffith at the stake." She scowled fiercely. "The man tortures cats!"

"You're on your own there." James stretched and sat up, turning sideways in the chaise and setting his shoes on the ground. "I'm not burning anyone. I vowed to do no harm." He brushed a lock of hair from his forehead and sighed. "On top of which, the evidence is unconvincing. Your Sir Reggie was scant on detail."

She stared. "I don't need to know the ghoulish particulars. You're not defending him? What if he broke into your house and swung Fezziwig around by his tail?"

"I'm having a hard time picturing it."

"He's a paragon of beauty, that's why." She hugged herself, eyes wandering the garden, which was densely planted, flowers clustered between azalea bushes and Himalayan rhododendrons.

Those pale purple stars of clematis—they were the same shade as Griffith's cravat.

She spoke in a whisper. "A handsome face can conceal unspeakable ugliness."

"You don't say," said James dryly. "To be clear, I can't picture Griffith holding Fezziwig by the tail, because Fezziwig would cut him to ribbons. That cat is a demon."

"Oh." Muriel deflated, pressing her palms to her temples.

"I have no idea what Griffith has done in the past or might be capable of doing. For all I know, he's another Vlad the Impaler." James shrugged. "But I always take hearsay with a grain of salt."

"Very mature." Muriel let her arms fall. "I always take hearsay with dried kindling and a match."

James regarded her, his mouth crooked, as though he couldn't decide between a smile and a frown.

"Muriel." He set his book beside him. "You are upset that Griffith wouldn't accept your commission. So am I, because I understand how much those illustrations matter to you, and because I'd imagined a passionate romance unfolding as the two of you bicycled along the shore, the wind in your hair, love poems spelled out in glistening seaweed upon the golden sand."

"Ha," she said as her heart gave an unwelcome thud.

"I wanted it to happen," James continued, coolly. "I even forgave you your willingness to abandon me."

Drat. That.

Abashed, she bit her lip. "You would have come along, of course." She squirmed, then yelped as wicker prickled through her skirt.

It was no more than she deserved.

She'd volunteered herself without sparing a thought for James, too caught up in the heat of the moment. But she'd have remedied the situation if it hadn't turned out as it did.

"I *was* going to ask you to bicycle with us."

"Thanks. I'd rather play tennis." James threw his arm over the back of the chaise. "The point is that Griffith made you feel something you haven't in quite some time."

"Not him. His art."

James arched his brows meaningfully.

"Fine," muttered Muriel. "Him too. I don't know how to explain that part."

"Attraction. Lust. Desire." James drummed his fingers. "It's highly explicable."

"I gave him a lobsterish look, didn't I?" Pain stabbed behind Muriel's left eye. "That's how you could tell."

"That, and the fact that you kissed him in front of me."

"I do manifest lust like a crustacean. Damn." She put her thumb on the ridge of her brow. "Thank God, it's over now. I want nothing to do with him."

"Hmm," said James. More drumming of the fingers. "What about a night in his bed, though? That wasn't a half-bad idea."

"Was it not?" she snarled. "Clearly, you haven't listened to a word I've said."

James considered her with a superior smile. "Either that, or I have listened entirely too well."

She knew better than to ask him to explain.

"Enough listening to me, then. It's your turn."

"My turn? You constantly dismiss all my wisdom. Why should I give you *more* priceless advice if you're going to ignore it?"

"I don't want you to say anything else about me. I want you to say something about yourself."

"Myself?" James laughed. "*I celebrate myself, and sing myself.*"

"James," she sighed.

"It's the beginning of a poem by Walt Whitman. You're going to America. You should know it. Shall I continue?"

"No. Quoting a poem is saying nothing."

"I couldn't disagree more."

She ground her teeth. "No poems. And don't tell me that it looks like rain."

He tilted back his head. A breeze riffled the leaves of the dogwood tree—like the rhododendrons, this particular species was native to the Himalayas. Shadows shifted across his face.

"It does look like rain."

"It doesn't." She inhaled sharply. "Tell me you'd rather not speak of it, and I'll stop prying. But please don't pretend not to understand me. You are consumed by some care. It ravages you."

She realized she could hear the sea, the steady breaking of the waves underlying the more ephemeral sounds: the humming bees, the rustling greenery.

After a long moment, James blew out a breath. "I can speak of it." A muscle in his jaw ticked. He opened his mouth, then closed it.

They sat in silence, listening to the waves.

Muriel finally said, "I can tell you my latest theory if that's easier. You can offer corrections."

"*Latest* theory?" His glance was both amused and wary. "How many have there been?"

"Several. I've been worried."

"So, you invented stories?"

"They each had their basis in observation. Ready?"

"God help me."

"Your heart was broken by a faithless rogue. A handsome, poetical dastard who lured you with false promises, then left you without warning. Despite his callous behavior, you have remained under his spell. You pined and pined, eschewing food, company, and the light. This trip is your chance to put all that behind you. My duty is to help you forget him, and to learn how to love again."

"Are you quite done?"

"Quite." She clasped her hands. "That's it, isn't it? I can see by your eyes."

"Blast my eyes." James blinked. "All this pollen. And that's *not* it. I don't need to learn how to love again. I need to live in a different world."

"There wasn't a handsome, poetical dastard?"

"No. No, there was a handsome, poetical French chemist named Gilles. He's hopelessly tender and alarmingly honest, and he didn't break my heart and I didn't break his. Both of us knew exactly how long the affair would last. It began last winter when I went to Paris." He paused, searching her face, then clarified: "As a representative of the commission inquiring into Pasteur's discovery."

Muriel nodded encouragement. When James had previously mentioned Louis Pasteur's treatment for rabies, and his own work publicizing Pasteur's method in England, he'd done so delicately, giving her abundant opportunity to slow him down or redirect the conversation, offering particulars only in response to specific questions.

Sometimes memories flooded her, and sometimes not.

Now she was fully in the present, with him.

"When did it end?" she asked.

"This spring. He was in England for nearly a month, helping me with my experimental study of—"

Again, a slight hesitation.

"The disease," said James. "Testing the action of drugs. Preparing recommendations. I've told you about my report."

"Yes." She nodded again. The report was cause for hope. James believed that rabies could be eradicated in Britain. But she didn't need to hear more at the moment. "About Gilles, though . . ."

"He's brilliant." James shook his head, a smile curving his lips. "But he can be careless. And the laws are different in France. Men like us have less to fear. I don't blame him."

"James." Muriel felt a rush of cold in her chest. "What happened?"

"It's still happening." His smile faded. "Letters I wrote to Gilles ended up in someone else's hands. Maybe he left them in a drawer in his hotel room. Or—he hated the London weather and bought himself a heavy overcoat. Maybe he didn't take the coat back to France. Maybe he gave it to a down-at-heel hansom driver, forgetting my letters were in the pocket. Maybe he was robbed of his pocketbook on his way to the train station. I can't ask him. He was only passing back through Paris. He's somewhere in the French countryside. Not that I would ask if I could."

He raked a hand through his hair.

"These letters." The cold in Muriel's chest was spreading.

"It's blackmail. What's ravaging me." He looked away.

They were alone in the garden. Even so, Muriel felt a horrible, creeping sensation, as though the hedges were filled with staring eyes.

Blackmail. How vile. How violating.

"I pay," said James. "And for my coin, I receive back my letters, one at a time. Whenever I think the ordeal is finally over, my blackmailer sends his boy round again." His short laugh was bitter. "I didn't realize how many bloody letters I wrote."

"Your blackmailer." Muriel sprang up. "The monster!" She paced a small, frantic circle. "Who could it be?"

"I don't know." James watched her patiently. He must have traveled already through every possible emotion.

She controlled herself. "The letters. Do they reveal . . . ?"

"That they were part of an exchange between two chaps affectionately buggering each other?" He lifted a shoulder. "They give the distinct impression."

Muriel's knees were shaky. It wasn't thirty years ago a man could be hanged for buggery. Even now the punishment could extend to penal servitude for life. But those convictions required proof the act had taken place.

"If they were published," continued James, "my name would be dragged, of course. Public scandal. Disgrace. Disinheritance. You know my father. And depending on the dispensation of my blackmailer, and the moral purity crusaders, I might even stand trial."

"For letters alone?"

"You were somewhere in the Indian Ocean when Parliament passed the Criminal Law Amendment Act. Gross indecency between men was made a misdemeanor carrying a sentence of up to two years."

"Gross indecency," echoed Muriel. "That's . . . vague."

"Deliberately so. It's a catchall. Extortionists are now proliferating more quickly than pimps."

She sank heavily into the chair.

"This is why I didn't tell you." James's expression was difficult to read. "Your worry has increased and mine exists in the same measure."

Muriel's helplessness besieged her—a dull, heavy feeling made worse by the acid sting of the injustice. She held onto her elbows tightly.

"No," she attempted. "I am more worried, and you are, therefore, less worried. It's the rule."

"A rule that depends on there being a fixed amount of worry. But worry isn't six apples, where you take four, so I have two."

"We are sharing the worry." She spoke with firmness, rising and crossing to the chaise. "That's what's important. Move over."

As soon as she settled beside James, he draped an arm around her, and she burrowed into his shoulder. It was a surprisingly comfortable position. James rested his chin on her head, and his breathing grew slower and more even.

"It wouldn't be difficult to discover Gilles's address," she said after a time.

"To what end?" James's voice was low. "He's not in danger. And nothing he could tell me would change the situation. He'd suffer agonies of guilt, and I prefer to think of him happy, in Provence, in a villa surrounded by . . . what grows in France?"

"Rosemary," she offered. "Lavender. Apricot and almond trees. Sunflowers."

"God, yes. Marvelous. Why cast a pall on all of that?"

"He might not see it that way."

"I see it that way." He said it in a tone that brooked no objections.

"All right." She lifted her head, scooting back to face him. She squared her shoulders. "What are we going to do?"

He returned her look, contemplative, then gave himself a small shake.

"Right now," he said, "we are going to do what people do at the seaside. We are going to fritter away the day. Recline under one of those tents on the beach. Watch the sand fleas hop about."

"You can read your novel." She was sitting on it. She raised herself up and pulled it free. "*Some Points on the Extirpations of Tumors of the Brain*." She read the title and let the book smack down on her thigh.

"What if we go down into town instead?" she suggested. "I can scout for a painter who isn't an unreasonably attractive reincarnation of Vlad the Impaler, and you can scout for a fisherman with an attack of the ague."

"Infinitely preferable," replied James at once. "I despise sand fleas. And bathing tents. Anything striped. You'll note I always wear solid colors." He stood. "Let me get my surgical bag. One of the maids told me her youngest sister slipped on the stairs the other day and broke her arm. The doctor set the bone, but I wouldn't mind paying a visit regardless. Fore Street, she said."

"Fore Street, then." She came to her feet and hooked her elbow through his. "Who knows? We might accomplish our aims with daylight to spare."

"In that case, I'm also scouting for a tennis partner."

"Failing that," said Muriel, "I can at least provide us with a proper picnic."

9

THERE WAS NO daylight to spare. Muriel and James found themselves completely occupied in the fishing quarter, where illness and injury were rampant. James's first visit, to the maid's sister, concluded with the grateful mother, Mrs. Grenfell, leading them to another cottage, up a steep flight of stone stairs into her cousin's sickroom, and from there, to another cottage, and another. As night fell, they wound their way back up to the hotel through lanes that reeked of fish oil and brine. Muriel's head still ached. She'd failed to approach a single artist, although she'd seen half a dozen painting in the boatyard, and more ducking into ale houses with their paint boxes and folded tripod easels. Thoughts of James's blackmailer assailed her constantly, so that her stomach churned. But James himself seemed invigorated by the day's work, and she let his improved mood improve hers.

The next morning, they returned to the harbor and parted ways. James went to look in on the Grenfell girl, and she went to canvass the artists of St. Ives. Most of them leased studios in crumbling buildings near the water. Not many of the artists were *in* their studios, but those who were toured her through repurposed sail lofts and netmaking factories. One overly inspired photographer had even established himself in an outhouse. Again and again, Muriel found herself stepping around heaps of netting and cracked spars to peer at oil paintings of girls peeling potatoes or ships on the harbor by moonlight. None of the paintings stirred her. So what, though? She should have learned by now to doubt the wisdom of relying on her own compass when it came to hiring an artist. She'd believed it would point her toward the sublime, and instead, it had pointed her toward a caddish, pretty-faced brute.

She attempted to commission a Bostonian in a long black cape, but he scoffed at her through his pipe smoke, speechifying on his dislike for the dainty and the tender. The following person to whom she applied—the wife of a man who took up the superior portion of their shared loft with his inferior pictures—said she hadn't the time. The most promising candidate actually painted floral subjects, lovely watercolors that brightened the tarry walls. Alas, he was to depart St. Ives on Thursday, for the Forest of Fontainebleau. He recommended a painter called Podge, but after spending a short, shocked interval in Podge's studio—rat *and* ferret infested—Muriel decided to give up, at least until tomorrow.

The afternoon was warm and calm, the thin scrim of clouds as radiant as pearl. She veered onto the beach—this one busy with working fishermen—and gazed out over the water.

"Muriel Pendrake!"

She jerked her head in the other direction. The man who'd hailed her was sitting in a battered old rowboat, an easel set up in front of him, practically between his knees due to the space constraints imposed by the thwarts.

She'd never seen him before. Doubtless he'd seen her at that blasted joust.

"Thomas Ponsonby!" He hollered the introduction, beaming. He had hair like a rooster's comb—in both color and direction of growth—and his green-checkered sack coat was buttoned only at the top button, revealing a blue-checkered waistcoat.

"Where's Raleigh?" he demanded, somewhat grandly, pointing at her with his paintbrush. "Off saving lives?"

"You know James?" Muriel approached. "From London?"

"From here. From the tiltyard. We repaired the fence together. He didn't mention it?"

"He did." Muriel's brow creased as she tried to remember.

"Did he?" Mr. Ponsonby grinned more widely. "Not surprised. It was legendary."

"Erm, yes." Muriel hesitated as details returned to her. *All thumbs* was the phrase James had applied to his fellow fence-mender. And something along the lines of *held the railing like it was a live eel*.

"We made a crack team." Mr. Ponsonby adjusted his straw boater, leaving a smear of blue paint on the brim.

"He's looking for a tennis partner." Muriel wasn't sure that James would thank her for this overture. *All thumbs* didn't recommend a man to racket sports. But Mr. Ponsonby lit up.

"Now?" He cast down his brush. "Serves you right," he told his easel, and vaulted from the rowboat. He was taller than Muriel had guessed, and immediately pulled one long leg up to his chest, gripping it just below the knee and balancing like a stork.

"Do you play?" he asked Muriel, switching legs. "Why don't we make a four? There's Griffith." He dropped his leg and waved.

Muriel tensed.

St. Ives was far too small a place. As was Cornwall. England. The Earth.

She turned by slow degrees.

Griffith was strolling toward them, in a top hat and a smoke-gray suit with a mulberry-colored waistcoat. He should have looked laughably out of place—the London bon vivant picking his way around piles of mackerel guts—but he carried himself with such easy assurance that she felt suddenly like an anxious caller, waiting to be received by the lord of the manor.

Idiotic reversal. *She* had ventured first onto this beach. And she cared not a whit that he'd declined to illustrate her lecture. That he'd declined to paint her nude.

Paint her nude.

Whatever had possessed her to suggest it? Her molars grated together in a half-swallowed cringe.

"He told me you're not riding with him." Mr. Ponsonby gave her a confidential glance. "But there's no hard feelings."

"I expect he replaced me within the hour." A pause ensued during which she tried and failed to hold herself back. "Who *is* riding with him?"

Mr. Ponsonby didn't have time to answer. Griffith was upon them.

"Don't look!" Mr. Ponsonby grabbed Griffith around the shoulders, facing him away from the rowboat, toward Muriel. "It's an atrocity. The picture is *so* horrifying I'm finally convinced I need a new occupation."

"What occupation?" Griffith's eyes met Muriel's. Smoke gray, like the superfine wool of his suit.

"Lamplighter?" Mr. Ponsonby released Griffith.

"I can picture you on stilts."

"Can you? I can't. Forget everything I just said. I was born to paint, and I will paint until I die." Ponsonby climbed back into the rowboat and sat, staring morosely at his easel. "Paint badly, that is."

Griffith's gaze had found Muriel's again. He leaned closer, a near imperceptible movement.

She perceived it. God, she perceived it from her tightening scalp down to her tingling toes.

"Hello, Penny," he greeted her softly.

"Hello, Mr. Griffith." Her reply was stiff with dislike.

He perceived *that*. His long lashes lowered as he studied her. "Exploring Downalong?"

That was what the locals called this lower part of town.

The question didn't require a direct answer, and courtesy failed to provide her with a ready alternative.

She looked at him, feeling overheated, and trapped, and wronged—and so, Lord, probably like a lobster in a pot.

A painful second ticked past.

He continued, "I could direct you to the studios of a few friends of mine. They're not flower painters either, but—"

"I've already visited several studios," she cut him off. He couldn't really imagine she wanted his guidance?

"You've found someone, then," he said.

"I have," she lied. She clenched her hands into sticky fists. "I couldn't be more pleased."

"Nor I, to hear it." His smile was sent by the devil. Its slightly crooked curve emphasized the symmetry of his chiseled features. It seemed to demand she kiss it into place.

Her throat went dry.

"Who is it?" he asked. "The painter?"

"You don't know him."

"How can you be sure?" The smile was in his voice now. "Were you talking about me?"

Bother. She rarely lied, and it never went well.

"He hasn't been here long." She tried not to blink. "He doesn't know anybody."

"I saw a great tangle of seaweed just over there." Griffith indicated the spot with a lazy tilt of his head. "Perhaps you should fetch him. And introduce us."

There was mockery in Griffith's voice. He could tell she was lying. A gentleman would play along, allow her to salvage her dignity.

He wasn't a gentleman. He was a fiend.

Irritation swept away her restraint.

"That's kelp," she snapped. "And it's as rotten as your heart."

For a satisfying second, Griffith looked shocked.

Mr. Ponsonby coughed. Her gaze flew to him. He was looking up at them from the rowboat, but at her glance, he bent abruptly and began to fuss with his paint box.

"You don't want it, then."

She turned back to Griffith. No trace of surprise on his face now. His eyes had a dangerous glint.

"The kelp?" She felt a hot itch climbing the back of her neck. Of course, the kelp. He didn't mean his heart. "It's useless to me."

He was studying her more closely still.

"I have fallen in your esteem." He sounded regretful. "Because I'm unable to illustrate your lecture myself."

"Unable?" When he put it like so, her anger seemed even more out of proportion. She wouldn't let him twist things around.

"You are unwilling," she said. "There's a difference. But that's not why I suspect a lump of diseased matter beats in your chest."

"Allow me to allay your suspicions," he drawled. His hand closed around her wrist, and the next thing she knew, her fingers were pressed to the side of his throat, sliding under the silk of his cravat. His skin was smooth and hot, and his pulse drummed steadily.

Her own pulse exploded into flutters.

"Everything seems in order with my heart." He tightened his grip on her wrist, thumb pressing the tender flesh between bone and tendon. "*Your* heart is beating rather fast."

She caught her breath and yanked her hand away. No one had observed them. The fishermen were concerned with fish, and the street above was all buyers and sellers, their attention trained on baskets and carts. Mr. Ponsonby had buried himself in that paint box.

Enduring Griffith's smug look alone was bad enough. His amusement enraged her.

She drew herself to her full height.

"What is your history with cats?" she demanded.

"I beg your pardon." His brows edged up. "*Cats*? I am universally beloved by feline kind. Cats trust me implicitly."

"That makes it worse."

"Makes what worse?"

Something clattered. Mr. Ponsonby had knocked over his easel.

"Clumsy," he said brightly. "Time for tennis?"

She couldn't break Griffith's gaze. This roiling tension—it wasn't normal, not for her. She had a quick temper, but she didn't usually feel as though a summer storm had been trapped under her skin.

"Not for me," she said. "I will never have time for tennis with a . . . a . . . double-dyed villain!"

After that, she'd no choice but to storm away. She couldn't bear to witness the moment Griffith's smile slid into a smirk. *Double-dyed villain?* It must have lodged in her head years ago, a phrase from a Drury Lane melodrama. If only a curtain could fall behind her, guaranteeing that this was the end. No further encounters. No further opportunities for foolishness. Her nerves had been stretched too thin. And Griffith knew how to strum on women's nerves like a lyre. Never again.

Were he and Mr. Ponsonby laughing as they watched her go?

She thought she did hear laughter as she reached the street and hesitated, spine rigid. But it was only the squawking of the gulls.

10

K IT ABIDED THE great Johan Gustav Svensson's studio parties only when the night was clear and the big double doors stood open, framing the moon-silvered bay. On those clear nights, the beauty of the view compensated—slightly—for the myriad irritations of the company.

In the foreground, the harbor, a shadowy forest of masts. In the distance, a lonely herring boat tacking round the point, or just the lighthouse, shining.

Tonight, there was nothing to see. Rain fell in sheets. The doors were closed, the windows shuttered. He could look at the art, of course. Svensson's paintings garnered the highest praise from academies all over Europe. He was the most important artist to take up residence in St. Ives, according to him, and to anyone who wanted to curry his favor.

Kit didn't look at the art. He looked at Ponsonby, who was standing with a posse of Svensson's admirers in front of one of the enormous exhibition paintings—easily nine feet high and nearly twice as wide.

Always a bit of a hanger-on, Ponsonby. Good-hearted but too eager to belong. Fame dazzled him. He'd begged Kit to attend this evening's gathering, but he seemed content to mingle on his own, swilling Swedish punch and laughing along to overheard jokes.

Bored, Kit circulated, an exercise in futility. Nothing to see, and no one he cared to talk to. Forty or so loud men, Bernhard and Takada not among them. The hot, smoky air stank of creosote and sweat. He found Ponsonby in the back of the studio, refilling his glass of punch.

"You're not *enjoying* yourself?" he asked.

"You say that like I shouldn't be enjoying myself." Ponsonby ladled punch into a second glass and pushed it into Kit's hand. "You never missed one of Burgess's salons." He meant Augustus Burgess, Gwen's older brother, onetime enfant terrible of the London art world. "How is this different?"

Kit set the glass down on the table. "You don't notice a difference?"

Ponsonby darted an uneasy glance around him. "Superficial differences. But essentially, with both, you have coveys of artists surrounded by art. Artists discussing art, complaining about art, making controversial claims about art. Everything you love best."

"Ponsonby," Kit growled. "There aren't any women."

"Women, ho!" The exclamation came from right behind him. "Who said women?"

A moment later, O'Brien, Craik, and Landon swarmed the table. The three mop-haired marine painters were Svensson's particular pets. Kit found them particularly obnoxious.

"Where are the women?" Craik jostled O'Brien in a failed bid for the punch bowl.

"Not here, which is my point." Kit stepped back to avoid their elbows. "A woman would get herself killed on the steps."

"Maidens fair," slurred O'Brien dreamily, sloshing punch into his glass. "They'd faint and tumble down."

"The problem isn't that they'd faint." Kit met O'Brien's glassy eyes, aware that he was wasting his breath. "The problem is their dress. You can't manage so long and steep a stair with skirts around your ankles, not without some kind of railing. I've suggested a rope." Kit frowned. "Svensson has yet to act."

"Bollocks." Craik burped it. "I'll tell him. We want women."

"It's not about what you want. It's about women having the option to come and go without risk to life and limb if *they* want." Kit slapped Craik on the back, hard.

Landon was grinning at Ponsonby. "You mended that fence the other day. Next time you should grab one of those dairymaids and prop a gate. Follow me? Prop a gate. Propagate."

Ponsonby chuckled.

"Nothing to grab in this room but our own pricks," grumbled Craik. "Svensson should have listened to Griffith. Chap's got the right idea."

"Grabbing women's not the idea," said Kit flatly. Landon and Craik exchanged a look.

"Someone needs a good frig," muttered Landon. Craik tittered.

A bead of ceiling plaster dropped into the punch bowl with a splash.

O'Brien startled, and the other men fairly screamed with laughter.

Kit turned to Ponsonby. He was laughing too, his face flushed with heat and drink and mirth.

"Enjoy," said Kit, and stalked off.

He'd reached the top of the stairs before Ponsonby caught up to him.

"Griff, wait."

"Why?" He stopped, looking down the precipitous flight. "You can carry on without me."

"Stay for cards? I'll get a game going."

"I'm tired."

"You're not tired. You're narked, I can tell. Out with it. What have I done?"

"I *am* bloody tired." Kit scrubbed a hand across his eyes. "It's what you didn't do."

"Didn't do? What *should* I have done? Barked at that chappie back there because he made a salty pun? Griff, if that's what you think, maybe you don't understand about chappies."

Now Kit laughed, the sound harsh. "Maybe I don't." He started down the stairs.

"Griff."

He twisted, at his own peril. Ponsonby was silhouetted above him.

"This is what you wanted." Ponsonby gripped the walls, leaning forward. "To be, you know, one of us. But chappies act like chappies. Around chappies, that is. So if you're *with* us, as a chappie—"

"Enlightening." Kit cut him off. "Don't get too sozzled. Chappie or no, these steps can break your neck."

He resumed his descent.

IT WAS RAINING too hard to bicycle home, not without fortification. Kit slouched into the Smack, feeling fouler than the night.

This is what you wanted.

Ponsonby's words rattled in his skull. He shed his dripping hat and coat and shouldered to the bar, ordered a whiskey, then another. The liquor burned down his throat.

This is what you wanted.

He ordered a third whiskey and sipped it, his eyes roaming the dim room. Fishermen in sou'westers and oilskins drank six-penny ale at the small, sticky tables. No women here either. A few slumming tourists were inspecting the paintings on the walls, gifts to the landlord from artist patrons. Gifts, or in some cases, attempts at payment.

The whiskey sent his mind roaming too.

He was four or five, lying in the grass alongside his nursemaid in Regent's Park, the two of them watching the young gallants ride by, so big and splendid on their stallions. His nursemaid was sighing. *What lovely, lovely gents.* And the gallant on the bay tossed them a wink as he passed. Kit had felt his own heart thunder with the hooves. There was nothing complicated about that moment. He'd twinkled with recognition, knowing he'd glimpsed his future self. He didn't wonder *how* he'd grow up to cut such a figure. Or what it would mean.

By the time he realized that his moody stare had settled on one of the tourists, the tourist was staring back.

The man's glossy hair was blacker than his suit, and gleams of light traversed its waves when he tilted his head to smile. His teeth were very white.

Kit looked away, perhaps too late to avoid misunderstanding.

When he'd first slipped out of his parents' house at fifteen, in clothing filched from his middle brother's wardrobe, he'd anticipated ecstatic freedom from men's gazes. On the street, in the Burlington Arcade, everywhere, he was shocked to discover *more* clinging eyes. He soon learned that he was seen not as a boyish girl but as a girlish boy, one of the mary-anns who worked in the alleys and lavatories, and in certain hotels. Thus began his education in the ways of the other West End, which had always existed, invisibly, all around him.

He was older now, and rougher, with calloused hands and broader shoulders, arms and legs thickened by years of training with shot-loaded dumbbells. Less appealing to men who sought effeminate lovers. More appealing to many others.

He tried to let his male admirers down gently.

He hoped tonight it wouldn't be necessary.

His fingers tightened on the tumbler in front of him. The rim sported a smudge he couldn't associate with his own mouth. He pushed it away and dropped his head into his hands.

Tomorrow. Tomorrow he'd ask Sally McDermott to accompany him on that blasted bicycle tour. Unless—hadn't she mentioned a sketching trip to the Somme?

Bloody hell. No Sally. Too bad, but there were other possibilities. Except—worse—he didn't have the sense to pursue them. Even now, his thoughts had begun to circle again around Muriel Pendrake.

She was too forthright to carry off a lie. Her angry blushes gave her away. She hadn't hired an artist, of that he was certain. What if he convinced Takada to devote a few days to her illustrations? She might feel grateful enough to renew her offer to ride. She might think more highly of him.

He shifted uncomfortably, and the barstool gave a derisive creak.

He stood to lose his bicycle shop, a considerable investment, his only financial security, given his increasing distance from both his family and his artistic livelihood. Winning this silly wager was a serious imperative. It behooved him to act accordingly. He should have begun training with a new partner yesterday. Instead, he was dragging his heels, revolving fantasies in the back of his mind. Fantasies that featured a woman with penny-bright hair. A woman who happened to loathe him.

A new thought nettled. This preoccupation—it wasn't *because* Muriel loathed him? Because he so disliked the thought of her dislike? He *would* feel gratified if he managed to convince her that he wasn't a villain, and that she was swimming, needlessly, against a current of mutual attraction. But he was entirely capable of letting her go, letting her swim off, low opinion unchanged. No, this wasn't about his ego, or his physical desire. He'd fixated for a different reason.

If she rode with him, the wager was as good as won. She herself had guaranteed it, and he believed her. She was all mettle.

He was slow to interpret the pressure at his side, someone leaning next to him at the bar. Lips brushed his ear.

"You're a pretty fellow. Are you as pretty down here?"

As the man whispered, he slid his hand over Kit's thigh. Kit grabbed a thick wrist before the groping fingers reached his groin.

"You've mistaken me," he murmured, turning his head. It was the tourist, of course. A man of middle years, a pretty fellow in his own right, with that thick black hair and luminous smile.

"I don't think so." The man spoke playfully, but with more heat in his voice. "Another inch will tell if you feel as I do. We'll see how it stands."

His fingers crept forward.

Kit plucked his hand away, the movement forceful but discreet.

"Better luck elsewhere," he said. The man froze and went deadly pale. Kit could read his expression all too well: the displeasure of rejection mingling with the fear of exposure.

He offered a smile. After a moment, the man took it, with a slight nod, and faded back into the depths of the room.

His departure revealed the presence of a second man, who must have approached the bar during the hushed exchange.

James Raleigh.

Kit rose, his eyes on Raleigh's face, which showed exactly how much he'd understood.

Everything.

As though they shared a single mind, he and Raleigh turned and headed toward the exit, stopping in the shadowy passage that led upstairs to the rooms for let.

"You're not a rake. You're a renter." Raleigh's tone was neutral.

Kit shook his head, which sent a twinge down his neck. Every muscle had gone rigid.

"I'm not a renter, in fact," he said. He paused. "You seem familiar with the type."

If Raleigh had pegged him for a male prostitute, it revealed as much, or more, about him.

Raleigh propped a shoulder on the wall. "All right. I'm a sod. Aren't you?"

The wind threw rain against the dark window glass, which rattled the panes like a handful of pebbles. What a filthy night.

"No," Kit sighed. "That fellow mistook me. Wishful thinking. It's not uncommon." He winked, a gallant's wink. "I appeal to all."

The set of Raleigh's jaw seemed to dispute the claim.

"Look," he said, low. "I think of Muriel as my sister. Tell me. What's your game? Do you also fancy women?"

"I only fancy women."

Raleigh's frown was skeptical. "I won't ask if you fancy Muriel."

"Dr. Raleigh," drawled Kit. "I'm beginning to think there's nothing you won't ask."

Raleigh gave him a grudging, sheepish look.

"Touché," he muttered. "Fancy whoever you please." He turned his gaze up to the low ceiling. "Well. This is awkward. Should we introduce a new conversational topic or go our separate ways?"

"Did you come out tonight for conversation?" Kit raised his brows. "Or were you looking for a lark? If the latter, that fellow at the bar didn't seem a bad sort."

"Good grief." Raleigh started, then laughed. "You're in earnest."

"Always. I'm particularly earnest about irony. Makes me feel modern."

"You're not offended, then, by my erotic dispensation? Or my suggestion that you shared it?"

"No." Kit smiled wryly. The tension in his neck and shoulders eased. "The social order offends me. Most theology. The doctrine of separate spheres." He ticked on his fingers as he talked. "Reviews of novels that spoil the effect of the plot. Overcooked carrots julienne. I'll leave it at one hand. You get the idea."

"Overcooked carrots. A true abomination." Raleigh wore a thoughtful expression. "I did worry, though, for a moment. I don't usually announce my proclivities."

"Of course not. We are meant to act as though certain desires don't exist. And yet society is set up to regulate or repress them, which rather proves the opposite. It wouldn't be illegal for men to kiss each other if some didn't want to do it."

Raleigh made a noise in his throat. "Our lawmakers all spooned together at Eton."

"It's *not* illegal for women to kiss each other," Kit continued slowly. "To make it a crime for women to kiss women would be to admit, publicly, that women kiss women, and that women kissing women is sometimes a matter of sex, not friendship. Erasure, not prohibition. Different but related tactics."

Raleigh's expression grew more thoughtful still. "The medical literature on sexual anomaly contains far fewer case histories of women."

"Because it's less common? Or because the doctors are men?"

"You sound like Muriel." Raleigh's mouth quirked. "The claim is that sexual inversion is a variation in the species, analogous to color blindness, or color hearing. Men have more variability, biologically, and so there are more male inverts."

Kit snorted. "The same argument is used to support the idea that there are more male geniuses. Biology can stuff itself."

Raleigh blinked, bemused. "As a man of science, I wouldn't go so far as that."

It had to be the whiskey that prompted Kit's next words, or some confessional quality possessed by the quiet alcove, combined with the fact that Raleigh had already confessed himself.

"As someone who wasn't raised to become a man," said Kit, "I would."

He held Raleigh's gaze, until a light kindled in the doctor's eyes.

"I don't particularly care what the medical literature has to say," he went on. "I've read some of it myself. I've read that female inverts are mannish. But I used to belong to a ladies' club in the West End convened by sapphists with perfumed skin and waist-length tresses and elaborate taste in corsetry. I've known toms who pass as men and others who pair dinner jackets with skirts in mixed company. Some women from the laboring classes put on trousers to get work. They might feel the trousers suit them, or simply that starving doesn't. There's nothing *but* variety. Is my friend Ponsonby's masculinity *real* while mine is an imitation?" Kit realized he'd swerved, that his speech had devolved into a tirade, but the venting came as sweet relief. "I swear to God he's been imitating *me* for years."

"Ponsonby." Raleigh hadn't looked away. "Your charming squire. That's what he called himself, when we were repairing that fence. Your squire, I mean. I added the *charming*. He was rather."

Kit grunted. "He has his moments."

"You of all people shouldn't dismiss medical literature. Sexology is a burgeoning field." Raleigh pushed off the wall and came toward Kit. "It demonstrates that anomalies are as natural as the norm, and that moves us closer to social acceptance."

"But the norm itself isn't *natural*, but rather customary. We're accustomed to dividing everyone into male and female, absolutely." Kit rocked on his heels. "And from what I've read, that's how the doctors describe inversion as well, in terms of those two categories. I'm saying we're more approximate. Not only the sods and the toms and the sapphists—everyone."

Raleigh tilted his head, musing. "You're saying the whole system of classification needs to change."

"I suppose I am." Kit stilled. "Discuss that with your sexologists."

"I'll have to brush up on my German." Raleigh folded his arms. "But I just might."

They looked at each other, the companionable pause rattling with more rain.

Kit sighed and pushed back his hair. "I hope you *did* come to the Smack for conversation. Otherwise, I can't imagine the disappointment."

"I'm not disappointed. This has been interesting, to say the least."

Raleigh took out his watch. "And now it's late. I should head back to the hotel, in case Muriel tries to drag me out of bed before the sun. Unless . . ." He dropped the watch back into his pocket. "A drink?"

"One drink." Kit turned. "I'm buying."

An hour later, they were both slumped over the bar, laughing about nothing they could remember.

"Do I have a chance?" Kit wheezed. It was likely a non sequitur, so he clarified. "A chance with Muriel?"

Raleigh nodded emphatically. "No."

"Was that a yes or a no?"

"Let me think." Raleigh put his tumbler to his temple. "Yes, no. You don't. Not a bloody chance." He started laughing again.

"Because . . ." Kit slumped further. "Because of what I told you."

"What? No, because she thinks you're a lazy, heartless, selfish, promiscuous blackguard whose talent finds its primary outlet in the torture of cats."

"I don't entirely understand the accusation." Kit wasn't sure he wanted to. "But I plan to make amends. I'm going to find her an artist."

"*You* should paint the seaweed," said Raleigh frankly. "If you want a chance."

"I cannot." Kit's words had begun to slur, so he pronounced each consonant. "It is beyond my power."

"At the moment I should say so." Raleigh put his hand in Kit's face and wiggled his fingers. "Neither would I wield a scalpel."

Kit batted at the hand, focused his eyes on Raleigh, and frowned. It was a bit frightening to get pissed with a man who fiddled in people's brains.

"Sober up," he commanded.

Raleigh turned his wiggling fingers into a signal to the barkeep. "Did she tell you *why* she wants the illustrations?"

"She wants them for her lecture."

"For her lecture," repeated Raleigh. "But there's more to it. She's a plant hunter. Knows loads about trees, shrubs, flowers—plants from all around the globe that people want to grow or use. Some American botanists—women, by the way—invited her to talk about her expertise. But then the patronizing tosser in charge told her she had to talk instead about the love of *seaweed*, as promulgated by Mrs. Alfred Gatty, an amateur algologist. Algologist. Algologist? It twists the tongue. Algologist. God. Where was I? The tosser. He did it to put Muriel in her place."

Even through his stupor, Kit felt a spark of anger on Muriel's behalf. Various profanities muddled on his tongue.

"Gah," he said.

"Exactly. She's incensed. And she's going to say so, during the lecture. Cheers."

The barkeep was refilling their tumblers.

"Why, then?" Kit laid a shilling on the bar. "Why the illustrations?"

"She wants to do what she was asked to do first, impeccably and impressively and inoffensively. For credibility. So it's more difficult for people to dismiss her as a raving termagant when she makes it rain fire at the end."

"She doesn't need paintings for that."

"I agree. But she thinks she does. *Your* paintings in particular. That watercolor—it's what gave her the idea. It has acquired for her a talismanic significance. The premise is misguided, but the cause is noble. To hell with patronizing tossers!" Raleigh lifted his glass. It left a sparkling trail in the air.

Kit shut his eyes. The darkness kept sparkling. To hell with patronizing tossers. His own bloody credo.

Only he couldn't paint the seaweed himself.

He couldn't paint anything.

He could try.

And fail.

Or . . .

Maybe he wouldn't fail. Maybe this was exactly the inducement he needed. Eyes still shut, he lifted his own glass and waited for the clink.

11

IT WAS NOON the next day before Kit could drag himself from the house, and even then, he cycled gingerly through the fields feeling like a tortured cat. Mrs. Pengilly from the neighboring farm had delivered his milk—loudly—well before seven. When the clock struck eleven, and he'd forced himself to stagger down into the kitchen, he'd failed to eat a bite of the breakfast he found congealed between two plates on the table. No fault of Mrs. Pengilly's, of course. He'd employed her for the better part of a year, and the wholesome meals never varied. Squinting against the light, he'd dunked hard bread in sugared black coffee until his brain revived enough to sift through the final events of the night.

Buying a bottle of port from the barkeep, passing that bottle back and forth with Raleigh as they lurched down Fish Street? Banging on the door of Takada's boardinghouse until the landlady threw it open, iron skillet in hand?

That had been real.

Riding home along the cliffs as the moon broke through the clouds, illuminating Muriel on a high promontory, naked but for those shooting boots, locks of coppery hair snaking around full, rose-tipped breasts? Climbing up to her on a perilous stair like the one that led to Svensson's studio, kissing her rain-wet lips as waves rose all around them?

That had been a dream.

She'd looked for all the world like a wicked Venus.

Now he tried to keep his bleary eyes on the rutted, half-dried mud of the path. Muriel wasn't naked on a ledge in the middle distance, awaiting his kiss.

She *was*, however, wearing those shooting boots.

It was the first thing he noticed when he finally came upon her, near Porthminster Beach, where the sands gave way to shingle and granite outcroppings. She was lying flat on a large rock, gazing into the water pooled in its center, those rubberized boots sticking out behind her. He stopped, transfixed, seized by an arousal so extreme he wondered if he were still dreaming, or at the least, still drunk. His pounding skull and sloshing guts refuted both possibilities.

She hadn't noticed him, so he cleared his throat.

No reaction.

"Penny," he attempted, too low. His voice didn't carry above the sound of the waves. The sea looked green as it broke between black boulders.

"Tide's coming in," he announced, overloud.

She turned her head. Her straw hat shaded her eyes. The curve of her lips did not seem friendly.

"You," she said.

"When it's high, these rocks are cut off from the beach." He already wished he'd picked a different opening.

She lifted her chin. This exposed more of her lovely face, and its rancorous expression.

"I know," she said flatly.

"It happens faster than you'd think. Don't want to look up and discover you're stranded. Or that we're stranded together."

He laughed.

She didn't.

"Well," he said. "G'morning." He scrambled up onto the rock and lowered himself down beside her.

"It's not morning." She turned back to the pool. "And I'm not inclined to take advice on tides from a man who fails to track the most basic effect of the Earth's rotation."

He wrapped his arms loosely around his knees. This was going about as well as he'd expected.

"*Unsolicited* advice," she added.

"I was stuck out here once myself," he said. "That's why I mentioned it." He scowled. Nothing like justifying your condescension with a testimony to your idiocy. "I'd the idea to paint a picture, of the sirens from the *Odyssey*. We stayed out too long and had to swim for it."

"We?" She rolled up onto an elbow. From this angle, he could see her eyes, dark and assessing.

"Me. And the models. I had to go back later for my easel, and the harp and the robes."

The crests of her cheeks grew rosy.

"Let me guess," she muttered. "The models. Josephine, Annabelle, and Violet."

He bit back a smile. "I'd no idea you were so lyrical."

"You are the one who paints sirens." She lay flat again and lowered her face over the pool. "Seaweed is too homely."

Her telling blush had warmed the air between them. Now, he felt a distinct chill.

"I sought you out today for a reason." His mouth was gritty, as though he'd swallowed sand on his walk over the dunes. "I thought perhaps we could talk."

"We don't have anything to talk about." She tugged up her sleeve, dipped her bare forearm into the water, and scooped a flat pink plant toward the surface.

He leaned forward to watch and caught a floral scent. Her scent. No primroses grew on this patchwork of wave-lashed granite.

He'd sought her out for *several* reasons, and it grew harder by the moment to rank or disentangle them. Winning the wager with Deighton. Surely that was primary. But if he could find his way back to art, by painting differently, and to a different end, for Muriel and her cause—that might matter even more. And if both goals could be attained with near simultaneity while he eluded his past? While he seduced and was seduced in turn?

A most favorable outcome indeed.

He breathed deeper, the air both salty and sweet. A loose lock of Muriel's hair was drifting in the pool, the dark filigree not unlike a marine plant itself.

This woman. She teased his senses, heightened his awareness. She distracted him from brooding over Lucy, but she also appealed to him in part because she reminded him of Lucy: frank and uninhibited, with a rough-and-tumble way of carrying herself, and eyes so sharp her glances could slice.

If there was a contradiction there, he didn't feel inclined to ponder it.

He studied her as she studied the narrow branchlets of the tiny plant.

"That was last summer," he said. "When I painted the sirens. This summer, I haven't painted a midge. A dot on canvas is more than I can manage."

She let the scrap of seaweed slip away. She withdrew her arm from the pool, rivulets running down her skin. "I don't understand."

"Something shifted." *He* shifted, on the rock, which dug uncomfortably into his sit bones, and looked out at the bay, rough with last night's rain.

He could sense her waiting and tried to find the words.

"The urge to paint used to seize me. It used to drive me out of bed in the middle of the night. I was determined to make great art. To be a great artist."

"You do. You are."

He looked over. She'd risen to her knees and seemed much closer, her face near to his. The wet lock of hair had tangled in the top buttons of her gown.

Her eyes were very bright. "That columbine study was just something pretty, you said. But I thought it much more than that."

Admiration of this sort used to puff his chest. Now he slouched, resistant.

"Do you know what all great artists have in common? The ones considered *truly* great?"

A line appeared between her brows.

"They're men." He answered his own question. "The exceptions prove the rule. Why is that?"

She drew back. "You assume that I agree."

"It isn't debatable. Raphael. Da Vinci. Michelangelo. Rubens. Rembrandt. Turner. I could go on and on. There's no list you or anyone could produce of female equivalents."

"Perhaps that is not because women are deficient." Her eyes were cutting him now, narrow and angry. "But because we haven't had the same opportunities."

He nodded. "It *is* far more difficult to achieve greatness as an artist if, for example, your education excludes study of the nude model, as is the case for female students at the Royal Academy Schools."

She'd put up her chin to argue. He saw the moment she realized that he'd said nothing to contradict—a quizzical little flutter of her lids.

He continued, the words coming faster. "And, of course, far fewer women attend the Academy in the first place. You need training to paint. Also, time and space. Money can buy a man all three. But not a woman. Her training is categorically inferior. Her time isn't considered her own. She can't close a door that her husband, father, son, or brother can't open. She is encouraged to *limit* her expression, to devote herself to ordering a household. She's taught that invention is beyond her. A man may face material obstacles to becoming an artist, but even a well-resourced woman has to battle social expectations, continually. How much less likely is she to paint a masterpiece?"

Muriel regarded him in stunned silence.

He felt a surge of pleasant anticipation.

"Mr. Griffith," she said coolly. "How much less likely are women to do *anything* when men will not stop yammering?"

The surge piddled into a nauseating slosh.

"Why, yes," he attempted, rubbing his brow. "That is what I meant."

"And what you exemplified."

"Erm." He felt as though his finger were poking his own brain. He used to silence male blowhards with that same pointed look Muriel was giving him now. He'd miscalculated, speaking so authoritatively from an experience she'd no idea they shared.

"You don't need me to tell you about women," he muttered.

"Or the tides," she reminded him. "Or the connection between women and the tides, as symbolized by sirens."

At this last, his lips tugged into a smile. She was thorough when it came to withering commentary.

"Just so," he agreed. "I've learned my lesson."

"I doubt it," she said, but she was softening visibly, her gaze more curious than outraged. "All right. Women rarely paint masterpieces, for the reasons you mentioned. What does that have to do with *your* painting? Or *not* painting, as the case may be?"

"It's why I stopped. I won't allow my works to confirm a harmful myth about the mystical talent of the artist."

"Oh, you won't?" Something about her tone made him uneasy.

"No, I won't." He persisted anyway. "Stories about artistic prodigies obscure the social conditions that determine the lion's share of success."

"Unbelievable." She was shaking her head.

"What is?"

"Your arrogance."

"Oh." He frowned. "That's what you gather from this? That I'm arrogant?"

"You are *insufferably* arrogant. And I am sorry I ever praised you. You don't think too highly of yourself to paint seaweed. You think too highly of yourself to paint at all."

"Look here." He bristled. "I wasn't suggesting that I *am* a mystically talented prodigy. I referred to all that nonsense as myth."

Her expression remained unchanged.

"You gave up painting," she said. "Gave it up out of *pity*, I take it? Pity for the unknown women who never attained their full potential?"

"Pity? Lord, no." He laughed a strained laugh. "In solidarity, perhaps. But it's more complicated."

"I see." She crossed her arms. "Women find it difficult to take lovers, far more difficult than men do. You haven't given up *that* practice."

He cleared his throat. "I don't claim to have made any systematic renunciation."

"Oh, so you're *not* England's Gautama Buddha?" Her voice dripped with sarcasm. "You want to remain a wealthy, pleasure-seeking rake, just not one who plies a brush?"

He smiled with clenched teeth. Perhaps this was all going rather worse than he'd expected.

"Solidarity with womankind," she mused. "How do you square that with refusing a woman's commission?"

"I don't." He held her gaze and spoke quietly. "I refused your commission because accepting did not feel possible."

She must have heard his sincerity. She bit her lip. One of her hands crept up, curled fingers nestled in the notch of her throat.

"There is a physical element." He admitted it stiffly. "These days, when I contemplate painting, I get headaches—like someone is twisting screws into my skull. A blank spot opens in my vision. It's not darkness. It's nothingness."

Her eyes were widening.

"My hands go numb." He shoved his hands under his biceps, two tight fists. "I chose to set aside my brush. Picking it up again won't be as easy."

She looked shaken, either by the disclosure itself, or by the fact that he'd made it, that he'd spoken to her in a voice rubbed raw. They were inches apart, face-to-face on a lonely rock, the sea rushing past on both sides.

He felt shaken too.

She recovered more quickly. Her brilliant eyes cleared, and the set of her jaw showed her resolve.

"You must talk to James," she said, with firm decision.

Longing produced a sudden cramp in his heart. She trusted Raleigh absolutely. His closest friendships had once been characterized by that same unwavering assurance.

"I did," he said hoarsely. "We talked last night. Not about that, about other things."

"So, *you* are responsible for his state." Her brows lowered. "I went into his room this morning and found him snoring on top of the bed with his shoes on."

"He shares the responsibility." Kit eased back, putting more distance between them. "If he knows how to cure a hangover, I hope he shares that too." A rueful smile edged his lips. "I feel like hell."

She was quiet.

"Wouldn't you rather he cure whatever keeps you from painting?" she asked after a long moment.

He tipped his head. "The social ill?"

"Your particular complaint." She seemed to be trying to look inside him. "It could have to do with the nerves."

"I'll manage on my own." He flicked his wrist, dismissive. "Nerves can be steeled."

"Indeed, they cannot," she said. "That's a figure of speech. You need a doctor."

Frustrated amusement crinkled his brow.

"You are relentless," he told her. "I need that. I need you. That's what I came here to say. I'm ready to paint again. Ride with me on that bicycle tour, and I'll paint anything you please."

"I don't think that's a good idea." Muriel was staring at Griffith's face. Usually, when she spoke with people, she stopped actively seeing them. That was how conversation worked. You didn't watch someone's mouth move. All the fleshy details faded away, so you could concentrate on the animating intelligence.

But Griffith never faded. His wicked beauty announced itself over and over, like a bloody trumpet. It was vexing in the extreme.

Too many parts of her felt too aware. Her damp forearm was rippling with gooseflesh, but then so was the dry, sleeved one.

She gripped her elbows.

"Headaches for you," she said. "Vexation for me."

Miles and miles of vexation.

Her own head hurt as she tried to assimilate all the new information.

"What awakened you to the woman question?" Her frown deepened. "Was it waking up with a suffragist?"

He gave her a wry look, his gray eyes glinting. "I count many suffragists among my friends."

"How uncharacteristically evasive." She said it in her sweetest voice. "I am correct, then. Your politics is based on pillow talk."

"Would that be so bad? If I listened to the women I bedded?"

Her gaze faltered under his. Esmé had educated her, and rewarded her progress, delegating tasks of increasing professional importance. But he hadn't *listened* to her, not when she'd expressed opinions that didn't conform with his own.

Nor had they shared a pillow.

She raised her eyes to find Griffith watching her.

Her mouth went dry, and her voice was scarcely more than a whisper. "I have seaweed to collect."

"Penny," he said, and his use of that silly nickname fluttered her pulse. "I'd hoped to be restored to your good graces."

"When were you ever in my good graces?"

He raised his brows.

That cursed kiss. He'd never let her live it down.

She went crimson. "I was much affected by the sun that day."

"It's sunny now." He studied her with interest. "Are you feeling a similar effect?"

She was feeling it, God help her. A fluttering within and a buzzing without. The beauty of the brisk, bright day, the rocks and the sea—a foil for the beauty of the man who sat before her.

"No," she muttered. "You're blocking the sun. And casting a shadow on the pool. No, don't move. I might as well find another."

She began to gather her scattered belongings: discarded gloves, pocket lens, chisel, hammer, oyster knife.

"Have I wronged you in some way?"

"Pardon?" She looked over, oyster knife in hand. He'd dressed more casually today, in a Norfolk jacket, with a gray cap instead of a topper, and he'd crossed his legs and propped his chin on his fist. The total effect was of boyish expectancy.

"Have I wronged you?" he repeated.

She scowled. She didn't like what the question made her confront.

Had he wronged her? He'd almost collided with her on the cliff path, but that was because *she* had started forward without looking, a fact he'd never mentioned. He'd kissed her, but that was because *she* had fibbed to James about seduction. He'd declined her commission, but even if he hadn't offered an explanation, she should have accepted his decision. She'd known as much in the moment, known that she was reacting too dramatically.

Clarinda Chiswick, and whatever poor cats had crossed the wrong quad at Eton—*they* might have more cause to complain.

"No, you have not," she conceded. "You haven't wronged *me*."

"Not you." He narrowed his eyes, suspicious. "Someone else?"

It wasn't worth it. She shook her head.

"What *did* you and James talk about?" she asked brightly.

He stared. After a moment, he shrugged.

"How you've been shabbily treated by a botanist in New York. It angered me. I find anger inspiring, as a painter."

"*That* is what changed your mind about the commission?"

"In part."

A possibility occurred to her, belatedly, and brought with it a hot rush of embarrassment. Good gracious. James hadn't been so drunk he'd joked to *Griffith* about exchanges involving nights in beds?

She winced. "James didn't propose anything scandalous?"

"No." Griffith smiled his indecent smile. "What did you have in mind?"

Damn her mind. It was suddenly a jumble of sweat-glazed images, clinging lips and legs, clasped hands, a tangle of mauve sheets, window curtains fluttering.

This was proof positive. Collaboration with Kit Griffith was a *terrible* idea. Erotic fascination without esteem—it felt lewd, sullying.

Exciting.

"A transaction." She sounded breathless. "That's all. You paint. I cycle. Nothing else."

"What else is there?" he murmured, a new glint in his eyes.

Her heart began to drum. "You start painting tomorrow. You can pick up the specimens at the Towans."

"You can drop them off at the bicycle shop. It's in the engine house near Tregerthen Farm. You start *cycling* tomorrow."

Fair enough. She gave a curt nod. Then, afraid he was going to shake her hand, she busied herself with packing her basket.

"Extraordinary."

When she turned her head, she saw that Griffith was lying at the edge of the pool. He twisted to grin up at her, holding her pocket lens up to his eye. His eye seemed to jump out at her, magnified to twice its size. The lens revealed, in minute detail, the curves of his lids, the black fringe of his close-set lashes. A silvery-gray star rayed out from his pupil. The rest of his iris was deepest, darkest blue.

Sensation shivered up her spine.

"Give me that." She reached for the lens. He handed it over and returned his attention to the pool.

"They look like chrysanthemums," he said, gleeful.

"The anemones?" She didn't need to see for herself. She'd already scrutinized the pool, poked the walls and turned over the little rocks. But she found herself stretching out awkwardly beside him. She rested her chin on her hands, her right elbow brushing his left.

"What's that one?" he asked, ignoring the contact, or perhaps he hadn't noticed. "A slug? Queer little thing."

"A sea hare." She glanced at him, at his perfect profile outlined against the sky.

He cut his eyes toward her. "I don't know that I've looked properly into a rock pool since I was a child. It reminds me of the colorful fripperies in a dress shop. All bright ribbons and beads and flounces."

"Slug spawn and fish ova and Rhodospermea," she said dryly. "Very fashionable."

He laughed, and she felt a delicious thrill.

"What's that?" he asked, looking down again. He reached out and touched the water's surface.

She tried to extend the line of his finger, to visualize where he pointed. The shallow pool was not more than two feet in length, studded with barnacles and anemones, sandy bottom a mix of empty shells and tiny locomoting creatures. Snails. Marine spiders. Who knew? The tattered oarweed fronds were stitched with wiggling red annelids.

Was he pointing to a jellyfish? A sponge?

"I can't identify many zoophytes," she confessed. "I'm not an expert on seaweed either, truth be told."

"Raleigh already told it. Some tosser changed your lecture topic."

"Professor Charles Heywood." She made a face. "I'm a British woman, so I must speak of seaweed. That's what British women do."

"Is it?" He sounded bemused.

"It's the stereotype in professional botanical circles. British women are seaweed enthusiasts. We collect indiscriminately and stick our innumerable specimens into scrapbooks in our shell-stuffed parlors. The professional scientists think more important work happens in laboratories than parlors. The scientists tend to be men, in case you're wondering. The women tend to be amateurs. Their contributions to science are largely ignored, or absorbed by their male correspondents."

She looked at him. He was looking at her. At such proximity, she could distinguish the blue in his moody irises without magnification.

Her throat constricted. She couldn't remember what she had been going to say next. His lashes lowered just a fraction. Her gaze dropped to his lips. She went so still that her breath stopped in her lungs. It was with a convulsive gasp that she jerked her head to the side and pushed up from the pool's ledge.

She stared at the curve of the bay, at the distant crescent of the beach, and then, horrified, at the swirling water that divided the rocks from the shore.

"Blast." She shot up to her knees. Griffith rose to his knees too, languidly, and considered the breaking waves.

"I warned you," he drawled.

"Warned me?" If only she could spit purple poison, like a sea hare. "You *distracted* me! I'd have moved to higher ground long before now if left to my own devices."

"We'll never know." He shrugged.

"*You* might never know. I know!"

This amused him, or the situation amused him. He was smiling faintly as he replied.

"The water's not deep yet. We can wade to the dunes. Give me your basket."

"I don't trust you with it." She jammed her tools and her gloves between the chutney jars. She stood in haste, then bent to grab the handle. The basket bumped against her legs and clanked.

"Suit yourself." He was up in an instant and bounding down the rock's slope, leaping out into the water with a whoop. He spun around to face her, and a waist-high swell knocked him sideways.

"Deuced cold," he called cheerfully. "Deeper than I thought. Can you swim? Beatrix couldn't swim. That complicated the last exodus."

Beatrix. One of the models.

"I'm not a siren," Muriel muttered. "But I *can* swim."

"What?" called Griffith.

"Soak your big head!" she yelled.

He grinned and snatched off his cap, shoving it inside his coat. He let himself tip over with a whoop and a splash, and floated on his back, limbs splayed.

"I've got something!" He righted himself and lifted a fistful of lime-green leaves.

"Sea lettuce." Muriel sighed.

"Do you want it?"

"No."

"Plenty of it, if you change your mind." He flopped over again.

It was hard to stay annoyed with him, splashing around as he was, like a drunken seal. *Hungover* seal. She skated down the rock on her backside and dropped into the sea, rising at once onto her tiptoes as the frigid water lapped her ribs, the basket clutched to her chest. A wave nearly overset her, and she staggered as she tried to kick her legs free from her twisted skirts.

"May I?" He appeared beside her, hair plastered to his forehead. She let him hook the basket over his elbow. He was taller, after all.

The next wave floated her into him, and he caught her around the waist, only for a moment. But as they waded toward the beach, his hand closed around hers, and she didn't tug free. It all felt suddenly, disturbingly good. The cold swirl of the sparkling waves. His warm, tethering grip. The way her feet kept lifting from the ground.

"I haven't gone swimming once since we arrived," she said, and he tutted and shook his head.

"I have to do this, then," he said. "To appease the holiday gods." He released her hand and turned, grabbing it again as he dove backward, pulling her with him. She shrieked and swam, or rather half swam, given the awkward drag of her clothes and boots.

When they reached dry sand, dripping and bedraggled, exhilaration turned them toward each other, and Muriel grinned up into his face, before she remembered herself and stepped away, catching her breath, reclaiming her basket, and her hand.

"I'm rather glad that happened," he said, a twinkle in his eye.

She shot him a dirty look. "That makes one of us."

He smiled, unconvinced.

She wasn't convinced either. That was the bigger problem.

Sand clung heavily to her boots as she trudged up the beach. He didn't pursue her, just called out as she neared the first bathing tent.

"Until tomorrow!"

12

MURIEL HAD A good memory and a better sense of direction. As a child, she'd spent her free half days as far from her cousin's shop as her feet would take her, exploring the forested hills and the heath, storing away the little details of the landscape so she could re-create her path home. Years later, she'd relied on her ability to make mental maps when she'd worked with local nurserymen in the northern provinces of China. Groups fanned out in the mountains, scouring for new cultivars of primulas and peonies, and she'd look up to realize she'd lost track of her companions. On each of those occasions, she'd found her way back to camp—not always quickly. But at least she'd never spent a whole night in a ravine, like Esmé.

The time had come, however, to admit defeat. It was noon, and birds were twittering, and she hadn't the foggiest notion whether to turn left or turn right. She and James had walked inland, across fields and up this long hill with its tumbled stone walls and old, unkempt orchard, and now the path diverged before them.

"Do you remember what they said?" she asked James, who was sitting on a stump, sipping from a flask.

"They wanted to sell me their goat." He held out his flask. "Sherry?"

"Not what they said about the goat." Muriel waved away the flask. "About which way we're supposed to turn."

"Sorry," said James. "I was too taken with the goat."

Muriel turned to survey the path's two forks. She had less of an excuse. As soon as the farm girls had heard Griffith's name, they'd begun to giggle and exchange covert glances, and she'd grown flustered herself, entirely unable to concentrate on the directions to the bicycle shop. Had she turned into such a harridan that she begrudged young maidens a bit of sighing over a handsome swain? Was it censure she felt? No, more likely it was protectiveness, the same as she'd felt toward Clarinda Chiswick. The girls seemed so innocent, and Kit Griffith, anything but.

"This way," she guessed. She picked up her hamper of dried seaweeds and started down the left fork.

"We were supposed to pass standing stones," she said with satisfaction, as a cairn came into view on the next hill, although she rather suspected navigating by cairns in Cornwall was like navigating by beech trees in Hampshire.

"And a stream," she said sometime later, and skipped across the little rill of water on flat stones, as James swung his arms wildly and teetered, having made a less felicitous choice: a slick and spongy log that crumbled underfoot.

It wasn't long after that they passed a farmhouse. The little boy chasing chickens in the yard brought them around the barn and pointed out the footpath.

Another quarter mile and Muriel saw the odd gray tower in the distance. She quickened her pace.

"I am quite sure I can ride a bicycle." She said it aloud, more to herself than to James. "This tour isn't a disaster in the making. I've gone on much longer excursions with men I barely know, by boat and by donkey and cart, and on foot, and it always turned out well enough."

She smoothed her hand over her skirt, one of her shortened, serge seaweed-hunting skirts, surely as practical for cycling.

"I dislike Griffith just the right amount," she continued. "He's not so odious in the moment that I recoil from the close association our bargain requires. And yet I remain conscious of his crimes and hypocrisies, and, therefore, on guard against his superficial charms. I have high expectations for his art, and low expectations for his behavior."

"Ah," said James.

A woodpecker began tapping, its steady tattoo ticking off the moments.

"That's all you have to say?" asked Muriel.

He gave her a placating smile. "Your speech seems very well calibrated."

"My *dislike* is well calibrated." Her brows pulled together.

"Isn't that what I said?"

Her scowl was accusatory. "You're not even on my side anymore. You're on the side of your drinking companion."

"I thought you and Griffith were now on the same side."

"When it comes to cycling and painting. Nothing else."

The engine house looked taller by the second, thrusting up from the ground like a phallic monument. Trust Griffith to have set up shop in a building that seemed to advertise virility.

Did he maintain an art studio as well? In this very engine house?

"You must examine him." She snapped her gaze back to James. "The symptoms he described are worrying."

James returned her look, brows high. "You worry for him?"

"For my paintings." She hefted the hamper so it rested again on her hip. "He told me he couldn't paint, and then that he would. I don't know what I'm to believe. If he does suffer from some malady, can he really overcome it overnight, by force of will?"

"I don't know," said James dryly. "On account of all the unknowns."

They walked along the perimeter of a pasture in silence, and perhaps they were both brooding about the unknown.

James spoke first. "Forbidding, isn't it?"

He was looking at the engine house. They'd arrived. The grass was haphazardly patterned with tire tracks. Several wheels leaned against the side of the building. The sign above the large window in front was perfunctory, bold black letters, no embellishments.

St. Ives Bicycle.
Sales. Rentals. Service.

Behind the glass, three Rovers stood on display, handlebars gleaming dully.

Muriel put down her hamper. "Mr. Griffith?"

She tried the door. It swung open, and she poked her head inside. The smell of metal, machine oil, and rubber assailed her. Nothing moved but the motes of dust suspended in the sunbeams.

"He's not here." She slammed the door and stormed back to James.

"We'll wait, then."

"No." She drew a breath. Her expectations for Griffith's behavior hadn't been low enough. "It was all a joke."

"Joke? What joke?"

"It didn't make any sense. I should have known better." She shook her head. "All his hand-wringing and chest-thumping about the plight of the female sex. It didn't make sense because he was pranking me."

Her insides shivered.

She whispered with her hand on her stomach. "He's laughing himself sick at Titcombe Hall as we speak."

"Titcombe Hall?" James blinked. "Why there?"

"It's where he lives."

"It can't be where he lives."

Her turn to blink. "What?"

"Titcombe Hall. That's Deighton's place. Don't you remember? He barked it at us."

She was staring blankly. Her memories from that encounter on the path centered on Griffith. The way he stood. The angle of his jaw. The curve of his mouth. The rough grain of his voice.

She gave herself a shake. "It's not possible. Lady Chiswick—she was talking about Griffith. She said . . ."

What had Lady Chiswick said, exactly?

Muriel moistened her lips. "She called him handsome."

"Oh, in that case, she *must* have meant Griffith. No other handsome men in St. Ives." James had begun to smirk. "Now who's lacerating? You once told me I'd aged well. Which I'm just realizing isn't very flattering, even on its merits."

"She was referring particularly to a cyclist."

"If she said Titcombe Hall, she was referring particularly to Deighton. He's not my cup of tea, but I can see how he'd have his adherents. Those calves. They're like young coconuts. And I believe his family runs Empire Tobacco, which is bound to put a shine on things."

The tickle in the back of Muriel's throat made her cough.

"She said—" Muriel coughed again. "She said she could tell I fancied him."

"Then Lady Chiswick seems to have made an incorrect assumption." James raised his brows.

He didn't need to say the rest.

So had she.

Another conversation might have undeceived them both. But since that morning over breakfast, she'd only glimpsed the unpleasant woman in passing. The hotel wasn't large, but she and the Chiswicks kept different hours. She hadn't seen hide nor hair of Sir Reggie, or Clarinda, to the best of her knowledge.

Clarinda.

Lady Chiswick wanted her daughter matched with Colin Deighton.

"Bother," said Muriel. "Griffith *didn't* do any bodily injury to cats?"

"I didn't what?"

She jumped.

Griffith had wheeled his Rover silently over the grass. He stood gripping the handlebars, glancing between her and James. He was windblown, just back from a ride, and he looked utterly appalled.

"You thought I'd harmed a cat? Deliberately?" His eyes were slits.

Her ticklish throat tightened uncomfortably. She emitted one more strangled cough. But her face was all the confirmation he needed.

"Good God," he muttered. "And you were willing to engage in civil conversation and share a small boulder?"

"I wasn't that civil." Muriel frowned. "And I didn't invite you onto the boulder." She studied him with increasing incredulity. He seemed to be taking her part. She narrowed her own eyes. "Are you mocking me? Or pandering?"

"Neither. I'm a lifelong friend of cats."

"The captain of the Mutton Wheelers isn't," interjected James. "Possibly. It's not confirmed. What I should say is a certain Sir Reggie has alleged malfeasance involving Colin Deighton and a cat. Muriel mistakenly assumed he meant you."

"Why?" Griffith hadn't taken his eyes from her.

"I misheard. It was hearsay. Hearsay I misheard." Muriel wanted to duck behind James, to hide her face, before she could expose herself further.

Gone in an instant. Her trumped-up impetus to eternal dislike. The flimsy bulwark it had erected between her mind and body.

She felt off-balance, hopelessly uncalibrated, and the longer she held his gaze, the worse it got. Her heart began to leap, tender and undefended.

A likable Griffith was far more dangerous.

"I brought specimens." She addressed him briskly. "They're dry, but they'll take on their natural shape and color if you put them in a basin of water. You can hang them to dry again, on a line, and return them to the basin whenever you wish to resume painting. The olive seaweeds are durable, a good place to start."

Griffith glanced at the hamper without seeming to see it, then back at her.

"I've never so much as flicked a cat's whiskers," he said. "Is there anything else I can clear up for you?"

She swallowed, a hundred inchoate questions muddying her thoughts. Why did he infatuate her? Was it a rakish trick, something he was *doing* to her, with full awareness? Something he did to all women? Was that what he'd meant by freedom? An open offer, the promise of pleasure with no strings attached? Was it worth it, the pleasure?

How did it feel?

"Nothing of which I'm aware," she said, and stretched her lips into a smile.

The woodpecker was tapping again.

"Well." She clapped her hands. "On to the cycling lesson."

_____

AN HOUR LATER, they were all three behind the engine house, Griffith on his feet, James in a wrought iron chair, and Muriel splayed like a starfish beneath a two-wheeled death machine.

Cycling was not intuitive.

She let her head roll to the side and considered the cheerful patch of oxeye daisies she'd just missed crushing.

"Much better this time," called Griffith. "Could you tell?"

James piped up. "I couldn't. More sherry?"

Muriel began to drag herself out from underneath the Rover, a complicated negotiation. Her skirt was tangled in the front wheel's spiderweb of spokes. As her legs slid free, she realized that her stocking had been torn by a pedal and that her flesh was gouged.

She sat up and waved Griffith away. She didn't want him hoisting her again, like she was a sack of potatoes.

"This makes me think we should stick to horses." James gestured to Griffith with his flask.

Griffith went to him and dropped into the adjacent chair, taking the flask and swigging deep.

"For one thing, horses can stand on their own," continued James. "They're also noble, intelligent creatures, beautiful to behold and capable of developing a rapport with their riders. Their legs do the work, instead of your own, which is another advantage."

Muriel stood painfully, straightening her rumpled skirt. She heaved up the Rover. It certainly couldn't stand on its own. And _she_ couldn't keep the blasted thing upright, not once her feet were in the air.

"Horses have to be fed and stabled." Griffith passed back the flask and crossed his arms. He'd shucked his jacket and wore only his vest and shirtsleeves. Muriel's eyes went straight for the swell of his biceps. A moment too late, she realized James had noticed the direction of her gaze. She snapped her eyes back to the Rover and concentrated on pushing it across the lawn.

"Bicycles were a novelty," said Griffith. "A toy for sportsmen. But the technology is advancing rapidly, and the price is falling, and low-mounts like the Rover mean women can cycle too, and they will, more and more of them. They'll cycle as fast as they please, *wherever* they please."

Muriel tried not to scowl. So far, she could only wobble slowly forward and accelerate sidelong, when she pitched to the right or the left.

"I mentioned that some of my medical colleagues fear that cycling strains the heart." James sounded sardonic. "It occurs to me the risk isn't to the cyclists but rather the pedestrians unprepared for the sight of so many female ankles."

Griffith snorted. "They'll get used to it."

Muriel glanced down. Even when she wasn't pedaling, her shortened skirt hit just below midcalf, revealing her lace-up walking boots and a bit of stocking besides. Shortened skirts made people stare, even nearer the shore. That couple she'd surprised—George and Margaret. They'd called her a *shocking-looking woman.*

"Or they won't get used to it," she declared, tipping up her chin. "But that won't stop us."

It had popped out before she could think. There was something rousing about Griffith's vision of shrinking distances and increased mobility, women going about their business on their own terms, facilitated by bicycles, which seemed suddenly marvelous.

The bicycle. A marvelous contraption—if it didn't kill you.

Griffith's appreciative look would have warmed her cheeks, but they were maximally flushed from her exertions.

She clenched her teeth, wheeled the Rover about, and swung her leg over the top bar. It curved down on this model—a drop frame, Griffith had called it. Designed for ladies.

"Ready to go again?" Griffith strode over. He stood very close, bracing the bicycle as she arranged her skirts and adjusted her grip on the handlebars.

As she revolved the pedals, he kept hold, moving with her.

"That's it," he said. "Eyes straight ahead."

The husky command made her want to look in his direction, and when he let her go, she was listing toward him, just slightly. In an attempt to restore equilibrium, she turned the wheel away from the approaching ground, which decision narrowed the distance all at once.

"Ahh!" she yelped as her elbow exploded with pain. She lay on her side, head ringing. Grass prickled her skin, and the warm scent of torn summer earth filled her nostrils. At least she wasn't learning on macadamized highway, or a graveled lane, or a cobbled street.

God, this tour would hurt.

James shouted, "Is it time for the sticking plaster?"

She rolled onto her back and blinked at the sky. Griffith's face appeared above her.

"You're doing quite well," he said.

She wiggled, resisting the urge to kick the Rover as she extracted herself.

"Mounting, balancing, pedaling, steering, dismounting." She pushed herself to sitting. "That's it? Five elements to master?"

Breaking it down thus made the task seem more manageable.

Griffith squatted, forearms on his knees. "Those are the basics."

"There are more," she said grimly.

"A few nuances. It takes a bit of skill, and strength, to manage momentum up and down hills. And the machine itself responds differently on different road surfaces. There's a trick to—" He must have realized his words were producing a decidedly negative effect. He smiled. "Not to worry. It will all be second nature before you know it."

She smiled too, a crazed smile.

Today was Friday. The Mutton Wheelers departed on Tuesday. At this rate, Griffith would have to run beside her, propping her Rover the whole way.

He rose and extended a hand. She clasped it. His strong grip made her knees feel weaker. She was upright in an instant but wobbling like a bloody bicycle.

"I have an idea," said James, musingly, leaning forward in his chair. "Muriel, what if you thought of the handlebars as bit and bridle?"

"You're not helping," she told him.

"Or *named* your bicycle, to establish a relationship?"

"Not. Helping." She grated it.

"You're the one who insisted that I come along," he huffed.

"Not for the cycling pointers."

He shrugged and plucked a book from his surgical bag. "I was going to suggest Cynisca, after the Spartan princess who won the Olympic chariot race."

"Cynisca." Muriel gave him a dubious look.

"I was feeling rather proud of it." He balanced the book on his thigh and drummed his fingers on the cover. "Boudica."

"I'm not calling my bicycle *Boudica*."

"Britomart? Belphoebe. No, I've got it—La Belle Dame sans Merci!"

"Daisy," blurted Muriel. She scowled with enough ferocity to preempt James's smirk.

He smirked regardless, a well-satisfied smirk.

Thanks to his *horseplay*, her bicycle had a name. A non-poetical, non-warriorlike name that probably struck fear in Griffith's heart. Fear that she'd plant herself in a field about five paces from the starting line, and that would be that.

She didn't look at Griffith.

"Daisies are hardy," she muttered. "They're extremely reliable. Also, they're quick. Quick to grow, I mean. Relatively speaking."

James was nodding along. "Brilliant." His lips twitched. "Now can I say *upsy-daisy* when you topple over?"

"I can't see how you'll refrain." She marched up to him and stuck out her hand. "Sherry."

He obliged her, and she wet her lips delicately, knowing the sherry was too rich to gulp. She'd underestimated her thirst. Her throat moved convulsively, and she tipped the flask again.

James eyed her with amusement.

"You should name *your* bicycle too," he said, as Griffith came to stand at her throbbing elbow.

"Agreed," Griffith drawled. "I'm thinking Vercingetorix. Or Buttercup."

Muriel sputtered and had to wipe her mouth on her sleeve.

"Buttercup," approved James. "And your bicycle club is . . ." He drew out the pause, grinning with anticipation. "The Flower Pedals!"

Muriel groaned, which made her battered ribs ache the more.

"Not another peep," she commanded. "Unless I need a spoke surgically removed from my backside." She slapped the flask into James's hand.

"On second thought," she added, "not even then."

ANOTHER HOUR LATER, she was lying in a bruised, sweaty heap, a rock drilling into her hip. Her only consolation—other than the fact that she did not, yet, have a spoke embedded in her backside—was that she'd traveled an appreciable distance from the engine house before an instinctive zigzag around a stick had precipitated her doom.

She levered up, palms on the grass. Griffith was loping toward her. The sound of a bell brought her head around.

A cyclist was spinning down the narrow road that wound past the farms. She pedaled smoothly, homespun skirt hiked to her knees, checked apron fluttering. A basket sat above her front wheel.

"Geddon, Kit!" she hollered as she flashed by, bright braids swinging across her back.

Muriel was still staring when Griffith dropped down beside her.

"Good form," he said. "I'd say you went fifty yards."

"*She* has good form." Muriel turned to him, unable to grudge the girl her admiration, even as disappointment with her own progress weighed in her gut. "She's a marvel."

"Martha Curnow?" Griffith stretched out his long legs. "She is. She rides like a fish in water."

"Whereas I ride like a fish on a bicycle." Muriel made a face.

Griffith's lips twitched. "You'll get the hang of it."

"You should have asked *her*."

He shrugged a shoulder. "She's farming stock."

The dismissive statement snapped her spine to attention.

"You want more polish?" She glared, curling her fingers in the grass. "I'm farming stock myself. The vulgarity comes out sometimes. Consider yourself warned."

His searching gaze roamed over her. "I wasn't voicing a personal objection. As I'm sure you know, farm chores begin before dawn and end after dusk. Her family couldn't spare her."

Oh. Well, that explained it. Lord, she was testy.

She gave a chagrined nod. "You taught her how to ride?"

"I did. After she convinced her father of the practicality. She sells eggs and cheese in town, and now she doesn't have to wait for the cart or walk the miles there and back."

"But there's the expense."

His gaze shifted.

"You didn't charge her." Muriel's eyes widened. "You gave her the Rover? Is she one of your . . . ?"

His gaze returned to meet hers. "You exaggerate my romantic profligacy."

"So *financial* profligacy is your line? My cousin was a shopkeeper. He made his customers pay ready money for every matchstick." She pressed with her knuckles until she felt moist grains of dirt on her skin. Something bid her continue. "And by his calculations, I worked myself more into his debt each day."

"I thought you were farming stock."

"This was after the farm."

He was looking at her too keenly. She gave herself a shake and winced as every muscle twinged.

"Miss Curnow," she said, bringing them back to topic. "She isn't anything to you. And you gave her a bicycle."

"It's a bicycle I used to rent out. I'm not losing much." He tossed his peaked cap onto the grass and scrubbed a hand through his hair. His expression was almost dreamy. "And she's gaining time."

"Because she can make her deliveries faster."

"And no one knows how much faster." A smile broke across his face. "She can skim minutes from the time she saves and linger on the High Street."

Muriel stared. "That matters to you?"

Such a small, nearly immaterial thing. A girl winning for herself a few precious minutes. Gaining time to look in a shop window or talk with a friend.

He swatted at a pollen-drugged bee, which continued its discombobulated loops.

"All the time in the world wouldn't mean she'd be allowed to ride with the Mutton Wheelers." He tipped his head. "Tootle off with a half dozen men on iron grasshoppers? Never." He laughed. "Iron grasshoppers. That's what her father calls bicycles."

"I was your last resort." Muriel rose to kneeling, over the protest of her knees. It was so obvious. How could she have imagined Clarinda Chiswick volunteering in her stead? What leisure allowed, propriety forbid.

She'd focused on Griffith's ability to magnetize women and ignored the hurdles in their way.

"Last resort," he agreed. "Also, first resort. There *were* a few middle resorts, artists of independent means and scandalous reputations. But the athletic one is off to France, and I suspect the others would have turned me down."

Her brow crinkled. "Why did you let Deighton goad you into this?"

Emotion flickered in his eyes, there and then gone. "Arrogance, stupidity, and righteous indignation."

He said it smoothly.

And that very smoothness pricked her intuition. That, and the charming way his features shifted into an even more handsome arrangement. It was *too* charming.

"You goaded him, really." As soon as she said it, the truth of it struck her. Griffith's wits were keen. Deighton couldn't outmaneuver him so easily. "You knew how he felt about women cycling. And how he thirsted for another contest. The challenge was as good as issued as soon as you said a woman could ride that distance. But you said it without anyone in mind." She shook her head slowly. "It seems an oddly big risk to take."

"Perhaps I thrive on risk."

"Perhaps you had an ulterior motive." She remembered his claim and repeated it archly. "Ulterior motives are the most interesting."

A muscle ticked in his jaw. His gaze bored into hers, and the gray of his eyes seemed to leach away the sunlight.

"I—" She shook her head, disconcerted. But the strangeness of the moment dissipated. A second passed, and he was smiling with characteristic irony.

"I had an ulterior motive," he said. "I just didn't know it at the time." He leaned toward her. "This victory will also be a victory for cats."

She laughed. Her laughter felt restrained. New questions queued on her tongue. But she'd pushed him enough already, in error. She wouldn't pursue an inkling, not now.

She had a bicycle to ride.

She surged to her feet, righted the fallen Rover with an *upsy-daisy*, and aimed it at the engine house. James wasn't reading any longer, and he wasn't alone. Redheaded Mr. Ponsonby occupied the other chair. Their conversation looked supremely spirited.

She climbed back into the saddle and flung forward before Griffith could reach her to steady the frame.

"I'm going!" she cried in excited disbelief. "I'm going!"

And she was. She was *going*, going at last, bowling along, the wind in her hair.

She heard Ponsonby's baritone. "Can she brake?"

"Not sure," said James.

Before the crash—the last of the day—she had time to experience the foretaste of victory, and to wonder how many ways she might win and lose in the weeks to come.

13

ON MONDAY MORNING, Kit rolled up a coat, a pair of trousers, two shirts and undershirts, four handkerchiefs, as many stockings, a cravat, and a nightshirt, and packed them into his knapsack, along with leather shoes and spats, a needle and thread, a jar of salve, a bottle of alcohol and tannins, toilet items, and assorted tools and parts.

He took the straps in one hand and curled his arm.

Twelve pounds, give or take.

His eyes strayed to the table, where he'd stacked Friday's purchases, art supplies from Lanham's on the High Street. He packed the sketch pad and pencils. The sketch pad was missing a few pages, all crumpled in the fireplace. Each page represented a failed attempt to capture the form of the seaweeds he'd floated in the wash basin. Those seaweeds were drying now, on a rack he'd assembled from a handful of loose spokes.

He didn't spare them a look. He left the knapsack on his workbench and rode to town, down Talland Road to Titcombe Hall, an imposing, many-gabled house, ivy-covered, with large bay windows.

He'd planned to talk with Deighton, to hold a parley of sorts, and discuss the route, but after a ten-minute wait in a dark, fussy drawing room stuffed with tapestry chairs and pompadour china, the door burst open, and an older man thundered toward him.

"You're Kit Griffith." It was an accusation. The man slammed a paper down on the table, the *St. Ives Weekly Summary and Visitors List.*

Kit knew perfectly well what it contained. Hawkings had stretched last Monday's events across two articles. One, a jaunty account of the joust. The other, a waggish announcement of the Mutton Wheelers' ten-day club run, including destinations, distances, and affiliated inns, and the terms of the wager.

"I've a mind to eject you from that chair." The man rounded the table, head lowered, a charging bull in Harris Tweed.

Even if they'd met on the street, Kit would recognize him as Deighton's father. He had the same wide neck and square jaw, and his deep voice boomed from his chest with the same aggressive volume, absorbed somewhat by the room's preponderance of draperies.

"Let me save you the trouble." Kit unfolded himself as Deighton Senior approached, which brought their faces into such close proximity that he felt a gust of hot breath.

"It was bad enough—my only son flitting about in knickers. Now he's a laughingstock, lampooned in a bloody gossip rag. Do you know what I was doing when I was his age?"

Kit closed his lips in a smile so he didn't voice his first thought. *Picking your teeth with human femurs.*

"I was expanding my father's tobacco company," snarled Deighton Senior. "I was overseeing the construction of a new factory, launching three new brands of cigarettes." He looked like he could light cigarettes off the hot coals burning in his eyes. "I was siring children. All disappointments. Girls. And Colin, who costs me considerably more than they do, with less chance of return." He looked Kit up and down. "You knocked him into a dunghill. You! You can't weigh ten stone."

"Closer to twelve," murmured Kit, which was true enough, with the knapsack.

"He'll even the score." Deighton Senior's upper right eyelid twitched. "I'm not giving him a choice in the matter. He will knock *you* into a dunghill, or he's forever disgraced. I'd rather die without an heir than suffer a weakling to carry on my name."

Kit tried to imagine his own father speaking so about either of his brothers, Clive or Holt, and could not. William Holroyd was a big man himself, and reputedly bloodthirsty in his business dealings. Within the household, he'd always been the permissive parent, over-riding his wife's objections to Kit's artistic pursuits and masculine outfits. When Kit had turned up at the dinner table with an Eton crop, unevenly barbered by a fellow student, he'd laughed and said it had decided him positively on the question of whether or not to in-vest in a Pyrenees wig company.

Would his father have cared more if his *sons* refused to perform as expected? Clive and Holt had both followed in his footsteps.

Kit stuck his hands in his trouser pockets and gave Deighton Se-nior a bland look.

"It was only a bit of fun," he said.

"Fun at my son's expense. He's the butt of a joke. But not for long."

"Sir," said Kit politely. "We're cycling the countryside together. The physical contest is now between each rider and the road."

Deighton Senior's lips drew back in a singularly nasty smile. "I wouldn't be so sure. You're leaving on two wheels, but you'll return on four, in a donkey cart."

Muscles tensed along Kit's spine, but he managed to shrug, cred-itably blasé.

"I called to discuss the tour with your son. If he's not at home . . ."

"He is not."

"I'll see myself out." Kit moved around Deighton Senior, slowly, and paused in front of a Sèvres vase set on an ormolu-molded stand. He plucked the freshest gardenia from the browning bouquet and threaded the stem through the buttonhole of his blue morning coat.

"Thank you for the flower," he said, glancing back at his host. "*A thing of beauty is a joy forever.*"

Deighton Senior released a growling breath of unadulterated disdain.

With a nod, Kit took his leave.

HE ARRIVED AT the Towans Hotel earlier than planned. Muriel wasn't meeting him until noon. He wheeled his bicycle through the

English garden and leaned it against the gazebo, inside which she was safeguarding her own bicycle, at his suggestion. He climbed the gazebo's three steps and sprawled on a bench to wait.

He'd mounted panniers over her rear wheel, so she wouldn't have to carry her belongings on her shoulders. He could tell they were still empty. She'd yet to pack.

Sensible. Why strain herself on their last training ride? He'd advise her, though, to test the weight before tomorrow morning.

He was facing the hotel and could see guests coming and going along the walk. The tall figure in white, with the tennis racket—that was Raleigh. Ponsonby was strolling with him. No easel. He held a racket too, and was either waving it for emphasis or demonstrating his forehand.

Kit considered jogging over, but in the end, he refrained, watching the pair's lively progress until the hedges screened them from view. He and Ponsonby hadn't directly addressed their quarrel—if that's what it had been—but they'd smoothed it over, and Ponsonby seemed to be making a point of avoiding the *chappies* he'd befriended at Svensson's party.

Or perhaps he was just more interested in befriending the doctor.

Kit's thoughts wandered until a new figure drew his attention. Muriel was approaching with long strides. She worked in the field, as a botanist. That explained her supple movement. As did the fact that she was a country woman, raised on a farm, or at least partially. She'd gone on to drudge for her cousin in a shop. He would never have guessed if she hadn't told him. Her accent was cultured, and she behaved so comfortably with Raleigh, whose every plummy inflection and gesture screamed blue blood.

He watched as she drew closer, pleasantly mesmerized by the sight of her, and by his speculations, all the things he wondered and was poised to discover.

"It's just us today," she called, in lieu of a greeting.

"Yes." He rose and steered her bicycle down the steps. "I saw our chaperones heading in the other direction."

She gave him a small, irritated smile. "Oh, please. Those two couldn't chaperone a turnip."

He smiled back. "Then they've been outdoing themselves."

Her cheeks went pink. Was she nervous? They hadn't been alone since their tête-à-tête on the rocks. He realized—all at once, with something like shock—that *he* was nervous. At a level below conscious thought, he'd spent the last days wondering how much—if anything—to divulge to her about his past, about his particular type of manhood.

His nervousness told him he'd decided and decided on *all*.

Unprecedented.

Back in London, when he'd used that other name, he'd felt discomfort when his lovers interpreted his body as feminine, when he sensed them desiring someone he wasn't. In Cornwall, his lovers met him as a man, and he kept his body to himself, engaging in erotic activities that allowed him to preserve his privacy.

The simplicity felt like luxury.

Suddenly, he didn't give a fig for simplicity.

She'd gone even pinker under his prolonged gaze.

"We've no need of chaperones." She said it forcefully, but he heard the slight hitch in her breath.

"I'm in complete agreement." He let his voice vibrate with innuendo. Flirtation was his favorite pastime, and it steadied him.

No need for nervousness either. There was some new ground to cover, but it wasn't without its well-worn grooves.

"I think we mean different things." She tried to frown but laughed instead. She'd been laughing more frequently around him. Every time, the sound sent a warm swell through his chest.

"And James and Mr. Ponsonby haven't been *chaperoning*," she continued. "They've been entertaining themselves. James won't admit it, but he likes cycling."

"Does he?" Ponsonby had convinced Raleigh to give it a try, and the four of them had spent Saturday and Sunday riding together on the field paths. Raleigh had taken every opportunity to compare the experience unfavorably to a gallop on a good hunter.

"Absolutely." Her nod was emphatic. "The more negative he seems, the more he's enjoying himself."

"Do *you* like it?" He found himself unduly interested in the answer.

She'd gone about determinedly mastering the mechanics. But did the momentum fill her with giddy joy, as it did him?

"I do like it, very much. Now that I don't topple over." She put her hands on the handlebars, and he let his remain where they were, their fingers nearly brushing, for a beat too long.

He released the bicycle, and she rocked it toward her, lowering her gaze to the polished frame.

"I think I'll get one, in New York," she said. "Although James said if I ride in the city, I have to promise I'll wear a pith helmet."

"Very protective," he murmured.

"Pith helmets?" She looked up.

"No." He smirked. "Raleigh."

She laughed again. "We look out for each other." Slowly, the laughter faded from her eyes, leaving an inexplicable shadow. "When we can."

His instinct was to cradle her face. To coax her confidence, and to pledge his assistance vanquishing any hardship.

Instead, he spoke lightly. "You're like a sister to him."

"He said that to you?" Her smile returned.

"He did. Although he didn't have to. It's obvious."

"He only has brothers, by birth. Older, thank God. I don't have any siblings myself." She paused. "Do you?"

He supposed he was looking at her too fixedly. But he didn't look away.

Older, thank God. An offhand comment, and an odd one, on the surface. But of course, Muriel had to know that her friend fancied men. The eldest son always bore the brunt of dynastic responsibility. Marriage. Children. It was fortunate for Raleigh, being youngest. Muriel was sensitive to that fact, and to Raleigh himself, to his right to live a life that didn't feel like a lie. Whatever her personal experiences, at the least she was aware that people loved differently. She was aware that alternate ways of being existed, outside the narrow limits prescribed by British law, church doctrine, and social convention.

That boded well.

Her eyes were searching his.

He hadn't answered her question.

"Brothers," he said. "Also older." So many years older they'd never paid him any mind. "We're not close, in any sense." He blinked, gathering himself. "Shall we? I thought we could take the inland route to Zennor. Ride on a proper road. Eat lunch at the Tinners Arms. Return on the cliff path."

"What would that be? Twelve miles?" She tipped her head thoughtfully. "Tomorrow we ride around thirty." She'd also read the paper. The Mutton Wheelers' first stop was Porthcurno, a village on Cornwall's southern coast.

"Not too bad," she added.

"Not a great distance, no." He felt compelled to correct a potential misimpression. "But it's the coastal route. We'll climb hills and round a promontory. There's rubble, and washouts, and wind. The going is steep."

She shrugged. "I'll dismount if necessary. I don't mind steep. Of all animals, I'm most like a mountain goat."

His brows shot up in amused surprise. A mountain goat, eh?

"Good, then," he said. "Agility is important. For the rubble." He paused. "And the rampaging bull."

She frowned. "What rampaging bull?"

"Deighton." He scratched under his cap. "Like father, like son. There might be a charge."

"You mean he'll charge *at* you?" Her voice rose. "This isn't a joust. We're all riding in the same direction!"

Perhaps he shouldn't have raised the issue, beyond asking her to pack some of Raleigh's sticking plaster.

He waved a hand. "Forget it."

She looked incredulous. "Forget that you said Deighton might attack like *a bull*? And what's this about his father? You know him?"

"Let's talk as we ride." He sighed. "It will help if I know I'm closing in on a pub. But first." He reached into his coat pocket. "I brought something for you."

"Oh." She bit her lip, and suddenly, she seemed to twinkle with shy expectation. Something went soft and vague inside him, and a funny, fleeting wish unspooled—that he had some kingly gift, precious gems, or the key to a castle.

He fetched up the length of lilac ribbon. "To trim your hat."

"But my hat has a ribbon." Confused, she touched her straw boater. The crown was edged with ribbon, wide and white.

"This one matches the lilac necktie I'll wear with my cycling coat. We don't have badges. Consider this our club color."

"Our club." She smiled wryly and put out her hand for the ribbon. "The Flower Pedals?" She shook her head. "I suppose it's fitting. For a botanist, and a dandy." She was eyeing his gardenia.

"First, I was a rake. Now I'm a dandy?"

"They're not mutually exclusive. And you can't deny it."

"I wouldn't waste my breath." He shrugged. "Denials are never convincing."

"True. Also, you're a dandy."

Now he laughed. "Fine. I'm a dandy. I adorn the world as best I can."

She rolled her eyes, but he saw how she rubbed her thumb over the ribbon, caressingly, before slipping it into her skirt pocket. His stomach tightened.

"You can adorn the world with your art," she told him. "Instead of your person."

"I can adorn the world with both." He winked, and then, to forestall her saying—or worse, asking—anything else about art, he turned, grabbed his bicycle, and pointed its front wheel toward the road.

THE VILLAGE OF Zennor was a stark smattering of low, gray cottages and a tumbledown church set under gorsy hills, the ground falling away in boulders on one side, to the sea. Even after she dismounted her bicycle, Muriel's arms vibrated from the ride over the bumpy, hard-packed road. The pewlike chairs in the pub added unnecessary punishment to her aching backside. But the pint and the pasties revived her spirits, and Griffith seemed to slip under her skin with every sidelong look, his attention caressing her very bones.

He chatted easily with the ancient publican behind the counter, and the pretty girls in mobcaps, his granddaughters. He drank two pints to her one, recounting the local legends, mostly involving bloodthirsty giants, whose comeuppances were meted out by smaller, wittier, more courageous opponents.

"So, you see," he said, grinning, "the folklore is on our side."

"*Folklore* will prevent Deighton from breaking you in half?" She sipped her beer in delicate disbelief.

"Among other things." He responded airily, then called for more pasties.

It didn't irk her, his inconsequential prattle. It was colorful and amusing, and it made *her* feel colorful and amusing, and pleasurably conscious of her body, despite the myriad discomforts produced by four days of cycling lessons. The more they ate and drank and prattled, the more she felt herself melting into her unforgiving seat.

How unexpected this all was. The sensations that engulfed her when he was near. The urges that disordered rational thought. At seventeen, she'd tingled under Esmé's regard, flattered and overwhelmed by his proposal, by all he offered. It was only later that she'd understood what he *didn't* offer. She'd come to recognize the contours of an inaccessible intimacy from the outside, via uncountable little snubs.

Over the years, she'd sorted out her confused emotions, and she'd locked some of them away—the ones that had no place in her marriage.

No longing, no lack. A simple formula.

Kit Griffith's least glance deranged her tidy equations. He seemed to see the tiny key hidden inside her. What if they turned it, together? Released some mad, molten force?

It would shake her to the core. But she'd lock herself tight again. She'd carry on, the same happy fortress as before. She'd forget—as she most often did—that her deepest being swirled with a wild, unmet demand.

But if Griffith met it? Met *her*, with equal force?

When their dalliance ended, she might yearn more than ever. She might have to live with the kind of loneliness from which she'd taken such pains to shield herself.

At that moment, Griffith said something utterly inane, and she laughed, laughed the ugly, booming laugh she usually tried to temper, and he leaned forward, elbows on the table, as though it were music, and he didn't want to miss a single note.

Loneliness became a distant abstraction.

She chased her laughter with a healthy gulp of beer.

DISASTER DIDN'T STRIKE until after they'd left the Tinners Arms and started spinning through the moorlands.

It took familiar form. Muriel saw the motion from the corner of her eye, a blur coalescing into shining wet teeth and a lolling tongue, a long body spiked with fur like a wire-bristle broom. Her blood ran cold. She flinched from the sound, but the low-pitched growl lodged in her ears. The world winked out. Or no, she'd hidden her face with her hands. She could still see the beast in the blackness, stretching as it lunged.

A bruising impact slammed away her breath.

Her ragged inhale had the pitch of a scream. She fought. She fought as hard, and as uselessly, as she'd fought that long-ago summer day, striking with her fists. But her blows didn't land on jumping muscle and knobby bone, and the smell in her nose wasn't excrement and blood, but heather and earth. She was thrashing the ground, face soaked with sweat, or tears, or both, and the growls had faded to nothing. With a gasp, she sat up, winching her eyes open. The light felt jagged. *Shining teeth.* She curled into herself, shoulders braced, gaze darting frantically.

She fixed on Griffith. He'd dropped his bicycle and turned back down the path, approaching at a run.

"Are you all right?" He fell to his knees at her side. "Did that dog cut in front of you?"

"It must have." She steadied her breathing. Just an ordinary dog. Friendly. A big, shaggy herding breed, with a place by the fire in a nearby farmhouse.

"You were writhing. You received some blow. To your head?"

"No." In truth, she'd no idea. She couldn't tell which part of her had hit the ground first. She was still numb.

"It happens." He sounded gruff. "Dogs make sudden movements, or horses, on the road. It's easy to lose control. Your hat." He leaned forward, face passing near hers, and tugged her hat from a heather plant. She took it from him, too clumsily. Her fingers pressed his, and the shock of that contact restored warmth to her veins. He moved his hand, dropping the brim of the hat, twining their fingers together. With his other thumb, he skimmed her damp cheek.

"You're sure you're all right?"

She felt her throat move convulsively. He meant had she injured herself. He didn't inquire after her oldest, most shattering hurt.

"Quite sure."

Esmé had struggled to conceal his restlessness when fear like this seized her, stalling their work. Her foible, he'd called it.

Griffith stroked a stray curl behind her ear. He was setting her to rights gently, with unhurried tenderness.

She exhaled. "I'm sorry I ever said your heart was rotten kelp."

The corners of his eyes crinkled. "Because it's an insult to kelp? Or because you finally recognize my fine qualities?"

A smile curved her lips. Her limbs felt looser, the fight flowing out of her. The dog was gone. It hadn't been *that* dog. She wasn't a child staring death in its jaws. She was a woman grown, on a warm heath, on a warm day, with a man whose eyes glinted with devilish suggestion.

Impulsively, she leaned in.

She laid her hand on his heart.

14

GRIFFITH TURNED TO stone. She couldn't feel his heartbeat through his coat. She couldn't feel the hard plane of his chest. The wool muffled all, surprisingly thick.

Time stopped.

He flicked her hand away, the action quick and somehow sharp. His brief, pincherlike grip didn't hurt, but pain bit into her regardless.

"Forgive me." She pulled back, sucking in her breath, mortified.

Oh, Lord. Excruciating error. This honeyed, heated feeling—it wasn't reciprocal. He didn't feel drugged by her scent, entranced by her lips. From the beginning, she'd misinterpreted his flirtation. She'd pegged too much to that one kiss, which he'd pressed upon her as a gallantry. He flirted as he breathed. Perhaps it wasn't even intentional, his flirting, but a side effect of making eye contact while dangerously beautiful.

He was making eye contact now. Her self-consciousness peaked. She wanted to bury her face in the prickly grass, but she'd feel more craven if she looked away.

"Penny." His voice was rough.

"Griff." She tried to smile. She was equal to the situation. She could navigate back toward teasing antagonism and preserve their nascent camaraderie.

Pressure kept building in her chest, threatening a new rush of tears. It would be hopelessly silly—to sob with thwarted desire. To sob because she'd forced this reckoning, and now, as a consequence, had to relinquish a gratifying daydream, in which *she* stirred desire too. Stirred his desire. *Ha*.

He was scrutinizing her, making some internal calculation, and she knew she *would* emit a sob if she had to hear him put it all into words. He'd already communicated his aversion with that flick of his wrist.

She'd spare them both.

"There was a caterpillar." She mustered the smile. "On your lapel, near the gardenia. I removed it."

He glanced down.

"It's gone," she said.

"There's no caterpillar on my lapel," he confirmed. He looked up. "There was, though?"

"There was." Her smile held. "You were helping me gather myself. I was returning the favor. Caterpillars chew through wool. You might have ended up with a hole in your coat."

"Nightmarish thought." His gaze roamed over her face. "You wouldn't be lying. About the caterpillar."

"Of course not." She blinked, too rapidly. "Why else would I have touched you?"

"I don't know." His gaze locked hers. "Perhaps for the same reason I touched you."

"Exactly. An exchange of services."

"I wasn't doing you a service." He edged closer, eyes bright. "I was succumbing to an irresistible temptation."

She swallowed hard. "Now who's lying. Me? Tempt you?"

The coals of that wondrous idea began to glow. Her pulse pounded in her ears.

She shook her head, and when she spoke, her voice was frayed. "You brushed my hand away."

"It was where you touched me, not that you did. I was afraid you might . . . It would be more awkward if you . . ." He swept off his cap and speared his fingers through his hair. "How to begin?" He cleared his throat. "There's something I want to tell you."

He looked at her broodingly. Brooding became him. His long lashes shaded his stormy eyes. The shape of his lips was temptation itself.

Her mouth went dry. "Go on."

"You asked me before what awakened me to the woman question. If it was waking up beside a suffragist."

She frowned. "If I recall, you dodged the question."

He didn't answer. The pause crackled with sudden tension.

"My God," she gasped. "You're *married*. You're married to a suffragist!"

"Married?" He started. "I'm not married to a suffragist. Far from it. I *have* woken up beside them, but . . ."

"Them," she echoed. "There have been suffragists plural. I thought I'd exaggerated your romantic profligacy?"

"Make it one. Only Rhoda is a member of the Central Committee." His forehead creased. "I was going somewhere else with this. For as long as I can remember, I have been most intimately concerned with women—"

She snorted, and he raised his brows.

"Women's rights," he finished. "I felt their lack keenly."

"Yes, you already said so. You informed me that women are disadvantaged as a class." She bent her lips in a sarcastic little smile. "Thank you, by the way. I might never have worked it out for myself."

"I was yammering, I know." He scowled. "*You* already said so."

"I felt annoyed at the time." She sighed and studied him. Rake. Artist. Dandy. Purveyor of bicycles—the sort that women could and would ride, into a more equitable future.

"I'm not annoyed any longer," she admitted. "I believe that your empathy is sincere."

"It was never empathy that drove me, but rage." He hesitated, rotating his cap in his hands.

"You see," he said on a breath, "I once lived as a woman myself."

She didn't see. Her mind was smooth. The words made hardly a ripple. She had to force mental movement. "I don't . . . You wore women's clothing?"

His lips gave a wry twist. "Not by choice."

"It had to be a choice." Her face warmed with bewilderment. "You can't wear clothing that doesn't correspond to you by accident."

He sat back on his haunches.

"Oh." She licked her lips. Her eyes slid to the masculine points of his chiseled jaw. His tanned skin was smooth, no hint of stubble roughing its fine grain.

She watched his beautiful mouth tighten.

He knew what she was doing, revising her inventory of his features.

She didn't let her gaze drop lower. She met his eyes. "You *choose* to dress as a man, then."

She had a vertiginous feeling, a reversal reversing itself, the world rearranging.

"You live as a man, but . . ."

"*But*," he murmured. "But what? A man can't have had a girlhood?" A corner of his mouth tilted up. "I live as a man, *and* . . ." He leaned toward her. "Can we start there?"

The moment stretched. His gaze heated the air between them. She detected his alluring scent mixed with the heather and gardenia. A small sound dragged from her. Something flared in his eyes, and he lowered his head, infinitesimally. She stared at his transfixing lips. They still wore the hint of a crooked smile.

God, she wanted to taste him.

A new wave of mortification crashed over her.

She scrambled back. Heat lingered in her limbs, but cold chased after. Oh, hell. She wasn't only surprised, she was humiliated. She'd imagined herself far worldlier than those sighing farm girls, when, in fact, she was hopelessly naive. A dupe in a game to which she hadn't received adequate instructions.

This was why she didn't play at love.

She felt a perfect fool.

She rose, unsteady, white spots blotting the corners of her vision.

Griffith was on his feet in an instant. He stilled her as she teetered, his strong hand closing on her elbow, as it had when they'd first met, when they'd stood together for the first time, in the field by the cliffs.

She drew a shuddering breath. He was staring down at her, with wary expectation.

She had to say *something*. Something adequate to the situation, to his revelation, to her bafflement. To this all-consuming desire.

Yes, she could answer him. *Yes, let's start there.*

"We should get back," she murmured, breaking his grasp. As she turned, she could feel his gaze between her shoulder blades.

Her hat was caught again in the heather. Her bicycle was a few paces off, on its side in the grass, looking like the skeleton of some alien creature. She retrieved both with clumsy haste.

She and Griffith cycled along the path, toward the cliffs, gulls floating overhead, seemingly motionless, suspended like her thoughts.

IT WAS NEARLY the dinner hour when they reached St. Ives, turning on the road that curved up to the Towans. The moment the hotel came into view, Muriel dismounted her bicycle. A light thud told her that Griffith had done the same. She couldn't risk glancing over. She didn't know what she'd say, or what she'd do. Instead, she pushed the bicycle up the hill, focusing on the hotel's massive stone terrace. Guests milled about, or occupied the wicker chairs, waiting for the dining room to open.

She spied Lady Chiswick seated beside a slender young woman with a shining knot of golden hair. Her stomach flipped as Lady Chiswick's head turned. Other heads were swiveling. A portion of the bored assembly had noticed her, and Griffith, and seemed to be tracking their slow progress over the grass with considerable interest.

She kept walking, her too-short dress swinging about her calves. She didn't want to stop at the gazebo, to make a tableau there with Griffith, for the world to see. Neither did she want to roll up to the terrace itself, sweaty and disheveled, whatever words she uttered to Griffith audible to anyone who chose to listen. She felt trapped, exposed in the spacious English garden as though on a great green stage.

Then she saw James. He stood near a potted palm at the corner of the terrace, with Mr. Ponsonby. *Thank the Lord.* He waved in greeting and started toward her. Mr. Ponsonby fell into step beside him.

She slowed, awaiting their arrival with bated breath.

"Muriel." Griffith's voice sounded low by her ear.

"I adore cabbage palms," she said, eyes fixed on the potted palm's profusion of swordlike leaves. "Their flowers have the most wonderful scent. I adore all trees, really. The other time I was in Cornwall, I botanized on Bodmin Moor and saw the Darley Oak. It's ancient, with an enormous hollow. Someone could live in it."

She'd like to climb into a tree hollow now.

"There was a ginkgo tree, in a valley in China," she continued, pulse racing along with her words. "The biggest I've ever seen. It had a similarly marvelous hollow."

"Muriel," he repeated.

"What cheer!" called James, drawing up to them. He was dressed for dinner, in a black evening jacket. "I was afraid you two had ridden off a cliff! Everyone's abuzz tonight." He lifted his hands, making a frame for his words. "Battle of the bicycles." He dropped his arms. "Bets *are* being taken. I expect a throng tomorrow morning at Titcombe Hall, to see you off."

"I'll be there." Mr. Ponsonby rocked on his heels. "Although how I'll hold my head up, I don't know. We played a four today. Took on Deighton and Butterfield."

"The elder," cut in James. "Turns out there are two Butterfields."

"More's the pity. One's bad enough." Mr. Ponsonby shook his head. "To make a long story short, they put us to rout. I feel positively wilted. I let the match point go by."

"Nothing you could have done," said James gamely. "Deighton serves like a cannon."

"It didn't help that I tripped over my own feet."

James grinned. "You heckled well."

"I heckled gorgeously." Mr. Ponsonby twinkled. "I'll give myself that."

"Deighton was frothing."

"I'll reprise my best insults at the starting line."

Muriel was following this volley in tense silence.

James caught her eye, a line appearing between his brows. "And how did you fare on your adventures? Where did you ride?"

"Zennor." She and Griffith spoke at once.

The ensuing silence felt unbearably thick.

"Lovely," said James. "Zennor."

Muriel's blush came on suddenly.

"I have to change," she blurted. "For dinner. Won't you all excuse me?"

She pushed the bicycle forward, causing James and Mr. Ponsonby to step apart.

"I'll see you tomorrow morning, then," said Griffith. "Half past ten at Titcombe Hall." She heard the hint of a question in his voice, but she was already past him, and she kept going, her spine far too stiff to permit even a nod of acknowledgment.

SHE SPENT A long while lying on the bed in her hotel room and emerged late for dinner, in an old blue dress that did little for her figure or coloring but at least covered her to the ankles.

In the dining room, she found James seated at a central table with two couples from London. They were deep in the fish course, and deeper in conversation. Something related to the Godrevy Lighthouse, and then to lighthouses more generally. She attended both the meal and her companions with but half a mind, smiling vaguely when James's voice turned humorous, picking at the roll on her bread plate, draining her glass without tasting the wine.

As dinner concluded, and diners began to rise, Muriel felt speculative gazes turn again in her direction. Heat crept up her cheeks as a toothy, middle-aged man detached from one of the lingering parties and made a beeline for her table.

"Mrs. Pendrake," he said. "Peter Lyons. Mark me now. I tricycle with my wife. We have a sociable, so we can sit side-by-side. She picks the destination, and I steer the way." He nodded in approval of his own words and continued in a louder voice. "That's the only sort of cycling compatible with feminine modesty. The sociable allows a lady to remain upright on a proper seat, while a man guides the machine, relieving her of unsuitable intellectual labor."

Muriel's eyes skittered around the room. People were inching over, forming a tightening cordon around the table.

"What *you* propose," scoffed Mr. Lyons, "is a disgusting stunt."

His mustache twitched as he waited eagerly for a response.

She stared at the mustache, feeling witless.

"Don't listen to that windbag!" This burst from a younger fellow, in a natty suit, with slicked-back hair. He shouldered his way up to Muriel's chair. "I put down a colossal wager. It's dogged as does it, my dear. Mark *me*, and ride for the win."

"Oh, pish." Another man approached, waggling his fingers in the air. "We all know she won't make it through the first day."

"And why won't she?" The woman sitting across from Muriel pushed back her chair and stood. "Naysayers dislike the idea of women on bicycles, because it draws attention to the scandalous fact that we have legs." Her glare bounced to Mr. Lyons, then back to the finger-waggler. "Legs we can use to send the wheels in circles, just as men do."

The finger-waggler shrugged, blue eyes shiny with complacency. "Mrs. Pendrake can bicycle down the lane, I don't doubt. But she won't be able to sustain the effort. Rivalry between the sexes is farcical. Women have inferior capacities. Our very brains are different. The female brain is five ounces lighter than the male brain, which correlates to . . ."

"Stop there, please, until I make my escape." Now James was on his feet, interrupting. "I can't talk brains on holiday. I made a promise. Mrs. Pendrake." He offered Muriel his arm. "Would you care to take a turn in the garden?"

Five minutes later, they'd pushed from the room, descended the terrace, and struck out toward the hotel's east wing. Muriel listened to the rhythmic crunching of gravel beneath their feet. The sun had painted the clouds with deep pinks as it slipped down below the curve of the bay.

Relief opened her lungs. She sighed and leaned into James. The air retained its mellow warmth, but the breeze felt cool, and the nightjars were churring in the scattered clusters of trees.

James turned them down one of the little paths that crisscrossed the geometric portion of the garden.

"You've been unusually quiet," he observed.

"Admiring the sunset."

"Not just now. Back in the dining room."

She released his arm, veering between ornamental beds toward a stone bench. He lengthened his stride and kept pace.

"It has been a day of surprises." She hugged herself. "There was a dog, on the ride back to town. A dog very like . . ."

She didn't have to say more.

James nodded sympathetically. "What did you do?"

"What I always do, but it was worse, because of the bloody bicycle."

"You crashed." He gave her a once-over. "All in one piece?"

She shrugged a shoulder and dropped down onto the bench. A pretty trellis arched above, covered with climbing roses.

"You told Griffith." James stood, considering her. "About your mother."

"Griffith told *me* something." She bit her nail, a habit she'd broken years ago. The stone bench was cold, and the shadows thickened beneath the trellis, but she squirmed, suddenly itchy and hot. She couldn't repeat what Griffith had said.

"Ah." James sat beside her and stretched out his legs. "What's that?"

She shifted on the bench. "I'd better not."

"Perhaps I know, then."

She turned her head sharply. James's face was carefully composed. Her breath blew out.

Holy God. He *knew.*

"How? How do you know?"

"Griffith and I had a conversation."

"That night? When you got potted and slept with your boots on?"

He nodded.

"But that was almost a week ago. And you didn't . . ." She clawed back a lock of hair. "You let me go on thinking that . . ."

She fell silent, a vein ticking in her temple.

She heard Griffith's voice.

I live as a man, and . . .

She gave her head a shake. "It wasn't for *you* to say anything. But *he* could have told me sooner."

The humiliated confusion flooded back, this time carrying a little hook of anger.

"He could have," said James mildly.

"You agree." She pounced.

James shrugged. "I'm not implying he *should* have. You didn't tell him why you were so frightened of that dog."

"It wasn't the time."

James tilted his head. "You get to decide when to disclose something deeply personal. And he doesn't?"

"It's not the same." She tried to think why. "He wasn't being truthful."

"Hmm." James brushed a rose petal with his index finger. "Is it that he wasn't being truthful? Or that the truth is more complex than you'd assumed?"

"Oh, God." She slumped.

I live as a man, and . . .

"That. The latter. Obviously. But I feel . . . I don't know how I feel. Intimidated, maybe." She rubbed her temple. "As if my brain was too small and suddenly stretched, but still doesn't fit enough new thoughts." She frowned. "That fellow wasn't correct? About the five ounces?"

"That fellow wasn't correct about bollocks, which weigh about a half ounce each, in case you ever hear differently." James waved his hand. "He probably read some drivel in a science column. I've looked inside all sorts of heads. There aren't any consistent features that meaningfully distinguish male brains from female brains, or, for that matter, English brains from Irish brains from Zulu brains, not so far as I can see."

She bit her lip. Her brain wasn't literally stretching, but she could feel it working.

She'd resented her treatment as a woman on countless occasions. She'd imagined what she'd have done differently if she'd been born a man. She'd never imagined *becoming* a man.

How had Griffith imagined it? How had he dared? Why?

"James," she said, and paused. "Is Griffith one of many?"

"One of many handsome men?" He shot her an aggrieved look. "No, if I recall, he's singular in that respect."

"James," she sighed. "My very handsome friend. You know what I'm asking."

He relented. "It's hard to take a count. You do understand how risky it is, to speak of these things."

She swallowed. In speaking, Griffith had put the life he'd built for himself in her hands. She'd been so focused on her own discomfiture that she'd failed to appreciate the enormity of it.

She closed her hands tight in her lap.

James glanced up at the clouds, faded now, all shades of gray against midnight blue.

"You've heard of female husbands?" he asked.

She gave a slight shake of her head.

"People raised as girls who live and marry as men. They're caught out from time to time, and it makes a sensation in the papers. Usually, the wives had no idea, or so the story goes."

"The marital relations, though." She flushed. "Aren't they . . . definitive?"

"Now we're getting technical." James narrowed his eyes. "Let's discuss the bedchamber another day. In any case, it's all up for debate. We can't ever know from those accounts what either spouse really thought of themselves, or each other, or their marriage."

The breeze stirred, perfumed with rose.

She wasn't—she couldn't be—now, at this very moment . . . But she was.

She was fantasizing about *marriage* with Kit Griffith.

Not an older don determined to mold her into the perfect helpmeet, to make her his doormat and his mirror.

A shameless rake tempted to touch her, to stroke her hair, to kiss her lips and. . . .

"There's a marquess of my acquaintance." James broke her reverie. "He hosts fancy dress balls for a very select society."

She looked at him. He was smiling a wicked smile.

"Not young misses, I'm guessing?"

"Men," said James relishingly. "Men with a taste for the nameless act. Some attend in silk gowns and chignons and dance the ladies' parts."

"You never mentioned this before." Had he thought her too puritanical? She sat up straighter and tried to modify her face into an expression of careless sophistication. It was only a temporary success. Her next thought rounded her eyes. "Do *you* wear a silk gown?"

"What do you think?" He leaned against the trellis, batting his lashes.

"Goodness," she murmured, struck by his elegant pose. No use pretending she wasn't amazed. When he held his head just so, she could picture his strong-boned leanness set off by a low-cut neckline, green silk brocade so that his eyes glowed emerald.

"I think you'd look stunning," she breathed.

"Oh." He seemed slightly taken aback. "I expected something more left-handed." He rolled his shoulders, a pleased, preening sort of motion. "I do look all right." He met her gaze and his turned thoughtful. "It feels like a costume, though. More than this does." He gestured to his evening jacket. "For a few of those gowned dancers, it might be the other way round."

"You and Griffith," she said slowly. "You share common ground, or at least an understanding. That's why he told you first."

"It was happenstance, really. A series of events led me to confide in him. He, in turn, confided in me. Fair play, you know. Trust."

Muriel's stomach dipped. Fair play. Trust. She hadn't shown Griffith either.

"Blast." She shot to her feet. "I've made a hash of things. I never even admitted there wasn't a caterpillar on his lapel!"

"Is that a euphemism?" James drew his brows together. "Or are you actually talking about an insect?"

"There *wasn't* an insect." She turned toward the hotel, a dark mass against the dimming sky. Lights twinkled in the windows. She'd propped her bicycle against the wall, behind that potted palm on the terrace.

She launched forward and almost tripped on the hem of her skirt.

God, skirts were abominably long if they weren't indecently short. She yanked it up to midcalf.

"Where are you going?"

"To the engine house." She called over her shoulder, breaking into a run. "I have to tell him."

"About the caterpillar?"

"Forget the caterpillar," she called.

Griffith had asked a question. *Can we start there?*

She'd clammed up. She'd nattered about trees.

But it wasn't too late.

Within a quarter hour, she'd coasted out of town and was pedaling after the weak orange light cast by her lamp, flying through the fields.

There was no light shining from the engine house.

Perhaps because of the conversation at dinner, she'd anticipated a beacon, a blaze in the night, like Griffith lived in the bloody Pharos of Alexandria.

Instead, she arrived to a dark tower.

She swung off the bicycle, shaky from exertion, craning her neck. Was he up there? Asleep? Surely it was closer to ten than eleven.

She extinguished the flame in the lamp, lowered the bicycle onto its side. She went boldly to the door and knocked. Nothing. She stepped back.

"Griff," she tried, and then, louder but more hesitant: "Kit?"

Grasshoppers were shrilling.

She wouldn't go so far as to throw rocks at the windows?

Damn it all. She dropped, kneeling to rake her fingers through the cool grass. Where *were* the rocks? The lawn was mostly rock, or that's how it had felt when she kept landing on her arse. Now not a pebble.

She sat, drawing up her legs. She'd wait. Alone, in the dark, on the damp ground. That didn't seem desperate. Or pathetic.

She waited, sitting, and then she waited curled up on her side, and then she wasn't waiting but sleeping, which she only discovered when she started awake, cold and stiff in pitch-blackness. Sandy-eyed, she squinted at the engine house, at where she thought it was.

Had he come home while she slept? What time was it now? Good Lord, was it already tomorrow?

Had she just made a worse hash of things?

She needed to pack. And sleep in a bed.

Could she do both?

Her knees chirped like crickets as she unbent her legs. She rode, not on the path between farms, but on the path *to* Tregerthen Farm. That is, she rode directly into a fence.

15

THE PALE MORNING sun shone down on Titcombe Hall with appalling brightness. As Kit coasted up the drive, he saw, through slitted eyes, a vast sea of hats and parasols.

So much for his hope that the morning hour would depress attendance. St. Ives's visitors had turned out in droves. He dismounted and pushed his Rover through the crowd, getting briefly stuck in the narrows between clustered pieces of wicker furniture.

"We arrived six days ago, and I've never been so dull in all my life." This was uttered by a girl whose skirts frothed over the sides of her chair. "The social calendar is sand, more sand, and if you're lucky, a starfish."

"What about this lovely party?" protested the girl whose chair was pulled close to hers. "It's not sandy in the least!"

Kit freed himself and threaded his way to a more sparsely occupied swath of lawn. A violinist was playing in a bower. Nearer the house, festooned tables had been laid with a breakfast buffet. Deighton Senior stood by the main entrance, looking florid and furious, neck bulging from his collar. A blond woman in ice-blue silk stood at his side, surveying the scene with a cold, unblinking gaze.

Kit stopped surveying them and surveyed the scene as well. Unease hollowed his chest. He didn't see . . .

There.

A burst of elation filled the sick, empty pit inside him. There. That gleam of penny-colored tresses. He accelerated. But at that moment, the owner of the penny-colored tresses changed course, presenting her profile. Sweetly freckled, short nosed. Utterly unfamiliar.

Elation fled. He parked himself by a hedge, indulging the deluded notion that his green serge jacket would allow him to blend into the shrubbery.

"Godspeed, young man," said the first person to wander past, a bespectacled grandmotherly woman, kind and twinkly. The next passersby snickered.

Yes, he was most certainly visible.

Did his head *look* as though it were about to explode?

He wished he hadn't stayed out drinking with Ponsonby until dawn.

No, he wished he were still drunk.

His nerve endings felt knife-edged.

She wasn't here. Did she mean to come at all?

"Too low."

This time it was a portly gentleman in an excessively tall topper. He'd approached with a woman—his wife, to judge by her long-suffering expression.

"Undignified," he said. "A saddle yea high." He thwacked the Rover's leather seat with his cane. "You might as well ride a New-foundland."

Kit grunted. "The Newfoundland might disagree."

The portly gentleman sniffed.

"Look there," he said. "*Those* saddles sit at sixteen hands."

Kit followed his gaze. The Mutton Wheelers had cycled into view, the spokes of their towering front wheels glaring in the light. They circled the fountain at the top of the drive, Deighton in front, his four wheelmen riding double file behind him.

"Is that a bugle?" asked the long-suffering wife, in a voice rich with horror.

One of the Mutton Wheelers was indeed holding a bugle. He sounded a piercing note. Kit and the wife winced.

Hell. This was hell. Kit made for the buffet. Maybe there was wine in one of those copper urns.

"Tea," said the footman, pointing to the urn on his left. He pointed to the urn on his right. "Coffee."

Kit glowered at both urns and then down at a chafing dish of sausages.

"Coffee, you said? Thank the Lord!" Ponsonby came barreling from nowhere, hopelessly rumpled and reeking like a distillery. "Coffee. A bucket, please." He turned to Kit. "I'm late. Am I late? You haven't gone yet. Bless you." He took a cup from the footman, gulped, and gave a yelp. "Bloody hot!"

Kit fought the urge to grab him by the shoulders. "Is she with you?"

"Who?" Ponsonby blew on his coffee.

Another bugle note sounded.

Kit's skin tightened. Last night, he'd refused to face this possibility. Hence the beer, the billiards, the whiskey, the cards, the imbecilic attempt to paddle a boat to the lighthouse, which might have been dangerous if remotely successful.

He checked his watch. Quarter past ten.

"I know what's to be done," said Ponsonby, knuckling his eye. He stood straighter, inflating his chest. "I won't cock it up. Have no fear."

Mother of God.

"Champagne?" Kit asked the footman. The footman shook his head.

"Ponsonby," said Kit, trying to keep his tone level. "*I* don't know what you're talking about."

"The cock-up with Coover. I'll make it right. Not whatever's cocked up between the two of you, obviously. The bit I bungled, when I told her you were here."

Kit began to intuit his meaning, despite the thicket of cocks and bungs.

"I'm sure she'll insist on making the trip, no matter what excuse I wire. But I'll send her packing before next Thursday, I swear. Her and Burgess and Nelly, and whoever else. She'll bite my head off and *chew*. She's not one for half measures. And Nelly will give me that *look*." Ponsonby shuddered. "But I will persevere." He lifted his coffee cup high, striking a valiant pose, then spoiled the effect by bringing the cup slowly to his lips for a timid sip paired with a preemptive wince. "Or maybe Nelly won't give me that particular look," he added, sipping again, with more confidence. "Now that I'm not trying to court her."

"You're not?" Whether Ponsonby was or wasn't still mooning after Nelly should be the last thing on his mind, but Kit frowned, intrigued. "Since when?"

"A few days." Ponsonby flushed a painful shade of red. "I still think she's ripping. It's just . . ." He emptied his coffee cup and pivoted back to the footman. "A spot more?"

Kit rolled his shoulders. The knapsack grew heavier by the second. Wonderful that Ponsonby promised to ensure he arrived back to a Sisters-free St. Ives. It didn't change the fact that his planned departure was suddenly in jeopardy. His bicycle shop. Perhaps more than that.

Had his instincts been so wrong?

Fifteen minutes remained. Should he race to the Towans? Force Muriel to say something he didn't want to hear?

You're not who I thought you were.

He could spit a version back at her.

I didn't see you as the sort who welched on a deal.

"Where's Raleigh?" Ponsonby glanced about. "Did he come with Mrs. Pendrake? Where *is* Mrs. Pendrake?"

Kit ignored this. He had to focus on the more relevant question.

What in bloody hell was he going to do now? Inquire if the long-suffering wife cared to ride for ten days on his handlebars? Or that beneficent grandmother?

"Hallo!" Bernhard was legging it toward them. "We're over there." The painter gestured at the knoll that rose in the wilder precinct of the garden, even beyond the group of lacy young ladies selecting croquet mallets. Kit squinted. Two easels on the crest. Takada, sketching.

"Instead of waves, today we study life and character," explained Bernhard. He spread his arms. "Panorama."

"I'm bad at people," Ponsonby sighed.

"You're fine at people." Kit managed a smile. It felt difficult to summon, but sincere. "One of the greats."

"Bad at painting people." Ponsonby flushed again and clapped a hand to the back of his neck. "Bad enough that anything else I do with paint *or* people seems better by contrast."

"Here," said Bernhard, pulling a shiny coin from his pocket. "Glückspfennig. For luck."

He handed it to Kit.

Kit contemplated the bright bronze disc in his palm, the German word marching around the numeral one stamped in the center. A lucky penny. Christ.

"Thank you." His voice scratched as he dropped the coin into his pocket. He checked his watch.

Seven minutes.

Two more ticked away as Bernhard and Ponsonby swapped artistic gossip, Kit staring at nothing, until Deighton crossed his line of vision. No bicycle. He was striding toward the house.

"Excuse me," Kit muttered, and hurried after. He'd do this fast. He'd jump from the ledge before it crumbled beneath his feet.

When he caught up, Deighton was already locked in conversation with Deighton Senior, or rather, gnashing his teeth while Deighton Senior delivered a harangue with his nose almost touching his son's.

"This is the last embarrassment," Deighton Senior was saying. "I ignored your tomfoolery. I permitted you to fritter away your time. But you've taken it too far. You fritter away *my* reputation." Deighton Senior stepped abruptly back, in disgust, and his hot blue eyes twitched to Kit.

"Bicycling was bad enough," he continued, still glaring at Kit. "Even before you associated your little club with a ponce and a virago."

Deighton himself hadn't noticed Kit's presence. "I'll win the bet, sir."

This recaptured Deighton Senior's attention.

"Oh, you'll more than win the bet," he snarled. "Remember what we discussed."

"Yessir." Deighton slouched.

"Stand up straight." The snarl became a bark. "When you return, you will put away childish things. No more bicycles. No more badges." He flicked the Mutton Wheelers badge on Deighton's striped jacket. "I'm sending you to Glasgow. You'll run the Scottish office."

"Glasgow?" Deighton went pale. "Sir. I—"

"It's decided. Trust me, you'll like the alternative far less."

Kit cleared his throat. Both Deightons turned to him, shoulders touching so that they formed a solid wall of animosity.

Skewered by their identical glares, he realized he didn't know what to say.

He'd misjudged everything. Consequences he couldn't yet bring himself to imagine were taking shape all around him. He didn't want to *say* anything. He wanted to release the howl that had been building inside since Ponsonby wired Lucy, and if he were honest, since long before that.

It stuck in his windpipe, closing off his breath.

"Ready, then?" Deighton shoved past, tight-lipped, cheeks waxen. He walked stiffly, with a self-consciously military bearing, back to the fountain where the Mutton Wheelers waited, each standing now beside his bicycle. The bugler was holding up two bicycles, his own and Deighton's. To his right, almost hidden by Deighton's front wheel, another cyclist waited. She inched her own wheel forward, and Kit saw her fully. Penny-bright hair coiled over her shoulder. Her hat was circled with a pale purple ribbon.

His fingers went to the matching silk at his throat as her searching dark eyes met his.

Air rushed in.

"Ready," he said.

AFTER A SCRUPULOUSLY polite round of introductions, the bugler played a call, and the Mutton Wheelers took a few running steps alongside their bicycles to mount. A moment later, they were tearing down the drive.

"Tallyho!" someone cried. Sir Reggie, by his voice. Muriel's gaze flew to him but landed instead on Lady Chiswick, who stood on the edge of the drive with a coterie of society matrons. They were staring at her. Their expressions spoke volumes. Or at least quoted selectively from the King James Bible.

Thou shalt not suffer a witch to live.

Face flaming, Muriel kicked up her leg. She straddled her metal broomstick. She was bedraggled from her awful night, which she'd spent mostly in the open air. She was far too tired to care what Lady Chiswick thought of her. Golden-haired Clarinda made one of a bunch of younger women, a little farther down the drive, all of them slim and fairylike in their pastel gowns. She caught Muriel's eye and sent her a wistful little smile.

Before Muriel could process her surprise and smile back, gravel crunched. Griffith rolled up beside her, already in the saddle. He looked slightly haggard in the morning light, which lent a wolfish edge to his beauty, and caused him to seem like more of a stranger.

She tried to read his expression. Was he angry? Was he ready to resume where they'd left off?

"Here we go," he murmured. With athletic ease, he went, pedaling past Lady Chiswick, past Clarinda, swooping down toward the bend in the road.

She swallowed, shuffled forward, and came to an abrupt halt, bracing herself as the bicycle tipped. She strained to pull it back to center. Her boot slid on the gravel, and a muscle twinged in her thigh.

Griffith had twisted to see if she followed. He applied the brake, skidding a half circle, and stopped.

She tried to telegraph confidence. She shuffled forward again, but the bicycle tipped, like an overloaded wheelbarrow. A few titters rose, and her panic rose with them.

This was going to end, right here, in front of Griffith and a laughing crowd. She'd let James push the bicycle most of the way from the Towans. She'd needed to walk, to wake up her legs, to ease the stiffness from her back.

Daft. She'd been absolutely daft.

"James," she hissed. He was somewhere nearby, somewhere in that swirl of chattering, cup-and-saucer-clinking onlookers. Surely he was watching and understood her distress.

An eternity passed, and then she heard his voice, matter-of-fact and commanding.

"Step aside, please. Step aside."

Finally, more commandingly still: "I'm a doctor!"

The crowd parted, and he emerged and loped to her. "I can't tell if you're on a bicycle or in a bear trap. Why aren't you moving? Why does your face look like that?"

She emitted a bearlike growl of desperation.

"The panniers," she explained. "Would you take this?" She reached into the left pannier and extracted her microscope. Then, after further consideration, her dissecting case, a wad of coarse toweling, blotting papers, and two pressing boards with leather straps and buckles.

"Golly." James bobbled her offerings. "At least you left your jars."

She frowned and began to yank jars from the right pannier, aware that people had begun to gawk. Griffith, she saw, had tilted his head.

"Well," said James philosophically, "at least they're half-empty. What's in this one? Liquid rubber? Forget I asked. Did you bring a change of clothes? Or is it nets and chisels all the way down?"

"I feel fabric," she confirmed. "But it might be oilcloth." Damn. The last few hours had been a blur. Questionable decisions had been made.

She balanced the last jar atop the pile in his arms. She felt naked without her collecting supplies—and she'd likely feel more naked come evening, when she had to climb into a musty old bed wrapped in nothing but the oilcloth—but the bicycle was distinctly lighter and better balanced.

She might actually make it out of town on two wheels, and back again.

James cursed and stopped a jar from falling with a steeply angled elbow.

"What would I do without you?" she asked, and he gave her his filthiest smirk.

"I can't wait to find out. Make it good."

Her gaze slid back to Griffith, and she tightened her grip on the handlebars.

"Tallyho," she whispered, and pushed off.

16

SHE AND GRIFFITH said very little to each other for the first several miles. They rode out of St. Ives, toward Zennor, and continued west on a rutted coastal path that hugged the cliffs, the sheer drop down to the azure water below too dizzying to contemplate. The wind blew strong and fitful, and it snatched at her breath and gave her yet another ceaseless task, apart from the steering and the pedaling: slapping at kitelike flights of her skirt. It was only when the path wound away from the cliffs, through hedged fields, that speech seemed possible. It wasn't a path anymore but a dirt lane, wide enough for two cyclists to ride abreast, and the air was sweet and still.

"Am I holding you back?" she asked, and he slanted her a look from beneath the brim of his cap.

"No."

The monosyllable didn't encourage further dialogue.

"You should catch up if you want." She tried again. "I know the way, more or less. Due west. If there's a fork in the road, I'll point myself at the sun."

"The sun's directly overhead."

"It is now." Her brows pulled together. She was attempting to consider his preferences, and he was making it difficult. "I assure you the sun will set in the west."

"Ah, yes," he said. "Because of the Earth's rotation. You've mentioned it."

She glanced over. His profile seemed hard, all ridges, the humorous curve of his lips compressed to a flat line.

"I thought you might mind that the others are so far ahead."

"I don't mind."

"They're probably gloating."

"They're probably bugling." He shrugged a shoulder, then sat up straighter, removing his hands from the handlebars. "Reason enough to stay out of earshot."

She had to will her eyes back to the road. He looked indolent, controlling the Rover effortlessly with his legs, arms crossed.

"I can't go very fast." Her front tire hit a stone and the impact vibrated from her wrists to her elbows to her teeth. She clenched her jaw.

Was she being considerate, urging him to ride ahead? Or cowardly?

"It's quite all right. I'm not in top form today." He paused. "Long night."

That was an understatement. It was also an opening.

She took a deep breath. "I know."

"You know?" Finally, some feeling in his voice. "You know what?"

"That you had a long night." Her blood began to rush through her veins, faster than her pedaling warranted. "I rode to your house."

"When?"

"Right after dinner. And then I . . . waited a bit."

From the corner of her eye, she saw him reach out slowly and wrap his fingers around his handlebars.

"And why's that?" he asked softly.

"I wanted to talk." She swallowed. The hedges had fallen away, and they were in open country, unbroken green scattered with rock formations, gray and strange against the horizon.

"I'd clammed up earlier. It was a rather feeble response." She stole another glance at him and thudded through a pothole, deep and avoidable. "I planned a whole speech. But you were occupied elsewhere."

He returned her sidelong look. "And now you want to know where I was and what I was doing?"

She blushed. She did, most definitely. "That's beside the point." She nerved herself, eyes back on the road. "I want to say what I intended to say. If you're interested in hearing it."

"Very."

Dammit. Her mind blanked.

After a minute, he made a noise, something between a knowing sigh and a scoffing laugh. "Right. Well. In that case . . ."

"I lied," she blurted. "There wasn't a caterpillar."

"No caterpillar," he repeated. "Noted. Is that all?"

She shook her head.

"I touched you to touch you." It was little more than a whisper. He heard her, though. She could feel the air thickening between them.

She licked her lower lip and tasted salt. "Since we met, I haven't gone an hour without recalling the feel of your mouth on mine."

The little silence was filled with the skittering ping of unsettled stones, the mechanical whir and creak of the bikes.

She was gripping the handlebars with such force she thought she might rip them away from the frame.

"I don't kiss people very often. Or ever, really. Only my husband, and only in the beginning. This is new for me—all of it. I want you." Cold sweat slid down her neck. She was saying *more* than she'd intended, her tongue loosened by the sleepless night, by the landscape, vast and wild, remote from her everyday life.

"But I have been wrong about you," she continued. "Again and again."

"I'm glad you were wrong about the cat," he murmured. "I couldn't live with myself."

She dared a glance. His hands were off the handlebars, tucked under his biceps. He wore a faint, ironic smile, but his eyes smoldered with quiet intensity.

"I don't want to get this wrong now," she said. "Yesterday, I was all mixed up by what you told me. To be honest, I'm still a bit mixed up. But we have ten days to . . ." Her voice caught. She wasn't sure how to exit the sentence.

Griffith's smile widened. "Ten days to see how mixed up we can make each other? What a glorious prospect."

Glorious? Try chaotic. Reckless. Irresistibly enticing.

Her feet went clumsy on the pedals. This wasn't the moment for her knees to turn to water. She focused on riding.

"Out of curiosity," he drawled. "How long did you wait for me?"

She bristled. "Out of curiosity, what time did you return?"

An impasse. He broke it by laughing.

She glared at him.

"The sun was coming up." He held her gaze. "I regret that I wasn't there to answer your knock."

The look in his eyes . . .

She had to swerve to keep their front wheels from touching.

"But I didn't expect you." He sounded amused.

"I should have expected you'd be out." She engaged her protesting muscles and corrected her course, surging up the slight rise in the road.

"More rest would have been wise," he said conversationally. It seemed toiling up hills didn't affect his breathing in the least. "But Ponsonby and I can get carried away."

She panted. "You were with Mr. Ponsonby?"

"And a couple of bottles. A classic combination."

She gulped for air. The road had leveled. And last night, Griffith hadn't been cavorting with a paramour, but drinking with a friend— heavily, to judge by his raddled appearance.

"It's an *unhealthy* combination," she told him. "James says alcohol causes degeneration and disease of the nervous system."

"Does he say it while swilling sherry?"

"Physician, heal thyself." She sighed. "It doesn't make it less true. I'm not judging."

"What, then? Fretting? Fussing?" His indignation was obviously feigned. Beneath it, he seemed pleased, as though no one had fussed over him for some time.

And maybe no one had.

Her heart gave a sudden lurch.

She trained her attention straight ahead. "I saw the sunrise too."

"Good God." His tone changed. "You waited all night."

"I fell asleep for some of it."

"On the drenched ground?"

Maybe she'd taken brazen honesty a step too far.

"I wouldn't say drenched. A bit damp, perhaps."

The pause extended. Then he said: "You should have let yourself in."

She made a face. "I'm not accustomed to letting myself into other people's houses."

"Desperate times."

"I wasn't *desperate*." She bit her lip. Was that how he saw her?

"Besides," she muttered, "we can't all be rakes like you, climbing trellises and crawling through windows."

"No climbing or crawling required. The door wasn't locked." He veered around something gristly. "I've never climbed a trellis myself."

She snorted. "What about an iron downpipe? Or a knotted lace curtain lowered from a garret balcony?"

"I appreciate the image." His voice was dry. "But I moved through the world seen as a woman for the first three decades of my life. Which means I followed a different version of the rake's rule book."

"Oh." Her breath puffed out. She felt awkward and almost painfully curious. "Trellises play a smaller role?"

He gave her a wry look. "Did *you* ever have to sneak past a chaperone to get a private word with a female acquaintance? Limitless energy goes toward governing what a woman says to a man. How she says it. Where and in whose company. But no one thinks twice if two wallflowers slip out of a ballroom. If a girl shuts herself up with another girl in the parlor, or even in her bedchamber."

"So you wouldn't scramble up to a balcony under cover of dark." She swallowed. "You'd just . . . call at the front door and walk up the stairs."

She pictured him in a gown, slinking through a lady's boudoir, slinking up to the lady herself, who watched him approach in her vanity mirror, shivering with anticipation.

She realized *she* was shivering, and she shifted on the dense leather seat, newly aware of the pressure it exerted on her inner thighs.

"Don't you miss the convenience?" she asked.

"Convenience," he echoed, and she cringed.

"Perhaps that sounded glib."

Suddenly, her front wheel dropped into a crater. The road was all craters. She could only brace herself and judder.

"This way!" Griffith waved as he turned, cutting a diagonal across the heath that swept down toward the sea.

She was gasping when she finally reached him, a stitch in her side, but soon her wheels were rolling on their own, pulled by gravity.

She felt lighter, speeding through the heather, cooled by the fragrant breeze.

Griffith had flung out his arms.

When the slope leveled, he put one hand on the handlebars and twisted toward her, his grin conspiratorial.

"My mother hoped I'd marry a title. Forced me to take classes in deportment. I despised them." He steered around a boulder, not a moment too soon. "Until I met Emma Sidnall."

"Of course there was an Emma." Muriel began to apply her weight to the pedals again, pushing through the goldenrod and eyebright.

He rode closer to her. "It never felt like convenience. More like recompense. All that vigilance, and yet some of us shared a blissful secret, right under everyone's nose. There *are* things I miss."

Her mouth went dry. She wasn't exactly sure what she wanted to ask. Men were motivated by sexual feelings. It made sense that they might want to couple with other men. But from what she understood, women responded to erotic advances with varying degrees of reluctance. The urge to initiate manifested rarely and—to judge by Esmé's reaction—indicated moral decay, or infirmity. She'd known pairs of women who traveled together, who lived together—for the companionship. Did they also crave each other's bodies? Did their affectionate caresses culminate in bliss?

If two lovers happened to be women, one of them *had* to initiate. Did that mean one played the man's part? Was that why Griffith began to gravitate toward male attire? Or had he assumed a new identity all at once, to escape marriage to a lord?

"What about you?"

She blinked. Griffith had posed a question to *her*.

"Me?" She pedaled more quickly. "There weren't any etiquette classes, or Emmas."

After their marriage, Esmé had taken pains with her elocution, but she didn't feel like revisiting those humiliating lessons.

"I fed chickens and collected eggs, and scrubbed things, and swept things. I took care of my younger cousins and did the bidding of the older ones. I didn't have a mother to hope I married anyone, let alone someone with a title. And I didn't share any blissful secrets, with anyone." She considered, then offered an amendment. "Well, James. But only in the sense that I knew he had something blissful going on with the son of his father's stable manager." She scowled. "Unfortunately, his father suspected. One day William was gone."

James had been heartbroken.

Griffith seemed to digest this. "They're aristocrats, I take it?"

"His father's a baron."

"And you descend from farmers. How did it happen, then? How did you and Raleigh become such great friends?"

She'd rather not revisit that either, not at present.

"He *is* a great friend," she said brightly. "He's going to repair the fence I knocked down."

She related the story of her mishap, pitching it in a far more comic register than she'd have thought possible, hours before, when she'd lain dazed on a tussock with a wooden rail on her chest, blinking at the indifferent spray of stars. He didn't mock her, and he didn't try to turn the subject back to their intimate histories. He related a series of mishaps, which put her own blundering into welcome perspective. Less welcome: her increased apprehension about the dangers posed to cyclists by geese.

They intersected a path that passed through a grim mining village, just a few granite terraces perched on a cliff, overlooking an engine house—this one still functioning, pumping water from the tin mine. There was a tavern, sooty and dark. They stopped for lunch, and she nodded off so many times over the hard bread and cheese that he eventually slid onto her bench, to act as a buttress.

After lunch, she rode even slower, and they didn't speak at all as they rounded the peninsula, sharing the exalted feeling that often surged in travelers when they reached Land's End, the westernmost point of England. The sea, so blue in the distance, boiled white around the columns of rock that rose near the crinkled brown cliffs. Gulls and cormorants wheeled above the high summit of the headland. The bright green turf was dotted with wildflowers. She felt no urge to collect them, even when they dismounted to stretch their legs. Everything seemed perfect in its place.

The sun was low by the time they curved east, following the southern shore, a succession of small headlands and coves, the cliffs rusty pink. When they clattered up to the Treryn Dinas Inn, their destination, its whitewashed façade was glowing in the dusk. Griffith and the man behind the desk talked in circles, until it became apparent that the Mutton Wheelers had paid for their rooms, and Griffith gave his coin instead to the skinny boy who carried her panniers up the stairs. Muriel followed him and found herself in a garret with a floor that sloped nearly as steeply as the ceiling and a bed shoved so close to the wardrobe its doors didn't open.

Just as well she'd scarcely a spare garment to hang.

When she descended the creaking stair to the vaultlike dining room, she found Griffith at a small table with a tankard before him. The Mutton Wheelers were the only other diners, but they'd finished their meal and risen from their chairs to crowd around Deighton, who sat hunched over a large notebook, writing, or drawing.

They straightened when they saw her. Butterfield, with the mustache. The younger Butterfield, much slighter, and sweet-faced, now that he wasn't blowing into a bugle. The two whose names she'd forgotten, one bulky and fair, the other lean, with black eyes and a shadow on his jaw.

"Mrs. Pendrake," said Mr. Deighton, with crisp correctness.

That was all. Not one of them spared her another glance.

"Sorry," she said to Griffith sometime later, starting awake and kicking his shin under the small table in the process. His toe came down on hers, the pressure light but insistent, trapping her foot.

"I'll go up to bed," she said, cheeks heating. She'd almost dipped her face in her bowl of half-eaten beef stew.

The word *bed* seemed to drift in the candle smoke. She had to say something else.

"I want to get an early start tomorrow," she added brightly. "So I can walk the shore before we ride."

"To what end?" His eyes shimmered in the candlelight. "You opted to leave your equipment behind."

"It was all too heavy." She shifted her foot, just a little, to better feel his weight bearing down. Her pulse was racing. "I still want to look, in case there's something extraordinary. I have a collecting bag, and I could always borrow a jar from the kitchen."

Actually, she doubted the kitchen shelves held glassware. The inn seemed too battered for anything delicate to have survived the centuries. The stew bowl looked like a hollowed cobblestone, and her wine had arrived in a dark gray pewter cup.

"But I'd rather bring you down to the seaweed than the seaweed up to you." She smiled, fiddling with the heavy, unnecessary knife beside her bowl. "You should see the plants in a natural pool, if possible. You'll get a fuller sense of them."

He was silent.

She stopped her fiddling.

"Which will help with your pictures," she explained. The shifting light in his eyes made her suddenly wary. "You do have a sketchbook?"

At his nod, her tension eased. "I've meant to ask about the bladder-wrack. You painted it? No trouble?"

He looked down at his hands, lashes black fans against his cheeks. "None."

He lifted his foot away and she slid hers back, feeling silly and sleepy and strangely bereft.

She stood.

"Don't do anything gladiatorial," she advised, glancing at Deighton. Griffith tipped back his head and smiled. Her eyes plummeted from his sharp jaw to the line of his throat and down to his collar, cinched by lilac silk. Was his pulse racing too? Because she couldn't think how to say good night without embarrassing herself, she turned on her heel.

She *had* packed a shift, as it turned out. During her last few moments of scantily clad consciousness on the lumpy mattress, she imagined him climbing to her window, then remembered, with disappointment, that the dismal little room lacked windows altogether.

17

WHEN THEY SET out the next morning, the fog had settled thick and wet in the valley, veiling the beaches and the bay. One bugle call became two, then three, then four, the shrill notes slicing at Kit's ears. He and Muriel were bringing up the rear of the column, and he wanted to fall back further, to separate from the wheelmen and spend another day in relative quiet, and with her alone.

She'd braided her hair, one thick, gleaming plait that hung over her shoulder. Right at that moment, it possessed more vivid color than anything else in existence. He couldn't stop looking at it as they cycled out of the village onto a narrow road that seemed to tunnel through gauze.

It was a good time to remind himself that she was bound for New York.

Whatever transpired between them, an ocean would soon intervene.

He'd learned to begin liaisons with the end in view, with finality as the main, mutually established fact. No muzzy-headed, naked whispering that projected forever togetherness. He kept the boundaries crystal clear, for everyone's sake.

The burnished tip of Muriel's braid seemed to smear his eyes with rich pigments. Cadmium red. Burnt sienna.

He hadn't done this in months—matched the world to his palette.

He looked away, overwhelmed by a predicament too complex to contemplate in its totality.

Last night, when Muriel had fixed him with that searching, dark gaze and asked about his painting, he'd slammed shut. He'd retreated from their newfound candor. He couldn't bring himself to tell her that his first artistic efforts had yielded nothing but crumpled paper and a painful sense of vertigo.

Because the truth would make her fear for her commission. That was one explanation for his dodginess. He was protecting her from anxiety—pointless anxiety. If he failed, he'd beg Takada to step in. She wouldn't go away empty-handed.

But no, it was more complicated. He was protecting himself. He didn't want to see his own fear of failure reflected in her eyes or to face what that failure might mean.

Something inside him was permanently broken.

He balked at the thought. Horrible to give it credence, but hell, quailing before that bladderwrack had been a bloody bad sign. Or perhaps only a bad start. Perhaps he'd redeem himself at the next rock pool. Hope remained. And yet—he wasn't in any hurry to put it to the test. He'd thanked his lucky stars for the morning fog, which had kept her—and him—from the shore. But if they did fall behind the others, if the fog lifted, she'd insist on stopping. This blasted ride was nothing *but* shore.

He flexed his hands. He might not redeem himself. She'd ask him to sketch the sea lettuce, and he'd fumble as she studied him, concern etching her brow.

Sea lettuce. That a marine vegetable could fill him with terror. He'd laugh, but sweat was gathering beneath his collar, despite the clammy air.

He looked again at Muriel. She was squirming as she pedaled, straightening then stretching forward, trying to ease the tension in her lower back. Cycling was the devil when it came to the spine, and to the delicate skin of the inner thighs. More than a rock pool, she needed a hot bath, steaming water scattered with rose petals and calendula, sprigs of lavender, or maybe heather. Hell, she was the botanist, not he.

She felt him looking and glanced up through mist-thickened lashes. Her skin was dewy, and her lips seemed plumper, the pink of damp shells. If he thought there was a chance that some hidden chamber of the Treryn Dinas Inn contained a copper bathtub and a tester bed, he'd have suggested they ride back posthaste.

"Penny," he said, and nearly jumped out of his saddle at a blast of sound.

She jumped too, and grimaced at the culprit, the younger Butterfield. He was a few yards ahead, bugle pointed at the sky.

"They're a bicycle club," she muttered. "But they think they're the cavalry."

"Young Butterfield thinks he's a trumpeter at the apocalypse," said Kit, but the bugle call drowned him out.

Somewhere in the distance, Deighton released an indistinct roar. Kit peered around and between the other cyclists and finally caught a glimpse of Deighton's blue-and-white striped jacket. His back was so broad his brown knapsack looked like a coin purse.

The elder Butterfield and Richard Kemble, the club treasurer, were riding behind Deighton. They both turned their heads.

"Did you hear that?" yelled Butterfield. He seemed to be yelling at Phineas Prescott, the club secretary, who rode directly behind him.

"What?" asked Prescott.

"Captain said stuff it!" yelled Butterfield.

"Me?" asked Prescott. "Why's he after me again?"

"Not you!" yelled Butterfield. "The bugle! Stuff the bloody bugle!" The bugle call cut off.

"You keep quiet now, Egg!" yelled Kemble. "Or tonight you're spit shining our shoes."

Even in three-quarter profile, Kemble looked fully disagreeable. He'd worn the same jeering expression at breakfast, when Kit tried to settle the bill for the rooms.

You're on our *club run,* he'd said. *The club pays. Not for too many nights, by the looks of you.*

Young Butterfield—or Egg, God help him—lowered the bugle. "Our shoes are canvas!"

"I don't bloody care!" yelled Kemble. "And I don't want to hear your voice either."

"I was playing the walk," whined Egg. "When I play the walk, we slacken the pace. It says so in the handbook. But the pace hasn't slackened."

Kemble and Butterfield weren't paying him any more mind. They'd accelerated, closing the distance with Deighton.

Egg looked at Prescott. "I was playing the walk."

"You were," agreed Prescott.

"There's fog," said Egg. "You don't ride at eight miles per hour in fog."

"We do." Prescott shrugged. "Until the captain decides we don't. Next time wait for him to tell you to play the walk."

"He can't tell me anything," protested Egg. "He's a mile away."

"You're supposed to ride with him!" Prescott shouted as the wind gusted, flinging a few cold droplets. "Bugler rides by the captain. It says so in the handbook."

"Captain's supposed to be courteous." Egg sounded sulky. "Also in the handbook."

"You can ride back here for now," conceded Prescott. "There are so few of us. But remember, formation matters. This wouldn't stand with the full membership."

Muriel gave a yelp. "Dear God. *More* Mutton Wheelers?"

Prescott and Egg twisted around and cut her identical looks of surprise.

"Sorry." She sat straighter. "Did I say that aloud? I could hear your conversation, and it's just—I hadn't realized you were so numerous."

Prescott gave a brief nod. "There are forty-eight members in total."

"We're the officers," added Egg. "This is an officers' excursion."

They faced front again.

Kit recognized Muriel's expression. She had more questions.

"And why *Mutton* Wheelers?" she asked. "Is it the association with toughness? I've found mutton very tender, in curries."

"Wouldn't know." Egg craned his neck to frown in her direction. "Not allowed to eat mutton. Training diet."

"We used to meet at the Shoulder of Mutton Pub," said Prescott, turning. "Now we have a clubhouse, but . . ."

A sudden flurry of shouts snapped both their heads back around.

"I don't see—" began Prescott.

"Cow!" Egg broke hard to the right. An instant later, Muriel did the same. Prescott and Kit broke left. The cow herself didn't move. She stood in the middle of the road with laudable calmness, her creamy brown flanks nearly invisible in the fog. They all missed her by inches.

Kit held his breath until he saw Muriel control her wild swerve. She careened back onto the road and steadied her wheel, face pale.

Anger stirred in his guts. With less than a week of training, she lacked experience handling her machine under duress. She might have gone flying into a furze bush, or worse, a boulder.

"Dismount and rest?" he asked her.

She shook her head. "We've barely gotten underway."

Yes, and what a start they'd made.

"Passing on the left," he announced. He swung around Prescott, and then overtook Butterfield as well, standing on the pedals, both for the added power, and because he did feel a bit too low to the ground in comparison.

He had to exert himself even more to pull even with Deighton.

"Foul weather," he remarked, when it became obvious that Deighton wasn't about to speak first.

"Didn't see you down there." Deighton grinned. "How's the mud?"

"Dunno." Kit grinned too. "Shall we try to knock each other into it? Get it out of the way?"

Deighton hunched over his handlebars. "No one's knocking anyone into anything."

"Your father suggested otherwise."

"My father—" Deighton reared. His front wheel skipped, and he jerked his handlebars, thinning his lips. "My father is not the captain of a bicycle club. Wheelmen follow the rules of the road. You'll end up in the mud—not because of me. Because you're halfway there already."

"Two of your officers nearly ended up under a cow. Due to your poor judgment." For a moment, Kit anticipated a kick to the head. Tension rolled off Deighton in waves.

"Reduce the rate of speed," said Kit evenly. "You have nothing to prove."

Deighton laughed, neck rigid. "This isn't the rate of speed I'd adopt if I had something to prove. I consider this a moderate pace. But fine." His posture relaxed. "I'll reduce the rate of speed. So long as you ride with me. No straggling."

"Fine." Kit sucked in a mouthful of salty air. It had the taste of a mixed blessing.

"Fine," repeated Deighton, and slacked the pace.

The next hours passed as predicted. Long intervals of hostile silence on the wheel punctuated by short periods of respite. The fog lifted at midday, and whenever they dismounted, he joined Muriel to admire the coastal scenery or ask her the names of the flowers threading the hedges. She didn't seem remotely bothered that he'd abandoned his place beside her, or that it meant they'd no time to explore the coves. She waved away his explanation as easily as she waved away his regrets. He shouldn't have felt surprised, let alone dismayed. He'd known she was self-sufficient. He admired her independent spirit. But he found himself wishing for some slight indication that she *was* bothered, just a little bothered, or at least pining for his return. At lunch, in Penzance, she was trapped between Egg and Prescott, and he watched her covertly, as she laughed and drank and brushed bright tendrils of hair from her face. *He* was trapped between Butterfield and Kemble, who were swapping facts about recent race results while Deighton paged through a copy of the Cyclists' Touring Club's *Monthly Gazette and Official Record*.

She bore her fate with better cheer than he did. Or was she actually enjoying herself? Egg, who couldn't be more than eighteen, had terrible manners. He shoveled his food with his elbows on the table and talked eagerly with his mouth full, encouraged by her smile. His eyes had begun to shine with devotion. Prescott had better comportment. He was likely in his twenties and far more restrained. He'd just said something that elicited Muriel's appreciation. Kit could tell from the way she angled her body and the lilt of her voice. She was asking him questions. They kept talking as they exited the pub, Kit skulking in their shadow, feeling vaguely villainous. The subject was birds. Prescott held his hand out, describing how the gulls in the St. Ives harbor took crusts without fear, and once, his whole pasty.

"I counted four different species," she said, and he said he'd counted five, and then it was comparing plumage to discover if their observations corresponded.

As they rode southeast toward the Lizard, following the curve of Mount's Bay, passing fishermen's huts and Coastguard cottages, Kit scowled at the birds he couldn't identify. He'd ride with her tomorrow, Deighton be damned. He'd sketch what seaweed had to be sketched. He'd throw in a portrait of a herring gull. End of story.

They cut inland to Helston and dismounted by the Loe. The gleaming waters of the lake were fringed with rushes and dark pines, and Muriel was instantly absorbed, wandering the bank in a reverie he didn't dare disturb. South of Gunwalloe, they dismounted again, and Kit turned to see that she wasn't among them.

"Where's Mrs. Pendrake?" He addressed Prescott, who rubbed his chin, where his black beard had sprouted densely since the morning.

"She'll be along shortly." He turned as though she might have already arrived. The road was empty. He turned back to Kit with less certainty. "She said she was going down to the shore. I offered to accompany her, of course."

"I offered as well," piped up Egg. "I'd have been the bigger help. My mother keeps a seaweed album."

"She told us to ride on." Prescott frowned. "It wasn't so far back. We can wait for her here."

"We're not waiting." Deighton pulled on the brim of his cap. "My guess? She hired a conveyance back to Penzance, where they have proper amenities."

Prescott and Egg exchanged a look.

"She didn't mention Penzance," said Egg. "She mentioned seaweed."

"You know women and their whims." Kemble shrugged and folded his thick arms.

"All mount!" called Deighton.

Kit was already on his bicycle, pointed in the opposite direction.

Deighton sneered. "Go after her if you're worried."

"I'm not worried," said Kit. "But she and I are a club. We ride together."

"You're a club?" Kemble chortled. "Just the two of you?"

"There's four at present." Kit added Raleigh and Ponsonby on the spot. Honorary members.

"And your name?" demanded Deighton.

Kit's brows pulled together. What the hell?

"The Flower Pedals," he said. "See you at dinner."

With that, he shoved off.

He *wasn't* worried. He should have known that Muriel would stop to hunt for seaweed without him, even if it meant cycling the last leg down to the Lizard on her own. Her decision grated, ever so slightly, or rather, the fact that she'd taken matters into her own hands, without asking his permission. It wasn't chauvinism, to consider himself the captain of their informally constituted club. He was the seasoned cyclist, responsible for her welfare, on the road, if nowhere else. Perhaps they needed a handbook, spelling some things out. He'd changed position in the column, true, without consulting her, but again—captain. And it wasn't the same as leaving the column altogether.

At least he could count on her common sense, and scrupulous attention to the Earth's rotation. She wouldn't tarry overlong. She'd learned firsthand that cycling in the dark was a perilous proposition. At any moment, she'd appear, spinning toward him, looking sheepish, or perhaps, not sheepish at all—happy. Collecting bag stuffed with kelp. He rode at a walk, to give her time, so he wouldn't inadvertently pass her turnoff before she'd reemerged. To his left, water rippled, a vast expanse, pale green by the serpentine cliffs, deepest blue at the horizon. To his right, walled fields made a series of rectangles that stretched across the low hills. It was early evening, hazy and warm. Wrens twittered in the hedges. Well, he thought they were wrens.

Annoyed, yes. But worried, no. That's why he rounded the bend and felt his blood turn all at once to ice.

Muriel's bicycle lay on the ground, at the base of a tree.

18

MURIEL WAS WEDGED in the lowest fork of an ancient oak. It wasn't as big as the Darley Oak, but its gnarled limbs answered to her purpose. She was safe. She repeated it to herself, fingers digging into furrowed bark.

I am safe. I am safe.

She almost believed it. She'd stopped shaking, but her chest was tight, heart giving quick, pinched beats.

I am safe.

A thud below shook loose her gasp. She swung her arm, snapped a dead, spindly branch, and stabbed downward with all her frantic strength. The branch connected.

"Holy God!"

She froze. A second later, the branch tugged from her hand, burning her skin through her glove. Another second, and it began to stab back.

"En garde, you bastard! What have you done with her?"

The husky voice was almost unrecognizable, tight with fury.

Almost unrecognizable.

She leaned forward and took a whack on the shoulder. "Griff?"

Wincing, she pressed back into the tree.

"Muriel?"

She leaned forward again, slowly. Griffith was standing beneath her like a swordsman, chest heaving, stick upraised. Her blow must have knocked off his cap. His hair was wild, and his eyes were wilder. They flashed over her.

"Blast!" He gave a shake and flung the stick away. He scrubbed a hand across his face, and when it came away, his expression teetered between shock and outrage.

"It's me." Muriel licked her dry lips and braced herself against the trunk, unbalanced in more ways than she could count. "I haven't cracked your skull?"

"No." He probed his head. "No, but it was a bloody good clout."

"You clouted back." She brought her bruised shoulder up to her cheek. "Did you think I was the banditti?"

"Yes. In a word." His laughter had a sharp edge. "First, I thought you'd collided with this tree. But then, yes, I thought bandits—or smugglers, really. It's Cornwall."

He stepped back, to look at her without craning his neck. The shadows beneath his cheekbones deepened as he clenched his jaw.

"What happened?" he asked, stance opening, gaze sweeping their surroundings. "Why are you up in a tree?"

"No cause for alarm." She swallowed. From her perch, she could see farther than he could. Linnets and yellowhammers rustled the hedges. There was a thatched cottage in the distance, a woman passing through an ivy-mantled garden gate.

No bandits. No smugglers. No beasts with blood-flecked maws.

She drew a long breath. "I didn't meet with any mischief."

"Something frightened you." His gaze swept back to her. "I'd have guessed you were simply after a bird's nest if you hadn't rained blows at my approach."

He was pressing for more information. But it would be easier to calm herself, and climb down, if she cleared her mind.

She lifted her chin. The glowing leaves above made a golden-green bell of serenity. "A woodpecker must live up here somewhere. Most of his feathered friends prefer the hedges, or the furze."

The pause lengthened.

At last, Griffith spoke. "You know a lot about birds."

She glanced down, relieved he'd taken her cue. "Not really. Prescott has a better eye. He spotted a pied flycatcher by the lake."

This earned her a grunt. "You two seem to get on well."

"We have plenty to talk about. We both appreciate the natural world."

"Delighted to hear it." Griffith's close-lipped smile didn't look delighted.

"Funny," he said, after a tense beat of silence. "You preferred to go down to the shore by yourself."

"Prescott's keen, but he would have gotten in the way," she responded slowly. "Egg too. They'd both have come along, and I'd have been minding them instead of the seaweed." She hesitated. "You understand."

He *did* understand, surely. There was a particular kind of work a woman had to do to manage the men who helped her unnecessarily.

His face didn't change. The fine hairs on her neck stirred with unease. He was seething, and not only with misplaced fury at her imagined attackers. Instinctively, she raised her defenses.

"It would have been tiresome." She frowned. "I only wanted a look."

"A look." Tiny muscles ticked near his temple. "Hardly worth separating yourself from the group."

The look had been worthless, in fact. She'd walked a small stretch of coarse sand and seen nothing but a few cuttlefish bones and egg cases.

Griffith was squinting at her now, his irritation plain.

"The others didn't wait for you."

She gave a huff. "I didn't assume they would."

"And me? Did you assume I'd continue as well?"

She bit her lip. Drat it. She hadn't intended to disrupt his ride. She'd simply followed the urge to beachcomb. And he'd been well ahead all day, vying with Deighton.

"I suppose I did assume so," she said. "I was quite prepared to ride alone. It's only fifteen more miles, fewer perhaps. I'm sorry you turned back."

"I'm not." His expression darkened.

She blinked at him. "Isn't that why you're angry?"

"Please. You're my wheelman. Wheelwoman." He waved a hand. "There was never any question."

She blinked again. "*Yours?*"

"Not in a proprietary sense."

"Oh." She furrowed her brow. "What's the other sense of the possessive?"

His expression grew darker. "Penny. You can't just disappear. What I meant is we're a unit."

She tilted her head. "Since when?"

"Since we started riding."

"And you're in charge of this unit? What you say goes?"

"Yes, dammit. Provisionally. I'm the one who knows the laws and the courtesies. I'm the one who can assess the condition of the thoroughfares and our machines. I'm the one who can fix a broken spoke and true a wheel." He sounded frustrated. "You're more vulnerable on the road."

This was undeniable. Also, irrelevant. She nodded. "And yet I'm accustomed to making my own choices."

His gaze bored into her. "Your choices affect me."

She glanced away, confused emotions welling in her chest. The simple statement pushed her strangely close to tears, as though his words had a broader meaning, expressed a sentiment she'd been longing to hear.

You are essential to my life.

She said nothing, heat building behind her eyes.

He folded his arms. "The choice to ride alone was foolhardy."

Her inner tumult made the criticism sting all the more. She wiggled herself into a more secure position and tugged off her gloves.

"You are overbearing," she told him, her voice cold.

"You are in a tree." He matched her tone. "Obviously, I wasn't overbearing enough."

They looked at each other in silence.

His thumb began to tap against his bicep. "Can we make a resolution? Going forward, neither of us strikes out unaccompanied. That's how riders get lost or left behind."

She shoved her gloves in her pocket and studied the pink mark on her palm. The instinct to refuse seized her. It would feel satisfying—and childish. What he proposed was hardly tyranny. Don't wander off. It was a basic principle, critical to social cohesion and individual survival.

She sighed. "So resolved."

"Good," he said, promptly.

"But if I see a promising cove, we're stopping."

"We'll stop." He paused. "If it's reasonable."

Reasonable could be negotiated. Griffith's temper ran nearly as high as hers, but he was fair-minded.

"All right," she said. "Good enough."

He brushed back his hair, grimacing as he touched a tender point. "Can we make another resolution? No whacking each other with sticks."

His grimace seemed a bit put on, and his eyes glinted teasingly.

"So resolved," she said, and felt her lips twitch. A spat was a spat with him. You had it out, and it was over. With Esmé, she'd often felt that she was living the long, punitive aftermath of a fight she couldn't remember.

"That was easy." He lifted his brows.

"You seem surprised."

"You have a truculent streak. I doubted you'd lay down arms."

"We resolved against sticks." She gave a small shrug. "Pelting with acorns is still permitted."

There was a little cache of last year's acorns in a declivity of the trunk. She took one in hand.

The teasing glint in his eyes became an intense glitter.

"Come down," he urged softly. "Then pelt me if you dare."

His low, goading voice sent a shiver along her spine.

She was beginning the awkward rotation that would allow her to drop to the ground, when staccato barking shattered the peace, sinister as gunfire.

She clutched the tree, every muscle gone rigid. Her heart seemed to rise into her throat.

Griffith turned.

"Ahoy!" He was grinning, grinning as slavering death hurled itself forward.

She shut her eyes, heard the thumps of a tussle. Panting filled her ears. She could almost smell the hot stench, wafting up to her in gusts.

"Good day to you too, mate."

There was a high-pitched whine. Griffith laughed.

He was safe.

She was safe.

She couldn't catch her breath. She let her forehead rest on rough bark, felt little particles shower her eyelids.

"Penny," called Griffith. "You're not stuck? Do you need a hand?"

"No," she croaked.

"Stop gathering munitions and come down."

Certainly, she answered. *Be right there.*

Her lips didn't move. She didn't move. The panting sounded unbearably loud. The next bark made her shoulders jump.

"I'll come up." Griffith spoke in a changed voice. "Do you mind?"

Those new noises—he was hoisting himself. She opened her eyes as he reached for a handhold above her head, sidling around her, larger fragments of bark showering them both. She flicked repeatedly at her eyes, and her hair. A hectic gesture that exacerbated the disorder of her thoughts. Where was her hat? She hadn't noticed that her hatpins had come loose.

"Truce," said Griffith. He'd settled himself on a long limb, legs dangling, one wrist resting casually on an upper branch. "Hold your acorns. I only want to talk."

Her stalled blood began to pump. She didn't look down. Death still bounded around the tree. She looked at Griffith, the play of light and shadow on his face.

"It's more comfortable over here." He shrugged his broad shoulders, the carelessness of the invitation belied by the glow in his eyes.

She edged out of the cramped fork and crawled onto the limb, then clasped the upper branch, turning so she sat as he did. Her right foot tingled. She'd had it jammed sideways so long it had gone to sleep. Griffith slid closer.

"You're afraid of dogs," he said, disarmingly direct.

A ray of sun lit his tousled hair and gilded his cheekbone. Now she suffered from a new form of breathlessness. His beauty almost hurt.

"I'm afraid of snakes," he offered. "I really am. I break out in a sweat." He frowned. "Sorry. That must seem trite in comparison."

His ruefulness moved her even more than the admission itself.

"Adders are common in Cornwall," she whispered.

He laughed. "That's not very comforting."

Indeed, it wasn't. Her ears flamed.

"James could tell you." She cleared her throat. "I'm clumsy with such things. Compliments. Words of comfort." Thankfully, her throat closed completely before she could add an explanation, embarrassing in its implied self-pity.

She'd heard little of that type of speech to date.

He touched her hand. For the tour, he'd donned buff-colored gloves. His leather-encased fingers skimmed her knuckles.

"Dogs are common everywhere." He turned her hand over. "You are uncommonly brave, to face them daily."

Air rushed into her lungs. *He* was graceful with compliments. He had the ability to make a person feel seen, and special. Knowing this should diminish the effect. He looked at other women with that same glittering gaze.

"Face them daily? Flee them, you mean." She shook her head. "It's *not* daily, thank God. Too often, though."

He considered her. "Remarkable that the fear doesn't keep you indoors."

"The only pleasure I ever found was out of doors." She realized, too late, how that might sound, and blushed. "Occasional terror doesn't weigh in the balance. Despite the nuisance."

"It's more than a nuisance," he said gently, concern in his eyes. "You were in agony."

Her discomfort increased. He'd observed her in an abject state, blanched and cowering.

"Nuisance to others," she clarified. "That's what's bothersome."

Frown lines carved down from his nose. "How is your fear a nuisance to others?"

"How isn't it?" She laughed humorlessly. "Shall I list the problems I've caused? Once I flung myself on the ground and crushed a rare orchid. My husband was livid. On two occasions, I panicked and threw an expensive lens into the undergrowth. Neither lens was recoverable. Then there was the time I made us miss a boat. The time I was the reason an expedition got cut short. The list goes on." Her temples began to throb. "Trust me, you'll find it a nuisance too if I let a perfectly benign retriever interfere with our timely return to St. Ives."

"Trust me, I won't." His smile was lopsided. "But perhaps I can lure the retrievers from your path."

"Your infamous charisma works on dogs?" She aimed for a bantering tone, but there was a catch in her voice. He couldn't create a charmed circle around her. No one could. Gratification bloomed inside her regardless, at the thought that he wanted to try.

"My charisma." He smirked. "I was thinking table scraps."

"I wouldn't bother. And I wouldn't worry. I *will* finish the ride." She nodded for emphasis. "Most dogs don't frighten me. It's only the large ones, with a certain kind of fur, a certain way of moving. A certain smell. Teeth that . . ."

She'd crossed her ankles and was grinding the bones together. Tendrils of emotion pushed at the cracks in the wall she'd built around herself. Usually, she cut them back.

"It's not the dogs themselves," she said at last. "It's a memory. They drag me into it, and then I can't get out."

His lashes had lowered as he listened. His gloved thumb traced the air above the pink mark on her palm.

"May I?" he asked. She acquiesced, half in understanding, half in bewildered faith. He lifted her palm to his lips. She exhaled. His mouth was silky, and she felt the slight suction of his indrawn breath, and then the damp tip of his tongue. Sensation twinned. The center of her palm seemed connected to the center of her being, which she located somewhere behind her navel.

It was a kiss. No one had ever kissed her there. Her hand was slightly cupped, as though the kiss were something she could keep. The intimacy made her head swim. She tightened her grip on the branch.

He lowered her hand, tucked it between them. "What frightened you today—it was an echo of something that happened a long time ago?"

"To my mother, not me." She looked up, through the branches. The leaves weren't so bright anymore. The gaps between had filled with gray. "But I was with her, in the yard. It came out of nowhere, the dog. It smelled like the bowels of hell, and it bit her before we could move. I couldn't make it let go. No one could. Mr. Wilson beat it with a shovel, and it still didn't open its jaws. Another neighbor had a rifle, and . . ."

She broke off and glanced at him.

He was looking at her steadily.

"Well," she said. "That dispatched it."

"Your mother's wounds." He hesitated. "They were mortal?"

She turned up her gaze again and watched the leaves shift in the wind. "Not at first. The doctor treated her leg. When the symptoms began, he came back, several times. Lord Raleigh paid the fees— James's father. Usually, he didn't extend himself beyond the Christmas dole of blankets, coal, and plum pudding. But news spread like wildfire. My mother was well-liked. A young widow. She always went to church. She sang in the choir. She had the prettiest hair. And she suffered so piteously. Everyone wanted to help, or gawk." She pulled a deep breath into her burning lungs. "The dog was mad, you understand."

Griffith made a soft sound, and his arm wrapped around her, strong and supportive. Feeling him there, without having to meet his eyes—it enabled her to go on.

"Mother had always been gentle," she said. "But she pushed away anything I brought her, violently. She broke our plates, our only pitcher. She had to be tied down. There wasn't enough sedative to keep her asleep. She strained against her bonds so that the bed thumped the floor. She made noises like I'd never heard. As though that dog's snarl was coming from her throat."

Griffith's arm tightened, and she released the branch above, trusting that he wouldn't let her fall.

"It went on for a week. I couldn't recognize anything about her. I drew near and my skin crawled with abhorrence." She softened against him, the words wringing her out. "Right before the end, Lady Raleigh drove over in her pony carriage, with a basket of cheese and grapes and beef tea. I remember she took the lid off the pot on the hob and pursed her lips at the cold oats, like she was in pain. She wanted to read to Mother from the Bible. She'd brought her youngest son, to teach him about charity."

"James." Griffith's chin came to rest on the crown of her head. Her cheek pressed the fabric of his coat, which smelled like soap and heath and some subtle, drugging scent that came from him alone.

"James," she said softly. "That's how we met. We stood in the corner, and he held my hand. He asked me about my mother's favorite things, what we liked to do together. He helped me see her again. And that helped me say goodbye." She twined her fingers together in her lap. "He wasn't yet twelve, because I was scarcely eight. But he knew how to give me something I needed more than charity, or even compassion. Even if we'd never spent another moment in each other's company, I'd have loved him forever." Her eyelids felt heavy and wet, and she realized she'd turned more of her face into Griffith's coat. She was too flustered, and too snugly secured, to move away.

"Do you know he researches rabies? There's a method now, to protect people who've been bitten by rabid animals. Hydrophobia can be prevented." She strove for businesslike briskness. "James says we're close to stamping out the disease altogether." She faltered, unable to present a façade, not now that she'd allowed it to crumble.

"I thought the advances would put my fear in perspective. But it defies perspective. It defies everything. When it comes on, I'm back there, in the yard with my mother, and the dog is lurching toward us. That moment—sometimes it feels like the only real moment of my life."

"It's not." His voice was gruff and low, and his body was solid against hers, and the reality of it flooded her from head to toe.

She lifted her head, angling her face up to him. His pupils had dilated. His eyes consumed her, dark and hungry. As her lips parted, a cool droplet splashed the corner of her mouth. The leaves quivered and began to dance.

"Rain." Slowly, Griffith withdrew his arm, giving her time to anchor herself. Catlike, he stretched his lean torso and levered himself up, climbing to higher boughs. "That sheepdog belonged to that cottage." He pointed with his chin. "I can see him behind the gate."

She heard the question in his voice.

"I can climb down now," she said. "Let's ride. Before the rain gets worse."

19

IT WASN'T LONG before the rain did get worse. For the first few miles, it pattered lightly, and they passed under bright breaks in the clouds. Even when it began to pour, they could see patches of sky in the distance, and as they crested a hill, Muriel heard Griffith shout with glee, and a moment later she understood why. Colored bands of light shimmered overhead and seemed to touch down behind the next hill. With one glance, they made an unspoken decision, standing simultaneously on their pedals. They rode faster, chasing the rainbow's end, until the clouds reconfigured, and the diaphanous ribbon dimmed to nothing. By then, Muriel was panting, collapsed on the seat, rain streaming on her face and up her sleeves. She was still wrung out from all she'd said, but she didn't feel depleted. Her chest ached, a hundred emotions expanding into the space she'd opened. As the road sloped down, the wind pushed at her back, aiding her effortless acceleration, and it seemed for a moment she might leave the ground and fly. She cackled for joy.

There was a gradual rise into more hills, and then they descended into a deeper valley. The clouds followed them down, nearly black, and suddenly, the rain came from all directions. It sprayed up from their tires, and blew in sideways sheets, and drenched them from above. They kept riding, but ever more slowly, as the road divided into rivulets.

"Dismount!" called Griffith.

"No!" she called back.

"What?" His shout was disbelieving. "Dismount!"

"We can't be far," she protested, splashing through a puddle.

"It doesn't matter how far we've left to go if we break our necks now!" came the response.

He meant her neck, of course. And she'd slowed them down enough already.

When he jumped off his bicycle, she kept riding.

"Don't strike off alone!" she upbraided him as she passed.

"*You* are striking off alone," he retorted.

"I'm continuing along the agreed-upon route!" She didn't trust herself to steer in the wet dark while yelling over her shoulder, so she yelled into the storm. "You are obstructing the path!"

She laughed wildly. Her skirts were soaked and slapped the bicycle's iron frame.

"Penny." He rode up on her left.

"I love storms."

"Penny."

"We'll make it in no time," she told him, blinking the water from her eyes.

"Dismount," he commanded.

At that instant, her front wheel plunged down into sucking mud. The world blurred, and she whipped around with the bicycle, limp as a rag doll. As she slid to a hard stop, her head jerked forward and back, and her outstretched foot skidded on the gravel.

"I dismounted!" she gasped, dragging her leg over the frame. The bicycle was perpendicular to the road. Her vision wobbled, and her neck seemed simultaneously too stiff and too loose.

She heard Griffith cursing as he circled back to her.

"That wasn't a dismount," he said. "That was a narrowly averted disaster."

"I hit a bit more mud than I expected." After the fact, she was trembling with nerves, gruesome versions of the spill she'd just avoided flashing through her mind. She fetched up a wobbly smile. "Now what? We walk to the Lizard?"

"We're going to walk to the inn in the nearest village." Griffith swung off his bicycle and came right up to her. "And leave tomorrow at first light."

"Won't it hurt your pride?"

"The hot meal and the dry clothes?"

"The giving up."

He shrugged a shoulder. "I don't care if Deighton celebrates a premature victory."

"I care, though."

"Picture the look on his face tomorrow, when we coast into Falmouth."

She shook her head. "Given that this is all my fault, I should get—"

"Penny," he interrupted. "If we're going to stand here in the rain, I'd rather not argue."

"That's a ridiculous statement. Arguing is *why* we're standing here in the rain. If we weren't arguing, we wouldn't be standing here in the rain."

"We could do something else."

"While standing here in the rain?" She scoffed. "And what's that? Play cat's cradle with a bootlace? Look for frogs?"

He pushed his bicycle away, took her face in his hands, and kissed her. She tasted rain, cool and clean, and then the heat of his mouth obliterated every other perception. For a heartbeat, she forgot everything. Forgot that they were ankle-deep in mud on a country lane, soaked to the skin. Forgot the bicycle race, and her lecture, Cornwall and New York. There was only this conflagration. Two mouths in the dark. His tongue slid between her lips, and she gasped. She let her bicycle fall as he pulled her against him. His gloved hands stroked the sides of her face, and then he was tipping her head, angling her chin, so he could kiss her ever more deeply. She drew a shuddering breath. Rain kept slipping down between them, rolling over their cheeks, into their mouths. She was going to drown, drown in rain and kisses.

Griffith broke away first, acknowledging the sounds she'd noticed only dimly. The clop of hooves and the creak of a wagon.

"Are ye spirits?" The old man hunched on the seat behind his horse was all but hidden by his greatcoat.

"Wayfarers." Griffith stepped forward. "Searching for a place to lay our heads. Is there an inn nearby?"

"Iss," said the man. "I'll take ye there."

"Terribly kind," said Griffith.

"It were never time wasted to do good," said the old man philosophically, and with just a touch of reluctance. "Get in, then. Weather's too dirty for a rat. Not that yer rats, nor spirits."

"No," affirmed Griffith. "Neither."

They loaded into the wagon, the bicycles causing their guide no small degree of consternation. Griffith crouched near to him, proselytizing about the wonders of the machine, or so Muriel thought. She couldn't be sure, pinned as she was near the back of the wagon, half under the bicycles' dripping rear tires. Eventually, she saw twinkling lights, which, as they drew closer, resolved into the small windows of a squat two-story building that seemed to swim toward them through a sea of total blackness.

The old man climbed down to assist Griffith with the bicycles.

"Do ye stable them?" he asked, sounding honestly confused, and Muriel hurried over to pluck necessary items out of her panniers. While the two men walked the bicycles around the side of the inn to the mews, she sheltered under the eaves, running her tongue absently along the inside of her bottom lip. When Griffith rounded the corner, his gaze arrowed to her mouth. She froze midlick, his knowing expression summoning a fiery blush. Her face was still red as they entered the inn. The old man led the way down a short corridor and into a large room dominated by an inglenook fireplace. A middle-aged woman and two half-grown boys occupied the benches set on opposite sides of the cheerful blaze.

"Mr. Hendy!" The woman rose. "What brings you by on such a night?"

Muriel found his mumblings unintelligible. She lingered just inside the door, eyes wandering to the bottle-crowded bar, where a few patrons had swiveled on their stools to inspect the newcomers. Battered drinking vessels hung from the low beams, and nautical memorabilia filled the niches in the stone walls. The stained shades on the gas wall brackets glowed with a grubby light. She started to shiver, the warmth of the room revealing by contrast the chill in her bones.

"I'm Mrs. Glanvil." The woman approached Griffith, and included Muriel in her sympathetic smile. "Stranded on the road, were you? Poor ducks. Our Mr. Hendy's a good soul. He's taken you to the right place. This is my family's inn, and the finest in Cornwall. You'll be wanting dinner, and a bath. My Jenny will see to it. She'll collect your wet things too, and wash and dry them. Just set the basket outside the door."

She turned.

"Tell Jenny now," she called, and both boys shot up from the benches. Mrs. Glanvil sighed. "Not you, Peter. You take the luggage. You do have luggage?" She turned back to them.

Muriel looked down at the bundle in her arms, a small dressing box and her wadded shift. Water dripped from the brim of her hat. She'd been pleased to find it—caught in the hedge by her bicycle—but it had done precious little to protect her from the rain. She could feel her braid leaking down her back.

When she looked up, she saw that Mrs. Glanvil's lips had bent into a concerned frown.

"We're traveling light," said Griffith smoothly, and gave the innkeeper his widest, most devastating smile.

"On bicycles, I hear." Mrs. Glanvil looked slightly dazzled—by the smile, Muriel suspected, not their means of transportation.

"You heard right," said Griffith, and Mrs. Glanvil blushed.

"You and the missus are bold ones."

Muriel coughed. "We're not—" She stopped herself. Mr. Hendy had come upon them as they'd stood locked in an amorous embrace. What was there to say? We're not anything so respectable as married?

"We're not . . . very bold." She coughed again. "A bath sounds lovely."

"Let's get you signed in," said Mrs. Glanvil to Griffith. "Then I'll show you up to your room."

Room. Singular. For the married couple.

Muriel's throat worked as she swallowed.

Griffith cut a glance at her, brows lifted questioningly. He'd try to get them out of it if she made a sign.

She gave a small shake of her head, and something kindled behind his eyes.

"We'll take your best," he said to Mrs. Glanvil.

The tub was some time filling, and so after Griffith returned from his transacting, they dripped awhile longer on the flagstones, Griffith standing Mr. Hendy several pints, although he limited himself to a single brandy, offering her the same, and clinking their glasses.

When they finally retired to their room, Muriel gaped. The tub was enormous, a great copper oval, capped with mountains of suds. Rose-scented steam curled toward the ceiling. A scrawny girl with carrot-colored braids was coming and going with linens and dinner trays, looking humid and surprisingly good-humored.

"That's all, then," she said, hands on her hips. "Dinner's there. Tub's there. Bed's there. Basket's there." Darting them each a swift glance, bright with curiosity, she whirled. "Evenin'."

The door clicked shut behind her, and they were alone. Muriel's eyes bounced between the tub and the bed. The bed was as big for a bed as the tub was big for a tub. Both seemed out of proportion to the room itself.

"You should take off your clothes."

Muriel's eyes bounced to Griffith. He was lounging against the wall, wearing the heavy-lidded expression of an inveterate seducer. She felt a flutter, and then a nip of annoyance, that he should find all of this so navigable.

"I've figured it out," she informed him. "You're *not* charismatic. It's just that some people are charmed by overconfidence."

"Are you?" He tossed back his wet hair and grinned.

Yes. When it came to him, she couldn't help herself.

She lifted her chin. "Not in the least."

His gaze traveled over her. "The laundry can't wait. Mrs. Glanvil's orders." He let his knapsack thump down on the threadbare rug. "I told her we're setting off early."

Laundry. Of course. She flushed, then frowned. Now he toyed with her. Her nerves were wound too tight for this type of teasing.

She enjoyed their banter, but she had to know where they stood, how far he wanted this to go.

"To be clear, then." Her brows knitted. "You *aren't* trying to seduce me?"

"Hell." He peeled off his jacket. "I hope I haven't given you that impression." The basket was just to the right of the door. In went the jacket. The vest. His necktie. He pulled his braces over his shoulders.

Muriel started, then spun. She faced the curtained window, pulse at a gallop.

On her wedding night, she'd waited for Esmé under the blankets, in a nightgown that buttoned to the throat. The nightgown hadn't come off in the course of the night. The act she and Esmé performed together had felt both insignificant and monumental. Beyond the ungainly mechanics, there wasn't much to it, and yet it signified that her marriage had been validated, that she'd crossed a threshold and put her old life irreversibly behind her.

This too felt like a threshold.

"Pasties, pilchards, heavy cake," announced Griffith, and she peeked over her shoulder. He was inspecting their repast, laid out on the rickety table, which had been jammed awkwardly between the side of the bed and the wall, to allow space for the tub.

"I could cry." He made a happy noise in his throat and hopped as he tugged off his stockings. He regained his balance, feet bare, and caught her gaze. "Here's the sequence." He sent the stockings flying at the basket. "First, strip. Second, devour food with irresponsible haste. Third, bathe."

She turned. "Shouldn't bathing come second?"

"Then the food will be cold."

"But if bathing is third, the water will be cold."

"That's why I emphasized haste."

"And we're naked in this scenario?" She'd hoped to sound wry, and a little scathing. Instead, her voice was hoarse.

"I skipped a step. We strip, then we quickly protect our modesty." His eyes were glinting. "That's optional, of course. Don't let me stop you if you prefer to dine in the buff."

"If I did, I *wouldn't* let you stop me." She paused. "I don't, though."

"We're agreed, then, on the plan of action."

She sighed. "How officious you are."

"Officious. Overconfident. Overbearing. Insufferably arrogant." He shook his head. "I'm surprised you like me so much."

"No, you're not," she muttered. "That's the most annoying part."

"You like me, then?" He couldn't hide his smile. "*So* much?"

"Stop talking," she suggested. "Or everything will get cold."

He was laughing as she sidled between the bed and the tub.

God above. She liked him. So much. Apparently, they were agreed on that.

She set her dressing case near the washbasin. Ducking as much as she could behind the tub, she struggled out of her dress and underthings, her stockings and shoes, and yanked her shift over her head. It was damp and badly wrinkled. She straightened, arms piled with filthy garments, and gave a squeak. On the other side of the tub, Griffith stood with his back to her, sliding his arms into his nightshirt. Her eyes followed the fabric as it slid over the taut curve of his bottom and curtained his hard thighs. As he padded to the table, she stared at the intricate play of muscles in his calves, her stomach tightening. She felt lightheaded. Too much exercise and too little food. Lunch in Penzance was a lifetime ago.

She dumped her clothes in the basket, shoved it out the door, and joined him at the table. At the first bite of pasty, she wanted to cry too.

"God, it's delicious," she mumbled.

"I've never tasted anything better." Griffith sighed. "Or more briefly."

She blinked. He'd finished his pasty with truly irresponsible speed. She intensified her own efforts.

"I maligned Egg in my mind," he said. "Earlier today, for his table manners. But I think I'm going to lick this clean." He was looking wolfishly at his empty plate.

"It's a sport in itself, maligning Egg." She took a sip of wine. "You saw how the others treat him. He says it was worse at school. And his father calls him *useless*."

"Seems you and Egg talked plenty as well."

"We did. He feels unvalued."

"Ah, yes, the upper-class English male has his cross to bear." As he turned his head, his ironical smile shifted. "An elephant could bathe in that tub."

"A baby elephant." The suds had flattened slightly, and the steam was more diffuse. The room had a pearly haze.

"Or the two of us."

Her eyes snapped back. He was sipping his wine, brows arched. Her mouth went dry. "Together?"

"Mmm." He nodded.

"You want to bathe together." Her pulse surpassed gallop. It began to whir. "Because that's how we ensure a hot soak for us both?"

"No, in fact, the tub's all yours if you wish. I don't need a hot soak. A tepid sponge bath will do the job." He put down his glass. His eyes were hooded, and his lips curved. "I want to indulge a purely salacious impulse."

"Oh." She felt breathless. "What would that involve?"

"You tell me."

Shyness gripped her so hard she could feel little pinpricks of anticipated rejection. "I'm not very imaginative."

"Everyone's imaginative."

She looked at the tub, heart pounding. "Couldn't you do the imagining?"

"I could," he said. "Is that what you want? You won't think me too officious, overconfident, overbearing, and arrogant?"

She looked at him. There was humor in his face, and something more.

"*Insufferably* arrogant," she whispered.

"Say if you do." His eyes were suddenly serious. "I'll stop at a word."

She gave a nod, and he was out of his chair. She caught another glimpse of his firm rear as he whipped off his nightshirt and sank into the tub. He went all the way under the water, then emerged, hair slicked back, soap dripping from his ear.

"Come here," he commanded.

She went on unsteady legs.

"Get in." He slung an arm over the side of the tub. Suds collected at his armpit. Glistening bubbles trapped themselves on the ledge of his collarbones. She rucked up her shift and stepped into the tub, hot water swirling around her sore, overstrained calves.

"Are you taking that off?" he asked, amused.

She flushed. "Shut your eyes."

He complied, and for a moment, she stared at his angular face, its hard lines and the soft, sly curve of his mouth. The black silk of his lashes. Someone—not her—could write poetry about such a face.

He was also flushed, from the heat.

She pulled off her shift and sat, tangling with his legs, water lapping up to the tub's rim.

"Now turn around," he said, and she floated, trying to rotate with minimum contact.

His arm wrapped her middle, and he guided her, until she sat between his thighs.

"I'm going to unbraid your hair," he said, with a raggedness to his voice that made her toes curl. She felt the gentle tugs as he set to work, separating the thick sections, moving up toward the roots. She was breathing deeply, sweat and steam beading on her cheeks.

"I've been wanting to do that all day." His fingers slid into her loosed tresses, combing and smoothing, stroking her scalp in slow circles. Time had no meaning. The steam was inside her now. She was hazed and drifting. He pushed the mass of hair over her shoulders and put his mouth on the nape of her neck.

She moaned and felt his smile on her skin before he pulled away. He kneaded her shoulders, and her neck, thumbs releasing the tense muscles along her spine. When he had her lolling with the relief of it, he reached over the side of the tub for the cloth and the soap. He soaped her with the same lavish thoroughness he'd devoted to massaging her aching back, lifting her arms one by one, turning her so he could lather her feet and calves. He held her gaze when he touched her breasts, and at her gasp, he let the soap slip and closed his hands on her hips. He towed her up his legs, until she straddled his waist, knees bumping metal.

For a second, he stared. Then he kissed her hard. He bent her backward, so that the weight of her wet hair dragged her head toward the water. She felt supple as a plant, as suffused with radiant energy, yet she drew it not from the sun, but from the questing heat of his mouth, the dark light of his eyes. He broke the kiss, and she sucked air into her lungs, hand flattening at the base of his throat. His pulse thundered through his jugular. He shared it, this storm of desire. Her excitement doubled. She stroked her palm down, over the solidity of his upper chest.

He caught her wrist. "Just there." He met her eyes, smiling wickedly as she jerked a nod.

"And how is this?" he murmured, fingers sliding to the crease of her thigh, fanning across her lower belly and teasing through the curls. "Here?"

He stroked the slippery inner flesh. A liquid sensation rolled through her, thick and sweet as glycerin. She collapsed forward, pressed her forehead to his, gasping as his finger stirred impossible sensation.

"Quick?" he asked, demonstrating. "Or slow?"

"Both," she gasped, but the slow strokes were torture, so a moment later she was moaning: "Quick, please. Quick."

She pulsed, her body seeming to tighten and dissolve at the same time. With a cry, she began to undulate against him, unable to curb the pleasure rising within her. Movements, noises—they were beyond her control. He stood, lifting her with him, water sluicing down, and pulled her up into his arms. Suddenly, she was sprawled on her back on fluffy towels in the bed, and he was pressing her down, heavy and urgent, his tongue deep in her mouth, his hand buried between her thighs.

She almost wished she'd said *slow*, that she could soften and sustain the quivers moving down from her belly, but she'd waited so long, for him, for this feeling—unlike any she'd ever known. She couldn't wait more. He had her on a knife's edge, tense and wild, and she was going to scream if he wasn't quicker, if he kept her there, if she couldn't tip over into bliss.

"Kit." His name was a plea. She moaned it as her spine arched, head pressing the mattress. He gave a purr of satisfaction and pulled back. Roughly, he hooked her legs over his shoulders, canted up her hips. She felt the tickle of his wet hair on her thighs, then his mouth latched, and she was lost. The whirlpool of pleasure sucked away all reason.

Sometime in the night, she woke up, alone in the bed, and for a few untethered moments, she didn't know where she was. She bolted upright. Before memory returned, Griffith rejoined her, and with him a strange comfort, as though she'd found something, or been found herself.

20

"BEHOLD!"

Griffith accelerated away from her, sprinting on his bicycle down the shady street.

"Behold what?" Muriel flew past primrose-covered villas, and out of the tunnel of elms, into the sunlight. He'd crossed a patch of grass and stopped to gaze down the steep slope at the shimmering blue of Falmouth Bay. He wore a crestfallen expression.

"The bay?" she asked, rolling up beside him. This was their first glimpse of it. They'd followed the coast around the Lizard, then swung inland at the Helford River, traveling the last miles to Falmouth through a verdant landscape of creeks and cornfields.

"It's picturesque," she offered. In his moody state, he was picturesque as well. Sulkiness did something unholy to his mouth. Warmth rushed through her, unrelated to the hours of continuous exercise.

Last night, that mouth had done unholy things to her.

She turned her flushed face into the breeze. "Is the inn nearby?"

He shook his head. "The inn's by the harbor."

"Then why are we here?"

"To hunt for seaweed on those rocks." He made a desultory gesture.

"Erm." She peered. The bay sloshed placidly below. "What rocks would those be?"

"Those magnificent, limpet-plastered rocks that you can't see because they're underwater." He knuckled a lock of hair off his forehead, pushing it under his cap with a grimace. "Falmouth has several beaches. Swanpool and Gyllyngvase are big and sandy and crawling with families. This one, which I swear to you exists—at low tide, anyway—is particularly interesting to algologists. Algologists? Bugger. *Algologist* is hard to say, even if you're not three sheets to the wind."

"You brought us here to hunt for seaweed." Suddenly, she was smiling, an over-wide, very silly smile. "What about the look on Deighton's face?"

"I will relish it when I see it." He shrugged. "But I realized I was far more eager to relish the look on *your* face. The look of delight when you beheld this . . ." The grimace returned. "This beach."

She couldn't contain herself. The boom of her laughter startled a seagull into flight. "You should see your own face. It's utterly forlorn."

"Is that so?" His brows lowered.

"Adorably forlorn," she revised, and his brows lowered further.

"You find my face funny." He leaned toward her, putting his face close to hers. "Or perhaps something is tickling the secret ticklish region of your body that I've mercifully made no attempt to locate."

"Is that a threat?" she whispered. Before he could answer, she was pitching herself off her bicycle. He lunged, and she shrieked and ran parallel to the bay, weaving around the daisies. He gained on her quickly, so she changed tack, bounding down the slope to the lapping waves. Here the bay hadn't swallowed the beach completely. She lurched along a narrow band of dry shingle, struggling to keep her footing. She heard his crunching steps, then his amused voice sounded in her ear.

"I thought you were nimble like a mountain goat."

"How nimble are *you*?" She gave him a shove. His arm shot out, and he tottered, swinging her with him. Her feet left the ground as they spun, locked together. When he set her down in the wet sand, he was laughing, staggering to keep his balance.

"I'm *fabulously* nimble." He wheezed. "If there were a candlestick, I'd jump right over." He jumped in place, sinking before he lifted up, and even then, barely leaving the ground.

"Hard to jump in sand," he muttered.

She rolled her eyes, then raced—nimbly—for the shingle as cool surf began to flow around her shoes. A moment later, he joined her.

She crouched to examine a shell, a peachy cowrie, no bigger than a fingertip.

"We could stroll," she suggested when she'd caught her breath. "See what we discover."

"Which way?"

She chose to walk toward the isthmus. He fell into step beside her, linking their elbows.

"No tickling," she warned him.

"Indeed not."

"I appreciate your forbearance." Her gaze glued itself to his gloved hand.

At dawn, she'd stirred and realized he was already awake, propped behind her, lazily stroking her hair. She'd slid her thighs together restlessly, unable to ask for what she wanted, until his calloused fingers had skated down her hip and worked the hard knot at the top of her opening, plunging inside as everything loosened, and cries burst from her lips.

"Self-preservation."

"Hmm?" She gave a little shake, looking up.

"It's self-preservation, not forbearance," he said wryly. "I know when I've met my match."

The light playing on his irises turned them to liquid silver.

On a shaky breath, she faced forward. The isthmus rose precipitously from the sun-spangled water, rock transitioning to wooded hillside. A castle stood on the hills' summit, like something from a fairy tale.

"Camelot," she murmured, half-dreamily, half in jest.

"A popular artistic subject," he remarked, after a pause. His voice was mild, but his biceps had tensed, and his stride changed rhythm.

"One of yours?" She stole a sidelong look at his profile.

"Oh, yes. The artists I grew up admiring painted knights and enchantresses. I had to try my hand at it."

"And?"

"*I am half sick of shadows,*" he said, in a manner she recognized, from James.

"You're quoting. From a poem?"

"By Tennyson. 'The Lady of Shalott.' Do you know it? The Lady is imprisoned in a tower, forbidden to look on Camelot directly. She must sit and weave the scenes she sees in her mirror. Eventually, she rebels. The reflected sight of a pair of lovers stirs her, and then Lancelot, who rides by on a warhorse. She leaves her loom. She leaves her tower. And for that, she dies."

"Golly." Muriel directed her frown at the castle. "You painted the unfortunate Lady?"

"I did a whole series. The Pre-Raphaelites all made drawings of her. In their illustrations, she's powerless by her loom, or floating dead in the river. I took more liberties with the poem."

"*I am sick to the back teeth of shadows.*" Muriel tipped her head. "I'd like it if the Lady said something emphatic, then galloped away on Lancelot's warhorse."

"You'd have liked my pictures, then."

"I've no doubt of that."

The silence between them felt warm and comfortable.

"The Pre-Raphaelites," she ventured. "I've heard of them."

"From people telling you that you look like you belong in one of their paintings?"

That was it, exactly.

She flushed. "Also, I've seen *Ophelia*, by Millais. He's a Pre-Raphaelite, isn't he?"

"One of the founders of the Brotherhood."

"It's an extraordinary picture, botanically speaking. I could have looked at the riverbank all day. The plant life seemed infinitely detailed." Her brow puckered. "Of course, there was death at the center of the thing. Another floating woman. Do I detect a theme?" She paused. "And does something about me suggest a watery grave?"

"It's your hair." He slanted a gaze at her. "The women in their paintings have long, thick, wavy hair, often red."

"My hair isn't *red*," she sputtered. "Have you ever looked at me?" She shut her eyes. "What color are my eyes?"

"Your hair gives off a reddish glimmer."

"My eyes."

"Brown. With a belligerent glimmer."

She opened them and blinked away the sparkles. The afternoon air had a dazzling clarity.

"What about *my* eyes?" He bent over her, batting his lashes. She laughed and was still laughing when she intercepted his kiss.

How did he know how to kiss like that? Like casting a spell and issuing an invitation. The buzzing was in her ears, not bees—every particle of her being, rearranging.

"Your eyes are also brown, are they not?" Her breath hitched as they stepped apart, ruining her delivery.

He raised an ironic brow. "It seems you are no close observer of my person. Shall I come closer still?" He moved toward her.

She skipped back, scandalized, and as happy as she'd ever been. "We're abroad, in daylight."

"We are," he conceded, glancing about the deserted shore. "Quite correct." He halted on the approach and held out his arm.

They began to walk again toward the castle.

"It occurs to me," he said. "You can see my Lady of Shalott, if you're inclined. Several of my Arthurian paintings sold to an American dry goods magnate with a private gallery on Fifth Avenue. I've heard he puts on excellent exhibitions."

She felt a bittersweet rush of emotion. Months from now, she might stand in a great gilded room, surrounded by strangers, and look upon pictures that recalled her to this golden afternoon.

"I'll make it a point to attend."

"How long will you stay in New York?" He sounded nonchalant.

"Indefinitely." She gave him a bright smile. "I'm going to teach botany at an academy for women."

"Wonderful," he murmured, with undoubtable sincerity. "And you have friends there?"

She looked away. *Friends* overstated it. "Fellow botanists. We write to each other and exchange our findings. I became friendly with the Satterlee sisters when they were researching in England. They founded the academy. They're the ones who arranged for my position." She looked back at him. "And the ones who set up my original lecture at Clinton Hall."

He nodded slowly. "What do they think of that fellow's meddling?"

Good question.

"I don't know. I haven't had a letter since it happened." She stopped walking and slipped her arm from his. "They're members of his botanical society—the Heywood Botanical Society. It's the most important botanical society in the whole United States. They depend on his connections for their fundraising. They've been equipping a lab, modeled on the Balfour Biological Laboratory for Women at Cambridge. It's an expensive project. Whatever they think, they're probably best advised to keep it to themselves."

Griffith's forehead creased as though he meant to object.

She turned to the bay. "They look like chicken coops."

He turned as well and tracked her gaze. "Bathing machines?"

A lone bathing machine stood a few yards away, a wooden hut on wheels, the waves washing nearly as high as the hubs.

He shook his head, a smile flitting across his lips.

"What?" She crossed her arms. "I know that look." Her cheeks scalded. "Good Lord. In a bathing machine? Really?"

"Penny." He widened his eyes. "Your mind goes to such places."

"I'm wrong?"

He sighed.

"What was her name?"

He turned his gaze up to the clouds. "Becky."

She snorted, and he dropped his gaze to her face, amused.

"I was thirteen," he said. "My family was on holiday in Ramsgate. She and I went into the bathing machine together."

Muriel's eyes wandered back to the bathing machine in front of them. Anything could go on inside those dark, hot little changing rooms, even in the middle of a crowded beach, with no one the wiser.

She gripped her elbows. "Pray continue."

"We'd only met the day before, but we were already in love. Well, puppy love." He laughed. "We changed into our bathing costumes in a white heat, to make the most of the time, the three jostling minutes it took for the horse to tow us past the breakers. No opportunity had ever been so perfect. Maybe it was too perfect. For some reason, I couldn't kiss her. I froze completely. She waited for as long as possible. Our driver began to shout, so she opened the door and jumped into the sea, without a backward glance. That was it. From then on, she avoided me like the plague."

She looked at him, trying to gauge his seriousness. "Did you mind dreadfully?"

"My suffering lasted about as long as our love. It was a bad day and a half." He shrugged. "I was a bit callow back then. Anyway, we weren't meant to be."

"Too perfect," she mused, eyes back on the bathing machine. Her heart began to race. "What would you say to another chance at perfection?"

KIT DIDN'T TAKE her meaning. It wasn't until she marched into the surf, casting a teasing glance over her shoulder, that the penny dropped.

He pursued her, then, with all deliberate speed, waves pushing against his shins.

Inside the bathing machine, he turned to pull the shore-facing door closed, and to pull off his leather gloves, which he rolled tightly together, one inside the other, and tucked beneath the waistband of his knickerbockers, into the pocket sewn into the front of his drawers.

When he turned to Muriel, he could hear his blood rushing through his veins. The space was small, and hot, and dim, and smelled of old sun-warmed wood. She was standing with her back to the other door, her hat in her hands, stray wisps of hair framing her face. She looked equal parts eager and nervous. The hat went around and around, the brim rotating through her fingers. The tip of her tongue swept the inner rim of her lower lip, leaving it damp.

"Becky could have kissed *you*," she said, voice sounding oddly hushed in the little room.

He stretched up his arms and put his palms on the rough wood boards of the ceiling. "Neither of us thought of that."

"Why not?"

He dropped his arms. "We were thirteen."

She nodded as her dark gaze assessed him.

"You're thinking something," he murmured.

Carefully, she hung her hat on one of the hooks in the wall, lingering a beat too long. With a sharp breath, she faced him. Two steps, and she launched into his arms. The impact knocked him back against the door, which held, thank God, and both of her gloved hands pressed hard on his nape. She dragged his head down, thrusting up onto her toes. Her lips crushed against his, slightly off-center, wet heat at the corner of his mouth, and then she corrected, her tongue stroking inside. It was the clumsiest, most arousing kiss of his life. He half laughed, half groaned, and let her plunder him. She seeped into all his senses, the taste and the feel of her inseparable from the breathy sounds, the indefinably sweet scent. He kept his need leashed, until her teeth scraped his bottom lip, and he reacted, pushing forward, fusing their mouths.

The atmosphere changed around them. The heat thickened. Time slowed. His fingertips glided over her silky cheekbones, her sweat-glazed throat. Her convulsive gasp shuddered something loose inside him. He dropped onto one of the changing benches, pulling her down, gripping her bottom as she straddled his thighs, skirts bunching.

"You're thinking something," she gasped. Her eyes were wide and dazed, her mouth glistening.

"I'm thinking I'm glad I'm not thirteen," he said, and hitched her higher. A little cry escaped her, and he knew she could feel the bulge of his rolled gloves between her legs. He could feel it too, rubbing his groin as she rocked her hips.

"What is that?" she panted.

"Something to please us." He flexed, driving up, and she moaned and ground harder against him. "Do you feel pleased?"

"I could be more pleased." She struggled for breath, twining her arms around his neck, a smile stealing across her lips.

"Is that a challenge?" He bloody well hoped so. "What if I please you more?" He flexed again, muscles hard as adamant. She sighed, eyes fluttering closed. "And more?"

She kissed him, a voluptuous, open-mouthed kiss.

He broke away. "And more?"

Her forehead fell onto his shoulder, and she bore down, stroking herself back and forth, the friction between them discharging sparks. They both shuddered with it. He imagined tearing her bodice like paper, baring her completely and luxuriating in her flesh. Every contour. Every texture. But here, now, the layers of silk and cotton and woolen twill added to the pleasure. Seams and buttons bit at them, and that pleasing leather dragged sensation from him to her, and her to him. His climax hit him like a storm. He jolted and gave a guttural shout, and she stiffened, inner thighs clamping hard enough to bruise. When she'd shivered and slumped, he lazed with her on his lap, arm under her skirt, fingers caressing the downy skin above her garters. The pad of his thumb traveled up and circled, moving in time with her slow, extravagant pulses.

Clouds of lust still billowed in his brain. He let his eyelids droop, memorizing her shape, the feel and weight of her. He'd sat up half the night at the table, looking at her, and looking at his sketchbook— the paper dry despite the sodden clothing at the top of his knapsack, which he'd laid out by the fire. The marks he'd finally made were depressingly inadequate. The room had been low-lit, and he'd tried to rely on shading. He'd focused on her hair spread in shining ripples on the pillow—to no avail. He'd thrummed with the urge—the old urge—to draw, to paint, to express what he saw and felt in the visual language he'd studied for more than half his life. She was naked in the bed, all lines and curves and rich tones, her strong features languid, and he knew exactly how to translate the dreamlike moment, how to compose it, how to give it depth.

And he could not. He could not.

He'd guided them to Castle Beach, steeled for another confrontation with the page. He wasn't sorry that it would wait for another day.

She seemed to sense that his mood had shifted. She brushed her lips across his neck, and then her tongue coaxed his attention back to the present.

———

BY THE HARBOR, Falmouth bustled, streets choked with sailors. The inn was a dingy building sandwiched between an ironmonger's and a ship chandler's, the windows of the latter papered with advertisements in half a dozen languages. He locked their bicycles in the back courtyard, then they entered the inn itself, a warren of darkly paneled corridors and dusty rooms that gave off the warm, yeasty smell of old beer. As Muriel inspected the display of model boats, he rang the ship's bell by the desk and inquired after rooms. The proprietor didn't have their names in his register. Deighton actually presumed they'd thrown in the sponge. With a suppressed snort, Kit made a reservation—two rooms, for appearance's sake. One last rotation through the inn confirmed that the wheelmen were elsewhere.

Elsewhere seemed a good place to be. He and Muriel wandered back out into the town. They ate pilau at a curry house near the quay, then wound their way to the shops. Muriel found a drapery that sold dresses off the rack and stopped to make a purchase. He bought Valencia oranges from a grocer, and they continued on with their parcels, circling back toward the harbor, or so he surmised from the increasingly potent odor of tar and rotten fish.

When the water came into view, Deighton came into view as well. He was a head taller than the men surrounding him, and so Kit had ample opportunity to observe his darkening expression as their gazes clashed.

"Oh dear," murmured Muriel.

A small crowd had gathered around a post upon which two men had planted their elbows. One was Kemble. The other was a thickset sailor in a scarlet cap. It took a moment to realize the wrestling had begun, they were both so still and silent. Kemble's veins made a bulging map on his forehead. The sailor's lips had peeled back.

Deighton cracked his neck as Kit and Muriel approached.

"Here you are, then," he said.

"Here we are." Kit smiled.

"Use your legs!" shouted Butterfield. "Damn it all, use your legs!"

"I don't know that you rode all the way south." Deighton's blue eyes looked hard as glass. "You might have cut east early."

"Orange?" asked Kit, plucking one from the bag.

"Yes, please," said Egg, reaching around from behind Deighton.

"Mrs. Pendrake!" Prescott had turned from the combatants. "Mr. Griffith," he added, in a more subdued tone.

"It's mandatory that you ride the entire distance," persisted Deighton.

"Check our cyclometers." Kit shrugged.

"You might have tampered with them."

Patience. With Deighton, patience came at a premium.

"We rode the entire distance," he said. "If my word doesn't suffice, you can examine the page I took from the register at the Top House Inn." He'd offered the puzzled innkeeper a pound to tear it out. "You'll trust your own signature, won't you?"

"Ingenious." Prescott looked impressed.

"He wasn't ingenious. He was ungentlemanly," Deighton snarled. "No one anticipates his word being doubted unless he's a liar and cheat."

"Or dealing with a liar and cheat," suggested Kit.

The crowd exploded into French-sounding hoots and hisses.

Kemble's arm had advanced by several inches.

"The hook!" shouted Butterfield. "Finish him with the hook!"

A laugh cut through the masculine uproar like bell song. It was a high, clear feminine laugh. Not Muriel's. She laughed like a flock of adorable geese.

He looked over his shoulder. A woman was gliding toward them. A dark-haired, flower-faced woman in a heavily trimmed biscuit-colored silk gown, with an underskirt of dusky rose.

Grace Swanwick, the diamond of the West End sapphists.

21

G LIDE ON.

He willed it as he faced front, heart pounding. Perhaps she
hadn't noticed him. Perhaps she'd been gazing at the ships in
the harbor. Perhaps she wasn't about to hail him with a name that
would cause the world to come crashing down.

"Mr. Griffith." Egg spoke around a mouthful of orange. "Do you
know the young lady?"

He pretended the contest absorbed him.

It did, in a way. A French sailor arm wrestling an English chappie
in sportswear, witnessed by a motley collection of crewmen hailing
from ports of call the whole world over. It was a fit subject for a
painting—not for a Pre-Raphaelite, perhaps. For a painter of modern
life.

"Mr. Griffith!" Egg spoke louder.

Hellfire.

Kit turned his head.

"Mr. Griffith," echoed Grace Swanwick.

He turned completely. She stood a foot away, and the knowledge
in her damselfly blue eyes was absolute.

"Miss Swanwick," he said.

Knowledge in her eyes, but not judgment. Hope and dread warred
in his chest.

Grace was unpredictable. She'd worked as an actress before Annie Groombridge had succeeded in wooing her from the stage, and her taste for drama knew no bounds. When Kit had met her, she was singing in Annie's Mayfair drawing room, the main attraction at the Hesperus Ladies Club's Saturday salon. They'd shared an instant rapport, which Annie had disliked at least as much as she'd disliked his trousers.

Had Annie come with her?

His eyes swept up the street. More sailors. Peddlers. Cornish women with baskets.

"I'd heard you'd gone to Cornwall." Grace's voice was pure and sweet. She could make a magistrate sob with a song.

Kit met her gaze. She'd lifted her manicured brows.

"But seeing you . . ." She twirled her parasol, allowing a theatrical pause, rosebud lips pursed, hand pressed to her shapely bosom. Kit realized that Deighton, Prescott, Egg, and several grinning sailors were hanging on her every word. "It is *quite* the surprise."

"I hope a pleasant one." Deighton stepped forward eagerly. "If not, but make it known, and I'll remove him from your company, and mine. I only fraternize with gentlemen."

Grace perused Deighton's person, from his monogrammed club cap to his canvas shoes. Her eyes swung back to Kit.

He caught his breath.

She smiled at Deighton. "No need to trouble yourself. Mr. Griffith is a perfect gentleman."

Kit exhaled through his nose.

"And you are?" Grace asked, still smiling. Kit glanced at Muriel. She was looking at Grace, her expression well-disposed and curious.

"Colin Deighton," said Deighton.

"Roger Butterfield!" cried Egg, at the same time, jostling Prescott, who'd also stepped forward.

"My wheelmen." Deighton glared as he acknowledged them.

Kit stopped tracking the introductions and explanations. His eyes had wandered up the street again. No Annie Groombridge. But there was Charlotte Tempest-Smythe, exiting a shop. Miranda Ellis followed. They headed his way.

Bugger.

"The hook! Dash it, man. The hook!" Butterfield began to shout again as the crowd erupted. Kit's head whipped around.

Kemble's opponent had forced their conjoined hands back to center.

Deighton rushed toward the post, clapping his arm around Butterfield's shoulder. Together, they bellowed insulting encouragement as a contingent of seamen in wooden clogs tried to drown them out by stomping the cobbles.

"Mr. Griffith." Grace drifted closer, addressing him alone, in a low, intimate tone. "But I can't call you *mister*. It's so . . . formal."

He hardly cared what she called him, or how she needled him, now that he felt assured she wouldn't let the wrong thing slip.

He shrugged. "Kit, then."

"Kit." Her eyes twinkled. "The surprise *is* pleasant. You've been missed at our salons. We wish you'd come back."

His smile had a cynical edge. "I doubt that's the prevailing opinion."

"Oh, don't let Annie sour you." She leaned even closer. "Henrietta hosts the salons now. *She* would be delighted by your presence. I'm sure she'll tell you so herself."

"Lady Chettam's here?" Kit's gaze flew up the street. Miranda and Charlotte had stopped to talk with a third woman he didn't recognize.

"I left her just now, at the curiosity shop. We're staying the week at the Falmouth Hotel. Henrietta. Myself. Amelia, Octavia, Rosanna, Miranda, Charlotte, Dorothea. Have you met Dorothea? You'll adore her. Who else? Hester and Celeste, of course. Virginia. You remember Virginia Potter? She's got a new mash. The girl looks exactly like Maggie, but you mustn't say so. We don't mention Maggie in front of either of them. Maggie is *not* here. Neither is Annie. Hardly any of us have seen her in months. *I* haven't. I moved out."

"And moved in with Lady Chettam," Kit guessed. It made a certain—dramatic—kind of sense as Grace's next move, leaving the grande dame of the Hesperus Ladies Club for her rival. Annie Groombridge and Lady Chettam had feuded before, over lovers, and over precepts, and the club had remained intact. But Grace was special. Annie had been besotted. "Is that why Doris and Mrs. McLaren aren't with you? There are factions?"

Grace sighed. "Some people are being silly. But everyone here is lovely, and that's what matters. You *must* pay us an evening visit."

Kit hesitated. "We're leaving early in the morning."

"I wasn't asking you to stay until morning." Grace peered up at him through her lashes. "Would you?"

The coquettishness was deliberately overdone.

His lips twitched. "Not a chance."

"I understand." She smoothed her mahogany chignon. "You're spoken for at the moment."

She cut her eyes at Muriel, who'd moved a ways off and sat on the steps of a stucco-fronted building, throwing dice with an elderly sailor.

He didn't realize he was wearing a moony expression until Grace laughed her musical laugh.

"It's all right," she said. "I'm spoken for too. You're both invited."

He hesitated again. Had she refused to grasp the fundamentals?

"You're inviting *me*," he murmured.

"Yes," she agreed.

"The gatherings are ladies only."

"Annie again." She made a face. "Silly goose. I think she's scared of toms."

"I've gone a bit beyond *tom*."

"So you have." She considered him.

"I don't intend to go back," he added quietly. "If I visit this evening, I visit as who I am."

She considered him for another moment.

"Well, then. Mr. Griffith." She nodded. "Half past nine."

She did glide on, her gait so smooth it seemed her feet didn't touch the cobbles. Kit's eyes bounced back to Muriel. His old and new lives had collided again. And yet, he didn't feel bruised this time, but rather bemused, and unexpectedly hopeful.

THE WARM NIGHT air was tipsy with the scent of wallflower and rose. Muriel found herself wishing the walk to the Falmouth Hotel were longer.

"Can we take a turn in the garden?" she asked Griffith, a figure of shadow and moonlight beside her. They could already see the lit-up hotel windows glowing through the trees.

"Let's," said Griffith, and linked their arms.

They fit together so well, strolling, their slow strides matched. When she kicked at her skirts, he pulled her into him, absorbing her little skip into their rhythmic pace. She kicked at her skirts often. She was glad she'd found a simple floral-print gown ready-made in her size, something to wear that wasn't shin-length with oil stains on the hem, but she struggled to readjust to all that cumbersome fabric about her ankles.

"I'm underdressed," she said grimly, picturing Miss Swanwick, beautiful and beribboned. For his part, Griffith had changed into an evening coat and trousers, his silk cravat folded crisply at his throat. It seemed he'd packed everything a man of fashion might require into that knapsack of his, except a top hat. He'd gone hatless, and left his hair unruly, which gave his elegance an appealingly raffish touch.

She almost wanted to see him stand again beside Miss Swanwick, to scratch some aesthetic itch. They made a gorgeous combination, like an iris paired with a peony.

She kicked at her skirt and sighed. "What if they won't let me through the door?"

"I'm more worried they'll try to keep you." There was a smile in his voice. "You will fascinate Octavia Jenkins."

"She takes an interest in botany?"

"She takes an interest in redheads."

"I'm not a redhead." She flushed. "You said they're a stargazing society."

He laughed. "That's what *they* say. I'm sure they stargaze from time to time, and Miranda Ellis writes horoscopes under a nom de plume. But it's a little joke. They're women born under the same star, so to speak."

Muriel slowed, looking up at the stars. "I've heard James use a similar expression. Men born under the same star. He also says *men for whom Greece is the holy land*. Or *men who are like the Greeks*. Because of something in Plato's *Symposium*. I haven't read it."

"A symposium was a drinking party." Griffith's voice turned dry. "Chaps got soused and said all sorts of things."

"You've read it?" She glanced at him from the corner of her eye. "But you don't care for the Greeks?"

"*Eros shook my mind,*" he murmured, "*like a mountain wind falling on oak trees.*"

His tone brought gooseflesh to her arms, as though a mountain wind really were blowing over them.

"That's Plato?" she breathed.

"That's Sappho, the greatest female poet of antiquity. Her poetry tells us more than Plato's philosophy about the creative life and the bittersweetness of desire. The Hesperus Ladies Club takes their name from one of her fragments. Sappho called Hesperus *of all stars the fairest.*"

"The evening star." Muriel stopped completely, head tipping further back. "I don't see it. There's the Plough. There's the North Star." She pointed. "That's your star, I think."

"The steadfast star?" He sounded amused. "My sweet, I'm far from constant."

It was a warning, gently put and worth heeding. He wouldn't be constant with her. But she'd meant something else, something deeper.

"I disagree." She started them walking forward again. "You've been committed to the same three things your entire life."

"Arrogance. Overconfidence. What was the third?"

"Art, love, and justice," she said softly. "Those are the three."

Silence stretched.

"That's rather grand, isn't it?" He shook his head, but his voice had a gratified gruffness. "Which star is yours?"

She studied the heavens, all the tiny white fires, impossibly distant.

"I've spent a lot of time like this, on ships at night, looking up. You feel doubly small, between the sky and the sea." For a moment, the turf seemed to rock beneath her, everything solid melting away. She leaned into him, anchoring herself with his warmth and strength. "When you're weeks on a steamer, there's nothing familiar but the stars. They make a pattern in the blankness, so you know you're somewhere instead of nowhere."

"Yours is the North Star too, then," he said. "The navigator."

Her throat swelled. She liked it too much, the idea that they shared a star.

"You *did* learn celestial navigation?" He nudged her, teasing. "Or did the sailors only teach you dice?"

"Teaching me dice was more lucrative for them." She giggled as she kicked her skirt, and he used it as an excuse to pull her all the way into an embrace. His fingers traced lightly up her ribs.

"I know what you're trying to do." She slapped at his hand. "It won't work."

His mouth pressed into her hair, and warm breath seeped to her scalp. She melted against him, and then his lips nuzzled her ear, and she gave a strangled shriek of laughter.

"It did work." His whisper tickled all the more.

She hadn't known her earlobes were so vulnerable. She writhed at the delicious torture, until he stopped her laughter with a kiss. He tasted of citrus and sorcery.

This already felt like part of her life. This ticklish, breathless joy. She could surrender to it, here, now. There was no harm in a thrilling summer fling.

So long as she didn't fall in love.

She wouldn't. She was resolved.

With a sigh, she wiggled from his arms and resumed the walk, her damp mouth tingling. "We'll be late."

"It's fashionable to be late." He caught up to her with a long stride. "But we can stargaze another night."

Another night. Seven remained, on the road. Seven more in St. Ives.

And then they'd part.

She turned her eyes on the hotel. "What goes on at meetings of the Hesperus Ladies Club?"

"A little of this, a little of that. There's food and drink, singing and dancing. Poetry recitations. Masques. Tableaux vivants. Bridge. Whist. Faro. The occasional lecture. The occasional lovers' quarrel." He sounded ever so slightly wistful.

"You went often?"

"Whenever I could." He paused. "Until the hostess forbade male attire."

She glanced at him. His jaw had clenched. "Why would she do so?"

"Several reasons, the most understandable being self-preservation. The neighbors were looking askance. At myself, Octavia, and Harry. I'm a dandy, as you know. Octavia dressed like a dragoon. Harry favored kilts." He gave a shrug. "Octavia switched to gowns with lace jabots, but Harry and I figured we'd rather bugger off. I'd been planning to relocate anyway. Not long after, I left for Cornwall."

"And became a man," she said, and blushed. "Maybe that's not the way to put it. Began to live as the man you always were." She blushed brighter. "I'm sorry if I've misspoken."

"Language is a crude medium." His teeth flashed, luminous in the dark. "Intention matters. Tonight, some of the ladies might call me by my old name, out of habit. And some might do so out of disrespect. I'd rather not hear that name, either way. But there's a difference."

Her shoulders had hitched with indignation. "It sounds like a continuum of disrespect to me. They should make the effort."

"My truculent one," he murmured. "Don't go scouring the grounds for acorns just yet. Perhaps they will make the effort. Miss Swanwick did."

"You're a man." She gnawed her lip. "You could join a gentlemen's club instead."

"And spend my evenings surrounded by gentlemen? It happens so often already. I'm not fond of men en masse." An ironic smile tipped up the corner of his mouth. "They're too embattled, always trying to prove their natural superiority, which gives the lie to the whole idea. The smart ones know it, so they're anxious *and* aggressive. I prefer the ladies of Hesperus."

Light from the lower hotel windows spilled onto the grass ahead. They passed in and out of bright squares, walking the length of the building toward the entrance.

"Your father's a successful businessman." She was thinking aloud. "Your mother wanted to wed you to a duke."

"A viscount would have done for her," he said dryly. "But yes, in essence."

Her brow furrowed. He'd grown up with every luxury, in one of London's affluent districts. Towering plane trees enclosing quiet streets. Redbrick townhomes built around garden squares.

Eyes and ears monitoring a daughter's every move.

"Didn't they have you closely guarded?" she asked.

"Apparently not, if I cavorted with sapphists." His eyes met hers, silvery with mischief. "But that's your question, isn't it? Did I elude my protection officers, or were my parents unfathomably lenient?"

"Your mother mustn't have been." Muriel remembered what he'd said of her. "She forced you to take deportment classes. She was trying to fit you into a mold."

"For a time. Mine was the stronger will." He raised a shoulder and let it drop. She knew he was willful. At the moment, he seemed pensive.

"Not to mention my father undermined her at every turn," he continued, a line between his brows. "He comes from a stolid West Midlands family of carpet manufacturers. No one wanted him to go to London, to dabble in finance. They swore he'd end up bankrupt and bedeviled. He felt like the black sheep. I think it made him tolerant of nonconformity. And my notoriety didn't hurt his reputation in the city. He's notorious himself, after a fashion. Known for wild investment schemes and unorthodox ideas. He likes thumbing his nose at polite society. He supported my enrolling in the Royal Academy Schools. Eventually, I lopped my hair and started running up bills at the tailors', wearing three-piece suits to dinner. Even then, he didn't balk. He called it *enterprising*."

Griffith grinned and brushed his hair back from his forehead. A lock sprang forward. If they had more nights together—a hundred, or a thousand—she'd brush that lock back herself, again and again. She'd become accustomed to the silken feel of it against her palm, and the skin of her inner thighs.

She swallowed. "What did your mother call it?"

"*Enterprising* wasn't the word." His grin faded. "The day I cut my hair she went sick to bed, and the next evening she sent false curls to my room. She wanted me to pin them on when I went to church and to balls. I obliged for several years. On my twenty-sixth birthday, I told her I was finished. No more church. No more society parties. I stopped sleeping at home."

"Those garrets in Chelsea," she sighed, with a flutter of her lashes. As she'd hoped, his grin resurfaced.

"I spent most nights on a cot in a friend's studio." Humor sparked in the depths of his eyes. "My mother took it badly—at first. But within a few weeks of my moving out, she'd transferred her energies to her dishwashing machine and quite forgotten me."

Muriel's brows winged upward. "Did I hear you correctly? She transferred her energies to her *dishwashing machine*? Not to her nieces or her cocker spaniel?"

"Dishwashing machine." He nodded. "She hates it when the servants chip the china. The machine is for washing dishes without excessive handling. You place them on wire racks that rotate on a wheel inside a boiler as a pump sprays hot water and soap."

"This machine works?" Muriel blinked. "She built it?"

"It works, and she's built several versions—or had them built. She doesn't hammer the metal, but she designed the thing, and it's bloody brilliant. If she were a man, she'd work as an engineer." He shook his head. "I can't even convince her to apply for a patent. She wants my father to do it."

He looked frustrated.

"Your mother is technological," said Muriel, musing. "You must have her to thank for your aptitude with bicycles."

His frustration transformed into startlement. "I suppose. I never thought of it that way. She disapproves of women bicycling." He frowned and laughed at the same time. "But she could probably improve on the Rover if she put half her mind to it. At the least, she could invent a better luggage carrier. Perhaps I should ask her."

"Would you really?"

"Good God, no." He crossed his arms. "I try not to introduce any unnecessary surprises into our correspondence. And I don't plan on visiting anytime soon, or anytime ever. In letters, I can omit. In person, I'd have to compromise."

She scrutinized his face. There it was, the willfulness. She could see it in the set of his jaw.

He caught her looking and smiled. "My brothers established a precedent for long absence. We're already a family that exists mostly on paper."

"Where are they? Your brothers?"

"Argentina. They're heavily involved in railways and refrigerated beef. I don't think they'll ever settle back in England. They both married Anglo-Argentine women. I've little to say to my brothers, so I fill my letters with illustrations of owls and hedgehogs for the children." They were moving through a pool of light, and she saw his features sharpen. "I haven't written in a while."

They'd almost reached the steps that led to the hotel's main entrance.

"My studio felt more like home to me than the house where I was raised," he said. "And my Sisters in art felt more like family than my kinspeople. The ladies of the Hesperus Club felt like family too. I couldn't talk to them about painting, but I could breathe among them, without the weight of the assumptions that pressed me everywhere else."

Muriel nodded. Their lives had been so different. But she understood what he meant. "The heath was home to me," she said quietly. "Not the rooms over my cousin's shop."

"You chose heath plants as your family?" The tenderness of his smile made her heart squeeze.

"And James. He rode on the heath. We'd meet by the pond and talk. But I never felt lonely there, even when I was alone."

They'd climbed the steps. In front of the door, he turned to her. "Did you often feel lonely?"

His expression was serious. Pale fire shone in his eyes. Her heart squeezed harder.

As a child, she'd studied and stroked and sniffed every flower and tuft of grass, so they could grow in her mind when she was back at her deadening labors or lying in the dark under the slope of the roof. But nothing kept the loneliness at bay for long.

Sometimes she'd wanted to howl from the ache of it.

He read the answer in her face and touched the pad of his thumb to her cheek. "Do you still feel lonely?"

She hesitated, chest constricting. She controlled her life now. It was, by and large, the life she wanted. And yes, the ache persisted, often below her notice.

Not when she was with him.

Music was filtering through an open window.

She tipped her head toward the sound. Given the grandness of the hotel, she expected the strains of melody to resolve into a chamber work by Haydn, Mendelssohn, or Mozart. Instead, she heard voices mount into a raucous chorus.

Her brows came together. "That isn't *Pirates of Penzance*?"

Griffith's gaze kept smoldering. But after a moment, he smiled, allowing the deflection.

"Lady Chettam is fond of comic opera." He turned back to the door and tugged it open. "We'll follow our ears."

Their ears—and a lanky, eager-to-please porter—led them between pillars and across the tiled mosaic floor of the hotel's entrance hall to a private drawing room.

Inside, chandeliers twinkled, casting specks of starry light onto the occupants, most of them on their feet, swaying with their arms around each other's waists or clapping their hands. A tall woman in a red guardsman's jacket strutted between the armchairs, belting words with astounding velocity.

"*In short, in matters vegetable, animal, and mineral, I am the very model of a modern Major-General!*"

The woman spun on her heel, saw Griffith, and cut off her song.

22

〜

MURIEL EXPECTED GRIFFITH to saunter forward and greet his old friends. Instead, he stood rooted in place, meeting the fixed stares with a fixed stare of his own. She realized in a flash that no one was prepared to break the silence. With every passing moment, the hesitancy on both sides deepened into an impasse.

Her mouth opened.

"*I know our mythic history, King Arthur's and Sir Caradoc's!*" The next lines of the song burst from her before she could think. "*I answer hard acrostics, I've a pretty taste for paradox.*"

She swung her gaze to Griffith, who looked frankly shocked.

She barreled on. "*I quote in elegiacs all the crimes of Heliogabalus.*"

Dear Lord, it was a mouthful. What followed? Songs from *Pirates of Penzance* were ubiquitous, but she'd never consciously committed them to memory.

The woman in the guardsman's jacket raised her voice. "*In conics I can floor peculiarities parabolous.*" Her brown eyes twinkled.

Muriel took a step toward her. She could feel her heart beating in her throat, but it didn't stop the words from emerging.

"*I can tell undoubted Raphaels from Gerard Dows and Zoffanies.*" A beat, and she had the rhyme. "*I know the croaking chorus from* The Frogs *of Aristophanes!*"

The woman in the guardsman's jacket was grinning now. She picked up the song where Muriel left off, gesturing to the assembled ladies. They began to chorus. The frozen room exploded into warmth and motion. A whippet-thin girl with sleek brown hair darted forward and grabbed Muriel's hands. Another girl, blond and cherubic, seized Griffith. Everyone was linking hands, forming a ragged circle, rushing as one toward the center, then hopping back, bumping the furniture. The song grew louder and faster as it raced to its conclusion. By the time the circle broke apart, Muriel's sides were splitting. She accepted the whippet-thin brunette's applause with an off-kilter curtsey and blushed as the woman in the guardsman's jacket gave her a salute. She looked for Griffith. He'd ended up near the piano. His hair was wilder, and he was slouching slightly, the picture of insouciant grace. He glanced at her with a crooked smile, and then the ladies surrounded him, all speaking at once. Affectionate exclamations pattered between eager questions. The cherubic blonde dropped onto the piano stool and banged a jaunty tune. Some remark made Griffith laugh.

All was well.

Satisfied, and far too sweaty, Muriel headed for the terrace. Three of the women intercepted her, their perfume preceding them as they swarmed, abuzz with friendly introductions.

"Champagne?" The fair one in pearls pressed a glass into her hand.

Muriel murmured her thanks, trying to match the woman with one of the names. Amelia Clarkson, she thought. A darker woman with straight black brows skewered her with a gaze.

"Are you a Gemini?" she asked.

"I'm not sure." Muriel blinked. This had to be Miranda Ellis. "I was born on the eighth of October."

"Libra." Miss Ellis and Miss Clarkson exchanged a speaking glance.

"Is that bad?" asked Muriel.

"Oh, no," said Miss Ellis. "None of the signs are bad."

A second speaking glance.

"None are wholly bad," she amended. She looked toward Griffith, so Muriel did too. He was in conversation with Miss Swanwick—resplendent in low-cut, crimson silk—and a smaller, older woman, the silver streaks in her dark hair glittering under the lights like her diamond earbobs.

"Kate is a Leo," said Miss Ellis.

"It could be worse," added Miss Clarkson.

"Kit." Muriel looked at Miss Ellis. "He goes by Kit."

"Kit," Miss Ellis agreed, easily. "Of course. Grace told us. Tonight, I used his natal chart to make a few calculations. You might find this interesting." She allowed a pregnant pause. "Jupiter is transiting his seventh house."

Muriel couldn't help herself. She pounced on the bait. "What does that mean?"

"Marriage," piped up Miss Clarkson.

"Or something like." Miss Ellis lifted her magnificent brows.

The two exchanged yet another speaking glance.

Muriel gave a tiny shake of her head and tried to speak lightly. "It would take more than Jupiter, don't you think? To make a person want to settle down?"

"Oh, but he does want to settle down," said Miss Ellis, with a mysterious smile.

"He told you that?" Muriel lowered her voice. She needn't have. Griffith was now on the other side of the room, as though by flitting about he meant to disprove Miss Ellis's claim.

"His chart told me." Miss Ellis fingered the shell cameo at her throat, of a Greek goddess, by the look of it. Or Sappho, perhaps.

"His chart." Muriel sipped her champagne, wondering if Miss Ellis was having her on.

"Kit's moon is in Cancer," offered Miss Clarkson.

Miss Ellis nodded. "He's strong but sensitive. Emotional stability is essential."

"I am a Cancer," interjected the third woman, Charlotte Something-Something. "I'm desperately sensitive. For example, Mrs. Pendrake, I cannot think you intended to slight me just now, but I cannot help but *feel* slighted."

"Charlotte," scolded Miss Clarkson.

"*Amelia*," retorted Charlotte Something-Something. "We both brought her refreshment, but she took yours and ignored me completely. Now I'm stuck holding two champagnes, like a jilted squire at a country ball."

"I'm sorry?" Muriel's forehead flexed. Charlotte Something-Something had a pretty face and a sulky mouth, and she was indeed holding two glasses. "The champagne was in my hand before I knew it."

"Because Amelia is an Aries. She must be first in everything." Charlotte Something-Something sighed. Miss Clarkson pursed her lips.

"I'm not upset, truly, with anyone," Charlotte Something-Something continued. "The sting has worn off. Here you are, my dear."

She passed a champagne to Muriel. Now Muriel was the one holding two glasses. She smiled at the women, wondering if they were all of them having her on.

"Hot as hades in here." The Major-General herself strode up to them, divested now of her jacket but no less martial in appearance. Her upright carriage was augmented by a long, tightly fitted cuirass bodice, gray as armor. "Does anyone care to join me as I seek fresher air?"

No one did, except Muriel, and so she and the Major-General stepped together onto the shadowy terrace.

"Call me Octavia." When she wasn't spouting rapid-fire nonsense in character, Octavia spoke with a slow, silky drawl. "I hear you're a bicycling botanist."

Muriel acknowledged this with a nod. "And you are a singer?"

"Seriocomic vocalist." Octavia struck a pose. "Music hall sensation. Star of the stage." She winked. "Did you recognize me?"

"Only your talent," said Muriel, politely. "Champagne?"

"No, thank you." Octavia lifted her own glass. "I usually drink one at a time."

"So do I," Muriel assured her. She contemplated the glasses in her hands with bemusement. "This has something to do with the zodiac."

The first notes of a quadrille tinkled merrily from the parlor.

Muriel raised her eyes and looked through the open doors. Couples had formed in the center of the room. Griffith was paired with an elfin young woman, slim and ethereal, with a pointy chin and a cloud of nut-brown curls. They passed close to the doors as they promenaded.

"Our newest member." Octavia followed Muriel's gaze. "Mrs. Dorothea Yarrow. Care to supplant her?"

"What?" Muriel curled her fingers more tightly around the stems of the glasses.

"As our freshman." Octavia's voice grew even silkier. "I'm delighted to propose you. Grace will second."

Muriel's gaze swerved from the dancers. "Me? A member of the Hesperus Ladies Club?"

She met Octavia's dancing dark eyes.

"I couldn't," she said, stiff with awkwardness. "I . . . I don't live in London."

"How disappointing." Octavia raised a brow. "I'd hoped you spent the colder months in town, when the plants are too withered by frost to be of interest."

This was wrongheaded on so many counts, Muriel laughed. "That's not how it works."

Octavia leaned closer. She really was quite tall, neither young nor old, and undeniably handsome. She smelled of sandalwood. "You're telling me tonight's all we have."

Muriel blinked. Was that what her comment had communicated? Carpe diem? Her head felt fuzzy, although she'd only drunk half a glass of champagne.

"I should tell you I'm not a sapphist." She blurted it out, then bit her lip.

Octavia pulled back slightly, a lazy smile playing over her generous mouth. "All right. Tell me." Her gaze turned wicked. "Like you mean it."

"I'm not . . ." Muriel gulped champagne, emptying the glass in her right hand. Heaven help her. "That is, I don't fancy . . ." She hesitated. She'd meant to say *women*. But did that imply she *did* fancy men, categorically? Throughout her life, she'd felt frissons with all sorts of people—because she admired their intelligence, or sensibility. If there was sometimes a physical component, well, she hadn't ever pursued it, until now. Or rather, she had with Esmé, but she'd found those brief, labored relations in the marriage bed oddly distancing.

She wasn't a sapphist, but maybe she wasn't anything else either.

"I don't fancy," she said, with a hard stop. That came closest to the truth. She looked again into the parlor. Griffith and Miss Yarrow were twirling. "Not enough to join a club based on the type of fancying I do."

Not unless there was a Kit Griffith Ladies Club.

Which, Lord above, there probably was.

The second glass of champagne now seemed indispensable and brilliant. She tipped it back.

"Enough to try out something new?" Octavia's flirtatious drawl sounded close to her ear.

Muriel's whole body tensed. The scent of sandalwood enveloped her.

"Octavia!" The cry came from the direction of the lawn. "What are you doing? You're too bad!"

Muriel swiveled. Two women—blond or graying, Muriel couldn't tell which—were marching toward them over the grass. The one who'd spoken pulled out in front, shaking a bouquet of heliotropes.

"I don't believe in *too bad*," called Octavia, but she slinked away from Muriel, palpably reluctant. "What were *you* doing out there in the hedges?"

"Stargazing," replied the woman with the bouquet, as her companion caught up with her and gasped out her own answer: "Flower picking!"

They were both blondes, Muriel could see that now. And both disheveled.

She blushed.

Octavia laughed.

"Virginia Potter." The woman with the bouquet drew up to Muriel. "You must be Lucy. I'm so glad to finally meet you."

"Muriel," corrected Octavia swiftly. "This is Muriel Pendrake."

"Oh dear." Miss Potter looked aghast. "That's what Grace said, isn't it? Muriel." She smoothed her messy hair with her free hand. "I've had *Lucy* lodged in my head. Kate used to go on and on about a Lucy."

"Kit." Muriel murmured it automatically.

"I've got all the names wrong tonight." Miss Potter gave Muriel an apologetic smile.

"This is Tilly Beresford," said Octavia, motioning at the other blonde, while cutting her eyes at Miss Potter. "Lest Virginia misspeak."

"Lovely evening." Miss Beresford beamed at them each in turn. *She* was lovely, with a rounded figure decorated with bows, some of which appeared to have been undone and hastily retied. Her big eyes rested on Muriel. "You're Lucy? An absolute delight to make your acquaintance. Virginia, give Lucy a heliotrope."

Octavia cleared her throat.

Oblivious, Miss Beresford plucked at Miss Potter's bouquet, then lifted a stem of purple blossoms to her dainty nose.

"We've imbibed rather a lot of champagne," confessed Miss Potter. "Smuggled a bottle down to the beach."

"We wanted to put a note in it," giggled Miss Beresford. "And throw it into the sea. But we hadn't paper and pen." She came forward to give Muriel the flower. "Oh." She stopped, looking between the glasses in Muriel's hands. "You like champagne too. Well, how's this?" She put the flower in the empty glass.

"Thank you." Muriel smiled weakly.

Lucy.

The first word Griffith had ever said to her. The name on his lips when she knelt beside him in the field. The woman he went on and on about.

Jealousy niggled, uncomfortable and unfamiliar. And foolish.

She and Griffith had no future. Why let his past torment her?

"There you are!" Miss Swanwick sailed onto the terrace, carrying with her the parlor's heat and heavy perfume. "And in good company, thank God." She took Muriel by the elbow and lowered her voice to a stage whisper. "I was afraid you were alone out here with Octavia. She's the worst flirt in the kingdom. An absolute menace. I must bring you back inside at once. Henrietta wants to meet you."

Muriel let Miss Swanwick tug her through the parlor, depositing her glasses and the drooping heliotrope on the mantelpiece. Another dance was starting, and before they could skirt the room to wherever Henrietta sat in wait, Griffith tapped Miss Swanwick's shoulder.

"May I?" He cut in deftly and whirled Muriel across the floor. The room blurred. He spun her too fast, and held her too tight, and she gave in to the giddiness, clutching his shoulders, a bubble of laughter in her throat.

The galloping rotations threw all thoughts of Lucy from her mind. She and Griffith danced every dance, until her feet were as sore as her knees.

They had to climb onto bicycles in the morning.

As the pianist bounced up to take refreshment and the dancers caught their breath, Griffith saw her eyes stray to the clock and nodded. "Time for the circuit of farewell."

It took another half hour, but, at last, they'd reached the door, and Griffith was bowing to Henrietta, Lady Chettam, a stately woman in late middle years. Despite her short stature, she managed to speak while peering down the length of her powdered and imperious nose.

"You must call on me in London," she commanded them both. "The salons start again in October." She focused on Muriel. "You will perform a duet."

Griffith made mild protest. "I don't sing."

"For which we're all grateful," responded Lady Chettam tartly. "I referred to Mrs. Pendrake and Octavia."

Muriel noted the humorous spark in her eyes. Griffith did not.

"Like hell," he grumbled. "I'll learn to sing."

Dancing had jettisoned certain things from his mind as well.

Come October, Muriel would live on a different continent. They weren't attending any sapphic salons, not together.

She didn't remind him on the walk back to the inn. Instead, they sang, loudly and off-key, whatever snippets of lyrics they could remember from popular ballads and drinking songs, until someone opened an upper-story window and shouted curses. After which they sang even louder.

23

K IT WATCHED A stripe of pale dawn light lengthen across the
floorboards. When it reached halfway to the door, he stirred,
easing away from Muriel, sliding from beneath her soft limbs
and silky curtain of hair. He crept to his own room, where washing
up and packing were the work of a moment, then clattered down the
narrow stair to breakfast. In the taproom, the smell of hot grease
overpowered the beeriness, and a girl in a white cap bustled between
tables delivering plates piled with sausages and eggs. He caught her
eye, placed a large, indiscriminate order, and plunked himself into a
high-backed chair at a table near the open fire. Butterfield and Kemble, already seated, looked up from their plates.

"You're chipper," observed Butterfield, his tone ungracious. "Enjoyed your night?"

"Yes, rather." Kit leaned back in his chair. During those first
strained seconds on the threshold of the parlor, he'd wondered if he'd
made a mistake, if the night were about to transform from midsum-
mer dream into nightmare. A great fist had seemed to close inside his
chest, choking off the air. Then Muriel had picked up Octavia's song,
her voice unexpectedly melodic, her throat flushed pink. His heart
began to beat again, and the shuttered faces of his friends opened one
by one. They hadn't all welcomed him with tact or comprehension.
Hester used his old name repeatedly, and Celeste had remarked, with

affectionate relief, that he looked the same and that she'd feared false whiskers. But by and large, the interactions had been comfortable, familiar in a way that didn't depend on his filling his prior mold. Only when he'd realized that Octavia had led Muriel onto the terrace did his emotions roil out of his control. He'd quickly contained his agitation. Muriel knew how to handle herself. And if she decided to dally with a female lothario, who was he to stop her? Bedding a woman didn't confer ownership. Still, his pulse had run high until she'd reappeared, at which point, he'd dashed forward and swung her into his arms. And later, he'd unbuttoned and unlaced every scrap of her clothing, and dragged his hungry mouth all over, licking every delectable inch of her skin, and . . .

"We would have enjoyed it too." Butterfield's sharp voice whisked the happy reminiscence from Kit's mind. "You and Mrs. Pendrake went to meet that gorgeous little creature—Miss Swanwick, was that her name? You could have been a trump and invited us along."

Mutton Wheelers at a sapphic gathering. Kit suppressed a shudder. "It was a private party."

"A party." Butterfield frowned. "I knew it. How many ladies? They were probably in want of gentlemen if there was dancing."

Now Kit suppressed a grin. "They were not in want of gentlemen."

"Says you." Kemble thrust his head forward. "I say you are in want of the fraternal spirit. Have we moved in on your territory? No! But you haven't so much as thrown us—"

Kit interrupted. "My territory?"

"Mrs. Pendrake." Kemble sounded impatient. "She's a nice bit of raspberry. And we don't even look at her! Then another fine piece turns up, and you keep *her* for yourself as well."

"You could look at Mrs. Pendrake, you know." Kit thanked the waitress as she set his coffee in front of him before turning back to Kemble. "You could talk to her. The key is treating her like a human being."

"Kemble *doesn't* know." Butterfield dabbed at his mustache with the corner of his napkin. "He's a Neanderthal."

"And you're a prig." Kemble poked at his tomato. "Five years on and you think you're still head boy."

That hit a nerve. Butterfield's nostrils flared. He folded his napkin neatly and returned it to the table.

"At least I *can* think." His gaze turned inward, and his next muttered words had the well-worn pathos of a mental refrain. "I should have gone to Oxford."

"Wish you had." Kemble shoveled the tomato into his mouth and spoke with a bulging cheek. "*I* should have beat that Frenchie. But you broke my focus."

"Why didn't you go to Oxford?" asked Kit, more to steer the conversation away from beating Frenchies than because he cared to find out.

"I am the firstborn Butterfield." Butterfield pushed his mushrooms to the rim of his plate with the back of his fork. "Firstborn Butterfields join the family firm at eighteen." He gave Kit a thin smile, all but hidden by his mustache. "Egg is going instead. He'll come up this term. I expect he'll get sent down again promptly."

Kit considered defending the unpromising adolescent on principle. It hardly seemed worth the trouble.

"And where is young Egg?" He sipped his coffee and looked around the room.

"In the courtyard with Prescott, wiping off the bicycles." Kemble glared at Butterfield's mushrooms, then at his own. "This training diet will be the death of me. No cutlets. No pork chops. No pudding. No pastry." He looked up as Kit's plate arrived, heaped with fried eggs and potatoes, two kinds of pudding, sausages, tomatoes, mushrooms, beans, fried bread, and a double serving of bacon.

"No bacon," he whispered, as though in pain.

Kit laughed and nudged the plate toward him. "Help yourself."

"Thank you, I will." Kemble speared a piece eagerly. Butterfield shook his head.

"What?" Kemble snarled. "Deighton's not here."

"Is *he* wiping off bicycles?" Kit didn't think it likely.

"He's negotiating with the proprietor," said Butterfield. "It's one of our objectives for this club run—getting more hostelries to affiliate with the CTC."

"Commendable." Kit raised his coffee, the toast ironic, but the sentiment more or less sincere. The Cyclists' Touring Club was the largest cycling organization in England, and one of the few that included women. Its mission to facilitate cycle touring involved securing discounted lodging rates for members and printing an annual directory of the establishments that offered them, along with maps and other guides. He thought back to the wheelmen gathered around the notebook at the Treryn Dinas Inn.

"You're recording the club run," he said as realization struck. "For the next edition of the *British Road Book?*"

"For a *Cornish Road Book*," corrected Butterfield. "The CTC wants more routes through Cornwall. More places of interest. More detail on road conditions. We're including paths too, for the adventurous. Noting everything down." He was noting Kit's plate, with a face that belonged in a Renaissance painting of a martyred Christian saint.

"You can have some too." Kit sighed. "Just leave me the eggs and potatoes."

Butterfield hesitated, glancing at Kemble, who'd pounced on the puddings.

"Perhaps a sausage," he murmured.

Kit finished his potatoes while Butterfield ate sausage with quick, furtive bites and Kemble grunted with rapture. His brain had snagged on an appalling thought.

He gave it voice. "Deighton's a consul, then?" CTC consuls were scattered throughout Great Britain. They brought inns and hotels under contract, and also supplied local information and aid to touring cyclists. Ideally, they encouraged esprit de corps among followers of the wheel—*all* followers of the wheel, men and women, old and young.

"He is." Butterfield took a second proffered sausage from Kit's plate. "As of this spring."

"Consul for Bristol?"

"Consul for Penwith."

Worse and worse. "He lives in Bristol."

"He plans to spend the bulk of every cycling season in St. Ives."

Kit brightened. There was a very large, very aggressive, Harris

Tweed–wrapped wrench in Deighton's plans. "Shame his father's packing him off to Scotland."

"Scotland?" Butterfield and Kemble spoke in unison.

"Scottish office." Kit had no idea what sorry fate *Scottish office* signified, but from the looks on their faces, the other men did.

"Glasgow." Butterfield balled his napkin in his hand. "He never said."

Kemble blanched. "Good God. They don't mean to send me to Glasgow with him? I can't go to Scotland. I have a fiancée."

"You remembered," said Butterfield dryly.

"I'll wire my father." Kemble pushed back his chair. "Tell him to ignore whatever he hears from St. Ives."

"Tell him to ignore the chairman of the company?"

"Why not? Chairman's a bloody lunatic, and everyone knows it. He'll get some other bee in his bonnet, and . . ." Kemble coughed as Deighton stalked up to the table. He looked even taller in the low-ceilinged room, pale cowlick nearly brushing the rafters.

He barked, "What the devil are you two eating?"

"Nothing." Butterfield stuffed the evidence into his mouth. "Poached herring," he mumbled.

"You were eating sausage and talking about my father." Deighton's face mottled with red.

"Bacon," said Kemble bravely, straightening his back. "In my case, it was bacon."

At that moment, a great marmalade cat, dozing by the fire, stretched himself, took a tottering step, and hopped onto the empty chair at the head of the table.

"Stay back!" Muriel must have entered the room while everyone's attention was occupied. She flung herself between Deighton and the table, arms outspread. "Don't touch him!"

"Touch who?" Deighton's jaw slackened in shock. "The woman's raving." He looked to Kit for confirmation. Kit looked at Muriel, who'd scooped the cat into her arms.

"I'm not raving," she said, composed but with fire in her eyes. "I won't stand by and let you misuse a defenseless animal."

Deighton's jaw firmed and his brows lowered. "That's a sack of fleas you're holding. I wouldn't touch it with a ten-foot pole."

"Better than beating it with a ten-foot pole," Kit remarked. "Delighted to hear you've put your school days behind you."

"What do you mean?" Deighton rounded on him. "My *school* days?"

"The years you spent learning Greek and Latin, and torturing cats."

"Griffith." Deighton's face was now purple. "We do not talk about *school*. It's not done."

"Sir Reggie did it." At Muriel's low assertion, Deighton rounded again, looming over her. His whole body quivered with rage.

She cuddled the cat protectively, then put up her chin. "It's true, then. You are a torturer of cats."

Deighton twitched, as though in denial. But no denial followed. Nothing followed.

"The ferry leaves in a quarter hour," he said at last, and turned on his heel.

KIT SPENT THE thirty-minute crossing to St. Mawes wedged between his bicycle and the side of the steamer. Most of the people on deck were locals, and therefore more interested in talking with the seven cyclists about their mounts than in admiring the sights.

"Which kind is faster?" chirped a gap-toothed boy of six or seven. He'd just been wrestled away from the life buoys hooked on the side of the pilothouse and was now attempting to climb Deighton's ordinary.

"The kind with the big front wheel," said Deighton, yanking the boy off the bike by the collar of his coat.

"The kind with the diamond frame," said Kit, indicating his own machine with a deliberately cocksure smile.

Deighton held the boy aloft, ignoring his windmilling arms and legs, and fixed Kit with a glare of feverish intensity. He hadn't calmed since leaving the taproom.

Needling him would be immature, and inexpedient.

Kit *almost* listened to his better angels and kept his mouth shut.

"The champion racer Teddy Hale set the hundred-mile road record on a high wheeler like that one." He pointed at Deighton's ordinary. "And then, a year later, he broke that record on a safety like this one." He flicked his bell so it emitted a short, cheery note of introduction.

"Hale's high wheeler wasn't like mine." Deighton gesticulated furiously with the boy, who shrieked with delight. "He rode an inferior model. *My* high wheeler—the New Rapid—is the best bicycle on the market."

Kit snorted. "Not by a long chalk."

As the ferry churned out of the shipyard into open water, he and Deighton went tit for tat with bicycle specifications, listing increasingly technical details in increasingly loud voices to an increasingly bored crowd. One woman seemed riveted even as they compared crank spindles and seat lugs, but it turned out she was trying to retrieve her son. Only Butterworth and Kemble kept hanging on every word, and—perhaps Kit was delusional—particularly on *his* words, the ones pertaining to the Rover's design and fittings. Muriel was out of earshot, closer to the prow, flanked by Prescott and Egg, all three of them gazing across the estuary toward the Roseland Peninsula.

Her shouts finally released him from the verbal duel. "Shark! Oh, how wonderful. Look!"

He and Deighton fell silent. Heads snapped around.

"It's a giant!" Prescott's exclamation floated back as well.

"By gad, look at that maw!" enthused Egg, his screeches even louder. "I never! What a blooming monster!"

Passengers jostled into the prow—not so many that Kit felt less penned in, but enough to block Muriel from his line of vision.

"Feed him Jago!"

The gap-toothed boy had been given a sweet and stood pressed into his mother's skirts, docile as a lamb, but this suggestion caused him to leap into the air. The girl who'd made it—his sister—seized him around the waist.

"No!" he howled, and twisted free. He beelined to Deighton for protection, clambering over the New Rapid's tiny back wheel and threading himself between the wheelman's legs.

"You again." Deighton's face registered confusion and shock in equal measure. "Get off."

The boy clung to Deighton's calf. "Jenny's going to feed me to the shark!"

"No, she's not." Deighton gave his leg a shake. "She's a little girl. What are little girls made of? Sugar and spice and everything nice."

"What are little boys made of?" Jenny crouched in front of Deighton's wheel, staring at Jago through the spokes. "Everything that tastes nice to a shark!"

Jago wailed.

"None of that," Deighton scolded him. "You're a man, remember."

"I'm a boy," sobbed Jago. "Sharks think I taste nice."

"Boys grow up to be men," snapped Deighton. "Men don't cry."

"We could feed Mr. Bicycle Man to the shark instead," said Jenny gravely through the spokes. "The shark might like him better."

Jago sniffed and nodded. He tugged Deighton's leg as Jenny tugged the wheel.

"Madam!" Deighton called to their mother, a touch of panic in his voice. "Madam!"

Kit angled his body away, tuning out the sounds of the tussle, which anyway merged with the general clamor on deck and the noise of the engines below. He studied the approaching landmass, houses clustered near the harbor, a verdant hill rising behind, topped by St. Mawes Castle. He'd first seen the castle at the National Gallery, in a painting by Turner. The canvas was washed with late-summer light, the sails of the pilchard boats like sheets of beaten gold, the hulls rosy, and the beach rosy too, flecked with silver fish.

The light today shone strong and clear, and the wind came fitfully from the west.

He imagined Muriel in the ship's prow, saw the scene as though it were a painting—not by Turner. No one could match Turner's sensitivity to landscape, but he peopled his canvases with puny, awkward figures, dismissible poppets, and the painting Kit pictured dwelled on Muriel herself. He styled her like the Lady of Shalott, in a medieval kirtle, hair unbound, but she didn't lie dead-pale in her boat, embowered by flowers of mourning. She stood proud and her dark eyes looked with unswerving brilliancy and directness on the world.

This went deeper than mere imagining. He *was* painting, albeit inside his head. He began to tingle all over, a combination of his own sudden giddiness and the restless salt breeze. If he did manage to put down real pigment, he'd weave all of his feelings into his brush-strokes. Muriel as the Lady of Shalott would draw the gaze with her beauty, but her eyes would ultimately direct the viewer's away.

Look with *me, not* at *me.* Her eyes would beam this message. *Let me show you what I see.*

A shark. Slug spawn. Seaweed. The rainbow's end. The evening star.

He laughed aloud—didn't he eschew romantic delusions? He needed to remember that she saw *him*, and that she might not see him as he wanted to be seen.

She might not see him as a man.

He sobered at once. The tingling became a sting, and he hunched his shoulders against the wind.

He wasn't a Neanderthal. Or a chappie. He hadn't been a school-boy, bullied and bullying, taught to dominate his emotions by dom-inating others—human or animal. He felt glad of it. Most days, he wouldn't wave a wand and make himself his parents' beloved baby son at birth. Most days, he was bloody glad he'd been a Sister, and a sapphist.

Had been.

He wasn't either now.

Did Muriel understand that, really? Perhaps the party had been a mistake. He needed a clean break. An existence that began the day he moved to Cornwall.

His stomach knotted, and when he soothed himself with the thought that it didn't matter what Muriel understood—she sailed out of his life by September—he felt it wrap around itself and pull into a hurting figure eight.

He'd rather the Mutton Wheelers make him sick than his own mind. He turned his attention back to the deck. Both children were gone. Their mother was likewise nowhere in sight.

He raised his brows musingly at Deighton. "I'd have heard the splash if you'd thrown anyone overboard."

Deighton pointed with his very square chin. A nearby parasol, held over a seat at a suspicious angle, began to giggle.

"They're hiding." He smiled an evil smile. "Up for a bit of fun?"

"I should have clarified," said Kit. "I'm not *for* throwing anyone overboard."

"Forget the brats." Deighton pulled at the brim of his cap. "This is about you and me. Let's race to Mevagissey."

Kit tightened his grip on his Rover.

He could say *no*, of course. Swallow his pride. Take the ribbing. Seem that much weaker. That much more womanly.

Dash it all. He didn't believe in those correlations, in that way of thinking.

But he was already saying, "Let's."

24

I WISH THERE WERE still wolves in England."

Griffith's statement hovered in the dark wood, tempting fate.

"To make the sheep less complacent," he explained, although Muriel hadn't asked. "They've lost the instinct to *scatter*." He made a scattering motion with his hands.

"To the left," she said, as the path forked. She was following directions she'd received from the innkeeper's wife. Griffith was following her—out of obligation, obviously. He'd brought his sketchbook, but he didn't seem interested in their destination—a cove known for its rock pools—and he didn't seem interested in discussing their evening with the Hesperus Ladies Club either, shrugging at her questions when he could easily have fleshed out various characters and their relationships.

No, he was interested in, precisely, *sheep*.

He'd griped about their role in the aborted road race for the duration of the walk.

"A solid wall of fleece!" He was still going. "Absolutely immovable. They were less like sheep and more like the foundation stones of the Bank of England."

"A monument," she muttered, unable to hold back. "A memorial to the great road race to Mevagissey that wasn't."

"It *was* a race." He hopped over a root—hopped higher than

necessary. "I was going to win it. Until we hit that blockade of sheep and had to call it off."

"The sheep. Yes, you've mentioned them."

"They'll get mentioned in the next edition of the *British Almanac*." Griffith scowled at the treetops. "They were a phenomenon. They composed the most numerous, slowest-moving, inconveniently positioned flock of recorded time."

She shook her head, amusement warring with annoyance. And disappointment as well.

She felt far too aware of the fact that they were alone, and that he'd made no move to kiss her. Far too aware of what her disappointment signified—she'd *expected* him to kiss her.

She cut another glance at him. He was rambling along, his gait athletic and almost hostile in its careless muscularity. The premature conclusion of the race had left him with too much unexpended physical energy. Or was his agitation the result of erotic restlessness?

Last night, after they'd returned to the inn, after he'd undone her with his clever fingers and wicked tongue, he might have lain awake, pent up with dissatisfied desire. He might have dreamed of release with someone else.

He might have dreamed of Lucy.

He met her gaze, briefly.

"I could almost believe Deighton plotted the whole thing," he said, not for the first time, and began to rehash the idea. It involved an implausible relay of telegrams, errand boys, and farmers.

She focused on guiding them out of the wood and across a sloping heath. The path to the cove started behind the barrow on the clifftop and wound steeply down to the granite boulders that backed the beach. She scrambled over them and dropped onto the beach proper. The tide was low, the tiny crystalline waves breaking some twenty yards away. Kelp carpeted the dry sand, sun-bleached and salt-encrusted. The air stank of sulfur.

She headed for the low-water mark, passing pools that glimmered like mirrors between the wide black rocks.

"Here!" she called back to Griffith, climbing onto a rock that delimited the upper boundary of the largest pool, rich with marine life. "I see a dozen species." None particularly rare, or worth collecting, but all as beautiful as jewels in the sun-struck water.

He came up beside her.

She kept her eyes trained on the pool. "They're mesmerizing, aren't they?"

She could feel him looking at her.

"Are you mesmerized?" he asked lightly. "Perhaps it's in the stars— your destiny is algolgalology."

"Algology," she corrected. "And no, I'll have had my fill of algae after this. My destiny is mycology. I can picture myself hunting mushrooms in the Catskills."

"Mushrooms." He sounded dubious. "The seaweed of the forest."

She gave a helpless laugh and a small shake of her head.

"The Irish moss of the mountains," he continued, encouraged. "Although, on second thought, the Irish moss of the mountains is likely . . . moss. The regular kind. And the sea lettuce of the mountains is lettuce. Does lettuce grow in the mountains?"

"Wild lettuce does." She sighed, feeling weary. He would persist in ridiculousness. "Anything else you want to say?"

There was a little silence.

"Forgive me." He spoke in a frank tone. "I've been acting like an ass."

Her gaze shot up and she met his changeable gray-blue eyes, a mix of storm cloud and sky. Their beauty took her breath away.

Proof enough that she was getting too attached, and that her own inability to modulate her feelings would be her doom.

"But you're not an ass." She cleared her throat and smiled. "I heard you're a Leo."

Now *he* laughed. "I'm sure you heard a lot of things from Miranda and the rest." He hesitated, a shadow chasing the mirth from his face. "I realized on the ferry that I find the notion somewhat disconcerting."

She drew in her breath, surprised.

The shadow vanished. His look was bright again, and teasing. "Ass isn't a sign of the zodiac, by the way, although it probably should be."

"Probably." She agreed automatically, peering up at him with new eyes. He was slouching with his customary rakish grace, cycling cap perched at an angle on his wind-mussed hair. He wore his self-assurance so easily. It could make you suppose he never needed to be assured.

She remembered the way he'd stood, frozen, on the threshold of the parlor in the Falmouth Hotel. *She* felt like the ass. All afternoon, he'd filled the air between them with obsessive monologues, and she'd failed to note the nervous undercurrent that sped his excited speech. She'd seen only the workings of an outsized competitive streak, and sexual frustration.

"You are disconcerted," she said slowly. "By the party."

He waved this away. "Not as disconcerted as I was by all those sheep."

"Kit."

"I like it when you say my name." His eyes flashed.

"God almighty," she muttered.

"That too."

She gave his shoulder a soft shove, and he caught her wrist, trapping her hand. His expression darkened.

"I don't like that you heard that other name," he confessed, voice tight. "I know you won't say it, but I don't like that you could even think it. I don't like that it's in your head."

"It's not." She responded instantly. "It is not in my head. I promise you. My head was far too full of Gilbert and Sullivan."

His former name *had* glanced off her. A different name stuck.

But this wasn't the moment to ask about Lucy.

She pulled away from him and snapped to attention, shoulders back, chin high. "*I know the Kings of England, and I quote the fights historical, from Marathon to Waterloo, in order categorical!*"

She gave him a salute, panting and slightly off-balance.

He smirked. It was a strange, sweet kind of smirk, filled with humor and relief and tenderness.

"You *are* the very model of a modern Major-General." He stepped into her, arm wrapping her waist. "What are my orders?"

The low growl ignited a fuse that ran all the way down her spine. *Burn for me. Burn for me as I do for you.*

One couldn't command such a thing.

His sinful lips had parted, and his eyes mirrored the light, like the rock pools, and with a sharp inhalation, she caught herself before she softened and forgot everything but the warmth of his mouth, the intoxicating scent of his skin.

"Seaweed," she murmured, breaking the circle of his arm. "Make your sketches."

"I was hoping for *make love to me on this rock*." He sighed and sat, legs crossed, sketchbook on his knee. "Seaweed it is."

She sat too, heartbeat slowing, and gazed into the pool. "This is what I wanted you to observe. Living plants. Their shapes and colors, how they move and catch the light." She glanced up and intercepted his stare. "You can stop observing *me*." She gestured toward the pool.

He grinned. "Your face is at least as riveting as that algae."

"You sound like James." She screwed up her face, but she knew her cheeks had gone pink. "The seaweed is down there."

"What was your original lecture topic? You never told me."

"Oh." For an instant, she gaped, nonplussed, then a warm glow spread in her chest. "Taxonomic practices. It sounds dull, but it's something I thought about a great deal during my last years in China."

"And?" He transferred his sketchbook to the rock and drew up his legs. "What did you think?"

"I won't lecture *you*." Her laugh was self-conscious.

"Please." His eyes held genuine interest. It melted the last of her reserve.

"Are you familiar with Kew Gardens?"

"I've been there, to the conservatories. And I've strolled around the grounds. They're lovely."

"They are lovely. But Kew is much more than a glorified park. It houses the largest collection of plant species in the world. The directors have been sending botanists to every corner for decades, bringing plants here, taking plants there, changing where plants are grown and at what scale. My husband was one of those botanists. He collected for Kew, and for plant nurseries in London and Truro, and he brought me with him. He died, of a fever, in Hong Kong. I continued."

"That must have been difficult." The gentleness in his voice was like a caress, its warmth seeping inside her, through the cracks in her wall of self-protection. She'd built that wall up over years, and he was bringing it down, in a matter of weeks.

"It wasn't," she said, too curtly. "Esmé's life was his work. He married me because I could help facilitate that work, and by the time he was gone, I knew exactly what to do to carry on his legacy."

Griffith kept looking at her, and she sagged a little and let herself feel comforted by his steady regard.

"I was seventeen when I met him," she said softly. "On the heath, in fact. I was malingering from my cousin's shop, and he'd gone out to botanize. He didn't live in Hampshire. He was visiting a friend. I took him through the cornfield to the beech wood, and to a clearing where I'd found a white wild orchid, and he seemed impressed I'd paid such attention to the landscape, as though it were an accomplishment and not a form of woolgathering. It was beyond gratifying. He was nearly twice my age, worldly and intelligent—an assistant to the superintendent of the Chelsea Physic Garden in London. He told me he was sailing for India, on a commission from a nursery. We boarded the steamer four days after the wedding. Our marriage was my apprenticeship as a botanist. That's what he wanted—an apprentice who'd stay by his side. And I wanted to learn. Well, I wanted to *leave*—leave Hampshire—first and foremost. In certain respects, we fulfilled each other."

She took a breath, shifting her gaze from Griffith's handsome face, too intent, and too ruminative, as though he were fitting together the pieces of her life.

"I never considered anything *but* taking up his commissions, not seriously. He'd trained me so well. I felt he was with me, every time I described a specimen or packed a bulb. I could hear his voice, advising me."

"You still hear him," said Griffith, low. "That was his voice, wasn't it? In the tree. He told you that your fear was a nuisance."

She studied the clouds.

Looks like rain, she could say.

She said instead: "I hear him less now."

How had she let this get so off track? She'd meant to talk about her lecture, not her marriage.

"I hear him less," she said. "And I consider his work—my work—in a different light. Mostly, we shipped ornamental plants to London. Pretty shrubs. We classified them first, according to norms set by Kew. Plants do have names before they're discovered by British botanists—names and local uses. But you need standardized nomenclature if you're trying to order the natural world in its entirety—to understand the whole. I was eager to contribute to that understanding, to compare morphologies and pursue the mysteries of photosynthesis, and hybridize lilacs in every shade of the rainbow. I took it for granted that Kew was the *center* of the world, the place where discoveries were made and knowledge was stored. Bit by bit, I realized how much local knowledge was being erased, and not to further some greater good. To enrich the empire. Naming and codifying species means better coordination between botanic stations in the colonies. Improving varieties means better yields on farms run by colonial planters, while workers sicken and die. I can't lecture on trade or foreign policy, so I chose taxonomy, as a way into a larger conversation about the consequences of merging a scientific system with an economic system. That was the idea, in a nutshell."

She waited as he mulled it over.

"Not dull," he said, cocking his head, gaze appraising.

"Also, not happening." She crossed her arms.

"Because of the tosser."

"Heywood." She nodded. "He's a professor at Columbia University and directs the lecture series, so he gets the final word."

"He disagreed with your analysis."

"Doubtless he would have. But no, that's not it. He only saw my title. He thought I should discuss something suited to my sex. He didn't explain himself, but *his* title for my new lecture made it obvious." She frowned. "'Gatty's Girls: Celebrating the Female Love of Botany.'"

Griffith's eyes narrowed. "Why did he pick Gatty?"

She shrugged. "It's the twenty-fifth anniversary of the publication of Mrs. Gatty's very popular book, *British Sea-Weeds*, in which she describes seaweed collecting as a charming pursuit and recommends it to women as an opportunity for light exercise and moral reflection."

"Not to mention debauchery on seaside rocks."

"She doesn't," said Muriel dryly. "She was extremely respectable. Hence Heywood's approval."

"Right." Griffith was thinking. "Why don't you give your original lecture anyway?"

She shook her head. "The new lecture has already been advertised. I need to engage with the topic. After I got the letter, I paced a hole in James's carpet wondering how. I decided to lecture *against* the female love of botany. Women can do more than notice and admire. We can make inquiries and conduct experiments. We can challenge received ideas. We're not only *hobbyists*. We can study, and work, and manage our own careers. I wrote it all out, and I included the story of the lecture itself, how Professor Heywood picked seaweed as my topic based on a biased assumption—which incidentally proved he was rot as a scientist and should probably get the sack."

Griffith seemed to be hiding a smile.

She coughed. "It was a bit zealous."

The smile emerged. "Might as well be hanged for a sheep as a lamb."

"Blazes." She had to laugh. "You're back to sheep."

He lifted a brow. "It was the relevant proverb."

"I burned that lecture." She put her palms on the rock. Its surface was very smooth and very warm. "I burned it after I saw your watercolor."

"Did you?" His expression became inscrutable.

"The way you painted the columbine. I can't describe the artistry. The effect, though. I can describe that." She searched for the words.

"Your watercolor reminded me that nature overflows the mind. That you have to feel to know. Artists don't lose sight of that. Scientists do."

"Anyone can lose sight of anything," he said, but he was staring like he'd never lose sight of her again.

Heat crept up her cheeks.

"It occurred to me I was making a mistake in speaking against the female love of botany. Not only because I don't want to get hanged by an audience expecting ardent descriptions of coralline. Because it's tantamount to accepting Heywood's terms, and the division between amateurs and professionals. There's a connection to be made between the refusal to take women seriously and the exclusion of native experts, the disparagement of different ways of knowing and the theft of resources. I'm going to address *that*, and the need to transform how and why we do botany altogether. But I'll get there via celebration."

She rose to kneeling, leaning out over the pool. Beneath the surface, plants formed a fairy-tale forest in miniature, pale pink and emerald, with fuzzy bursts of crimson.

"With your paintings in the lecture hall, the audience will feel like they're *in* a rock pool."

She dipped her finger in the water, drawing a silver circle above the *Plocamium cartilagineum*, then reached further to brush the feathery tips of its red branches.

She withdrew and saw that Griffith's face had darkened, his eyes more storm cloud than sky. Her gaze fell to his sketchbook.

She hesitated. "Has it come back?"

"Come back?" He echoed her blankly.

"The headaches and numbness. You painted the bladderwrack, but perhaps you're suffering a recurrence, as with malaria."

He gave a slow shake of his head. "It's not a recurrence."

"Good." She bit her lip. His face didn't communicate *good*. He looked away from her then, out to sea. She tried to think of something else to say, but she'd been talking herself blue, and so she let the silence stretch.

Her heart beat in her ears—ten loud beats—before he spoke.

"I told you I had two real families in London."

She nodded, but of course he couldn't see her, so she said, "The ladies of the Hesperus Club. And your Sisters in art."

"My Sisters in art," he repeated. "The Pre-Raphaelites formed their Brotherhood. We formed a Sisterhood, while we were students at the Royal Academy Schools. Four of us. Musketeers of the brush and chisel. Three painters and a sculptor. I was the rabble-rouser. I spent nearly as much time perfecting our manifesto as I did painting." He paused. "I broke with them officially in May. It broke my relationship to painting. It broke something inside me."

"I see." She did, and she didn't. She bit her lip, puzzling it out. "Was there some disagreement about artistic principles?"

"No."

"You left because it didn't make sense for you to remain in a Sisterhood."

"Correct."

"But then why such distress? Surely your Sisters supported your decision."

He gave a strangled laugh and turned back to her, lifting her hand and threading their fingers together. His palm felt as warm as the rock.

"Lucy thinks I'm Judas."

Lucy.

She tightened her grip on his hand. Of course. His headaches and numbness, the blackness that swallowed his vision when he lifted the brush—all symptoms of heartbreak.

"Lucy is your . . . Sister?"

"We founded the Sisterhood together. No one knows me better."

"Then she can't think you're Judas." It burst out, with the ring of truth. How could Lucy know him and think such a thing?

His eyes clung to hers, vulnerability in their depths, and then his irises turned steely.

"We vowed to take the art world by storm, as women artists. To support each other, as women artists. To champion women in the arts. I betrayed that vow."

"By being who you are?" She sat motionless. "You can still champion women in the arts. You're not a woman artist yourself, but you know what it's like to be a woman artist, and you can lend your support as a man. It might go further, in fact."

"That's the rub." His face set in harsh lines. "Everything I do goes further, *because* I'm a man. We vowed to fight that reality, not benefit by it."

"But that's too simple." She slid toward him, until their folded legs touched. "Earlier this summer, I had dinner with a Russian naturalist in London. He's writing about the significance of cooperation in the animal kingdom. It's brilliant work, a challenge to Darwin's focus on competition. The whole table debated his ideas in the liveliest fashion. After he left the restaurant, someone told me he'd been jailed in Russia for fomenting revolution with the peasantry. And that he was born a prince."

There was a pause. Griffith's face didn't alter.

"Sometimes people in better circumstances use their resources *to* fight," she said, pulse racing as she held his gaze. "And everyone benefits in some way from unjustness, even overworked, malnourished factory girls in Whitechapel. They make their tea from plants grown on plantations in India that pushed families off their land. We're all of us bound up in the same web, and evil is done in our names every minute of the day. I never thought about the tea plantations when I was a girl. I never thought, *I am a citizen of Britain, and this is a cup of blood from the colonies.* There were things I didn't question. I question more now, but I still don't have the answers. You can leave painting to your Sisters and sell safety bicycles, because safety bicycles help emancipate women, but do you know where they get the rubber for the wheels? The Amazon. The rubber tappers are subjected to unthinkable brutalities. I'm not suggesting we do nothing about human suffering. On the contrary, I think we should do everything we can. But that involves participating in the world we're trying to change. You can't participate blamelessly in the world. Blamelessness can't be a precondition for action."

The lines in Griffith's face cut deeper. He looked exhausted.

"I know," he said. "Lucy does too. If I had to guess, I think she feels more abandoned than righteous. I'm acquainted with that sensation, and what it does to you. I felt it when she married, despite my best efforts. It wasn't the same between us. He came first. The duke."

Muriel was quiet. Lucy had married a duke, and Griffith was jealous, and she was becoming well acquainted with *that* sensation indeed.

"I didn't tell her. I moved to Cornwall, and I didn't tell her why. I let her think it was the light. The goddamn painterly light." He shut his eyes briefly. "I was going to tell her, but she figured it out before I had the chance. She went to my show this winter in London. She didn't know it was mine. *Kit Griffith* meant nothing to her. But she recognized my style. We were each other's best critics. She made me the painter that I am—that I was." He released Muriel's hand, and spread all ten of his fingers in frustration. "I visited her not long after. She came to the door, and she looked at me like I was . . ." The fingers balled into fists.

"Kit." Muriel rose to her knees and touched his face, the proud promontories of his cheekbones. She looked at him like he was *him*—the man who made her heart beat faster and her mind expand. The man who made her whole being ache as though every particle had tensed to keep her from tumbling off some ledge.

Irony registered as a painful twist inside her chest. It took him all but admitting he loved another woman for her to admit the truth.

She was already tumbling.

His eyes swept her face, and he kissed her. His arms slid up her back. Instantly, her body was languid as honey. The air buzzed all around her, and their tongues slid together, slow and sweet. He pulled away first.

She gave him a wobbly smile, breathing hard. "Make love to me on this rock?"

He raised his brows. "What about the seaweed?"

"Good point." She heaved an exaggerated sigh. She'd meant it as a joke, after all. "Never mind, then."

"Damn." He put on a rueful expression. "I've lost my touch as a seducer."

A hundred subtle emotions were marching across his eyes.

She wondered if hers looked similar.

He glanced at his sketchbook. "I'll just observe the seaweed, if that's all right."

They adjusted themselves, looking down into the water, no longer touching, the sea air moving between them. Muriel emptied her mind of the past and the future, and she watched the underwater plants sway in currents invisible to the eye.

25

I *HAVEN'T DOOMED MYSELF,* she thought as she rode along the edge of the moor. *This may yet end well.* The wind blew hard from the north, heavy with the threat of rain, and the clouds pressed down, gray as the scattered moorstone. Steering a straight course was next to impossible, though hunched on their low-mounts, she and Kit had an easier time than the men inching along ahead, their tall, flimsy bicycles looking ready to spin in circles, like enormous weathervanes.

She wasn't worried about the storm, still miles off, pulling strength from the sea. It had chased them inland, beneath spiraling birds, all the way to Bodmin Moor, the sight of which made her blood sing. On similar heathland, she'd first found comfort and purpose. The desolate, gorgeous, pulse-thumping landscape served as a reminder.

There was hope for life after Kit Griffith.

Over the past four days, she'd tried to reckon with her realization at the cove—that despite her firmest resolve, she was falling in love—and to catch herself mid-plunge. She might as well have tried to reverse gravity. It wasn't just her lust-crazed lobster eyes on stalks. The feeling was that of her whole heart popping out, swollen and tender, extending beyond the protection of her ribs.

The night before last, at the inn in Callington, she'd drifted in and out of sleep, her limbs intertwined with his, the sensation delicious and so satisfying it seemed complete—warm and rounded off.

Yesterday, as they pedaled toward Bude, she'd experimented with the idea that this time together was enough. Yes, she was smitten, but that didn't spell disaster—her life spinning out of control, whirling around some incipient lack. She'd carry the fullness of these golden moments with her. By dusk, mental clarity had faded with the light, and as she dismounted at their destination, the gooseflesh was spreading on her arms. When Kit walked past her into the hotel, his sidelong glance knocked the air from her lungs. Knocked the notion of golden moments from her mind. It wasn't enough. The time. The closeness. Her want yawned wide, and it terrified.

Today, she didn't feel that terror, the sense that her heart might leap from her chest altogether and leave a billowing void. She drew strength from the moor's solidity, the granite within the rolling hills. This liaison wasn't everything. Its loss would be bearable. The earth itself gladdened her, as it always had—soil woven with roots, sending up green fuses that met the sun and exploded in life. She could smell summer-warmed rock and dry heather and the wind's wet edge of rain. Renewal, not doom.

This may yet end well.

A swirl of young starlings caught her eye. They streamed above and grew smaller and smaller, disappearing over the moor.

She'd lagged behind Kit, so she accelerated, coming up on his left.

"Do you think we'll make it to Newquay?"

He hollered as a gust tipped him toward her. "I think we might get blown clear to France!"

France. Where James's poetical chemist ate apricots in a rosemary-hedged villa. Those two lovers had been sundered by circumstance and neither resisted, content with a fond farewell.

She hollered back. "I've never been!"

At that instant, the wind tore her hat from her head and sent it whipping toward France without her. Kit vaulted to the ground and was after it, neck craned to track its tumble through the unruly sky. And that was why he caught his foot in the bramble and pitched forward onto his face.

By the time she'd jerked her own bicycle to a stop and run to him, he'd rolled over onto his back. She dropped to her knees in the prickly grass. His cap was gone, and his hair was rumpled, but his eyes were open, and his gaze seemed to strike through to her core.

"Penny," he drawled. He wore a wry smile. They'd been arranged just so before, her kneeling, him sprawled out. On that previous occasion, other names had hovered on his lips.

"Penny with the hat that ended up in Normandy." She flopped over and lay beside him, looking up at the racing clouds through the branches of a stunted hawthorn. "Penny with the penchant for sea lettuce."

"The one and only Penny," he murmured, which shouldn't have made her heart skip. He'd given her that nickname *because* its reference was singular. "My spine's been dented." He sat up with a groan. "Should have taken this off." He swatted at his knapsack.

"It's so lovely here." She shut her eyes and sank her consciousness into her heels and tailbone, her elbows and the back of her head, flattening more of her body against the ground. When she opened her eyes, she felt simultaneously heavy as the whole world and vanishingly small.

"Do you remember when we met, you said you wake up bewildered, and I said I do too." She watched tiny leaves shake loose from the hawthorn and fly. That hoary old hawthorn had grown over decades into the very shape of the wind, the whole of it bent like a bow, leaf after leaf shooting free.

"I remember," Kit responded after a pause. "It's a feeling of being adrift, in time or space." He cleared his throat. "Or in yourself."

"Do you ever feel the opposite?" She shut her eyes again. "As though you know exactly where you are, and who you are, and everything else turns around that certainty?"

She heard his intake of breath. "Rarely."

"It's a rare feeling. I feel it in places like this." She felt it also in his arms.

New York lacked for heath, and moors, but surely, in the forests of the Hudson River Valley, there'd be some mossy clearing or forgotten orchard where she'd know such peace again—alone, but not lonely.

She opened her eyes. The clouds looked darker. She didn't want to move.

"Penny. About your lecture."

She registered his tone with faint alarm.

"I have something to tell you."

She sat up, into the wind. "What is it?"

"There's no painting of the bladderwrack. I tried, but . . ." His jaw tensed. "I failed. Still can't draw a midge. Or a kelp."

She drew back. She'd suspected, hadn't she? She'd discounted her intuition, choosing instead to believe a lie.

"You said you'd painted it." Her voice was thin and accusing, and she burrowed her gloved fingers deep into the grass.

He went a shade whiter beneath his tan. "I'd hoped to make it true. I was afraid if you knew, you'd give up on me. I was afraid I'd give up too."

"You *are* giving up." It was written all over his face. "Why now?"

"We're almost back where we started." He slumped, his bleak expression fit for the gallows, as though the loop they'd been cycling around Cornwall was a noose and their return to St. Ives would cinch it tight around his neck.

It seemed years ago that they'd passed by Land's End, the westernmost point on the circumference of their journey, and passed through the Lizard, the southernmost. Now that they'd reached the Devon border in the village of Kingsand, and swung north as far as Bude, and west again, they were closing in on victory—one sort of victory.

"We'll win the bet," she whispered.

"You'll fulfill your side of the bargain." He ran a hand over his face. "It is evident that I cannot fulfill mine."

Resignation wasn't his way. He looked and sounded unfamiliar.

"You still might," she protested, and he gave her a bitter smile that seemed wrong for his mouth.

"I can't even draw *you*." His eyes moved over her, and she wondered at his inflection. Should it be easier to draw her than a midge, or a plant? Yes, for him, aficionado of the female form.

Dark emotion welled. She'd once offered to let him paint her body, and with every passing day, she found herself offering more of herself, *finding* more of herself, body and soul, and it was turning her inside out.

The terror returned with the force of all she could lose, borne on a gust of wind that stung her cheeks like a slap.

"I don't give up on you," she said, through numb lips.

He stared, eyes nearly black, and then he looked away.

"Shigeki Takada will take the commission instead, I'm almost certain. He's not a flower painter either, but he's meticulous and harmonizes his tints like no one else. His pictures won't disappoint." He looked back at her, wind plastering his soft hair to his hard cheekbone. "I *am* sorry."

He was. She could see it. He was sorry, sad and sorry, and after all, his disappointment had to outweigh her own. He was an artist who couldn't make his art. She couldn't imagine anything comparable— banishment to the moon, perhaps, where nothing grew.

She reached for his hand and squeezed.

"You're not angry?"

"I'm not angry," she confirmed.

"Another thing about your lecture, then." His gaze sharpened. "Your friends, the botanists who invited you to New York. You said they haven't written. Have you written to them?"

"I sent a letter before I left for St. Ives."

He nodded. "You explained your plan? Told them that you'll critique Heywood's intervention and the ways botany has been put in service of the powerful more generally?"

Her hand twitched in his. "I asked logistical questions pertaining to my arrival."

He kept looking at her.

"Kit," she said. "Celebration and sea lettuce aside, there remains a very strong possibility my talk will create conflict." She'd thought he understood. "I don't want the Satterlees implicated in my quarrel."

"It's not *your* quarrel. You are not belaboring a personal grievance. You are taking a stand in accordance with your principles. Do the Satterlees share them?"

He appeared resigned no longer. His eyes were silver fire.

"I believe they do," she said softly. He *had* understood. He'd understood everything. He'd listened to what she'd told him, and he challenged her now on a point of strategy. He advocated for a collective effort, and it made sense that he would. He'd come of age rabble-rousing with his Sisters, musketeers of the brush and chisel.

All for one, and one for all.

"Then write them," he said.

"I *could*." She licked her lips. They might support her, if pressed, but at what cost? "Heywood wields enormous influence."

"More reason to band together. The Satterlees are from New York, yes? They must have yet more friends. Heywood's voice is louder than yours, and theirs, but perhaps not louder than a chorus."

She hesitated, hit by a wave of longing. His being was as beautiful as his face. How had she ever thought him vain and capricious? The surface glitter distracted from the substance.

"So you'll write?"

She shook herself. "I will consider it."

A pleased smile drifted across his mouth. "You need comrades." He reached out, caught a loose lock of her windblown hair, and gave it a gentle tug—a comradely tug.

Her huge, unprotected heart lurched.

She managed to smile back. "Such as you?"

He inclined his head. "If you'll have me."

She swallowed hard and locked his gaze. That was just it. She wouldn't have *him*. She'd have distant affinity, another correspondent, albeit one whose letters didn't go into the pigeonholes of her desk. She'd keep them beneath her pillow, or in the carved box she'd ported around the world, battered container of her few sentimental trinkets.

"Comrades," she croaked, and pumped his hand, which made him laugh and tug her to her feet.

THEY'D BEEN RIDING for less than half an hour when thunder burst the iron-gray vault of the sky. Kit felt a corresponding explosion in his head. The ground seemed to shake. Day turned to night, pitch-black and demon-ridden. The wind's moan became a roar, and raindrops hard and sharp as teeth bit his face.

He tried to speak to Muriel, but wind snatched the words away. Wind had unraveled her chignon, and her shining hair fanned, twisted, and fanned again. Her face was pale and undaunted. It told a story: she'd traveled the world and weathered worse.

He didn't signal for them to stop. She had the look of a woman who'd ride through hellfire, and besides, there was nowhere *to* stop. The moor might have been the middle of the sea, for all the harborage it offered.

His vision flickered. Brilliant blades of lightning carved the clouds.

Muriel's rippling hair flashed red.

In that moment, he couldn't tell if he'd been struck by a bolt, or if she had. The illumination was blinding in its intensity and outlined every detail of her face. He felt seared, and his nerves jumped when the thunder crashed. He realized he was pedaling faster, out of a mad impulse, as though he could throw out his arms and pull the lightning from the sky, pull it away from her. He wanted to protect her with his life.

Hubris.

He twisted and called out, feeling both agitated and absurd. "You weren't struck by the lightning?"

"I don't know." She caught up to him, eyes wild and bright with excitement. "Would my fingers still be this cold?"

"You're laughing." He squinted and confirmed it for himself with a low mutter. "She's laughing."

She bared her small white teeth. "I told you I love storms."

The wind rayed her hair around her head.

The inside of his chest felt molten.

She was the storm. For two weeks, she'd been sweeping through him, frenzying his blood, flooding him with desire, leaving great swaths of happiness and whirlpools in his thoughts that went round and round a question he couldn't ask, or even finish.

What if, what if, what if.

But he'd brood about that later.

"Take care when you brake," he advised her. "The road is treacherous." He turned his eyes on it. If they slid over the verge, they'd plunge into the pathless waste where gorse would claw them to a standstill.

The rumble of thunder was constant now. There was more debris in the wind than rain.

"It's like being shaken in a box of rocks!" Muriel's shout sounded muffled.

"What's not to love?" he shouted back. If she laughed in response, the thunder drowned it out. Something pricked his jaw, and something else pricked the corner of his eye.

He didn't think she was laughing, not anymore.

They battled forward.

In the distance, tiny twin flames appeared, burning through the murk. They seemed to hover, and then to lower down from the air.

A trumpet blasted, and blasted again.

His first thought was of the end. The end of the world. A great red dragon whipping his tail, casting the stars to earth, as in William Blake's illustrations for the Book of Revelation. And then he blinked and understood.

Bicycle lamps. The Mutton Wheelers were coasting down a hill, coming toward them.

A dumbfounded laugh escaped his lips.

The storm was apocalyptic indeed if it had prompted Deighton to double back to ensure their safe passage.

He raised his arm. After a long moment, Deighton saw him and did the same. Egg blew the halt, and the wheelmen stopped, dismounted, and turned their machines. No one said a word as Kit and Muriel joined the column. Egg blew another call, and they were off.

The pace was slow uphill. Kit had rain in his eyes, in his mouth, in his ears. When the ground leveled, he tried to call for a halt, but it was like shouting underwater. No one heard. As they began to descend, into a wooded valley, the mud beneath their wheels moved with them. They weren't riding anymore but sliding. The wind kept slapping them with stinging debris. And then a drenching gust hit like a fist. Kemble went over, knocked flat into Butterfield, and Prescott and Egg crashed into them from behind. It was no good braking. Kit swung wide and shot off a ledge, or that was how it felt. All he knew was that his wheels left the ground. His stomach rose up, and then the bicycle came down, hard, and he bounced off the seat into a heap of muddy leaves.

He lay on his stomach, dazed, feeling not pain but a kind of heaviness, only dimly aware of the rain pattering on his back, as though he'd become one with the mud. He was some time tottering to his feet. He dragged the Rover from a bush and staggered with it toward the scene of the crash, the wind shoving at his back. He let the Rover go, let it tip, when he saw the other machines scattered over the earth, Muriel's among them.

Penny! This time it was like shouting in a dream. He was screaming soundless screams. Because he saw her now too, or at least he saw a lock of hair bright against the hard, wet ground and the curled fingers of a gloved hand. The rest of her was obscured by the circle of crouching wheelmen, all staring down with expressions of horror.

His approach had a nightmarish slowness.

Prescott turned a pale face to him. "We've killed her!"

"It's your fault." Kemble met his gaze, eyes wild. "Bringing a lady on a run. You killed her!"

"I'm not killed." It was Muriel's voice, faint but more than faintly annoyed. "Give me some air."

The wheelmen opened the circle, Egg releasing a tiny, relieved sob. Kit realized he was on his knees, and that the rain was sluicing straight down from the sky with the gushing velocity of a cataract. He helped Muriel stand, and they splashed after the wheelmen to the relative shelter of a tree.

Deighton punched the trunk. "This was a bad idea."

"Evidently." Kit raised his brows as Deighton shook out his hand, teeth bared in a grimace. "Also, we should have walked downhill." He turned his gaze to Muriel, watching as she shifted gingerly, testing each bone and joint. She was white to the lips, excepting the streaks of mud on her cheek, but her eyes were clear and focused, and nothing seemed broken.

"No, I mean *she* was a bad idea." Deighton moved his jaw from side to side. "This farce has gone far enough. She can't continue."

Muriel's brows met. "I'm not staying here."

"It's too dangerous for you to ride on. You were already lagging so far behind, I had to turn the column around for you. Then you *fell*."

"Everyone fell."

"I did not fall, madam." Deighton's right eyelid was twitching. "You will stay here, with Griffith. I will stop at the next village and have someone send a carriage."

"That's not how this works," interjected Kit. "If she wants to ride on, she rides on."

"*You* want her to ride on." Deighton widened his stance, edging Egg out of the protection of the tree's canopy. "You put your own interest above a lady's safety."

Kit frowned. "Convenient, is it not? Your concern for her safety furthers *your* interest."

"Griffith." Kemble was frowning too. "Facts are facts. She has . . . organs."

"Organs." Egg looked acutely embarrassed, in addition to bruised, scraped, and very, very wet.

"The brain is an organ," Muriel reassured him.

"Women have a limited supply of animal vigor," announced Deighton, glaring vigorously all around him. "When they overuse their brains, it depletes a certain other organ."

"Hair?" guessed Egg.

"Hair isn't an organ," said Prescott.

"Then why does thinking too much make you bald?" asked Egg.

"I refer to the *female* organ." Deighton went red. "The necessary one, for wives, and mothers."

The wheelmen were all suddenly concentrating on their muddy shoes.

Did Muriel want to be a mother? Kit felt and instantly resented a sharp little jab in his gut.

Her eyes had focused on Deighton.

"A woman using her brain depletes nothing. Except perhaps the egos of mediocre men invested in the idea that they're automatically superior to half of humankind. Research finds that the female brain is no different from the male brain." She drew a breath. "Which I confess, in present company, I doubt."

Butterfield murmured to Deighton out of the side of his mouth. "That was an insult."

Deighton made a belated sputtering noise.

Egg tittered.

Deighton barked at him. "Go wipe off the bikes."

"In the pouring rain?" Egg blinked.

"We're riding to Newquay," said Deighton. "It's not riding to us. We're wasting time."

Kit shook his head. "Riding in this storm is dangerous, period. For once, why don't you use the correct organ?"

Deighton's lip curled. He opened his mouth and roared. But no, it wasn't Deighton roaring. This roar was loud as thunder, and went on and on, longer than any human breath.

Muriel reacted first, running toward the sound, Kit giving chase. The ground sloped steeply, and Muriel skidded to a stop at a precipice, which, Kit realized, was disturbingly close to the spot he'd landed when he'd flown off his bike.

It provided an unobstructed view down into the valley.

Deighton, Kemble, Butterfield, Prescott, and Egg were only a moment behind, and so all seven of them stood and watched as the dark wave swept through it, destroying everything in its path.

26

M Y GOD."
  Kit wasn't sure who'd spoken. He wasn't sure what he was
  seeing. It made no sense. Everything below was chaos. Instead
of copses, fields, cottages, there was churning water, nearly black
with debris. Treetops protruded, and roofs.

What had been a riverside hamlet was now *within* the river, almost fully submerged.

Fence posts were spinning in the currents. Branches. A chicken
coop. Other bulky shapes he hoped were hay bales but feared were
sheep.

"Is that . . . ?" Kemble clamped his arm. "In the water there . . ."

"Yes." Muriel answered, and her certainty sent a cold prickle
down Kit's spine. She had excellent eyesight, years of experience
identifying small, half-hidden things.

"Where?" asked Deighton. "What?"

"A child," she said. "By the oak."

Kit was focused on the tiny form, bobbing and flailing. Kemble
was still holding his arm.

"We have to do something." Butterfield turned to Deighton. All
the wheelmen did. They looked lost, overwhelmed, and strangely
childlike themselves as they awaited their orders. Deighton stood
stock-still, rain streaming down his face. His eyes were vacant.

"Captain?" urged Prescott.

He shook himself. "We'll ride down at once."

"No, we won't."

Every head snapped toward Muriel.

"That will take too long," she said. "We'll go this way."

"Off a cliff?" Butterfield blanched.

"It's not quite so steep as that. You'll have to pick your path carefully. The rocks will be slick, and the earth may crumble. Take small, sideways steps, and try not to lean back. Unless you need to sit and slide. There's no shame in it. Ready?"

She gave them a rallying look, gaze landing briefly on each of them in turn. Kit found himself nodding, even though his stomach churned like the water below. She didn't pause to acknowledge his nod, or to solicit Deighton's response.

She turned, hunching slightly against the wind, and ran parallel to the hillside, away from the sheerest drop.

Kit tensed. The low roar of the river had made a strange silence in his head. He watched, frozen, as she shifted her horizontal motion, angling down, then zigzagging back, then angling down. Half the hillside seemed to cave beneath her feet. She was carried with it for several seconds, during which Kit forgot how to breathe, then she lunged and snatched at a sapling, swinging herself to firmer ground. She skidded, skipped, and didn't stop. She hadn't misrepresented herself. She *was* like a mountain goat.

Kit was not. He'd never plunged over the edge of such a dauntingly perpendicular slope, at least not deliberately. He felt dizzy as he started forward.

The wheelmen didn't move.

"I can't." Butterfield's voice cracked.

"Sit and slide," called Kit, as his feet shot out from under him. He slid on his arse over mud and wet grass, found his feet for a few hopping steps, then slid again. Plummeting off a literal cliff could hardly have brought him down to the valley floor faster. This was a kind of plummeting, plummeting by giddy stages. He reached the bottom with shocking rapidity, heart banging out of his chest. Muriel was already wading out through knee-high water.

The next moment his breath exploded, his whole body jolting with a sudden impact. A hand grasped his collar to keep him upright. He made a strangled noise and jerked free. Deighton stood behind him, panting. He might have banged into Kit by accident or aimed for him, so as to break his own momentum.

He met Kit's eyes without apology. "How do we find the boy?"

It was a reasonable question. Without the bird's-eye view, Kit had no idea where to start. Acres of water spread before them.

"We follow her," he said, and waded after Muriel.

"He was by a tree." Deighton lurched along beside him. "But which? They look the same."

"Not to Mrs. Pendrake."

"And why is that?"

"She's a botanist." Kit gritted his teeth. Had Deighton learned *nothing* about his traveling companion but the fact that she contained the female organ? "Botanists can discern subtle distinctions in trees."

"Mrs. Pendrake can pick out a tree she saw from the top of that mountain? In the midst of all *this*?" Deighton's disbelieving gesture brought home the point. The flooded valley seemed alien, even things that should have been familiar difficult to recognize in their strange new context. Chickens were roosting on chimneys. A pink armchair drifted by.

"She can," said Kit. He wasn't sure of that either, but he needed to believe it. He needed to believe that *someone* could interpret this devastation and tell them what to do.

"There!" Muriel had stopped to point. She stood fifty feet away, in water as high as her waist. "That's the one." She cast a bright glance at Kit, expression torn between hope and fear. "The big sessile oak."

"He'll have got himself up into it." Deighton lurched faster, trying to run. With a grunt of frustration, he shoved his cap inside his coat and dove.

Kit did the same. The current was pushing him off course as he swam, and objects he didn't care to identify battered his legs and arms.

What if the boy *hadn't* got himself up into the tree?

He wouldn't think of the alternative, that tiny bobbing figure swept away, slipping down beneath the choppy waves.

Deighton reached the oak first, grabbed a branch, and hauled himself up. His head and shoulders disappeared in the dense foliage.

Kit heard him halloing, saw the leaves shake as he climbed higher.

"He's not here," he shouted down to Kit. "Dammit all." He sounded almost shrill. He climbed higher, higher than any little child could climb. Kit rolled onto his back in the water, looking up into the gray sky, blinking against the rain, lighter now. He let the current tug him.

"Griffith!" Deighton was screaming now. "Griffith!"

Kit tilted his head in time to see him jump. He had a long way to fall. The resulting splash slapped Kit in the face, and then Deighton was rising up from the water below him with the violence of a kraken.

The ensuing struggle dunked them both.

Kit wrestled himself free of Deighton's grasp and shot to the surface, choking. "What in the bloody hell are you doing?"

"Saving your life." Deighton treaded water furiously. "You were immobilized by cramp."

"I was *floating*, on purpose, to check the direction of the current. I think . . ." Kit didn't want to say it. The current was sluggish and slow, but a tired, cold, terrified child could hardly have resisted. The current would carry them to wherever he'd fetched up.

Kit let the current tug him again, away from Deighton and the oak, and bumped an obstruction that didn't give way. It was an enormous branch that must have curved down from the oak's trunk, so that most of its length was underwater, except for the leaves and smaller branches at its distant tip. A thin arm was hooked among them.

Kit did feel a cramp then, in the soles of his feet, and he felt too all the hope and all the fear he'd seen shining in Muriel's eyes.

He swam, the strokes jerky and frantic. At last, between the green leaves, he glimpsed a small, wet, bone-white face. Water lapped the boy's chin. His eyes were half closed, and his lips were blue. He was alive.

"Thank God," breathed Kit, and sank—just for one wet second—with relief.

Deighton towed the boy to the knoll where the hamlet's stunned residents were gathering. He swam a one-armed backstroke, bracing the boy protectively against his chest. Kit followed, grimacing, trying to shake the spasms from his feet.

A woman broke away from the huddled crowd when she saw them. She stretched out her arms, a wail emerging from her throat.

Deighton staggered through the shallows, and the woman raced toward him, a fierce blur wrapped in a sodden shawl.

"God bless you," she gasped, as she gathered her son to her. She was smiling at Deighton through her tears. "God bless you."

Deighton stared. The woman's attention was drawn immediately back to her son. She soothed and cuddled, bundling him in her shawl.

"At your service," mumbled Deighton, far too late. He looked at Kit, who'd hobbled over to stand at his side. There was something soft and awed in his face that he schooled quickly into a surly frown.

"Let's go," he said, and stalked back into the flood.

The sun was breaking through the clouds, and light glared on the water. Boats had appeared, sculled by grim-faced men. The rescue effort was underway in earnest now. Rescue would eventually become repair, and these Cornish folk would rebuild their lives, together. Kit hesitated, wondering if he had a further role to play, or if he was intruding on other people's pain. No one paid him any mind. On the knoll, the mother knelt, rocking her son with her lips in his hair. Some women, and men, stood conferring, and some were striking off in different directions.

Kit turned and scanned for Muriel. She was trudging with Deighton, heading back toward the hillside, looking from time to time over her shoulder, for him. Hesitation evaporated. He went after her as fast as his feet would allow.

When the three of them arrived at the base of the hill, Deighton addressed the wheelmen, who hadn't made it farther than the water's edge. Butterfield and Egg looked to have had a particularly rough way down.

"The boy's safe." He fitted his crumpled cap on his head. "We found him."

Was it the royal *we*? Or was Deighton crediting the collective effort? Muriel blinked and caught Kit's eye. He gave a conspiratorial shrug, delighted by the answering twitch of her lips.

"Back to the bikes." Deighton tucked his chin and pushed between Kemble and Prescott, tackling the hill with long strides. Butterfield looked up toward the hilltop. His face was so vividly expressive of misery, Kit felt the absolutely ludicrous instinct to give him a hug.

"He's scared of heights." Kemble sneered.

"I'm not." Butterfield straightened.

"After you, then." Kemble bowed and made an ushering motion.

"Ladies first." Muriel glanced between Kemble and Butterfield. "Mr. Butterfield will come up behind me." She gave Butterfield a lovely, muddy smile. "Just watch where I step and put your feet in the same place."

He was too petrified to resent her aid, let alone reject it. He nodded.

"How did you become such a champion stepper?" asked Kemble, later in the climb, when Muriel's zigzag path had them walking toward each other, at different elevations.

"She's a botanist and a plant hunter," snapped Kit, from yet lower on the hillside, annoyed. "She has traveled the world over. Do none of you know that?"

"I know it," offered Prescott, from behind him.

"I know more," said Egg, from behind *him*. "Mrs. Pendrake didn't tell Prescott about the giant panda."

Kit was regretting the question.

"She didn't tell *me* about the giant panda," he muttered.

"Please tell us," said Butterfield fervently. It was clear he'd prefer listening to anything other than the thoughts in his head. He hadn't looked up from the ground once.

"What's a giant panda?" Kemble was walking away from Muriel now, scowling. "I've never heard of such a thing."

Deighton stomped irritated, impatient circles on the brow of the hill as the rest of them finally struggled up to him, talking loudly and longingly of favorite meals. The topic was a non sequitur introduced by Kemble after Muriel concluded the tale of the giant panda, and everyone was hungry enough to find it inexhaustible.

Kemble had launched on a paean to roast duck sauced with brandy, claret, and port, which a hot blue glare from Deighton cut short.

"We can't ride to Newquay." Deighton's hands were in fists. "We won't even make it to Padstow." His throat worked above his wilted necktie, as though the next words were hard to get out. "It is decided. We ride inland."

Kit looked at the sky. The sun still winked through breaks in the clouds, but to the north, a line of thunderheads towered. More weather was coming. And floods likely rendered the coastal paths impassable.

Deighton was using the correct organ. No wonder he was irritated.

Kit opened his mouth to congratulate him, then figured it would do more harm than good and took himself over to the pile of bicycles to see what, if anything, had to be set to rights.

ALL THE MACHINES were serviceable, but only barely. The journey to Bodmin was sloppy, slow, and painful. There was flooding there too, in the town center. Overflowing drains. Swamped shops and houses. They chose to lodge on the highest ground, at a former coaching inn, the Travellers Rest, where the red-nosed, white-haired innkeeper ceded the old tack room to their bicycles, then ushered them into the bar.

Night was falling, and the storm had regrouped. Wind raged noisily along the narrow street. There was no roast duck on the menu, so Kemble had to content himself with chicken. Kit savored the warmth more than anything. Wind slicing through damp clothing as he cycled had chilled him to the bone. Deighton spent most of the meal simmering in silence at the head of the table.

"We were supposed to ride to Newquay." Deighton shoved away his emptied plate, which nearly forced Kit's plate off the table. "Bude to Padstow to Newquay. That was the plan. And tomorrow, Newquay to Porthtowan to St. Ives. Now we must do it all tomorrow, rain or shine."

The windows rattled, and a man eating alone in a booth whistled. "Lord, she's blowing now."

"We are on a *ten*-day run." Deighton crossed his arms, clutching his biceps, revealing fingernails bitten to the quick. He looked supremely ill at ease. "It was printed in the paper. With all the destinations. Everyone in St. Ives is taking bets on whether or not *she* will complete the run. If *none* of us do?" His eyelid was twitching again.

"There's no controlling the weather," said Muriel. She'd raked her hair into a messy braid and somehow exuded command. Now that Kit considered it, she *had* been commanding the Mutton Wheelers for much of the day. The experience seemed to have shifted the balance of power. Butterfield and Kemble were both nodding along to what she said.

"I control myself." Deighton dropped his hands to the table and gripped the edge. "And my club. We will complete the run tomorrow, even if there's a tempest."

"Tomorrow, then." Muriel raised her glass of ale.

Deighton snarled. "*You* should take the train to St. Ives. We're going to be riding excessive miles, through excessive mud. And this time, I won't turn back for you."

"Understood." Muriel sipped. "I'll take my chances."

"I'd put my money on Mrs. Pendrake," said Butterfield, with an admiring shake of his head. "When I saw her go charging down that cliff . . ."

"What are you saying?" Kemble started. "You can't put your money on *her*. That means putting your money against *us*."

"Does it have to mean that?" Butterfield smoothed his mustache.

"It's not the end of the world if she completes the run. The Rover is a well-designed machine. We wouldn't be the only club switching over."

Kemble was gawking. "We'd have to let women in the club."

Butterfield shrugged. "Frankly, I don't see the problem."

"In the club means also in the *clubhouse*. It's squalid!" Kemble paused. "I suppose the women might make it less squalid. They could tidy. Maybe even embroider our emblem on chair covers." He seemed to be warming to the idea.

"We could call them the Wheelettes." Egg perked up as well. "Or the Muttonettes."

Kit wondered if Deighton was about to flip the table. His knuckles were white and veins bulged in his forehead.

But at that moment, the bar flooded—not with water—with people, more and more, all disheveled, with slightly dazed expressions. The innkeeper's wife answered Deighton's questions as she stacked the emptied plates, and overheard snatches of conversation supplied the rest. These weary souls were marooned rail passengers. Sections of the line connecting Bodmin with Wadebridge were underwater, and a tree had come down and blocked the train bound for Truro. Some of the passengers had waited hours for seats in the plodding, insufficient three-horse omnibus that had started from Bodmin to collect them. Others had trudged through fields and along roads thick with mud.

Chairs were in high demand, so Kit, Muriel, and the wheelmen rose. Rooms were going to be in high demand as well. They'd already taken theirs, but as the wheelmen trooped upstairs, Muriel hung back with a significant look.

"We should share," she whispered. "For the common good." She flagged down the innkeeper's wife as she bustled by.

"I think there was a mistake." Muriel smiled at her, but her eyes slid back to Kit. "My husband and I only need *one* room."

My husband and I . . .

That phrase on Muriel's lips instantly conjured all the warm fantasies he usually tried to fight. He and Muriel traveling the world together, or even better, staying at home, *their* home, mostly windows to let in light for all the plants and to facilitate his painting. Late nights. Late, lazy mornings.

He gave his head a rueful shake, dispelling the visions.

Even so . . . *My husband and I.* It lingered like a sweet taste.

He let it. There was only so much sweetness a man could resist.

27

❧

THE LONG DAY had strained Muriel beyond her limit. She stripped off her filthy gown, washed, changed, and crawled into the bed, eyelids sliding down with the weight of sandbags. Through her torpor, she was vaguely aware that Kit was padding around the dark room. She rolled onto her side and watched him through her lashes. He was tossing his necktie on a chair, crossing in front of the fire, backlit, face in shadow. Her lashes fluttered down. When she lifted them, he was standing at an angle to the fire, shirt gaping at the neck, golden light on his bare throat and collarbones. He looked honey-painted, and beautiful, and the air seemed to shimmer around him. He was watching her.

"I like . . ." Her whisper trailed off. She started awake and met his gaze. "Your eyes," she finished.

"My brown eyes." He teased her with a smile.

"They're not brown." She wiggled into her pillow. "They're . . . eternity."

"You're asleep," he observed. "I don't think eternity is a color. If it was, I'd have bought the pigment."

"They're silvery, like stars, and stars are in the heavens, and the heavens are eternity." Her lids drifted back down. "And when you look at me, I feel like I'm at the center of the galaxy." She heard herself suddenly, realized with vague alarm that this speech was more incautious than her leap down the escarpment. "Don't worry, though," she murmured, maybe to herself, maybe to him. "I know it's not personal. It's just a property of your irises."

She heard his soft tread and felt the mattress dip as he sat.

"Penny." He brushed his fingers over her unbound hair. "Of course it's personal."

"Personal with many persons." She was slurring her words. She wanted to say that she wasn't hurt, that she understood the goodness of his rakery, that every farm girl and bluestocking and suffragist and widow should share this magical feeling, and so she could share him. Not that he was hers to share. And if he was, maybe she would insist that certain things—just a few—were personal to the two of them only.

"Many Muriels," she slurred. "Curtains, knees, pugs, seaweed."

"I've never been one for lasting attachments." His voice was low. "You know that."

"Why?" She wasn't asleep. She was drifting between sleep and wake, which was far more dangerous. Just alert enough to ask questions her slumbering inhibitions should have silenced. "Because you wanted someone you couldn't have?"

Lucy appeared at the bedside, beautiful in her bridal gown. The room grew tall and vaulted. It was a church, and Lucy waved goodbye to Kit and glided toward the man who waited by the altar. He wore a jeweled crown. He was a prince. No, he was a duke. He was Charles Heywood, chasing her through the lecture hall, out into the busy New York street, which teemed with staring strangers.

Sometime later, she opened her eyes. Kit was behind her, his arm around her waist, their legs tangled, his chin in her hair. He'd washed too, and smelled of lemon verbena. She breathed deeply, settling herself in his arms, relaxing something so deep inside that she felt like the sigh she released. Sometime after that, the storm woke her. Her pulse jumped with every crack and thud.

"Are you frightened?" Kit's breath sifted through her hair.

She gasped at the next thud.

"So am I." His smiling lips brushed her ear. "This storm is blood-curdlingly gothic. Let's hope it's over by morning."

Morning. When they'd ride, rain or shine, to the rugged north coast and west to St. Ives. This was their final night on the road. Thank God she'd fallen asleep before she'd spouted any more foolishness. Eternity. Lucy. Her eyes were wide open now. The fire had burned low, and the air on her face felt clammy and cold.

"I'm not frightened." She wriggled around, facing him.

"Nor do you seem tired," he drawled. "And we need our rest for tomorrow."

"I can't rest in this weather."

"Hmm." His eternity eyes glimmered. "Let me help with that." His lips covered hers, all silken heat and greed, and she let him consume her, surrendering to sensation. Her fingers twisted in the thick silk of his hair, the slide of tongues between their joined mouths sending licks of fire down to her belly, her legs, her curling toes. She jumped as the wind shook the walls, and he laughed a dark laugh, lifting away.

"So tense." He pushed her onto her back and kicked off the blanket, cold air dropping into the void, making her shiver. "Pull up your shift."

She blushed and lifted her hips, tugging the cotton up to her waist. The bed's white dimity hangings took on an ethereal quality. Shadows from the fire's flickering coals wheeled above. Her shiver became a full-body shudder of gothic excitement.

"Higher, please."

The crisp demand made warmth rush between her legs. She rolled the fabric up, exposing her breasts. She had gooseflesh from the chill, and he chased it with his hand, stroking up her belly, rolling her breast beneath his rough palm.

"Will you take off your shirt?" Her voice hitched. He hadn't ever, except for that first night, in the tub. He always kept himself partially clothed, and she'd learned not to let her hands roam. "I want to see you too." She swallowed, momentarily shy. "And touch you."

He lay still beside her, her heart thumping into his motionless hand.

"That's not something I often do." He spoke slowly. "I have difficulty trusting that I will be seen how I need to be seen. And touched how I need to be touched."

"Can you show me? Show me how?"

"It's late." His hand began to move again, fingertip dragging between her breasts, then over her nipples, which responded with exquisite agony. "Someday perhaps you could touch me like this. Or like this." His teeth replaced the fingertip, and she arched her spine, helplessly encouraging the torment. He drew back with a rasping breath. "And we could lie like this, skin against skin." He eased onto her, shirt rubbing on her sensitized breasts. His mouth was on her neck and her jaw, suckling her lower lip, until she sighed, and their tongues met. He broke the kiss.

"And you could see and touch me everywhere. There are parts of my body I might wish otherwise, but I can still enjoy them." He hesitated, looking down at her. "With someone able to understand that neither *man* nor *woman* comes down to parts. Either could have any."

"I understand," she said, but perhaps there was a shade of uncertainty in her tone. At any rate, he didn't tear off his nightshirt and fall upon her naked. He rested his forehead on hers, and she felt the gossamer movement of his lashes. Her mind was turning and turning. A man could have had a boyhood or a girlhood. A man could have a smooth jaw and calloused palms, or a beard and smooth palms. He could have a muscled chest, or a soft one. She tried to think how best to express her thoughts. It was all so complicated. Or stunningly simple.

I love you.

She was far too awake to say that.

"Speaking of parts," he murmured. "Would you like to see my cock?"

Her mind lurched, and her reply was a stutter. A stuttered *cock*, no less, which made her cheeks glow like coals in the dark.

"I have several. Wood, glass, stone, rubber. *Very* soft leather packed with wool. I only brought one." He paused. "*See* was a euphemism, by the way."

"Oh," she said, faintly. "*Would you like to see my cock* didn't sound particularly euphemistic."

"Mm." She could hear his grin. "Here's the proper question. Would you like me to fuck you with my cock?"

Sweat dampened her throat, anticipation coiled between her legs, and she gave a little whimper.

"Is that a yes?"

"Depends on which you brought," she managed. "It's not the stone one?"

He laughed and stroked a thumb down her side. "Too heavy. I'm traveling light."

"I warned you I'm not imaginative." She laughed too, shakily. "I certainly can't imagine a stone . . . That is, a—" She coughed. "Cock. Of stone." Except maybe she could, because every moment she was coiling tighter. Intrigued. Excited.

"You might find you like it. It's hard, of course—harder than most—but smooth. I'd warm it first. And oil it. Nothing I use on bicycles, I give you my word. And I'd fuck you with it slowly, using my hand to control the strokes."

She pressed her thighs together, a pulse beating at their apex.

"And the one you did bring?" She tried to make her breathing more even.

"Packed leather. I fit it in a leather harness. Which leaves my hands free." His hands were roaming lower.

She moaned, unable to restrain herself, and he repositioned, shoving apart her legs. She couldn't wait another second, and he obliged her, no more caresses. He leaned forward and put his mouth on her. Her moan became a groan, a deep, desperate sound that she could hardly believe she was making. He pulled with his lips, lapped with his tongue. She forgot the cock. She was rolling against him, lost in the rapture of the moment. He slid two fingers inside her, working her with a slow, churning motion, and then stroked faster, once, twice, three times, and she screamed, convulsing as thunder broke, dark vibrations traveling through her. The next clap of thunder started it again, delicious tremors that took her apart. Kit sprawled on her legs, purring his satisfaction like a lazy cat. Finally, he stirred.

"Don't go anywhere," he said, as though she had muscles and

bones, as though she could do anything but puddle on the bed like silk.

When he returned, he knelt at her feet, legs spread, nightshirt rucked up. His cock jutted, dark and curved, larger than she'd pictured. The sight motivated her to prop herself up on her elbows. He stroked his hand back and forth, up and down the length of it.

"Can you *feel* with that?" she whispered.

"I'm not frigging myself." His teeth flashed. "I'm warming the leather. Any pleasure I derive from this particular action is sourced in my mind, not this phallus. But the mind is powerful. And my desire to be inside you is more than physical."

He lunged and came down atop her, bracing the bulk of his weight with his arms. "Do *you* want me inside you?"

God, yes, she wanted it. She wanted it now, and tomorrow, and next week, and next year, and *someday*, and forever. She pushed up and kissed him, wrapping him with her arms and legs as he slid into her by slow degrees. He rolled his hips, lodging himself deeper and deeper. She was pinned, filled to the brim and quivering. She traced the taut muscles of his back, dug her nails into the hard curve of his buttocks, urging him on. He changed the angle of her legs, pressed her knees higher, thrusting faster, his teeth on her throat, and her peak slammed her head back into the pillow and kept coming on. She heard her cries mingle with the storm, and she couldn't tell if he'd cried out too, or if she'd reached the heights alone. She held him close, breathing his scent, unable to speak. She drifted off with him inside her, and woke up briefly to the sound of thunder, his body curled around her, his arm slung possessively beneath her breasts. And then, despite the storm, despite everything, she slept like the dead until morning.

28

IT WAS STILL raining at breakfast. The bar was even more crowded than it had been the previous evening, and a mood of agitation prevailed. The storm had disturbed everyone's rest and continued to disrupt travel. Muriel squeezed between tables at which the talk was nothing but complaints about the beds, the weather, the train, the tea, and the toast. Her only concern was *getting* tea and toast. Cold, burnt—it made no difference. She was groggy, sore, hungry as a bear, and she required sustenance for the grueling ride ahead. She'd have eaten grubs.

There were no grubs in evidence, and no free tables. She had no party to join. The wheelmen were in the tack room, attending to their machines. She'd peeked in on the way to the bar and seen Kit crouching by a Rover with his shirtsleeves rolled up. He had a smudge of grease on his cheek, and hair in his eyes, and the muscles in his forearms were doing interesting things as he changed the angles of his wrists. She'd realized she was giving him that mortifyingly lobsterish look, so she'd hurried on, before anyone could remark it.

Now she clutched at her rumpled skirt, wondering if she could make herself very small and perch on the edge of a bench at a table of strangers, or if she'd better return to her room and gnaw a seaweed specimen.

A woman noticed her distress and scooted down her bench voluntarily, opening a space.

"You can sit here." She was around Muriel's age, with a tired face and energetic hair, curls escaping her bun and corkscrewing in all directions.

"We're terrible company," warned the woman sitting across from her. She seemed as though she'd be very good company, on less trying occasions. She had a sprightly air. Her smocked silk dress was a conspicuous shade of pink.

"And anyway, we're about to leave." The woman to the right of the woman in pink set down her teacup. Her eyes were a fathomless blue.

"We're not even guests here," confided the woman in pink.

"My thanks." Muriel sat, a little confused and wholly charmed.

"We're at the White Hart," the woman in pink continued. "But the kitchen flooded, so there was nothing to eat."

"Oh dear." Muriel surreptitiously surveyed the adjacent tables, trying to pick plausible husbands from among the diners. None passed muster. These women were elegantly eccentric and seemed incongruous with the general run of stranded families.

They traveled in their own society. Perhaps they were sapphists. She smiled. Her imagination *had* improved. Since meeting Kit, her sense of possibility was ever expanding.

"Were you on the train to Truro?" she asked. Sapphists or no, she'd wager they were bound for a resort. "Is Penzance your destination? Or St. Ives?"

The curly-haired woman's face clouded.

"St. Ives," responded the blue-eyed woman, with a peculiar emphasis.

"No." The curly-haired woman crossed her arms. "We're returning to London."

Muriel's smile slipped. Clearly she'd interrupted an argument.

"St. Ives is lovely," she murmured.

The women seemed to have forgotten she was there.

"I can feel it in my heart." The curly-haired woman pressed a hand to her chest. "We were stopped by fate."

"For heaven's sake." The woman in pink frowned. "We were stopped by rain."

"There's no fixing this." The curly-haired woman whispered it to herself. She looked wan, lines bracketing her mouth.

Muriel cleared her throat, preparing to excuse herself, but the woman gave a shake and addressed her friends in a brisk tone.

"You two go. The only thing you did wrong was follow my lead."

"You're not our leader," said the blue-eyed woman mildly.

"You have cold feet," the woman in pink suggested. "There's no reason to turn back now."

"I don't think . . ." The words wrenched in bursts from the curly-haired woman's throat. "I don't think that . . . *he* . . . will forgive me."

The blue-eyed woman took her hand across the table.

"Lucy," she soothed. "It was a long night. Finish your tea. You'll feel better."

Muriel sucked in an audible breath.

The woman in pink heard and shot her a friendly wince. "Terrible company, as I said. Apologies."

"Not at all." Muriel hardly moved her lips. She was rooted to the bench. She didn't blink.

Not Sapphists. Sisters. Kit's Sisters. Kit's *Lucy*.

She was certain. Everything fit. She understood their conversation. She understood everything.

Lucy might have broken Kit's heart, but she'd broken her own heart in the process. She'd come to Cornwall to make things right, and maybe still could.

"Wait!" Muriel bolted up as the women rose. All three looked at her with amazement. As well they might. She was wringing her hands.

"Is something the matter?" Lucy was all solicitude. In an instant, she'd put aside her own turmoil, giving Muriel her complete attention. She had a frank gaze, inquisitive and kind. She was a *duchess*, for the love of God, but without an ounce of pretension. Every bit as interesting and attractive as Muriel's jealousy had painted her.

"You're leaving." Muriel's mind blurred. Should she detain them? Should she tell them Kit was in the next room?

"Back to the White Hart." Lucy tipped her head. "To pack our bags in the hopes we're not stuck here forever."

Muriel's veins felt like wires.

This way, she could say, and lead them right to him. He'd look up from his bicycle, sweaty, surprised, and heart-stoppingly handsome, and he'd drop his wrench, and Lucy would pale, and perhaps they'd start forward at the same moment. They'd fall into each other's arms. Kit deserved that. He deserved a magnificent reconciliation. And he deserved also to choose when and how and if it happened. Lucy had hurt him, badly. They all had.

Muriel couldn't spring them upon him, not without fair warning.

"Of course." She nodded. "Good luck, with everything."

As soon as the three women had walked away, she collapsed on the bench and stared at the remains of their meal, the teacups and plates. The woman in pink had folded her napkin into a rabbit.

She would tell Kit as soon as her legs were in working order. He would do with the information what he wished.

Her hands balled into fists in her lap. A sneaky, slippery, treacherous thought began to writhe in her brain like an eel.

What if she *didn't* tell Kit? She could keep the encounter secret. She could keep him for herself for one more week.

Her heart hammered.

All she had to do was nothing. Lucy and the others would board a train to London. She and Kit would spend seven golden days together in St. Ives, six silver nights. She wanted that time, all of it, so intensely the prospect of losing an hour robbed her of breath. There was precious *little* time, in the scheme of things. To share under such constraints meant unreasonable sacrifice. She'd been fuzzy-headed last night, overestimating her own selflessness. But love wasn't stingy, or dishonest. And she loved him. She loved Kit Griffith. His eyes, his hands, his voice, his swagger, his soul. Lucy loved him too, perhaps in the same way she did. And when the world went dark for Kit, hers was the name that called him back. Lucy was his light.

What was Muriel's love if it interfered with that light?

She sat perfectly still, sick with desire and guilt, hollowed out by poisonous temptation. Even her appetite had deserted her.

She ordered breakfast regardless. She needed strength to decide her next move.

KIT HAD DONE what he had to do in the tack room. He'd taken off his pedals, and Muriel's, cleaned and rethreaded them, replaced a spoke and adjusted the rest, checked the brakes, and generally assured himself that the day's problems wouldn't be mechanical in nature. Now his head was swimming from the fumes of the cement Butterfield had used to re-adhere his front tire to its rim, and he was more than ready for a second breakfast.

Kemble had the same idea. "I'm bloody starving."

He beat Kit to the door and jogged into the hall, as though the two of them were competing for the very last kipper. Which maybe they were. An ungodly number of people had been coming and going since dawn, their voices and footsteps a constant din. Probably they'd descended on the bar like a plague of locusts.

"I need a blacksmith." Egg spoke in a small voice, slumped against a wall, cracked leather halters and frayed ropes dangling all around him.

"Abandon the thought." Deighton was using a rag to polish his badges. "We ride on the hour."

"On the hour?" Prescott checked his watch and exchanged a look with Butterfield, whose stomach growled audibly. An instant later, they were gone.

"But I can't ride with a broken handlebar. I thought it had come loose yesterday, but look, it's actually broken." Egg turned to his bicycle, propped against the wall beside him. "Just *look*."

Deighton did not look. "Don't pout. You're a Mutton Wheeler. You can ride."

"But—" Egg's expression turned plaintive.

With a muffled curse, Kit forsook all hope of second breakfast and stalked to Egg's machine. A proper fix *would* require a blacksmith, but he could rig up a temporary solution, quick and ugly. He'd unscrew the handlebar from its socket and jam in a broom handle. There was a broom in the tack room, but not a saw. He'd have to break it. Very ugly. Maybe he could sand the edge.

"This is doable," he told Egg.

"Doable? And you'll do it? Oh, ripping! I'll run for a bite, then?" Egg's eager question was hardly out before he shot from the room.

Kit worked for several minutes to remove the broken handlebar before he realized that Deighton hadn't departed. He was standing with his legs spread and his arms crossed, watching him.

"Yes?"

"That machine belongs to *my* wheelman. You don't have to fix it."

Kit exhaled. "You're welcome."

Deighton grunted.

Kit stuck out his lower lip to blow hair from his eyes and cleaned grit from the socket. The room was quiet. Deighton hadn't moved.

Kit sighed. "I don't have to fix it. Like you didn't have to turn back for us yesterday. Or attempt to save my life." He paused. "We'll leave to the side the fact that you almost killed me."

This time Deighton's grunt sounded almost humorous.

"You're welcome," he said.

The silence wasn't companionable, but neither was it murderous.

The crack of the broomstick beneath Kit's shoe sounded like a gunshot. The diameter was close, but not an exact match, slightly too small, which was preferable to the alternative. A bit of cement would do the trick.

Kit had just completed the cementing when he felt something brush his leg. He glanced up, but Deighton was in the same position.

"Cat," said Deighton, and there was, in fact, a cat in the tack room. It went slinking around the bicycles and then rubbed itself against Deighton's calf.

Kit squared his stance.

"Do you expect me to fall to and start *torturing*?" Deighton looked affronted. "What in God's name do you think I'd do to it?"

Kit shrugged without lowering his guard. "I don't want to find out."

Deighton was glaring at the cat now, a glare that seemed powerful enough to crisp its fur. The cat wove between Deighton's legs, oblivious. It was little more than a kitten, gray and fluffy, with big eyes in a round face. He bent and scooped it up.

"Easy," said Kit warningly.

But Deighton was cradling the cat in his arms, much as he'd cradled the half-drowned boy. His glare had dulled, and he studied the cat with a wholly new expression, flummoxed and a little bit sweet.

"I slapped cats at school." He said it grudgingly. "Is that what you want to hear? Fine. I confess. I slapped cats. Only toms, though. I slapped them to make them fight. To make them stronger." A knot formed on his brow, and he muttered the rest: "It was for their own good."

Kit looked at Deighton for a long moment. He was still studying the cat, his short, colorless lashes trembling.

"I see." Kit focused again on the repair. "Was it good for you?"

"To slap them?"

"To get slapped." Kit spoke quietly. "Or thrashed, or whatever it was." He guessed *slapped* wasn't the half of it.

Deighton's glare was hot again. "I'm strong, aren't I?"

Kit nodded blandly. "Indeed. You could toss me overhand into a dunghill."

"Exactly."

"Your father wants you to." Kit raised a brow. "But you haven't."

"Yet."

"You won't." Kit would put money on *that*. "You're an obnoxious blowhard, but you're a sportsman. As you once told me, you follow the rules of the road. You'd rather face your father's wrath than compromise your integrity. *That* is strong. Standing up to a bully, instead of bullying in turn. Strength and violence aren't the same thing. But I think you already know that."

Strength and violence and manhood aren't the same thing, he

could have added, but didn't because Deighton's eyelid was already twitching.

"Ha," said Deighton, without conviction.

Kit wiped the grease and cement from his hands with a rag. Deighton had set the cat on the saddle of his bicycle. The cat remained in place, gazing tranquilly at Deighton over the handlebars.

"Another thing I think you know," said Kit. "You can tell your father to hell with Scotland."

Deighton was too thunderstruck for fury. "And he'd say to hell with me. He'd disown me. I'd lose everything."

"You'd lose a lot." Kit knew a thing or two about the price of defiance. "Not everything. And there's much to gain. The life *you* want to live."

"What's this about?" Deighton narrowed his eyes. "Your life is that bicycle shop. Which is about to be *my* bicycle shop. Worry about yourself."

"I'm not worried about losing the bicycle shop."

"You can't wheedle it back from me. I have plans for it."

"I won't wheedle, because I won't lose." Kit cocked a brow, curious despite himself. "What plans?"

"Second clubhouse." Deighton looked at the cat, who looked back at him. "Ferocious little fellow, isn't he? I wish I could bring him with us. We need a mascot. I'd call him—" A sudden noise turned his head.

"Mrs. Pendrake," he finished.

"Mr. Deighton." Muriel was breathless, as though she'd run from the bar, when in fact, she'd walked at a deliberate pace, each measured step reinforcing her determination. "I must speak with Mr. Griffith before we go."

"We are going *now*." Deighton fixed his eyes on her. "And I must first urge you again to spare yourself the physical strain and the probable injury." His eyes dipped, and he took in the sordid state of her gown, which yesterday's misadventures had torn, stained, and misshapen. "The impropriety," he added, with a hint of a blush.

"I know you must." She gave him an impatient smile.

He kept looking at her, slow to realize this was her only answer. When he did, he snorted.

She stepped aside to let him stomp from the room.

"Butterfield!" She heard him bellowing in the hallway. Someone else was shouting too.

"Train's running! Train to Truro!"

She ignored the commotion. The room was cluttered, redolent of rubber and old horse, with one small, cobwebbed window sieving the dismally thin light. Kit and a cat on a bicycle were regarding her with glowing eyes.

"Lucy is here," she breathed. "Here in Bodmin."

Kit didn't blink. She tried and failed to decipher his expression.

"They're at the White Hart." She approached him, pulse thudding. "Lucy and two other women."

He gave his head a slight shake. "No, they're not. They can't be. They'd have come and gone by now."

She stared at him, and the longer she did so, the more his face resembled a mask. "You knew." She struggled to comprehend it. "You knew they were on their way to see you."

"Weeks ago. Ponsonby told me."

"And so . . ." She remembered her intuition that *Kit* had goaded Deighton into their wager, not the other way round. Here it was. His ulterior motive. She stepped even closer, peering up at him. "You got yourself embroiled in this contest, to evade them."

How perfect. How painful. She'd wheeled away with him, wheeled all around Cornwall, but fortune's wheel had brought him to Lucy, regardless.

She had the power to relieve *his* pain, at least.

"I was right." Shoots of real happiness pushed through the choking overgrowth of envy. "Lucy doesn't think you're Judas."

His lips parted, but seconds passed before words followed. "You discussed me?"

"I only sat beside them. She was speaking to her companions."

"You were eavesdropping." He crossed his arms, thumb tapping at his bicep, a line of doubt between his brows. "What did this *Lucy* look like?"

"Sad," she said. "This Lucy looked sad. She looked like a person deeply sorry that she'd harmed someone she loved." She cleared the rasp from her throat. "Deeply sorry that she'd harmed *you*."

"She said my name?" His gaze was dark. "What name did she say?"

Muriel hesitated. "She didn't say any name."

"Ah." He held his mouth in a hard shape she'd never seen. "I wonder which she'd have used."

"I don't know." She glanced away from him as the cat jumped down from the bicycle, landing lightly. Part of her wanted to stop here, but it wasn't the better part. She'd made her decision, and she would represent what she'd gleaned as fully as possible.

"I do know her intentions." She looked back at Kit, holding his gaze. "She wants to mend things."

He was still. "Perhaps she can't."

"She can't, and you can't, if you don't try." Slowly, she reached out and touched his wrist.

"I have tried." He caught her fingers and squeezed. "I've tried all sorts of things. I've tried to forget. I've tried to distract myself." His thumb swept back and forth across her knuckles, absently, but there was no mistaking his meaning. "Nothing has worked."

A sick shiver raced over Muriel's skin. Her mouth tasted like sand.

He'd tried to *distract* himself.

She was a *distraction*.

The idea cut like a rusty blade, leaving a nasty residue behind. It was one thing to share a man's life briefly, and intensely. It was another thing to let that man use you to *hide* from his life.

For the first time, she felt lonely in his presence. She was in a tiny, dirty, unfamiliar room, in a town where she knew no one, and where she didn't plan to stay. Her life was made of such rooms and such places, adding up to nothing and nowhere. All at once, she missed James, desperately. She missed the home she might never have. She missed Kit, even as he stroked her skin.

She pulled her hand away. The cat streaked by.

"They're returning to London," she said. "Or Lucy is. She lost her nerve. To see her, you'd have to go to the White Hart, right now."

He paled. He was far paler than Lucy had been in her vision. He looked like a ghost.

"No time," he whispered, and there was triumph in his voice, and defeat. The room filled with wheelmen, pushing between them, pushing them apart, in their eagerness to claim their bikes.

29

WITHIN MINUTES, THEY were lined up on the street, standing by their bicycles in formation, making final adjustments. The rain had stopped, and the air smelled earthy, with a cool nip.

Muriel glanced at Kit as he rolled his Rover even with hers. He'd tugged on his coat but hadn't buttoned it. He was still pale in the gray morning light and looked dazed.

He was making a mistake.

He caught her eye and summoned a grin. "Ready?"

This was it. The last push to the finish. She wasn't ready. She was unsettled, with a splinter in her chest like something had broken.

"Ready," she said. Over breakfast, she'd fought her way to honesty, rubbing herself raw, and now this one white lie burned like acid on her tongue.

She wasn't ready, but she'd ride.

A cart was clattering toward them, blocking their way, and Deighton delayed the *all mount* to let it pass. As the sound faded, a new one reached her ears. It seemed to come from right behind her.

A hoarse, sustained growl. *That* growl.

The street disappeared. The inn. The men and their bicycles. Her terror belled until it was bigger than she was. She was inside it, in the yard, and the old images surged. Her mother turning, her smile slow to fade. The dog's lurching gait. Its leap.

"Penny." Kit had heard the growl too. He leaned toward her. She saw him through a mist, through veil upon veil of grief and fear.

"You're here," he said quietly, and then, after the slightest hesitation: "*We* are here."

His eyes shone. Those eyes seemed far, far away, but they were made of starlight, and starlight could travel an impossible distance. It reached her. Here. Now. Those other images drained of color and scattered, wisps of the past, floating back to where they belonged.

"And there's a fossilized-looking collie a few yards away," he continued, a smile warming the silver of his gaze. "He's old as the hills, with very few teeth and enormous dignity of bearing. He can't hurt you. I promise."

She nodded, without looking away from his face. Her blood began to flow again. All her muscular aches gathered in her chest, where that cold splinter still lodged, its point aimed at the plumpest, softest region of her heart. Oh yes, she *was* going to yearn for this man, in the months and years and decades to come. She would yearn bitterly. For her, this wasn't distraction. This was life itself, at its sweetest. And she wouldn't regret a single moment.

If Kit rode with her now, would *his* regret haunt him?

"There *is* time," she blurted, and grabbed his arm.

"Penny." He gave a minuscule twitch, of confusion or dismissal.

"You and I resolved that neither of us would strike off, but we can make the choice together to split up." She gulped, aware she was speaking out of turn and that she couldn't live with herself if she didn't continue. "To win the wager, *I* must finish the run today, not you. Don't go to Lucy if you don't want to. But if you do, don't let anything stop you. Not this."

Not me.

He was staring, a kindling hope in his eyes.

"Are you certain?" he whispered. His pinkie hooked hers. She looked down at their linked little fingers, skin hidden by the dirty leather of their gloves.

She was certain. That wasn't a lie. And she was certain too that letting go of his pinkie would feel like tearing away a part of her own body.

"All mount!" Deighton bellowed it from the front of the column.

She let go. She swung up her leg and sat astride her bicycle.

Kit's eyes were blazing.

She wished her own eyes could inscribe a message on the back of his skull.

Good luck. I love you. Goodbye.

She pushed off. The wheelmen were already in motion, bumping over the cobbles.

"What's going on?" Deighton had twisted to look over his shoulder. "Griffith, where are you going? Have you lost your mind?"

She also allowed herself a backward glance.

Kit was riding too, but in the other direction, riding hard for the White Hart Inn.

HE FOUND THEM in the busy coffee room, Lucy, Gwen, and Nelly. They were absorbed in a discussion—Lucy scowling, jabbing a hairpin into her frizzy curls, Gwen sketching as she spoke, Nelly tapping her cup with her spoon. His knees almost buckled at the sight. To stand on the outside of their little circle, peering in—it felt ghastly and perverse, and for a split second, *he* felt ghastly and perverse, for separating himself from them, forcing a new reality that caused everyone discomfort. Betraying his best mates.

By being who you are?

He heard Muriel's indignant voice, and the split second passed. He strode to their table. "You wanted to see me?"

His words drew three pairs of startled eyes.

The hairpin slipped from Lucy's hand and splashed into her tea. Gwen was so reserved her emotions rarely reached her face, but she stared in open-mouthed surprise. Nelly yelped.

"How are you here? *Are* you here?" She stuck her fingers in Lucy's tea and yelped again. "It's hot."

"Hotness is tea's only defense against fingers." Kit's pulse was crashing, but his voice sounded dry. "You got what you deserved."

"I wanted to get the hairpin." Nelly leapt up. "To poke you, in case you're a mirage." She grabbed him in a rib-cracking hug. She worked in clay and marble and had the arms of a discus thrower.

"Ow!" She stepped back. "You pinched me."

"In case you're dreaming." Kit's lips twitched. So did Nelly's, and he saw over her shoulder that Lucy's did too—twitched and held in a tentative smile. Nelly tugged him, and he sat down beside her.

A good thing. His knees *were* buckling.

"Should we order more coffee?" Gwen's expression had smoothed, but her color was high, and her Fra Angelico blue eyes had a slight squint—her version of beaming. "The kitchen is flooded, so there's no food, but the coffee's rather good."

"Why are you dressed like a golfer?" Lucy laughed, but tears sparkled on her lashes.

"Cyclist." Kit glanced down at his jacket. "I'm on a cycling tour. Or I was. It's a long story."

Silence fell between them, filled with the hum of other conversations, and the roar of blood in his ears.

It was such a normal occurrence—the four of them gathered around a table—that the awkwardness seemed out of place and extraneous, an irritation they could brush away, like a buzzing insect. Only they couldn't. That wasn't how this worked.

He picked up a spoon, to have something to do with his hands.

"How was your exhibition?" he asked Lucy. "At the New Gallery?"

"Oh." She swiped at a stray curl, gaze skittering sideways. "I hardly know. Critics said some positive things." She hesitated, looking vacantly toward the corner of the room.

The pause lengthened, excruciating.

"I kept wondering what *you* would think." She inhaled, and slowly, she brought back her gaze, until it met his.

"Your show, last winter." She was going pale, which made her look more freckled, more like the scrawny orphan he'd first met. "I loved it. I didn't say so."

He swallowed. No. She'd said other things. He wasn't sure he could endure their repetition.

As he stared, Lucy's chin formed its characteristic point, and her gaze turned narrow. She was girding herself for a headlong charge, right here and now.

"I couldn't believe you'd kept it secret." She seemed to grow taller, hair bristling. "I couldn't believe that you hadn't shown me the pictures first. That you wouldn't take the credit, for yourself, and for us, and for . . ."

"Women?" Kit set down the spoon with an acid smile. His ribs felt sharp. If he breathed too hard, they'd slice his lungs.

"I asked myself if you thought the pictures were too daring, and the idea made me furious." She clasped her hands so tightly her knuckles turned white. "We *dare*. That's what we do. It's why we formed the Sisterhood. To dare together." Her fury had built anew as she spoke, but it had a beseeching quality, as though she were afraid he'd contradict her.

He didn't. He didn't say anything. His palms were damp.

She slumped, fury fading, until her face held only entreaty and wonderment.

"I went back to the gallery," she said, the heat gone from her voice. "I went back again and again. There was one picture in the Arthurian series—*Half Sick of Shadows*, you called it. The Lady of Shalott in her tower, and out the window, Sir Lancelot, riding through the barley sheaves on his warhorse. You used the same model for both. The lady and the knight had the same face." She bit her lip, studying *his* face. "I kept thinking about the picture. I tried to buy it, but an American collector beat me to the lot. You're the rage in New York."

At that last, her eyes lit up with fierce elation. They'd always reveled in each other's accomplishments. A good review. A good commission. A good sale. Good placement on the wall at the Royal Academy's Summer Exhibition.

And yet—impressing a fusty, famous, well-connected Academician never satisfied him as deeply as impressing *her*. Lucy would give his canvas a certain sharp-eyed look and begin to bounce on the soles of her feet, like excitement was lifting her off the floor, and his heart would lift too. The Sisterhood amplified their efforts as artists, and helped them gain external validation, but in a certain sense, it made external validation unnecessary. Made it clear what audience mattered most. Why they painted, and for whom. He'd muddied all that.

Nothing was clear.

Perhaps Lucy had forgotten for a moment the circumstances of his American debut.

"*Kit Griffith* is the rage in New York." He pronounced each syllable with slow deliberateness, and he braced himself. Her eyes were honey-colored, but they could sting.

"That's what I said." No sting. Just a glowing gaze. She smiled, a wider, surer smile than before. "*You* are the rage in New York."

Suddenly, his heart was in his throat, stopping his words. He felt pressure at the back of his eyes.

"You did dare." She whispered it. "*I* didn't. *I* was the disloyal coward. I jumped to the most superficial, self-serving conclusions. I preferred to think you'd fabricated Kit Griffith out of thin air, to join the enemy, for your own profit, or as a prank you didn't let me in on. But that wasn't it."

He shook his head. "It wasn't the intent. The effect, maybe." His heart was sinking fast, and he uttered his prediction hoarsely: "You think that just as inexcusable."

"I don't think anything you've done is inexcusable." She regarded him, expression as serious as he'd ever seen it. "Blaming you for betraying us was easier than transforming my idea of . . . well, *us*. Who you are, and who we are. I let everyone down, including myself. *Kit*." Her tongue tripped a little, and she flushed. "Kit—I'm sorry." She grabbed her tea, took a nervous gulp, and sputtered.

"Hairpin," murmured Kit, with sympathy.

Gwen handed her a napkin.

"I should have written," she gasped as she recovered, making a face and dropping the hairpin on the table. "But you weren't responding to letters, and—"

"What do you mean?" he interrupted. "Whose letters didn't I respond to?" He looked at Gwen and Nelly. "You wrote?"

"Often." Nelly glanced at Gwen, who nodded.

"Until you wrote to Lucy and quit the Sisterhood." Gwen rolled her pencil between her fingers. "We realized you might not want to hear from us."

He had wanted to hear from them. More than he'd been willing to admit.

He frowned. "I collected my mail in Camborne every week. I received none of your letters."

"Camborne?" Now Nelly was frowning. "Not Camelford? Thomas swore it was Camelford."

Thomas Everett Ponsonby. The bloody bungler.

"Why in God's name did you ask him?" Kit groaned. "I'd written you both with the address."

"Yes, well, we lost the address." Nelly cut him a defensive look. "I can't find any of my correspondence. I kept it in a box that I needed for a new set of chisels, and I thought I'd transferred it to my writing desk, but it's not there. And you know how absent-minded Gwen is." She gestured at Gwen, bent over her sketch again.

"Thomas sounded absolutely certain." Nelly scowled, and the exasperation in her black eyes was all for Ponsonby. "I should have remembered how *he* is."

Kit winced, feeling a pang of compunction. "Go easy on the chap. He meant well."

"Oh, he always means well." Nelly gave a shrug. "I'm always easy on him, considering. I should go harder."

"To crush his hopes," agreed Gwen, still sketching. "It would be a kindness."

Nelly sighed and began to pleat her napkin with precise but agitated movements. "We kissed *once*, under mistletoe. Mistletoe! I'd kiss a warthog under mistletoe. I told him that. I have abundant holiday spirit. He acted as though we were betrothed. Even after he snapped the toe off my Persephone, and I chased him out of my studio with a hammer."

"That was an accident, with Persephone," interjected Kit. He'd been there in Nelly's studio when Ponsonby fell over her cat's water bowl and landed on the base of the plaster cast model. The night lived on in infamy.

"My point is that I couldn't say anything worse to Thomas than I've said already." Nelly sipped her coffee. "He's uncrushable."

Lucy snorted, and Kit caught her eye, and they shared the look he'd thought they might never share again, as though they were of one mind. He brought the spoon to his lips, to catch the grin spilling off his face.

"We do have to thank Thomas for his wires," conceded Nelly. "Otherwise, we wouldn't have made this trip."

Kit removed the spoon, and now his grin was going everywhere. "We have to thank Muriel as well."

"Muriel?" Lucy's brows went up.

"Muriel?" Nelly wore an arch smile.

Gwen lifted her head from her sketch.

"She sat with you at the Travellers Rest. That's how I knew to come here, to find you before you turned back."

"Turned back?" Lucy looked blank.

"To London."

"*Muriel* told you that we were turning back . . . to London?" Her tone was incredulous.

"That *is* what you said." Nelly struck a diplomatic note.

"True," said Lucy. "In a moment of despair. I can see how *Muriel* might have believed it. But Kit, how could *you* believe it? Have you ever met me?"

It was a fair point.

"You weren't turning back, then." He scratched his nose.

"Obviously." Lucy scoffed.

He folded his arms, looking from her to Nelly to Gwen. "We could have had this conversation in St. Ives."

He could have continued cycling. Accompanied Muriel. Seemed like less of a weakling for failing to complete the run. He tried to frown, but the corners of his mouth kept turning up.

Anyone who thought him weak could stuff it. He'd see Muriel in St. Ives, when he introduced her to his three best mates.

Happiness bobbed like a buoy inside him.

"We'll have other conversations in St. Ives," Lucy declared. "We need to rewrite our manifesto. And you haven't heard our idea."

"First, I want to hear about Muriel." Nelly leaned forward.

Gwen waved an arm. "Where did everybody go?"

The formerly bustling coffee room was notably emptier.

Nelly furrowed her brow.

Kit blinked.

"Bugger!" Lucy jumped up. "The train!"

30

THEY MADE IT to the platform seconds before the train to Truro steamed into motion. Even the first-class carriage was full, and they found seats together only by the grace of two jovial young men eager to retire to the smoking lounge for the sake of the ladies.

"You should have taken your private railcar." Kit arched a teasing brow at Lucy as he settled across from her.

"Anthony wanted me to take it." She set her bag on her lap, a better-quality bag than the battered one she'd lugged about as an art student, but still, a workbag. "Too much fuss."

"He gave this venture his husbandly approval?" Kit felt the jab of Nelly's elbow. Sometimes his teasing went too far. He'd wounded Lucy in the past, implying that her marriage to the Duke of Weston was a form of subordination.

Chastened, he cleared his throat. "How is Weston? And how are the girls?"

"Wonderful." Lucy opened her bag and pulled out her sketch-book. "I can show you."

"Dear God, no! Desist!" Kit covered his eyes with his hands. "I've seen enough depictions of Weston's bits to last a lifetime."

"I haven't," murmured Nelly. "He's quite a specimen."

Kit lowered his hands and saw that Lucy was scowling at them both. The first painting she'd ever exhibited was a nude of Weston, as scandalous as it was successful. He'd played muse to her ever since. In Kit's opinion, teasing about Weston's willingness to drop his trousers was permissible until the end of time. The duke's devotion to Lucy's art—his devotion to *her*, full stop—was his finest characteristic.

Nelly might disagree.

The sketches Lucy showed him were of her daughters, twins, just beginning to toddle when he'd seen them last.

"They're with Anthony at Stratton Grange." She named his—their—country seat, smiling a little wistfully at her drawings. "I'll join them next week."

Kit gave the sketches their due, nodding as he returned the sketchbook. "Beautiful."

The drawings *and* the children. Lucy had managed to combine her roles, so they seemed compatible, integral even, each to the other—artist, wife, mother. Aristocrat, less so. Pomp and circumstance still put her back up—she dressed herself in the mornings and gritted her teeth through society functions—but she'd also used her station to advance the causes she supported, with Weston's help.

Kit leaned back in his seat, contemplative.

"Would you have imagined," he asked, "when we were nineteen years old, just starting in the Antique School, that we would one day take a train together to the sea—you a duchess, and I a gentleman?"

"I'd have imagined winged pigs before this." She laughed, shaking her head, and then, slipping into the East End cant that once peppered her speech: "Life's a rum go, ain't it?"

"That it is," he murmured. Lucy's accent had changed over the years. *She* had changed, but he still recognized the half-feral girl, impassioned and ambitious, loyal and kind. He hoped that—in some sense—he remained recognizable too.

He tipped his head. "What would they think of us? Our nineteen-year-old selves?"

"They'd think we're a dream come true." She gave a happy sigh and flicked at the window curtain. The landscape whirring by was lushly green, only a few broken branches and puddles scattered in the fields to show the storm's path.

"So." She turned back to him, expression suspiciously innocent. "Who is *Muriel*?"

He told them, as much as he *could* tell them, in a busy train carriage, as a man of honor and discretion. When their curiosity was appeased, they told him their idea.

"The Siblinghood?" he repeated.

"It's not sonorous," Lucy admitted. "But it captures the spirit."

He gave them all a doubtful look. "The Sisterhood is women artists dedicated to supporting women artists. You don't want to change or obscure that."

"We want *you*, though," said Gwen. "Stop moving."

"Are you sketching me?" He stilled, swerving his eyes to peer down at her sketchbook. "I don't look half-bad."

"The *Siblings*," said Nelly. "I think it's brilliant."

"It was your idea," guessed Kit, and Nelly sniffed. He laughed and scrubbed a hand over his face.

"Sorry," he muttered, as Gwen made a beleaguered noise and lifted her pencil. "And thank you all, truly."

The three of them waited, watching him, love and hope and excitement written plainly on their faces, even Gwen's. They were his friends, his Sisters, and their desire to bring him back into the fold was profoundly moving, and perhaps . . . not *exactly* in line with his own sense of things.

He opted for absolute honesty. "I confess I'm unsure about *Sibling*." Nelly's sniff became an offended huff.

"I'm not opposed to it," he said. "But I might rather something else. Maybe you stay Sisters, and I'm a cousin. Maybe we won't figure it out today."

Lucy nodded. "We have all week."

"Or this week," he added, wryly. A frown puckered her brow. She opened her mouth to protest, then checked herself.

"It's well begun, at least," she said, relenting but determined.

"Another thing." His heart skidded to a stop. The buoy of happiness turned to lead in his chest and plummeted to his stomach. He pushed himself to speak through a clenched jaw. "I can't seem to paint at all these days." He put on a mocking expression, a cover for his wavering composure. "My ability to participate in any circle of artists is currently hypothetical."

"What do you mean—you can't paint?" Lucy's eyes narrowed.

So he told them, too, about burning his easel, about his subsequent headaches and shaking hands. He told them haltingly, tension locking his neck and shoulders, then sat in silence, eyes on the window.

"It's because of what I said." Lucy'd gone rigid too, her steepled hands pressed to her bloodless lips.

"Don't worry. You're not so powerful." He sighed, and suddenly it was easy to speak, to let the most maudlin formulation slip out.

"I abandoned the Sisterhood," he said. "And then I abandoned art." His laughter seemed to shred his throat. "Too late, I discovered that art had abandoned me."

"Kit." Lucy lowered her hands. "*You* are not so powerful. You can't banish art from your life by burning an easel. Art is extremely tenacious. How else could it persist in the face of so much misunderstanding and rejection?"

"Ha," he muttered, but as he looked at her face, its familiar, nononsense expression, he felt the lead in his gut begin to lighten.

Her gaze faltered and then firmed, as she came to some decision.

"I couldn't paint," she confessed. "After Anthony built me my studio. It was so grand, I felt like an utter fraud. I couldn't paint for a month."

"I don't remember that." He crossed his arms.

"I didn't tell you." She went pink. "Any of you. I was ashamed. I let you think I was preoccupied with married life."

That he did remember. "You and Weston spent all of that April holed up and cooing at each other like doves."

"You thought I was with him, and he thought I was at the studio. Really, I was going for soggy, horrible walks all over London, hating myself for squandering what ninety-nine percent of the people I passed could never ever have."

"Lucy," said Gwen in a soft voice. "Why?"

Lucy looked at her, then at Kit. "You know what it was like for me, before. I painted in a little, dark room, on old canvas, with cheap brushes and not enough of anything. Not enough light. Not enough space. Not enough time. Not enough *pigment*. Suddenly, I had everything, and it should have made painting so much easier—the possibilities were limitless. But I'd always made art in *response* to limits, and I didn't know myself as a painter without them. I was so overwhelmed I couldn't begin. My head didn't pound, and my hands didn't shake, but my feet propelled me miles and miles, sent me anywhere but the studio."

"You invited me to share the studio with you." Kit frowned as he reinterpreted events. "I thought it was because you felt guilty for avoiding me. But it was because you needed me to help you stay put."

"And to help me feel like myself again." Lucy chewed her lip. "I wish I'd tried to explain, but it felt so vile—whining about luxury." She paused. "I know our situations aren't the same. But I also know you and art haven't done with each other yet. You'll meet on new terms."

"Perhaps." He moved his shoulders, loosening his neck, the motion agnostic. Lucy's smile was suffused with faith. It thawed him to the marrow.

"All right," he allowed. "I hope so."

"Enough talk." Gwen tore a sheet of paper from her sketchbook and folded back the top quarter too quickly for anyone to glimpse what she'd drawn there. "Let's play."

She passed the folded paper to Lucy.

Lucy's eyes twinkled.

"Kit," she said. "Meet Mr. Malkin, the bird-cow in spats." She bent her head and began to sketch.

"We've already met." Kit snorted. "I invented this game."

"Don't look." Lucy hid her sketch with her left hand, right hand flying. "Voilà!"

She folded the paper again, concealing all but the thinnest bottom sliver of pencil marks. She passed it to Kit.

"Mr. Malkin, the bird-cow in spats," he muttered, extracting a pencil from his knapsack. The first time they'd ever played, they'd produced a drawing of exactly that: Lucy's cat, Mr. Malkin, with the torso of a bird, the legs of a cow, and the feet of a dapper young man.

Hence, the name.

"Hurry up," said Lucy.

He examined the edge of Lucy's sketch. Had she been drawing scales?

"No thinking," she said, so he filled his segment quickly, more scribble than sketch, the coils of a serpent. He folded the paper down and passed it to Nelly, just as Lucy handed him another.

"I started this one," she said, so he elongated the neck, draped the shoulders in a flowing toga, contributing the midsection of a Roman senator.

They kept passing papers, and his pencil kept moving, scrawling chicken feet and shading tiger stripes. It *was* drawing—but drawing with four hands instead of just one. Connecting lines that a friend had begun, and another would continue.

He felt fine. Better than fine.

Maybe his hand shook a little, but maybe that was because he was laughing as he clothed a walrus in a tartan waistcoat and put a horse on a bicycle.

"You start one," said Gwen.

He didn't hesitate. He drew a woman's head, her hair windblown into snaky locks. She had strong features and fine dark eyes, and he would have gazed into them if Nelly hadn't clucked with her tongue.

He folded the paper and passed it on.

When the collective sketches were unfolded, on the platform in Truro, they all laughed at the impossible creatures, neither fish nor fowl, though many included appendages of both.

Kit claimed the drawing of Muriel for himself. She had butterfly wings and octopus arms. The mouth he'd sketched smiled up at him, as though she marveled, and approved.

31

I T WAS EVENING before he went to Titcombe Hall, where a merry crowd had been milling on the lawn since midafternoon—the predicted arrival time for the touring cyclists.

"Oh my," murmured Lucy, walking beside him up the drive. "I didn't imagine quite so many people."

"They're staring at me," said Nelly, putting her hand on his forearm.

"They're staring at me." Kit plastered a smile on his face.

"You're both stupendously vain." Lucy glanced over her shoulder at Gwen, trailing after them in a cobalt-blue gown with a Watteau back. "They're staring at Gwen."

"They're staring at me," repeated Kit. "Because I'm arriving on foot, instead of by bicycle."

"With three beautiful women." Nelly gave his arm a tug, steering them onto the grass. "Some of these chaps look impressed."

Some of them did. Kit spotted O'Brien as the man bowed his head in deference, hair flopping on his forehead. He stood with his regular clique: Craik, Landon, and a few other of Svensson's toadies. They were clustered around a statue of Venus on a plinth, guffawing as Craik painted her hair yellow and someone lewder pinked the tips of her breasts.

"I say, Griffith!" Landon jogged forward. "You've tripled the ladies and lost the bikes! Not a bad trade."

"Bikes are on their way." He didn't stop walking. More and more heads were turning toward him.

The populous edges of the lawn had a fairground atmosphere. Children shrieked, and couples wandered the hedges. Young men were setting off rockets. Two boys—fishermen's sons who often ran errands for the artists—had turned up on a pony, now cropping lilies in a flower bed.

Closer to the house, the gaiety was that of a garden party. Well-heeled guests gossiped in groups of basket chairs. Badminton was underway, and servants circulated with silver trays of lemonade and claret cup.

"Libations!" Nelly swerved from his side.

Lucy followed.

Kit took another step, looking after them, and ran smack into a wall of tweed.

Deighton Senior.

"Pathetic!" The man glared at him with vicious glee.

"Forfeit, did you?" Arthur Hawkings appeared, notepad in hand.

"Not at all." Kit watched Hawkings's pencil move. "I expect Mrs. Pendrake will pedal up the drive in less than an hour."

"We expected the Mutton Wheelers hours ago." The pencil kept scratching. "What happened?"

"Waterspout on the moor." Kit found himself talking in note form, for the reporter's benefit. "Fell behind schedule."

"What happened to you?" Hawkings looked up. "Why didn't you ride with them?"

Kit's eyes locked with Deighton Senior's.

Nothing to do with your son, he considered saying. *He's a better man than you are.*

But it wasn't his battle.

As the pause drew out, Deighton Senior's gaze flared with triumph.

"Because he was planted in a dunghill," he told Hawkings. "Write that down."

"Is it true?" Hawkings asked.

Kit shrugged his most quotable shrug and strolled after his Sisters.

"Griff!" Ponsonby vaulted into his path. "What in the hell? Where's your bicycle? Are you—"

Kit grabbed Ponsonby by the shoulders, spun him around, and pointed between the basket chairs, guiding his gaze to a tree and the three women gathered beneath it.

"I swear to God," said Ponsonby. "I didn't know they were here. They must have arrived today."

"They did." Kit pounded his back, grinning. "We arrived together."

"You patched things up?" Ponsonby grinned too, and hooted. "I knew you would." A split second later, his grin closed up like an umbrella. "Oh, hell."

He ducked behind a hedge.

"Erm." Kit ducked behind the hedge as well.

"I've *busted* things up, with Nelly." Branches rustled as Ponsonby crouched and wedged himself *inside* the hedge.

Kit rocked on his heels, nonplussed. He was glad now that Ponsonby had been out earlier, when the four of them called at the Oatridges'. The poor fellow needed time to collect himself.

More rustling, and then: "She can't see me?"

"No one can see you but me," said Kit dryly. "Which means everyone will think I'm communing with a shrub." He went deeper into the greenery, until a tall camellia bush hid him from the festivities completely. "No one can see either of us here. You can come out."

A negatory rustle.

"She won't take it too hard. The bust-up. Unless you busted up another of her sculptures." Kit paused. "What have you busted up, exactly?"

"My word. Our *bond*. I told her I'd wait forever. I knew my feelings had changed, but I hadn't planned to act until I'd broken the news. But now . . ."

Kit stepped closer to the hedge, peering through the leaves. "Now what?"

Ponsonby spoke in a hoarse whisper. "I snogged another chap. Not that Nelly's a chap. I mean, I snogged someone else."

"You snogged a chap?" Kit blinked.

"He's much more than a chap. Is it shabby of me, though? A shabby thing to do to Nelly?"

"Far from it," said Kit automatically. "She'll be relieved."

"Relieved?" Ponsonby drooped like a basset hound puppy.

"Resilient, I mean. Heartbroken but resilient. Who are you snogging?"

"Who do you think?" Ponsonby reddened. "James."

"Muriel's James? James Raleigh? The doctor?"

"You're shocked." Ponsonby sounded devastated. "Because we're incompatible? He's so useful, and I'm so useless? I've nothing to offer?"

"You've plenty to offer. I can think of a hundred reasons he'd like you." Kit cleared his throat. "I didn't know you might like him, in that way."

"I'd be a fool not to like him in every way." Ponsonby's eyes began to shine. "I've snogged chaps. Not since school. Not sober, anyway. And not since Nelly. But he's . . . There's no one quite so . . . He's truly . . ."

As he listened to Ponsonby stutter, Kit folded his arms. His smile was so enormous it hurt his lips.

"You've got it bad," he observed.

"I didn't realize until we went to the lighthouse." Ponsonby was smiling now too. "Grenfell took us. He's a huer. That's Cornish for craggy-looking bloke on the clifftop who watches for fish. He was a little too eager to skive off and row us out there. I could sense something about him, an *intention*. I thought he was after James, and it made me bloody wild. I wanted to hurl him out of the boat. But James would have done something brave and useful to save him, and I couldn't have *that*. So I heckled Grenfell a bit, to see if he'd hurl *me* out of the boat."

"Because then *you* would be the recipient of Raleigh's brave and tender ministrations?" Kit groaned. "Ponsonby."

"You don't have to tell me. I ended up provoking James far more than I provoked Grenfell. He almost hurled *himself* out of the boat, he was so aggravated."

"I suppose then *you* could have saved *him*. Except . . ." Sudden doubt surfaced. "Can you swim?"

"In a shallow fountain, if I'm drunk enough on champagne. Otherwise, I sink like a stone." Ponsonby winced. "But no one had to swim. And I couldn't have been more wrong. Grenfell was after the lighthouse keeper. As soon as we reached the island, the two of them skipped off, to check the lobster traps. Have you heard that one? Check the lobster traps?" He snickered.

Kit raised his brows.

"Anyway," said Ponsonby. "I was left to explain my appalling behavior to James. And there was really only one way to do it."

"You snogged him?" Kit pounced on the answer, laughing with delight at Ponsonby's expression. "Well done."

Ponsonby cocked his head proudly. "It was an inspired moment."

"I'm inspired. This is a painting." Kit took a step back. "You look like the Green Man, with all that foliage around your face."

"You want to paint me?" Twigs snapped boisterously as Ponsonby bounded from the hedge. "As a pagan god? Would you give it to James?" He shook leaves from his shoulders, then went still, eyes widening. "Wait. Griff. Are you *painting* again?"

"I seem to be." He affected nonchalance. The alternative was too embarrassing. Frolicsome leaps through the garden, like a baby goat. "I took Lucy, Gwen, and Nelly to the harbor. Lucy brought a paint box and a few boards, and we . . ."

Shouting punctured the background hum. It started far away, at the circuslike fringes, and swept up to the house.

Kit started running before he could think. He reached the drive and glimpsed the source of the excitement.

A cyclist, pedaling madly, hair blowing about in glorious disarray. Sparks from the rockets floated above, showering the dusk.

"Pendrake!" The man who hollered it must have bet good money. The name was a victorious roar.

Ponsonby took it up, sprinting past Kit. "Pendrake!"

Kit shook himself and sprang again into motion, but now the going was slower. The crowd had flowed onto the drive. He could hear Muriel yelling but couldn't make out the words.

He shouldered his way forward.

"She's calling for a doctor," someone said.

"Blimey!" The exclamation sounded right in Kit's ear. "Deighton took a cropper!"

"Knocked his lights out!"

"Oh, but here he comes! Look!"

Bugle calls added to the cacophony.

Finally, Kit pushed to the front. Bicycles were scattered on the gravel, and all the riders were on their feet, except for Deighton, who sat dazedly with Raleigh crouched beside him.

"Mrs. Pendrake finished the run, and she finished *first*." Hawkings was speaking loudly, soliciting comment from the spectators. "Who expected it?"

He jotted down responses, a barrage of largely untruthful affirmations intermixed with sniffs of moral opprobrium and sour grapes.

"We rode together." Muriel spoke up. Her stockings were black with mud, and as she swiped at her hair, she left a stripe of mud on her cheek. "I only went ahead after the accident, to fetch James—Dr. Raleigh."

Deighton climbed to his feet. He'd lost his cap and a purple knot had formed above his left brow.

"Luckily, he has the heart *and* head of an ox," Raleigh pronounced, rising as well. "But his collarbone is broken."

"I don't feel it," muttered Deighton.

"How do you feel about losing the wager? Exchanging mounts and permitting women into your club?" Hawkings waited, pencil hovering.

"Don't answer that." Deighton Senior stormed over. "And you, Hawkings, for shame. Boys clowning isn't a story. My son had you all on. He's done with his club. It doesn't exist anymore. He is going to lead Empire Tobacco's operations in Scotland. Put that in your paper."

"I am not done with my club," said Deighton.

"What was that?" His father rumbled the question like a threat.

"I am *not* done with my club. I'll go to Scotland, but I'll cycle there." Sweat stood out on Deighton's face. "And eventually, I'll open a Cycle Works. It's my dream."

"Your dream." Deighton Senior looked disgusted. "Go to the

house. You're unfit for company." When Deighton didn't move, he seized his arm. Deighton ground his teeth together so hard Kit heard a crack.

He moved to intervene, but Raleigh got there first.

"Unhand my patient, sir," he said crisply. "He has a serious fracture, and you are doing him harm."

"I don't feel it," repeated Deighton, but his voice had gone threadbare.

Deighton Senior's neck bulged, but he let go, glaring.

"What kind of bicycle will you manufacture in your works?" asked Hawkins. "High wheelers or safeties?"

"I will be guided by my knowledge of both the best bicycle models and the bicycle market." Deighton was sweating copiously, but he managed to sound like a creditable version of his blowhard self. Which very nearly filled Kit's heart with affectionate relief.

"Safeties, then?" prodded Hawkings.

"Time will tell." Deighton frowned. "And for the record, our club already permits women. Mrs. Pendrake is a Mutton Wheeler."

"A Muttonette," offered Egg, trying to catch Hawkings's eye.

"We voted her in at Porthtowan," continued Deighton. "I wouldn't call this *losing*, exactly. Her victory is our victory."

Kit laughed. Deighton's hard gaze swung to him, but when he realized Kit wasn't laughing *at* him, his expression mellowed.

Deighton Senior had turned an alarming puce.

Raleigh thought it alarming too. "Take a deep breath."

Deighton Senior did not. He pivoted and shoved through the crowd.

"All right, then." Raleigh's expression said *good riddance*. "Come with me." He beckoned to Deighton. "Let's see about your shoulder."

Hawkings had begun peppering Muriel with his questions.

"Excuse me," called Kit, and Hawkings glanced in his direction. So did everyone else. Kit smiled liberally in all directions. "I hate to interrupt, but I must borrow the champion."

Muriel watched him approach, and when he reached her, he had to tense his muscles to keep from sweeping her into his arms. He took her elbow instead. "She deserves a toast."

———

"I THOUGHT YOU'D be in London by now." Muriel didn't lean into him as they walked across the grass in pursuit of champagne. She was acutely aware of her filthy dress and filthier gloves, and of their altered relationship. He might not want her to press against him as intimately as before.

"London?" He released her, and they faced each other. "Why would I be in London?"

She was too tired to construct careful sentences.

"Lucy," she said, and watched his face soften. It hurt like the rack, and then, the thought of his hard-won contentment dulled the pain. She smiled. "You accepted her apology."

He lit up. "She came to St. Ives. They all did."

Muriel's mouth turned dry. "And will she leave the duke?"

Kit looked at her without comprehension.

"It will be like that, then," she said, and a knife twisted inside her, for all of them—herself, Kit, Lucy, and the duke—each allowed only a sliver of bliss.

"Like what?" Kit hesitated, then drew a sharp breath. "Good Lord. Me and Lucy? *That* is your meaning?"

Now *she* was uncomprehending. "You're in love with her. She's in love with you."

"Penny." His eyes glinted. "You weren't trying to arrange a match between me and my dearest friend, a happily married duchess and mother of two?"

Her pulse was quickening. "I thought it the likely consequence of a reconciliation."

He stepped toward her, his proximity scrambling her thoughts. "I am not in love with Lucy. I have never been in love with Lucy. I couldn't feel more fully that she was my sister if we'd shared the same cradle."

"Oh." She exhaled a shaky breath as some secret tension left her body. Her eyes fixed on his waistcoat, peeping out from his magenta jacket: gold, embroidered with sunflowers.

"Penny," he murmured. A bright current carried warmth from the crown of her head down to her toes.

One last week, then.

She lifted her chin, met his gaze, and tottered. Too much cycling. She'd forgotten how to stand. His hands wrapped her shoulders.

She couldn't breathe.

His dark stare unnerved her. It was raw in a way she'd never seen.

"Penny," he began. "What I feel now is—"

"Mrs. Pendrake." The reporter signaled to get her attention. "You haven't had your champagne. But we want to photograph you before it gets too dark."

Kit backed away from her smoothly, with an easy smile. He wasn't going to finish his sentence—now, or ever.

Heart drumming, she looked with dazed disappointment from the reporter to the stocky man with the camera.

"Photograph *me?*"

"Capture your victory, for the front page."

The stocky man was already setting up his camera.

She frowned and scratched at the mud on her cheek.

"All you need to do is get back on your bicycle, and your fellow riders will lift you up, like so, above their heads." The reporter raised his arms enthusiastically.

Egg was approaching, rolling her bicycle.

"We'll cheer," he promised, offering her the handlebars. Prescott, Kemble, and Butterfield crowded close.

"This seems unwise," she said. More people were forming a ring around them. She felt a cold stare drilling into her like a diamond point. Of course. Lady Chiswick. The woman's whole face was puckered, like someone had pulled a string on a drawstring bag.

Thou shalt not suffer a witch to live.

Muriel's frown deepened. And then, a wicked satisfaction curved her lips into a smile.

Maybe a minute or two of levitation was in order.

She straddled the Rover. "High as you can, boys."

Kit trotted over and gripped the frame with the others.

"One, two, three."

Her feet left the ground. The wheels left the ground—not simultaneously. She tipped forward, then back, and then she was hovering, six feet in the air.

She could see the fading glimmer of the ocean.

She filled her lungs. The air smelled faintly of salt, and more strongly of smoke and grass and strawberries left too long in the sun. It smelled of summer, and she drew more and more into her lungs, so she'd never forget.

The camera shutter popped.

32

꒰ ෴ ꒱

TIME THAT WEEK went topsy-turvy. She took naps at noon and
watched meteorites shower down from midnight until dawn,
lying in the grass, head on Kit's shoulder, every nerve wakeful
and crackling. She ignored the inexorable sweep of the clock hands
and instead divided portions of the day and night by her own unhurried transits, to the rock pools, the cove, the beach, the tennis club,
the Towans, the engine house. The holiday felt endless.

And then, abruptly, she reached the end.

It was the final day. She packed her specimens and Kit's paintings.
She picnicked with Kit, Lucy, Gwen, Nelly, Thomas, and James. She
and James took a farewell walk on the beach while Kit and Thomas
bathed.

"You told me you despised anything striped," she reminded James
in a murmur, noting where his gaze tended. "And Thomas is always
dressed like a barber's pole."

Thomas was at that very moment splashing with high knees through
the surf in his red-and-white striped bathing costume.

"I must have been feeling contrary," sighed James. "Stripes are the
very spice of life."

Kit tackled Thomas around the waist and down they both went.
The splash sparkled.

She could stay longer. The thought was a sparkle.

She and James had their tickets, yes, and he was due back at the hospital, but she didn't strictly require the two full weeks she'd allotted in London to put her affairs in order. James wouldn't mind. Thomas had changed *his* ticket and planned to travel with them. If anything, she'd get in the way.

There was so much left to do here.

She and Kit hadn't yet gone to the lighthouse.

He hadn't shown her his old canvases.

They hadn't discussed the contents of the letter she intended to send the Satterlees.

She hadn't modeled for his picture, of Cynisca, princess and charioteer.

He hadn't climbed the trellis below the balcony of her hotel room.

She hadn't helped him overcome his fear of snakes.

He hadn't told her all his stories of Cornish giants.

They hadn't played cards, or dominoes.

They hadn't sung a duet.

They hadn't seen *The Pirates of Penzance* on the stage. Or gone ice-skating. Or boating on a river.

The thoughts kept coming, sparkle after sparkle, and things to do *here* became things to do in general, became a desire that a few additional days in St. Ives couldn't slake. Pointless to pursue. Besides, Kit hadn't asked her to stay.

Final day turned to final night.

The train departed in eleven hours, and she was breathing in gasps, sprawled naked on her back in his bed, the moonlight silvering the window.

He turned his head, and she felt his hair tickle her inner thigh, and then the heat of his lips, the swipe of tongue. And then he was filling her, and she was stretching around a warm, smooth hardness so big she knew she would break. She would break if he pushed any deeper. If she felt it press against the aching center of her being. He pushed. It pressed. She broke. Liquid burst from inside her.

She cried out, helplessly, in pleasure, and then she fisted the sheets in shame. Damp was spreading beneath her trembling thighs.

"God, that was glorious." He sounded reverent as he withdrew.

She pressed her hand over her eyes. "Your bed, it's ruined."

"Baptized." He stretched out alongside her. "I'm pleased as the pope."

"This isn't the moment to talk about the pope." She gave a weak laugh. "I can't believe I did . . . whatever that was."

"You like my stone cock." He kissed the side of her face, hand massaging her pubic bone. "It happens sometimes, at climax."

"People evacuate entire pitchers of liquid?" She wished she could sink through the wrinkled, wet sheets, like they were ocean waves. "It's obscene."

"Mm." His hand massaged lower. "Obscenely lovely."

Esmé's face hovered above her in the dark, lips thinned with revulsion at the very idea of her arousal. She blinked it away. Kit was the one looking down at her, at her flushed, bare body. Her breasts were swollen, and moisture glistened on her thighs, and *lovely*, he'd said, *obscenely lovely*, and his glowing eyes, his touch, made it true.

He was in his nightshirt, his own obscene loveliness shrouded from view, and she contented herself with fumbling her hand through his hair, stroking his brow and his nose, and his lips, until he sucked her finger into his mouth. She sighed, and he rolled on top of her.

"I'm going to miss you," he murmured.

Her lungs crumpled.

I'm going to miss you. How different that was from another five-word statement, the one she could imagine him saying instead.

I can't let you go.

She whispered against his mouth, the words nearly lost in his kiss. "I'm going to miss you too."

She slept and woke. The moon had moved to the corner of the window. She could feel that Kit was awake, on the other side of the bed, tense and restless.

She swallowed. "Would you like me to . . ." She didn't know what to offer, but she wouldn't let that stop her.

"I want to do anything you want," she whispered.

Kit lifted his head. His hair was tousled, and his eyes were heavy-lidded.

"Is that so?" The corner of his mouth tilted up as he regarded her. "In that case, perhaps you'd frig me with those lovely fingers."

Her excitement bloomed, a new variety. She reached out, pulled him back to her, hand working up beneath his nightshirt. She stroked his hard thighs, hesitated, and stroked higher. With a shuddering sigh, she put her palm on him, and then her fingers, reveling in his heat. He growled encouragement as her fingers moved, faster and faster. He backed off, straddled her legs and knelt, yanking the nightshirt over his head. His smile was wolfish now, sharp-edged in the moonlight. With another growl, this one pure exultancy, he fell upon her. She cried out at the gorgeous shock of skin on skin. He was hot and hard and smooth and rough and soft, and he rubbed himself against her, rocking his hips in a rhythm that had her writhing. She held his shoulders as they ground together. White-hot heat obliterated her sense of her body's boundaries. He threaded their thighs, their limbs an aching knot they pulled tighter and tighter together. Their motions slowed, but the pressure built and kept building. She sent her moans into his throat, and then the blaze went everywhere, sensation uncontained. He jerked, teeth on her neck, his own cry of release hoarse and so obscenely lovely she wanted to lap at it like cream.

At some point, they unthreaded, and he flopped onto his stomach, head turned toward her on the pillow. She lay on her side, running her fingers down his back, over his muscled rear, which summoned her attention more fully than could the rarest plant to ever give leaf. His beauty cramped her heart.

Her hand meandered, as they drifted in and out of speech, as the moon continued to inch away behind the window glass. It felt so good to lie with him naked in this moment, every part of each of them offered and received and honored.

"Thank you," he said in a low voice, after a long lull.

"For what?"

He rolled onto his back, trapped her hand against his breastbone. "For urging me to try, with Lucy. The estrangement had eaten away at me. In some ways, I'd begun to feel like a stranger." He touched their conjoined hands to his mouth, which curved in a smile. "A handsome stranger, but a stranger nonetheless."

His hot breath tickled.

Her heart cramped harder, and her words ghosted out. "It is such a beautiful thing, to know you."

He guided their hands down, rose on an elbow, and kissed her, a soft, slow kiss.

Sometime later, they lay on their sides, facing each other.

"Do you think you'll ever reform?" she asked, idly brushing the tousled locks back from his forehead.

His brows shifted, just a little.

"Me, a reformed rake?" He sounded playful, but his lower lip took on a brooding fullness, almost a pout. "My sweet, rakes don't really reform. They marry when it's expedient and give their wives the clap."

"But you're a good rake. You've followed a different rule book."

"I'm an honest rake," he said. "I know what I have to offer." He flung an arm over her waist, drew her closer, and this time, when he kissed her, it was wickedly lascivious.

"No," she said at last. "That's a fraction of what you have to offer."

"Perhaps," he conceded. "But marriage isn't in the cards."

"Why?"

"Please."

She flushed at his sardonic tone. "Marriage is in the stars, though. Jupiter is transiting your seventh house. And you have a Cancer moon."

"First algology, now astrology." He sounded sleepily amused. "I'm guessing this is Miranda's doing."

"She's the one who told me about Jupiter and the moon." She hesitated. "James told me about female husbands."

He made a noncommittal noise in his throat.

"You *could* marry," she insisted.

"Who?"

Her blood came to a complete stop in her veins, but it was a rhetorical question and he continued with hardly a pause.

"If they can, sapphists make their lives with each other. The ones who want *me*—well, as I've mentioned, I have difficulty trusting that they see who I am."

"If you're lumping all sapphists together, you're not seeing who

they are, individually. A sapphist might very well want you for you."
She drew a breath. "So might women who aren't sapphists."

He didn't refute either possibility. He looked more awake, but his
gaze had gone dark.

"Anyone I married would find as much danger as security in the
arrangement. The courts would strip her married name from her if
my past were discovered. The public would castigate and pity her.
That's not something I could rightly offer."

"Marriage *is* dangerous." Esmé's face was there again, above her,
then gone. "There are rewards, but risk is always part of the equation.
It can seem like a cage in the best of circumstances. And husbands
are so often violent or unfaithful or disinterested. And wives have so
little recourse."

"You're hardly recommending the institution."

"I'm not trying to recommend it." What *was* she trying to do? In
any event, her mouth was still moving. "The only thing I recommend
is . . . growing roots with someone."

"It's always plants with you." He was teasing, retreating into rail-
lery. She shut her mouth, shut her eyes. The splinter in her chest reas-
serted itself, a little prick to the heart.

She willed herself to sleep, and as the silence extended, wondered
if he'd drifted off himself.

"Children." His whisper floated between them. "Children are
commonly considered chief among the rewards you mentioned."

She opened her eyes, looked into his.

"Did you want them?" he asked.

Her reply stuck in her windpipe. She had, and she hadn't.

"*Do* you? Want them?"

"I don't know," she said, truthfully.

"My wife would know she wouldn't know that particular joy."

Another diversion. Did he even realize?

"Kit." She curved her hand on the back of his neck. "Children are
orphaned and deserted at horrifying rates. You can create whatever
kind of home you wish, with whomever else you invite into your life."

He let her draw his head close.

"You claimed you don't trust your lovers to see who you are. I think you're afraid they *will* see who you are. You keep your attachments brief to prevent the possibility. If you're not seen fully, rejection can't touch you fully. If you were seen—it would brutalize. It would hurt so badly you might feel it wasn't survivable. I know. I felt it once. I felt like I'd flayed myself, peeled layer after layer, showed everything, wanting him to want me. And he didn't." She felt it now, a ghostly trace of the panicked agony that had ripped through her in the days and weeks following her wedding, before she'd understood and made peace with the terms of the marriage. "But it is survivable. You must hazard it. Not to love. You're good at loving. To *be* loved."

He pulled back, hard, and she dropped her hand.

She'd crossed a line. They were down to a fistful of hours, and she'd become reckless.

"Or maybe you truly do prefer summer flings," she said.

His voice didn't rupture the hush. It was the barest scrap of breath.

"Is that what this is?"

She didn't answer. Her heart pounded in her ears as she waited for *his* answer. After a few moments, she turned, putting her back to him. She heard him sigh, and a few moments after that, he pulled her against his chest, wrapping her in an embrace. When the sun replaced the moon in the window, they were still lying in each other's arms.

The sun stroked her cheek. What if she *were* a plant, nourished by light? Light was more ubiquitous than love. It warmed her, and so did Kit's skin, his breath, his hand heavy on her hip. The awareness that had struggled up at the first touch of gold subsided into the darkness. And this was where the roots grew—in the sweet, deep, dark. She burrowed down, blissfully mindless. Plantlike. When her lashes fluttered next, Kit was cradling her closer. The sun was high. It was high, and the birds were chirping, and . . .

She shot up with a gasp. "I'm late!"

SHE ARRIVED AT the platform uncombed and out of breath. James and Thomas left off pleading with the conductor.

"Here she is," said James, relief and concern on his face as he looked her over.

The conductor's expression was sour.

She turned to Kit, who'd raced with her through the fields and through the narrow, winding streets of St. Ives, and there was so much more to say, and do, but the time had run out. A few rote words were exchanged. A hand was extended and clasped. They might have been strangers. Her face felt like rubber. Kit's eyes told her nothing.

"Muriel," murmured James. "Not to rush things, but we're well past all aboard."

She nodded. She boarded. By early evening, she was back in London.

33

"Go to London," said Lucy, underlining the words with a slash of her brush through the air.

"I can't have heard that right." Kit was sitting in the grass by her easel, painting small rocks.

"Go to London," she repeated. "Look at you. You're languishing. We've been painting en plein air every day since she left, and every day your complexion looks more like moldy cheese. It's pitiable."

"We agreed not to talk about this."

"We didn't agree on anything of the kind. You've been avoiding the subject."

"Fine. I'm happy to continue with avoidance."

"You're *not* happy. That's why I'm telling you to go to London." She dropped down beside him. The amber-toned sunlight held the first hint of autumn. Beyond the cliffs, the sea was silver with fish. The pilchards were running.

"I'm happy," he said, not entirely dishonestly. He had his Sisters again. Lucy was leaving for Stratton Grange, and Nelly and Gwen had gone south to Newlyn, but that was immaterial. He had Sisters. He had art.

"She's on Gower Street," said Lucy. "I have the address from Ponsonby."

"You're persistent as the croup," he told her. "And I don't see how you'd trust an address from Ponsonby."

"It's James Raleigh's address." Lucy smiled, wryly. "So he has a vested interest."

"What, then?" Kit set down his rock and his brush and hugged his knees. "I should ride up on a white horse and plight my troth?"

"I was picturing a bicycle." She gave a tiny shrug.

He pictured it too, then shook his head. "I don't think you understand."

"I understand what I saw between the two of you." A smug note crept into her voice. "And this avoidance. It's not like you to clam up." She paused. "You're afraid of letting something out."

"Funny." He flung back, crossing his arms behind his head. "She said I was afraid too." He frowned at the sky. "I am dauntless when it comes to affairs of the heart."

"Affairs." Lucy's voice was pointed.

He propped himself on an elbow to glare. "Are you judging me? Of course you're judging me. You and Weston are so sickeningly sweet on each other, you think all people should mate for life, like swans."

"Do swans really mate for life? Or are they a symbol of love because pairs of them touch their heads together and form hearts with their necks?"

Prescott would know. Kit only scowled.

"Oh dear." Lucy's eyes began to dance. "You're a swan! You presented yourself as a strutting peacock, but you're a hopelessly devoted swan. You're afraid of letting out a telltale honk! Or hiss." She hissed loudly, stretching out her neck.

"That was the worst swan imitation I've heard in my life," Kit informed her, without being sure he'd ever heard another.

She pursed her lips, curled her fingers, and made a heart with her hands.

"Stop it," he growled. "I've no wish to be tied down."

He wouldn't feel tied down with Muriel, though. He knew that already. He'd grow. She'd grow. They'd grow together.

He was in love with her. It wasn't his usual casual besottedness. God have mercy, Lucy was right. He was in *swan* with her.

He'd been aware, hadn't he? This whole time? It felt cataclysmic to articulate it, even to himself. Volcanic pressure built in his chest. Any moment, the smoke would pour out of his ears.

Lucy's lips were trembling.

"Honk," she whispered.

He'd best remind himself of the facts.

"Whatever you saw between us," he said, "it's over. She's headed for New York."

"And it wouldn't make the remotest bit of sense for *you* to go to New York." Lucy rolled her eyes. "What ever would you do in a grand metropolis famed for art and culture, with galleries and museums lining the streets, and your first patron already on the hook?"

He ran his fingers through his hair, fidgeting.

Lucy held his gaze until he stilled. The irony faded from her face. Her expression was serious. "You're sure to meet absolutely brilliant American artists. And they'll meet you, for the first time. You can start fresh, as you please, how you please. With one stipulation. You must write, every single day, because I'll miss you fiercely." She blinked, eyelashes suddenly spiky with moisture. "We all will. But we'll live vicariously through your adventures, and we'll celebrate your conquests." Her smile was watery and wistful. "Kit Griffith, our New York cousin."

"We didn't decide on *cousin*," Kit muttered. "And I haven't decided I'm going to New York." His brow knotted. "Perhaps it makes sense." It did make sense. Far more sense, for him, than a lifetime rusticating in St. Ives. A pain in his gut twisted his lips. "But not if she doesn't want me."

In that case, nothing made sense.

The back of his neck felt hot.

"She thought *we* were in love," he said, and Lucy looked genuinely surprised.

"You and I?"

He nodded. "And she brought us together regardless."

"Admirable, generous woman," said Lucy, with feeling. "And perfect for you. You'd torment a jealous one."

He flinched. "You assume I'd be unfaithful?"

"No, not if you swore fidelity. But you're an incorrigible flirt."

"I'm a flirt," he confirmed, grim with self-knowledge. "You're right. I'd flirt with a hatstand. It's harmless."

Lucy shrugged.

He squared his jaw. "I'd always put her first, before anyone else, before anything."

"Before all the hatstands," murmured Lucy. "Lovely."

He ignored her. "I wouldn't rest until she was certain of me." His neck felt hotter.

Lucy sighed, thoughtful, then nodded. "I'm glad to hear it. She put your happiness before her own, after all."

His pulse picked up. "That's your interpretation?"

"Of course. She brought us together, thinking we were in love. That proves she loves you enough to want love *for* you, even if she loses by it."

"Or it proves she *doesn't* love me. She never said she did." His voice was getting gravelly. "On the contrary, she said I'd arranged my life to prevent anyone from loving me." He cleared his throat. "So, I can't see that she would. Love me. She's too intelligent. She knows me too well."

"Kit."

"Is that how I look at Ponsonby? How awful for him."

"Kit." Lucy's expression smoothed, but her voice was still tinged with patronizing amusement. "Just . . . let her."

"What?"

"Let her love you. Confess your love to her. And then, let her love you."

He was watching Lucy's lips move, because all at once, he found words hard to parse. Listening didn't supply him with enough information.

"She might not."

Lucy's smile was gentle. After a long moment, he realized she wasn't planning to offer him surety.

His heart was pumping lava.

Muriel might. She might not. One thing was certain. She *couldn't* if he didn't open himself up enough to give her the chance.

"So," said Lucy at last, picking up her sketchbook, "will you go to London?"

He reached into his pocket and closed his fingers around a cool metal disc. He pulled it out.

Lucy's smile reversed into an appalled frown. "If you have to flip a coin, *don't*. Forget I encouraged you, and God save women from indecisive rogues. Muriel deserves better."

He looked at the copper penny in his palm. He'd been carrying it since Bernhard pressed it upon him that anxious morning at Titcombe Hall.

He hadn't intended to flip it.

Perhaps he'd thought to kiss it, for a little extra luck.

"I'll go tomorrow," he said, and closed his hand.

34

❦

MURIEL THOUGHT SHE heard the faint chime of the doorbell, so she poked her head into the hall. Nothing. She drifted forward and paused at the top of the stairs. The house was silent. James had the day free, but he and Thomas had gone out immediately after breakfast, their secretive smiles and overall air of mystery stopping the questions in her throat. She'd watched them stroll past the drawing room window, feeling a little pinch of hurt, until James gave a skip of spontaneous delight and swung around the lamppost, head thrown back and arm outflung, shouting to the rooftops. Some line of poetry.

Eros shook my mind.

The little pinch of hurt eased, and her eyes misted, and she'd hoped the happy lovers were embarked on a marvelously romantic spree. Pistachio ices, flower gardens, a French restaurant, the theater, a private ball. Thomas was due a bit of fêting. Over the past several days, while James worked long shifts at the hospital, and she retrieved the portfolios of specimens she'd lent to the Royal Botanic Society, Thomas had lain in wait, lurking in the entrance of a terrace across the street, never taking his eyes from James's doorstep.

I don't have anywhere to be, or anything to do, he'd explained. *And finally I can put that to use.*

When the blackmailer's boy had appeared, on the third day of his vigil, he'd followed him to Piccadilly, to the Burlington Arcade and the Albemarle Hotel, and finally to a flat on Tachbrook Street. He'd pushed inside, surprising the boy, and the flat's occupants as well, three men gathered around a table sorting pawn tickets and polishing watches. Caught red-handed in a thieves' den, they'd turned over James's correspondence and wasted no time pinning the blame on an absent accomplice, an unemployed valet, fled now to Canada.

Muriel listened for another sound, struck by a chilling thought. They'd celebrated too soon. The blackmailers were at the door, prepared to make more mischief. She heard a muffled thud and gripped the banister, blood running cold. A moment later, Fezziwig scampered up the steps.

The house was quiet again. She exhaled. She'd imagined the chime.

There was no one at the door.

She returned to the desk in the blue bedroom, picked up her pen, and reread the final paragraph of her lecture. In a month, she'd be delivering it, to a crowded hall, in a new city. No matter what happened after that, she would adapt, and on balance, she felt far more hope than fear. She could envision a sufficient existence for herself; more than sufficient—very pleasant. She'd develop a closer friendship with the Satterlees, and together they'd expand their botanical academy, opening its doors to women from all walks of life. Some would go on to study at universities, changing who did science and how. She'd take pride in her students' experiments in the laboratory, in their research, in their sense of possibility. On the days she didn't demonstrate or lecture, she'd travel to mountains, marshes, and meadows, to the forests and the seashore, familiarizing herself with the plants of New York.

Red columbine grew wild there. You could find it on wooded hills with clayey soil, and in the crevices of slate ledges, and at the rocky borders of streams. She would find it. She'd find many things.

She rolled the pen between her fingers.

A bell rang.

Not her imagination. Not the doorbell either.

Her eyes moved to the open window. The lightweight curtains

billowed with a warm, rose-scented breeze. She walked over, batting away the sheer fabric, and she leaned out.

Her heart gave a queer knock.

Kit stood below in the courtyard garden, his top hat under his arm.

"I tried the door first," he said. "I was about to climb the trellis."

The world tunneled. No more buildings. No more lime trees. He stood very straight, the well-tailored lines of his plum-colored morning suit marking the limits of her vision. His handsome face was so clear it seemed to shift with his emotions, his eyes a mix of darkness and light.

"You can't climb the trellis." She fought for breath. "There's no trellis."

"I was about to scale the brick, in truth." A smile tugged his lips. "But that makes it sound like I'm here to commit a burglary."

She choked on a laugh. "You're not?"

"No."

"Why *are* you here?" She steadied herself with a fist on the window frame. His gaze slid to her fist, then back to her face. He stepped closer.

"To extend an invitation."

"An invitation," she echoed, brows drawing together. "To dinner?"

"I do have something in mind for this evening, yes. I rented a sociable, and I thought we'd ride to Hyde Park."

Her stomach folded over and cramped. A jaunt in the park. An evening's entertainment. Then he'd be off. What had *she* thought? That he'd come to London just for her?

"Thank you, but I am already engaged," she said hoarsely, the lie heating her cheeks.

His smile faded. Her heart beat painfully fast, and she longed to retract her words. It was cruel, though, his sudden appearance, after she had acclimated to a reality in which his kisses played no part. It felt like a test. How many goodbyes could she withstand without breaking completely?

"I should get back to my writing." Her knees had begun to tremble.

"Your lecture?" he asked, his interest plain, and she stopped breathing, overwhelmed by a vision. The two of them lounging in each other's arms in the park, on the soft meadow grass, surrounded by corn marigolds, talking until the sun went down.

"Is it going well?"

She only nodded. She'd learned something from him, *with* him, about love, about how *she* loved, and she knew that she couldn't dip in and out of it. Love for her had too strong a current.

"I'd like to hear it," he said. "Which means I should let you finish it."

Hear it. Not *read* it, months from now, enclosed in a letter. A slip of the tongue. Easily made because he didn't register the difference. To him, the difference didn't matter. The distance didn't matter.

She felt the worst pinch yet.

She drew back, and as she did so, she saw the sociable. It was parked behind him, wide and unwieldy. The tall wheels framed two seats and sets of pedals.

The question burst out. "How on earth did you ride that alone?"

"Awkwardly." He was still looking up at her. "Overconfidently. I didn't expect I'd ride alone for long."

He was mocking himself, and she supposed he deserved it, but she felt even shakier as she pictured him riding away.

"I'm sorry," she whispered.

"Don't be." He shook his head.

"I just . . . can't." Now she was shaking like a leaf, and he noticed, his eyes darkening.

"It's my fault," he said. "A wiser, humbler man would have arrived on foot." He paused, studying her intently. "You told me once I was insufferably arrogant."

"Once?" She let out her breath and managed a smile.

"You also told me I could create whatever kind of home I wanted."

For a moment, she couldn't think. She couldn't speak. She stared, unable to swallow around the lump in her throat.

"I believe that," she croaked.

He took a breath. "I want to create a home with you."

The lump in her throat tripled in size. Her pulse drummed so loudly in her ears that she didn't trust she'd heard him correctly. Hadn't her ears been playing tricks on her?

But no, the doorbell *had* rung. He'd rung it. And the next chime had been the bicycle bell. There was nothing wrong with her ears.

"Penny," he said, "I invite you into my life. That's why I'm here. A holiday isn't enough. A summer isn't enough. I want us to pedal this ridiculously large tricycle to Hyde Park, and then to New York, and then to the moon, or Jupiter, or both. I want miles and miles, and hours and hours, at your side. I want to sit in the front row of your lecture—not to admire my own paintings, however superlative—to admire you. Your intellect and courage. You don't need me there, I know. But if you'd feel even remotely emboldened by my presence, I swear nothing can keep me away. I want to join your battles, whether it's to help negotiate a truce or to head up a charge. I want to bring you comfort, like a heath plant. Heath plants are perennials, or at least I think they're perennials. Are they perennials? Never mind. In any case, I want to love you perennially. I'm an awful flirt. I've been known to make eyes at Augustinian nuns, and friends' grandmothers, and when I was presented at court, I made eyes at the queen. I fed on sighs and glances and furtive touch. I've never asked for anyone's whole heart. Until now. Penny, I am here to ask for yours. I am here to offer you mine. It's not rotten kelp, but it's not without flaws either. I don't have to tell you. You see them. You see all of me. I *was* afraid you wouldn't, and then I was doubly afraid when I realized you did. Accepting your love means accepting myself. In the past, I've loved as an escape. This is new. Loving you is terrifying and exhilarating and all I most desire. So, please. Say something. Anything. I can survive rejection. What I couldn't have survived was your leaving London in any doubt about how I feel."

She clung to the window frame. His expression grew increasingly uncertain as her silence stretched.

"You're not in any doubt?" he asked. "I was jesting about the nuns. Mostly. Reverend Mother Cecelia had a miraculous—"

She spun. She went sprinting across the room, pounding through the hall, down the stairs, her skirt hiked to her waist. Pretty speeches weren't her forte. She needed to throw herself into his arms, to press her heart to his, to breathe him into her lungs.

The front door resisted.

She twisted and tugged the bronze doorknob, uncomprehending.

Jammed. The latch was always sticky, but Thomas had gone at it yesterday afternoon, taking it apart and cleaning off the rust. She could still smell the vinegar.

It *had* to open.

She attacked the door like a fury. Her love was on the other side. Or rather, he was in the courtyard, looking up at an empty window as the minutes ticked by, thinking . . .

Dear God, what must he be thinking?

She stumbled back, dizzy from her efforts, breathing in erratic bursts. When she regained the window, she was so lightheaded, she had to blink away the floating spots before she could confirm what her sinking heart already suspected.

He was gone.

KIT HAD CLAIMED he would survive rejection, but as he supplied the motive power needed to propel the sociable down the street, he wondered if he'd exaggerated his resiliency.

He had declared himself. He had offered himself. She had not been swayed. He had seen the last he'd see of her: a beautiful, stunned face high above him.

He steered to the curb. The pain in his chest bid him hold still, and he obeyed. He closed his eyes, the carriages and pedestrians making a dull roar all around.

He sensed that someone had come up to him and was hovering, too close. His skin prickled and his eyelids gave an unwilling flutter.

Go away.

He couldn't endure an exchange with a stranger, with anyone. There was a hole in his middle, and if he moved, if he spoke, he might get sucked through and disappear completely.

Go away, he thought. *Everyone, go away. London, go away. Go away, go away.*

"Kit."

He opened his eyes. Muriel appeared, dark brows tensed, chin upraised. He'd seen that determined expression before, but never fixed on him in exactly that manner, as though he were the prize to be won.

Awe parted his lips. He didn't feel small, but rather overwhelmingly aware that he was a part of something vast, something infinite. This unfamiliar awareness—it was humility. Had to be. He felt *humble*, even as hope and pride swelled his heart.

"Penny," he said. She was gorgeously disarranged, locks of bright hair streaming over her shoulders. Her myrtle-green tea gown had an *en coeur* neckline that trained his attention on the rapid rise and fall of her breasts.

He swallowed. "You ran."

The breath she drew was wheezing and accusatory. "I'd have ridden with you instead if you'd waited."

"I did wait." He peered into her deep brown eyes, trying to read her thoughts. "I waited until your removal from the window became an undeniable answer."

"I removed myself from the window to go out the front door. But I couldn't get it open. One of Thomas's projects around the house was unsticking the lock. He seems to have made it more stuck."

Thomas Everett Ponsonby.

Kit laughed, and it soothed his raw edges. He hadn't imagined laughing again so soon. He hadn't imagined *her*, wedging herself between the sociable's tiny front wheel and the enormous wheel to his left, her skirt brushing his knees.

"You opened it eventually," he murmured. She'd opened the door in time. She'd run to him. She was here. He was here. So were dozens of passersby, but he didn't care. Let them crane their necks and gawk.

"I didn't exactly open it," she said.

He blinked. "Then how . . . ?"

"Drawing room window." Her cheeks flushed. "You were already riding away." She pressed closer, and her scent encircled him. "I couldn't let you go."

He pulled her down onto his lap. His elbow thwacked the wheel's rim and the hard seat dug into his thighs, but the moment her body touched his, the emptiness inside him filled with a warm light. It was akin to the feeling that sent him to the easel, a bright incitement to make life bigger, to bring something new and beautiful into being.

Her eyes were shining. "I think we're each meant to take our own seat."

"My love," he said, "I don't anticipate us doing what we're meant to do very often."

He kissed her. At some point in the lengthy process, his hat toppled, and at another point, he heard a scandalized gasp, and then a few titillated jeers. He lifted his head reluctantly. A small crowd had gathered on the sidewalk. He treated them to a devil-may-care grin and gathered Muriel more fully against him, feet fumbling for the pedals. The wheels groaned and began to roll, and they left the gaping throng behind.

MURIEL SAW TWO options—slip off Kit's legs, or strangle him to stay put, which couldn't improve his already compromised steering.

They were listing *across* the street on a long diagonal, and a cab had to corner sharply around them, the driver cursing a blue streak.

"Stop!" Bizarrely, she was laughing. She confronted a very high likelihood of spilling onto the pavement, getting crushed under the wheels of an omnibus or trampled by horses, but the gory prospect couldn't dim her incandescent joy.

She strangled him, arms winding tight around his neck. Her face pressed into his jacket, which smelled deliciously of his soap and his skin, and she was still laughing as she heard the approaching thunder of a larger carriage.

"This isn't funny," she said, and smothered her maniacal giggle in soft wool. "Stop, please. I'm begging you."

"I'm trying," Kit muttered. "Difficult to work the brake from this angle."

She could feel them turning, and before long, the traffic sounds faded. They slowed enough that when they hit the curb, the jarring impact didn't dislodge her. She extracted herself from the tangle of man and metal, brushing at her skirts as she staggered onto the sidewalk. She didn't recognize the street, narrow and quiet and tree-lined.

Kit followed her onto the sidewalk, pulling off his gloves.

He took her hands, and she shivered at the contact. He possessed the world's most electrifying palms. Suddenly, she couldn't feel her feet. She had the sensation she was floating. It took acute mental effort to ground through her heels.

"I have questions," she said.

"About Reverend Mother Cecelia?" A grin shaped his mouth. "So do I." His eyes were gleaming like quicksilver. He liked to ruffle her, and she gave him a ruffled look, lest he discontinue the practice.

"Leave the woman her sacred mysteries," she sniffed. "It's nothing to do with nuns."

Shyness stole over her. Her voice dipped. "You're coming with me to New York."

"Was that a question?" He sounded amused. His hands traveled up her forearms and gripped her elbows. "I am coming with you to New York."

"What about your bicycle shop?"

"Sold to the Mutton Wheelers, with a few stipulations."

"Your parents?"

"They'll have three sons in the Americas. I don't know if I'll ever put it to them that way. But I'll write newsy letters about Wall Street and Fifth Avenue."

"Your Sisters?"

"They'll visit."

His arms came around her, and his lips found her throat. She tipped her head back, and her vision went pale blue with smoky London sky.

"Other questions?" His lips moved over her pulse.

She smoothed back his wild hair and slid her hands to his nape. "I love you."

He lifted his face. "I hope that's not a question."

He wasn't teasing. He was solemn, a vulnerable softness in his gaze.

She shook her head.

"You're sparkling," she whispered, in wonderment, before realizing that her eyes had filled with tears.

"There's so much I want to give you," he murmured. "Nights of exquisite pleasure. Early mornings of exquisite pleasure. Midafternoons, if you're not teaching, and I'm not in the studio, although—let's be frank—I'm not opposed to giving you exquisite pleasure in the studio. I like a well-furnished studio, upholstered chairs, lots of fringe. Where was I? Evenings of exquisite pleasure. Exquisite pleasure in the Catskills, surrounded by fairy rings of toadstools. Exquisite pleasure at the shore as we sample America's bathing machines."

She was laughing in his embrace, which made the tears slip down her cheeks. He kissed the damp skin below her eyes, and the salty corner of her mouth.

"I want to give you my name," he said. "Or we can invent one together. Kit and Muriel Pengriff. I think it has a certain dash."

She stared. "Pengriff."

"Griffindrake?"

"But you've begun to build a reputation as Kit Griffith."

"I can begin again. New beginnings keep me young."

"We can see." She swallowed hard. "We have time to decide." All of August had been a race against time, the sands running down, and then, just as she'd thought the end had come, there was so much more.

She trembled, and his grasp on her tightened.

"I have something to give you now," he said.

"Exquisite pleasure?" She glanced to the left and the right. The street was quiet, but it was a street in Bloomsbury and hardly deserted. On cue, a curtain twitched in a window.

"Don't tempt me." Kit growled it against her ear, and her skin heated everywhere.

She wiggled away, smiling, and he pulled a stone from his pocket.

"Our badge," he said. "Rather, the design for the badge. We won't wear painted rocks. I'm thinking sterling silver and enamel."

She took the stone. He'd painted a wheel, spokes threaded with daisies and buttercups. She traced the letters with her fingers. *K&P*, the stone read.

He cleared his throat. "The final version will say FPTC, for the Flower Pedals Touring Club."

"I like this one," she said. "For Kit and Penny." Her heart overflowed, and he was sparkling again. The world was sparkling.

"We should pedal on," he said thickly. "They'll have started to worry."

She looked up at him, brow flexing.

"Raleigh and Ponsonby." He gave her an adorably sheepish smile. "They're waiting at the Serpentine with a celebratory picnic. Champagne. Strawberries. I think Raleigh's selected a poem or two, so prepare to be regaled."

"Oh," she said, and then: "Oh."

"I got to town yesterday," he admitted. "And did a bit of scheming."

His face blurred. She had a ticklish feeling in her throat.

"You *were* overconfident," she breathed.

"Not *over*confident, as it turns out." His smile was widening.

She laughed and gave him a push. He caught her wrist, trapping her hand against his upper chest.

"Also, I was ready to fail," he said. "To look an utter fool. I was ready to risk everything for this, for you."

She stepped into him and kissed his wicked lips.

"They'll have eaten all the strawberries by now." He sighed against her mouth. "Next time I pledge my life and love to you, I'll go about it differently."

"Next time?"

"Tomorrow, probably. Every day after that."

She was laughing through her tears, and *his* eyes looked suspiciously bright as they climbed into the sociable.

"This really is much better with two," Kit remarked as they pedaled together down Tottenham Court Road. "I'm so delighted you seduced me."

She cringed a little at the memory, both happy and abashed. "Is that what happened?"

The wind was riffling her hair, cooling her wet face and tingling lips. He linked their elbows snugly.

"Yes," he said. "And it's happening still."

She shut her eyes briefly, and opened them to dazzling light, the beams of late-summer sun painting the crowns of the trees with gold. A fallen leaf went twirling by. They rolled on toward the park, and she was laughing again, joyful beyond words.

HISTORICAL NOTE

As I mentioned in my Dear Reader letter, I wrote *A Shore Thing* in close conversation with my partner, a gender and sexuality historian. Mir Yarfitz researches trans and queer people of the late nineteenth and early twentieth century. He is himself a trans man, and we live a trans and queer life together in the twenty-first century. We were both assigned female at birth and have related in various ways over the years to our femininity, masculinity, and sexuality. I've always wanted to set a love story like ours in the past and to get the chance to involve him more deeply in my writing process. Mir helped me come up with the vision for *A Shore Thing* and showed me how to find new details in the archives. He contributed research, discussed every chapter draft, and brainstormed with me about how people in Victorian England might have thought and talked about gender and sexuality. This book couldn't have happened without him. Fiction is my thing, and history is his, so we sat down and wrote this historical note (and the discussion questions!) together.

WE'RE OLD ENOUGH at this point to have watched terms come and go. In the 1990s, people in our communities used words like "queer," "genderqueer," "dyke," "FTM," and "MTF." Now we use terms like

"AFAB," "AMAB," "nonbinary," "transmasculine," and "transfemi-nine." In the 1880s, "queer" was beginning to pick up the resonance of same-sex attraction, but no one said "transgender" or "gay" or "gender nonconforming," and "homosexual" and "heterosexual" had not yet entered common usage. Terms (sometimes but not always negative) then in circulation included "sodomite," "molly," "invert," "sapphist," and "tribade." The distinction that has been made between LGB (sex-ual orientation) and TQ+ (gender identity) was not drawn until later in the twentieth century, in part driven by respectability-minded gay and lesbian activists trying to prove that loving women did not make women masculine, and loving men did not make men feminine. How-ever, in earlier periods, and throughout the world, this line between sexuality and gender has never been firm, and people with varied ap-proaches to gender and sexual practice have often been grouped to-gether and seen one another as comrades.

We both felt that Kit was a trans character, but Kit couldn't have thought of himself using the word "trans." It's impossible (even for historians) to access the self-perception of people who aren't around anymore to tell you how they identify, and what they think and feel. Historians do know that people have lived and loved in all sorts of ways in all sorts of times and all sorts of places. But in the nineteenth century, people who lived and loved outside societal norms left scant records in their own words.

All history (not only historical fiction) involves anachronism. Whether deliberate or not, every writer of history and historical fic-tion interprets the past in terms legible to the present. Our hope for this book wasn't to create a perfectly accurate portrait of England in 1888, but to put the past and present in conversation. Our hope was to contribute to the growing canon of queer and trans love, to use historical fiction to tell a story readers would enjoy now and that might help point the way to a future in which everyone understands that people outside of the gender binary exist, have always existed, and have the right to do so fully, on the terms of their choosing.

Early in *A Shore Thing*, Kit and James share a moment of recog-nition that leads to an exchange of confidences. Kit is accustomed to being perceived by men seeking sex with men as a possible partner and has no negative judgment of "mollies" or "sodomites." While James may not have met someone like Kit before, he has read about "sexual inverts" in international medical journals, and would also have read newspaper stories about the era's most famous British "female husband," James Barry. At the time the book takes place, the field of sexology was just developing. Sexologists interviewed "deviants," seeking them out in jails and hospitals. They asked them about their childhoods, fantasies, and partners, and made up categories of normal and abnormal sexual desires. Many sexologists, such as Karl Ulrichs, John Addington Symonds, and Magnus Hirschfeld, were themselves practitioners of "man-manly love," and tried to convince judges, religious leaders, and the general public to view their subjects as sick rather than sinners or criminals. This medical model has persisted and has sometimes been used strategically: trans people themselves advocated in the 1970s for including transsexuality as a diagnosis in the DSM as a way to get surgery and hormones. However, it is important to understand that there is nothing wrong with LGBTQ+ people. The sickness lies in a social system that considers some lives "normal" and others "abnormal." This system creates situations of emotional distress and physical danger for those who don't fit the norm. The system is what needs to change, not us.

James mentions attending fancy dress balls where he dances in gowns. This is historically possible. In the late nineteenth century, big cities around the world had boisterous queer nightlife. British inns, taverns, and coffee shops housed private "Mollies' clubs" from the early 1700s, where people we might today consider gay and trans held dances, weddings, and other functions. Individuals assigned male at birth generally had more freedom of movement than individuals assigned female, but they also risked greater police, legal, and tabloid attention. Arrest records place gay men, transfeminine people, cis sex workers, and other working-class people at the same brothels and parties. Class, race, gender, and colonial position affected who would be prosecuted and punished, and how. Nonetheless, such spaces could enable gender and sexual outsiders to build community and kinship ties across hierarchies of privilege.

In Victorian society, sex between women was usually treated as though it wasn't even a possibility and could therefore sometimes hide in plain sight. Female husbands, if brought to court, were charged with fraud rather than any sexual crime, as none existed on the books. Newspaper stories in which female husbands were "discovered" often commented that the decision to live in male clothing must have been driven by the need for more work opportunities: better pay, less harassment, the chance to leave a small town and fight in a war. Their wives were described as deceived. This reporting didn't allow that transmasculine people might have desired women, or that others might have found them sexually desirable even knowing their "secret." We have to rely on imagination to fill in the gaps.

In recent decades, some things have gotten better for queer and trans folks: more legal protections, broader acceptance. At this moment, however, attacks on trans people and their rights have become political currency. Bills are being passed to forbid trans girls from playing sports, to deny young people lifesaving health care, to ban books for even mentioning the existence of gay or trans folks. And the epidemic of violence against trans women of color continues. We don't think fiction and romance will save the world, but we do believe that imagination is vital to personal and social change. When things are hard, art can provide a place of dreaming new possibilities, and be a source of strength in making them real. History can also show us that people pushed to the margins have always fought for justice, and sometimes won.

If you are interested in learning more about trans history, you might start with Susan Stryker's classic *Transgender History*. In more recently published books, Kit Heyam's *Before We Were Trans* tours the world through history, art, and literature; Jen Manion's *Female Husbands* contextualizes some of the fascinating stories that our characters might have seen in the British press; and Emily Skidmore's *True Sex: The Lives of Trans Men at the Turn of the Twentieth Century* tells eighteen similar stories in the United States. Jules Gill-Peterson's trailblazing *Histories of the Transgender Child* centers race in the development of medical responses to children's genders. Contemporary trans memoir is a large and growing genre, and we recommend exploring it, to hear people telling their stories in their own voices.

Natalie Wynn's YouTube video essay series, ContraPoints, uses fabulous set and costume design to explain contemporary trans issues to a broad audience. If you or someone you know is still grappling with some of these concepts, the GLAAD Media Reference Guide is regularly updated online to follow the constant evolution of terms and identities. And if you are looking for works of fiction that critique this world, imagine alternate worlds, and manifest queer futures, there are plenty of them out there. We've recently read and loved books by Ryka Aoki, Rivers Solomon, Torrey Peters, Kai Cheng Thom, Akwaeke Emezi, Bishakh Som, Jordy Rosenberg, Joshua Whitehead, and Ray Levy, and the list of brilliant trans, Two Spirit, and nonbinary writers goes on.

Thanks so much for reading *A Shore Thing*. We hope you enjoyed it. Collaborating on this book brought us a lot of joy. We got to walk the cliffs in St. Ives and visit the hotel where Kit and Muriel sang and danced with the sapphists in Falmouth. We got to touch fabric samples from 1880s cyclists' regulations manuals in the British Library. And, like Muriel, we learned more than we wanted to learn about seaweed.

Joanna & Mir

A
SHORE
THING

JOANNA LOWELL

READERS GUIDE

DISCUSSION QUESTIONS

1. Muriel and Kit live happily ever after, but even happily ever afters require emotional work, compromise, and encounters with various obstacles. In your opinion, what are the biggest relationship challenges Kit and Muriel will face as they build a home together in New York? Are these challenges mainly societal or interpersonal? How can they be overcome?

2. Suffragists were big fans of bicycles. Susan B. Anthony said of bicycling, "I think it has done more to emancipate women than anything else in the world." What new freedoms did bicycles open for women? Why did Deighton insist that penny-farthings were superior to safeties? What do you think it would have taken for men like him to accept women bicycling?

3. Today we tend to think that sexual desire defines a person's identity: a man attracted to other men is a gay man; a person attracted to people of all genders is pansexual. Sexologists in the late nineteenth century were just inventing the opposing concepts of homosexuality and heterosexuality, along with the idea that sexual orientation was an unchangeable part of the self. Muriel's attraction to Kit and experience with the sapphists lead her to wonder if she should start thinking differently about herself. Is her desire defined by attraction to a particular gender, and does that matter? What about Ponsonby's?

4. As a trans person living in a period when hormones and surgical interventions were not available to make his body more congruent with his gender, Kit relied on binding, packing, clothing, and other material (rather than medical) methods of living his gender in the world. Across the span of trans and queer history, these methods have been (and continue to be) far more prevalent than hormones and surgery. While trans and nonbinary people are often singled out for consciously performing their genders and modifying their bodies, feminists have long called attention to ways in which all people, whether consciously or not, use clothing, makeup, exercise, and other techniques to embody their genders. What strategies have you used to embody your gender? How have they changed over the course of your life?

5. How do the non-trans characters in the book embody their genders? How do you see them struggling against the limits of Victorian gender norms?

6. Kit's conflict with Deighton and Deighton's father goes beyond disagreements about bicycles, into the meaning of masculinity itself. As Kit spends more time in all-male spaces, he finds he doesn't like most of what he sees. What do you notice him objecting to? Although his life would have been easier if he were assigned male from birth, Kit reflects that he is grateful for his experience of female socialization. Why?

7. Deighton and his father also fight with each other over the meaning of masculinity, although they seem to agree that it involves dominating others. Can masculinity exist outside of domination? What alternative models of manhood do you see in the book, and in the real world?

8. Muriel loves her work and is proud of her self-sufficiency. What struggles has she faced as a female botanist, seeking to make a career for herself with, and separate from, Esmé? How has she confronted them?

9. Muriel has felt lonely for much of her life. How has she internalized the emotional damage from her relationship with Esmé and the death of her mother? What strategies has she used to keep herself safe? What is it about Kit that allows her to let down

some of the walls she has built? Do you think there are some boundaries that are important to retain, even within intimate relationships?

10. Both the sapphists and the women artists in the book have created Sisterhoods to respond to specific social challenges. What similarities and differences do you see in the forces that brought each group together? Under what circumstances might all-women spaces still serve an important purpose? How can trans and non-binary folks also find mutual support?

11. Blackmail was a common threat faced by wealthy gay men in Britain, particularly after the passage of the 1885 Criminal Law Amendment Act. Before you learned of the source of James's stress, what did you imagine it might be? What do you think of James's story arc? Do you believe he and Ponsonby have a future together?

12. Romance novels have increasingly centered female pleasure, focusing on women's orgasms, consent and communication, and a broader range of sexual acts. Do you think social norms around what does and does not count as "actual sex" have similarly evolved? How might this differ in queer and straight relationships?

ACKNOWLEDGMENTS

Many, many people helped me along in various ways as I wrote this book, more than I can name here. I am so lucky and so grateful to have you all in my life.

A special thank-you to my agent, Tara Gelsomino, who believed in Kit's story from the beginning, worked with me tirelessly on a half dozen versions of sample chapters, and very early on gave the book its title, which made it feel like it might actually exist one day and kept me going. And to my editor, Kate Seaver, for getting what I wanted to do and shaping the narrative with her expert editorial pruning shears in ways I couldn't. Thanks also to the Berkley team for the vision and support. And to Katie Smith and Rita Frangie Batour for the beautiful art and design. And to the Berklettes, and, in particular, Elizabeth Everett, who I look up to so hard my neck hurts.

Huge thanks to my colleagues and students at Wake Forest University, and to WFU itself for funding my research trip to Cornwall, where I had friendly and frightening encounters with seagulls and the chance to spend time in the St. Ives Archive and at the St. Ives Arts Club. Thanks to the members and volunteers of both those organizations for the warm welcome, the tours, and the local and historical knowledge.

Meredith Lee was my generous and astute first reader. They're a busy, brilliant scholar in the field of trans studies, and I'm humbled by the gift of their time and care.

Sarah Evenson provided insight, enthusiasm, and empathy every step of the way, as well as invaluable feedback. Their own creative work inspires me. Support trans artists! Sarah-Evenson.com.

I couldn't write anything without my comrades in narrative: Joanna, John, Brian, Art, Julia, Brad, Dona, and Radhika. Your co-thinking makes words feel possible.

Les compañeres—you give me fuerza. Chemlawn, Ian, and Jesse—all my most memorable bicycling happened with you guys. It wasn't always well-advised, but I regret nothing. Sarah—Frankie's tea party scene got cut, but I put in something else for you. Jessica—our teaching taught me so much about, among other things, hand flexes, hazelnuts, and the future of Fanny Price. Rian—our talks as I wrote this made it easier to manage everything else. Stiv—the blue flame burns bright. Corinne—style and substance. Nico—it all began with you.

Thanks to Mama, Aunt Rhetta, my brother, and the Ruoccos, for a lifetime of storytelling, acceptance, and very, very loud conversation.

Joey Ruocco—we go on together always.

Mir, my love, we finally had romance *and* romance! Amazingly, happily, our relationship survived.

Photo by Mir Yarfitz

Joanna Lowell lives among the fig trees in North Carolina, where she teaches in the English department at Wake Forest University. When she's not writing historical romance, she writes collections and novels as Joanna Ruocco. Those books include *Dan*, *Another Governess / The Least Blacksmith*, *The Week*, and *Field Glass*, coauthored with Joanna Howard.

Ready to find
your next great read?

Let us help.

Visit prh.com/nextread

Penguin
Random
House